DESTINATION MOON

A NOVEL BY

LUCHIA MILLER

ISBN: 978-0-57868-548-9

For Mom and Dad

To move, to breathe, to fly, to float,

To gain all while you give,

To roam the roads of lands remote,

To travel is to live.

~Hans Christian Andersen~

It is not in the stars

To hold our destiny,

But in ourselves.

~ William Shakespeare~

* * *

TO THE MOON AND BEYOND!

ORION GALACTIC AIRWAYS (C)

Do you long to explore SPACE, travel to the new COLONY PLANETS?

Are you a 'PEOPLE PERSON'?

Willing to live OFF WORLD?

Orion Galactic Airways, is currently seeking able bodied Women, Men, and Alien Beings, between the ages of 21 and 35, for the position of OFF-WORLD FLIGHT ATTENDANT.

Applicants must be: Aged: 21-35 (or Alien equivalent)

Height: 5'1" to 6'5" (weight in proportion to height)

A citizen of Planet Earth, Earth Federation Colony, Space Station, or Registered Alien (Allied Planets).

Seeking applicants who will uphold our 135 year tradition of premium customer service. To view the full list of requirements or to apply, eye-scan, oriongalactic/owfa. We look forward to hearing from you!

* * *

1

THE TRAINING FLIGHT

MARCH, 2079

Lift off in thirty minutes! Spring could feel the butterflies in her stomach as her first StarShuttle loomed in front of her. She clasped her shaking hands under her trainee folder, planting a wide smile on her face as the crew shuttle came to a stop in front of Spring's ride to the Moon. She gazed out the window, feeling a little shy around the real flight attendants in their cobalt blue uniforms while she wore her trainee uniform: a drab burgundy two piece suit with a white collar. She caught her reflection staring back at her in the window, a confident looking young woman with honey brown skin, large brown eyes. Confident? She was scared to death.

The StarShuttle looked massive to Spring, but not as large as the StarShips her class had studied. She could see why it was a 'Shuttle' and not a 'Ship'. It vaguely resembled the old fashioned jet airplanes, only larger and wider, a sleek triangle shaped combo of the ancient Concorde mixed with a classic Boeing. It sat on a flat metal launch pad that blended with the blue-gray chrome of the shuttle itself. The glare of the rising sun cast a reflection on the small rectangular mirrored, solar passenger windows, bouncing of the glossy fuselage. Three scary rear engines let out occasional bursts of steam, wafting up to the dark blue Orion tail with the golden shooting star emblem. Spring tore her eyes away from the ship, staring up at the morning sky. She could just make out the ghostly shape of the full Moon, disappearing in the yellow and pink sky. She was going to up there! She would be on the Moon in a few hours!

Spring glanced back at the JFK StarPort, her eyes barely making out the cluster of spectators on the long observation deck. Even at this early hour, crowds eagerly lined the rails, most with high powered cameras no doubt. She smiled as she spotted the tiny shapes of children, their faces pressed against the glass rails or held in the arms of a parent. She had been one of the kids on the observation deck eleven years ago. A twelve year old tourist from Virginia Beach, with frizzy hair and an oversized, 'I Love NY' sweatshirt that matched her big brother and little sister's.

She could still remember the excitement coursing through everyone on the deck. It was her families first and only trip to New York, and somehow her parents had managed to snag tickets for one of the nighttime viewings. The Moon flights were still pretty new back then, (the shuttles were smaller), she couldn't imagine how much her parents had paid for a family of five. Spring would never forget the sheer thrill of watching the StarShuttle rise up into the crisp night sky, lights blinking on its wings as it shot up into the air. She had watched until it was nothing but a glowing speck, headed toward a crescent shaped Moon.

"Ready to fly, girl?" Spring jumped, looking up into the smiling pixie face of Miki, her mentor on the flight. The rest of the crew had already disappeared through the boarding door. Spring was the only one still on the crew shuttle. Even Gina, her snooty classmate with the perfect hair and to die for designer shoes had boarded. Her own brand new pumps squeaked with every step. Spring ran a hand over her hair, making sure her thick black curls were not escaping her regulation ponytail. Her head felt like a shellacked helmet of hairspray.

"Sure!" Spring smiled brightly, before taking a deep breath, standing up to follow Miki. Ten minutes later, Spring is standing between two empty row of seats, watching as passengers began to board.

Everyone is dressed in their best: stiff new jeans, shiny shoes, glossy new highlights. They make their way down the single aisle slowly, taking in the dark blue seats, ultra white side paneling, the purplish-blue cabin lights. There is a collective library style hush as they take their seats, examine their harnesses, glance out the specially made wide porthole sized windows.

Spring watched as an elderly man stood in his row, gazing down at his seat. He looked as old as her Gran-Libby, at least ninety. His silver hair trimmed neatly, courtesy of a recent haircut. His dark blue suit had the synthetic sheen of polyester, but it's new and his white shirt is sharply pressed.

She stared at him, thinking of Grandpa Sven, as he gazed curiously around the cabin, his wrinkled hands leaning against the headrest of his seat. She wonders who he is, where he's going. He looks in her direction, his crinkled eyes shining, a small smile on his face. Spring smiles back. He nods, saluting her.

* * *

"Ladies and gentlemen welcome aboard Orion Galactic's flight 822 to the Moon." The captain's voice is temporarily drowned out by cheers and loud applause in the cabin. "We have a smooth eight hours and nine minutes today, that will put us on the Moon at around...uh, 545pm. For those of you traveling for the first time on a StarShuttle, our launch pad will begin to rise up in a few minutes." The captain explained, "This will assist us in obtaining the proper position for lift off. Once the launch pad has lifted, we will then start our engines. This may sound a bit like thunder, but that's normal. Flight Attendants, prepare for lift off."

Miki took her seat, folding down a blue chair attached to the wall in the back galley, right beside the exit door. Spring stared at the door's red emergency handle, feeling a little dizzy. *Lift off.*

"Here's your seat!" Miki gestured cheerfully toward a folding seat beside her. It was so small! Dark blue with very little padding, its saving grace was the slight curve of the bottom. Spring folded the chair down, sitting beside Miki, buckling herself into her harness with trembling fingers, pretending she was in a training module and not the real thing. The harness pressed tightly against her chest.

As soon as she sat down, the plane shuddered once, then a sound that reminded her of a giant electrical elevator filled the cabin. The shuttle rose up, inch by inch. Spring could hear a few excited squeals in the cabin. She still could not believe every seat was full. One hundred and ten passengers. The shuttle came to a halt at a ninety degree angle, hovering silently for a few minutes, then the engines roared to life, one at a time, sounding exactly like thunder, shaking the shuttle, filling it with a vibrating hum. Spring let out an odd sounding giggle, thin and tin like. The harness seemed to press tighter into her chest.

"Breathe, Spring."

Spring looked sideways at Miki, suddenly realizing she was breathing shallowly. Miki's voice was firm but calm, her eyes reassuring. Spring gulped in some air, breathing deeply, glancing back at Miki, nodding a silent thanks. Her eyes stung a bit. *Just like riding in a plane, silly. Breathe.*

"It's okay," Miki said in a voice barely audible above the engines, "I was totally in your shoes last year. Hell, we all were once! You'll see."

"No turning back now." Spring gulped in more air. She forced her eyes to focus on the secured galley compartments and ovens, made of shiny stainless steel.

Suddenly, the engines quieted, almost to a purr, and the throbbing of the shuttle stopped. Spring cast a surprised look at Miki just as the engines took on a deafening roar, and her body was sucked into her seat. Lift Off! Her skin and face felt like they sliding backwards over her cheekbones in rippling folds toward her hair, exposing her teeth in a smiling grimace. Her stomach felt like it was caving into her ribcage, hiding for cover. She felt sick. She squeezed her eyes shut. *This is it! Can't get off now!*

The shuttle roared for a few minutes more, then nothing but a smooth, gentle hum, as it arched upward and the morning sunshine outside of Miki's passenger sized window in her door, turned inky black. A feeling of weightlessness came over Spring before the shuttles systems kicked in, returning gravity to normal. It felt like a normal AirShuttle. She still kept her eyes closed .

"Spring! Open your eyes!" Miki said, "You don't want to miss this... look!"

"Ladies and Gentlemen, planet Earth on your right hand side," The purser announced proudly, "You are now officially, Off World. We now invite you to sit back, relax and enjoy your flight to the Moon."

Spring opened one eye cautiously, gazing past Miki, who graciously tried to flatten herself against her jumpseat. Spring blinked, her eyes widening, "Oh my god! It's so beautiful!" She could hear the awe and emotion in her voice, impatiently blinking back the wetness in her eyes that threatened her view of Earth. She had never seen such a glorious sight as Earth, blue, swirling with white. She leaned forward, pressing her hand against the cool glass of the window, watching as Earth moved slowly under her hand. "Home." She whispered. "That's our...Earth?"

"What a sight, huh?"

Spring nodded, tasting salty tears. "I can't believe I'm here seeing this! It's so...I...I never thought it would ..." She trailed off, her voice thick, tears dampening her cheeks, "It's just so ...wow!"

From the sniffles and loud nose blowing, she could tell the passengers were as moved as she was. Several clapped, while many oohed and awed. She had the impulsive urge to clap herself, exchanging a wide smile with Meri. For once Spring did not feel like the underachieving failure in her family. Her brother may be a cadet at the Earth Federation Academy, but she was the first Stevens going to the Moon!

"No matter how many times I do this," Miki said as she stared at Earth, "I'll never get tired of seeing home. Hands down, my favorite part."

"But, isn't the Moon home for you now?" Miki shook her head. "Earth will always be home...but hey," She leaned closer to Spring, her voice full of mischief. "There are a few places that give Earth a run for its money!" "You mean, Eden? The colony planet?"

"Eden's okay." Miki allowed, chewing on her lip thoughtfully, "First colony planet and all that, but I mean the planets belonging to others, like Endari or Zantan. The men there are...out of this world! Try checking out some of those, 'cause that is where the action is!" Miki grinned, her eyes twinkling.

Spring thought of her classmate Jorge and his Etrueleon mom. "What about the Etrueleons? Have you ever met guys from there?" The Etrueleons were the first alien race to publicly make contact back in 2031. They had provided the Terraforming formula. Of course Spring had never actually met an Etrueleon. Unless holograms in third grade history class counted. And Jorge looked more like his human dad than an Alien. Only difference was that his eyes looked a bit like a lizards and he had a slight bump for a nose above his mouth. His nose probably made wearing sunglasses impossible.

Miki shrugged, "They're okay, I guess." The seatbelt sign went off, Miki unbuckled her harness, bouncing up, stretching, "The Endarions are better, easier on the eyes! Hardcore types. Sexy. Come on lazy bones, time to make the donuts!" She opened a storage compartment in the wall, pulling out her folded serving smock, before sliding a look Spring's way. "My grandpa always said that."

Spring took one more look outside, her eyes roaming over the thousands of stars, before unsnapping her harness. She stood up on rubbery legs, smoothing down her trainee uniform. "Hardcore?" She frowned. *Did they look like lizards? Klingons? Vulcans? Sexy Vulcans?*

Spring stood off to the side, watching silently as Miki turned on the four large food meal replicators in the wall. They hummed loudly to life. It was hard to believe that behind the four twenty inch long rectangular doors, there were enough meals for one hundred people. Almost at once, the delicious aroma of breakfast filled the galley. Next, Miki was pulling out stemware and glasses, setting them on the fold out counter in front of the intimidating, drink dispenser, full of as many blinking lights as the flight deck.

Spring stepped forward awkwardly, "Here," Miki said handing her a square silver lined tray with a small, blinking computer attached to the side, "Start at row ten, and take down drink orders. I'll have them ready for you when you get back. The orders show up on that screen over there." Miki pointed to a blank screen by one of the replicators.

Another flight attendant came back, fastening her blue smock over her white blouse and blue pants. She smiled at Spring before picking up what Spring assumed was the meal manifest tray and heading out. Spring stared down at the blinking tray, before planting a bright smile on her face, "Be right back!"

* * *

"Ladies and gentlemen, we have been cleared to land onto the Moon's Milky Way Lunar International StarPort. Please stow your carry-on luggage and refasten your harnesses. We'll be landing shortly, thank you."

The purser's PA was music to Spring's ears as she moved down the aisle, checking harnesses, before wearily plopping down onto the jumpseat beside Miki. Her cheeks hurt from smiling and her hands still shook from the heavy drink tray.

"Think you can do this?" Miki asked as Spring buckled her harness. Spring bit her lip, thinking of her semi-disastrous turn at the drink devil.. err dispenser during the second beverage service. The floor still felt slightly sticky under her feet. Chris, (the only guy on Miki's crew) had looked impressed; he had never seen the dispenser sprout five drinks like a water fountain. Miki had kindly pointed out that it was a good thing they had both ducked when they did, avoiding the spray of drinks, while Chris deactivated it. Of course, this was after cleaning up the cute guy in 16C's bout of space sickness in the aisle. In that instance, Spring had been very grateful for the artificial gravity on the shuttle.

She settled in her seat, watching as the shuttle slowly began to descend over the dark, nighttime terrain of the Moon. A few twinkling lights were visible from the nearby city. Her breath caught as she saw a fleeting glimpse of the Apollo site, with its illuminated stiff, American flag surrounded by the ever present, clear habitat bubble. Larger identical bubbles enclosed the city and StarPort. It always struck her as odd that the Moon was not Terraformed. Maybe it had to do with tourism on the Moon. After all, everyone expects the Moon to look grey and...Moon-like. She felt a smile tug at the corners of her mouth, as the shuttle picked up speed, coming in for a landing, "Nothing to it, piece of cake."

* * *

ORION GALACTIC AIRWAYS tm
Travel to the Moon...TODAY!!

ORION GALACTIC AIRWAYS introduces affordable fares to the Moon from our 5 Earth based StarPorts! Travel in relative comfort in our spacious, **Galactic Plus© class**, aboard the streamlined Boeing 907!

Enjoy luxurious amenities at competitive pricing! Choose from LAX,JFK,LHR,or our newest StarPort, BMS (Berlin Merkel StarPort) in Berlin,Germany!

Fares start at:

ADULT: $25,000 and up *

CHILDREN: $15,000 and up*

EARN discounts and mileage when you sign up for our Frequent Flyer program. For more information or to make a reservation, blink-scan OrionGalactic.

We'll see you on the Moon!

* All prices are subject to change. All fares are in the global Ceres dollar.

* * *

2

MILKY WAY LUNAR INTERNATIONAL - MLI

The cabin filled with applause and cheers as the shuttle landed smoothly, touching ground on the Moon. It landed like an old fashioned airplane, except it took up only a few feet of the runway, before slowing down gracefully, taxiing toward the MLI terminal. Miki graciously tried to flatten herself against her jumpseat, so Spring could have a clear view of the StarPort. Spring leaned forward as far as her harness straps would allow, taking in the sand-like terrain that sparkled like fine sugar, contrasting with the smooth black tarmac and bright blue-white lights that lined the way.

"Ladies and Gentlemen," The purser's voice interrupted the cheers and clapping." Orion Galactic Airways, would like to welcome you to the Moon's Milky Way International StarPort. Current local time is five thirty-five..."

"The buildings are so low!" Spring murmured as they taxied closer to the bubble encased StarPort. The StarPort looked like a life-size snow globe, a dome of shimmering, protective glass, supported by towering beams of silver that rose up in vertical curves toward the top. "It's like a snow-globe," Spring glanced excitedly at Miki, "I don't know...I keep expecting a giant hand to come and shake it, you know?" She laughed to herself, shaking her head.

"Wait till you see the main city." Miki said in a bored voice, "It's like a goldfish bowl."

The Moon was achingly familiar and foreign all at once, set against a black sky filled with stars and the twinkling lights of passing ships. They taxied past a shuttle warehouse encased in a protective dome of asteroid resistant glass, 'Fly Orion Galactic' was lit up in red lights on the roof of the warehouse. Neighboring warehouses advertised, such ancient airlines like Delta, and Virgin. Boxy Landrover style vehicles zoomed by the warehouses on small paved roads, occupied by people covered head to toe in protective suits, with mirrored face shields.

The shuttle approached a towering dome of glass and metal beams, the snow-globe StarPort. A space traffic control tower, (STC), stood a few feet away from the dome. Sphere shaped and with a disco ball mirrored top, it definitely claimed the title of off world 'space needle'. The StarPort was ablaze with lights, showing nine circular levels. She could see the dark silhouettes of people moving around inside, the tiny figures of two children skipping ahead of an adult. Her eyes could make out the welcoming neon sign of her favorite bookstore as one of the stores based in the solid looking center of the clear StarPort. Spring exhaled, suddenly surprised that she felt a little afraid of the Moon until she saw the humans (or humanoids) walking around. She found herself smiling as she watched figures moving through the clear, tube shaped jetways that led to or from a couple of parked shuttles. Shuttles of different sizes and shapes, some in shiny chrome, others in black, a few in white. *This place is enormous! This is so not a dream...I'm really here, on the Moon!*

"The StarPort is packed! Is it always like this?" Spring clutched her jumpseat as the shuttle parked onto the launch pad with a vibrating shudder that rattled her teeth. Almost immediately, an accordion shaped tube inched its way forward, unfurling into a fluid shape as it locked against the shuttle with a loud suction noise. The 'Fasten your seatbelt/harness sign' went off, and passengers bounced up, ready to leave.

"Flight attendants, prepare for arrival and cross-check." A voice crackled over the PA. Miki and Spring stood up. Spring jumped a bit as her jumpseat loudly snapped back into its folded position. She swayed, grasping the top of her jumpseat for support. Miki squeezed past her, disarming the nearby door by pressing a simple 'disarm' button. Spring could not tear her eyes away from the red emergency handle.

"Yeah, this place is always busy around this time." Miki said absently before picking up her interphone, "Hi! Door three-right is disarmed!" She hung up the phone, glancing at her watch, "I think I'll be able to make it to IKEA before it closes. Whoo hoo!"

"IKEA? There is an IKEA on the Moon?"

Miki popped some gum into her mouth, offering Spring some. Spring shook her head. "Yep. It's in Lunar Prime East. Nice area. Kinda expensive, but then everything here is. I practically live on PB&J sandwiches! You have your C.O.E passport, Spring? You're gonna need that for customs again."

Spring retrieved her bag from the galley storage compartment, pulling out her 'Citizen of Earth' passport card with a flourish. "Ta dah!" She glanced down at the credit card sized passport, wincing at her deer in the headlights picture on the upper left corner, and the miniature picture of Earth in the upper right corner. It was amazing that such a simple blue and grey card held so much information, from her race, (human), to her fingerprints, dimpled smile and the mole on the left side of her neck. Curly black hair and brown skin. Her favorite part had to be the 'Planet of Birth' section.

"I thought I only needed it for 'Exit Earth' stuff. Do I have to clear if I'm deadheading back?" She thought of the Earth Exit procedures and the physical and mental exam everyone had to go through, (even crew), before each flight. She had watched as a flight attendant from another carrier was sent home in tears because he had a nasty cold.

"You'll need to flash it here too." Miki grabbed the ID card, examining it before handing it back, smirking. "Spring Raine Stevens?"

Spring gathered her purse and trainee folder, following Miki as they headed up the empty aisle. She stopped a few times, trying to see Earth out of the passenger windows, but was only met with the painfully bright lights of the StarPort ramp. She gazed down at the empty seats with their crumpled blankets, feeling oddly sad and alone. The passengers were on their way to colony planets, starbases, adventures on the Moon, and she had to go back to Earth.

Spring caught up with Miki and the rest of the crew at the boarding door, Gina, (who had worked up front and never set foot in the main cabin), posed for pictures by the cockpit. She made the poor purser take the same shot over and over until she was satisfied. The pilots were long gone.

"Nice meeting you both!" Spring reached out, impulsively hugging a surprised Chris, then Miki. "Sorry about the soda machine!" Then to Miki, "Thanks for everything, hope you make it to IKEA."

"Thanks! You did a tastic job! We'll see you on the line in a few, as a regulah!" Miki squeezed her arm as she went past her. "Oh, have a safe flight back too!" She waved.

"See ya in a few months!" Chris nodded to them as they stepped into the jetway tube. Spring stumbled under the jetways moving sidewalk, hastily grabbing the rail, her eyes glued to the Earth. It hovered surrounded by darkness, a sliver of its left-hand side was cloaked in shadow, the rest of it cradled in a blanket of white clouds, mixed with blue. Home. Beside her Gina was snapping away, tears rolling down her cheeks. Miki stood behind Spring, jabbering away on her phone, her back to Earth. Spring dug through her purse, finally dragging her clear phone out, her shaking fingers fumbling to turn it on. The phone beeped to life, smiling Spring lifted it up, aiming...Earth was gone!

The jetway ended, bringing them into the entrance to the customs area. She looked up at the thick, blocky, 'Welcome to the Moon' sign as it zoomed overhead under the fast moving sidewalk. The sidewalk ended at the start of a long stainless steel hallway, covered with large images of the history of the Moon, and human space travel. In between each image, a moon shaped light hung embedded, some were full, others crescent shaped with the iconic 'man in the moon' face. In illuminated alcoves, life size mannequins modeled bulky spacesuits from the twentieth and early twenty-first century.

There was even a small section devoted to the famous twelve flight attendants, known as 'The Twelve'. The first flight attendants in space back in the 50's. One of their baggy, jumpsuit style uniforms and clunky space boots were on display, along with pictures and footage of their tiny 8 seater shuttles. Spring grew up idolizing one of the twelve, Jackie Bleu. A glamorous woman with dark brown skin and curly hair, someone that looked like her. She was secretly relieved that uniforms were more attractive now. Passengers stood awestruck in the 'Visitor', 'In Transit' and 'Resident' lines. Spring followed Miki to the 'Crew' line. She tried not to stare too hard at the varying uniforms of the airline crews waiting in line. Crews stood in line dressed in everything from micro-mini's to uncomfortable looking shiny bodysuits. One crew sported clear space bubble helmets.

"I think I got some passable shots of Earth. What about you?" Gina gestured toward Springs phone. "Oh!" Spring turned it over in her palm, staring at the most recent picture. Her shoes.

* * *

Spring and Gina's return flight was delayed, so they had a few extra minutes in the gatehouse. Although slightly smaller than the JFK StarPort (built on old Floyd Bennett Field, on an island near the old JFK airport), it felt foreign, more sterile. People walked around in a half shocked, dream-like state, as if they still could not believe they were on the Moon or were just too terrified to go further into space. Being on the Moon reminded you that you really were far from home. If you left your lights on at your house on Earth, you couldn't fly or drive home from the Moon.

"That flight was so easy! My trips to Rome were harder than that." Gina said loudly, applying bright pink lipstick that matched her cheeks. Gina had that 'genetically altered' look. Sharp cheekbones, lips so full they looked swollen. Lashes only a giraffe could get away with shaded her artificially bright eyes, while her tiny waist looked more deformed rather than hourglass."Didn't you say your mom was a flight attendant too? Like, she's 100 or something like that?" Gina asked, running a hand through her brassy, highlighted hair.

"My grandmother was a flight attendant." Spring answered, her eyes on a couple sitting by the floor to ceiling windows, leaning into each other. Spring's mind automatically went to Wesley: wondering what he was doing at that very moment. On second thought, she didn't want to know what he was doing. She already knew whom he was probably doing it to. She looked away from the couple, feeling that painful tug in her heart. *Stop it, Spring. You're on the Moon...the Moon! Wes is thousands of miles away...millions even. He's engaged to someone else now.* "She used to fly out of JFK back in the day for Orion's 'Airways' side." Spring turned her attention to a departing StarShuttle launching into space.

"Maybe I flew with her." Gina yawned, snapping her compact shut. "I flew with, like, a ton of dinosaurs. Those old hags fly nothing but international."

"Really? She retired back in the 50's. Were you flying then?" Spring asked innocently. Spring stood up, walking the few feet to the ticket counter. Gina followed closely behind, her spiked heels clicking loudly.

"No! Do I look like I'm that old?"

"No, not at all." Spring replied. Gina smiled smugly. "You don't look a day over ...uh...thirty-five?"

Gina glared at her. "I'm twenty-eight." She snapped.

"Hello, there! I have your seats." The agent handed them two seat assignments, "Seats six C and D. Boarding level seven. Have a good flight back to Earth, ladies."

"Um…Thank you!" Spring took her card, trying not to gape at the gate agent's long neck, high forehead, and wide, cat-shaped eyes and expertly applied makeup. She had tentacles pulled back in a tidy ponytail. The agents answering smile faltered a little when she glanced at Gina. "Enjoy your flight back to Earth." The agent repeated herself.

"Now boarding levels six and higher for flight 8226 to Earth." Announced another agent by the jetway door. Spring pulled a gawking Gina toward the jetway, "Hi there!" she said cheerfully, handing over boarding pass.

"Wow. Did you see her hair?" Gina whispered loudly as they buckled their harnesses. "Can you imagine trying to style that nightmare? Disgusting."

"I don't know," Spring said evenly, observing the working flight attendants in action, helping a group of teens and their tired chaperones in bright yellow shirts. She looked away, glad she was sitting at the window, her mouth curved in a faint smile, "There are worse things."

"Like what?"

Spring smiled wider, watching the silhouette of a couple embracing by the terminal windows, "Like being a bigot." She slid a look toward Gina.

* * *

"So, how was it? Totally magnif huh?" Pam asked as soon as Spring wobbled into the dorm room. Spring was a complete contrast to her roomie Pam. While Spring was petite and top heavy, Pam had a model's tall waif-like figure along with reddish blond hair and green eyes. She also had the aura of privilege that came from growing up in Greenwich with nannies and private schools. Whereas Spring's curly hair was so dark it appeared ink black, seemed to compliment her dark skin and amber colored eyes. She came from a solidly middle class, military family.

Pam lay on her stomach, surrounded by notes, while Jorge sat on the floor loudly reciting StarPort codes. A classic sci-fi movie flickered on the wafer thin TV, while at the same time music blared from the left hand corner of the screen, while text messages were displayed on the right. A half eaten box of pizza sat on the small table by the window, the smell of green peppers, onions and pizza crust, made Spring's stomach rumble. On her bed a neatly folded note was propped against the freshly made pillow. She stumbled over to her bed, wishing that the party would move to Jorge's room. Just once. She wanted the room to herself. Perhaps take a long three minute shower.

"Hey, gorgeous!" Jorge waved, before turning back to his notecards. "JTK. Oh, yeah...J.T. Kirk international on Mars! You think they'll ever name a StarPort after Darth Vader?"

"Earth was amazing! And I loved the Moon!" Spring quickly skimmed over the note, written in Pam's loopy handwriting, "What time did my parents call?"

"What time or how many times?' Pam snorted, "Your mom called three or four times I think, guess they want to hear about your flight."

"I'll call after my shower." Spring moved toward her dresser, awkwardly stepping over Jorge's notes, pulling out an Earth Federation Academy T-shirt her brother gave her and some yoga pants. "I forgot to check in with them." She leaped over Jorge's legs, heading toward the bathroom, "Pam, you're so lucky your parents didn't call non-stop when you left for the Moon."

Pam looked up at her with unreadable eyes, "Guess you're right." she said with a peculiar twist to her mouth. "Charity galas are a bit more important than the Moon." She looked down at her notes, blinking rapidly, "They're probably still pissed I'm not a Prima with the ballet or a carbon copy of my stuck up sister. But hey," she said in a tight voice, "someone has to be the family black sheep...huh?"

Silence. Spring exchanged looks with Jorge.

* * *

Spring waited until Pam and Jorge had gone downstairs, before calling her parents back on the TelVid. Her mom answered on the first ring, "Well! It's about time, missy! How was the Moon? Hold that thought, honey…" Her mom stared fixedly at the screen, "Command Text." Spring's mom said to the screen, waiting a few seconds for it to flash a proceed message. "Marc! Spring is on the TeleVid! She's back from the Moon!" Her mom winked at her grinning, "Just a sec honey, wait till your dad's on."

"Where's Dad? Is he running errands or something?"

"No, he's in the kitchen…why?"

"You're sending Dad a text when he's down the hall?"

"Sure, why not?" her Mom shrugged, glancing down the hall. "It's better than yelling down the hall, right?"

"Where's Summer, Gran- Libby?" Spring asked looking over her mom's shoulder, her eyes roaming over the familiar beige living room, with the floor to ceiling bookcases. Empty bookcases. Most of the books were piled on the smooth area rugs near the twin moss green couches, like miniature skyscrapers, leaning precariously in the gentle breeze from the open balcony doors. Mom was reorganizing again.

"Huh? Oh! Summer? Summer's out." Her mom said distractedly, as if she just remembered her youngest child. It always amazed Spring that her big brother was named Hunter and not something seasonal like,Winter or Fall. "And your grandmother is busy taking her art class. Marc!"

"Got it! Hey, Space Girl, how was the Moon?" her dad's smiling face popped up in a separate box, the blaring lights of the kitchen behind him. The kitchen looked so stark compared to his yellow and black 'Retired' T-shirt. Behind her dad, cluttered mixing bowls and colorful ingredients lined the counter. A couple of tall pots threatened to boil over on the stove. Spring glanced at her mom. Her mom wiggled her eyebrows at her, while Spring bit back a giggle. Dad and his experimental dinners.

Spring filled them in, carefully omitting the drink dispenser fiasco. "I can't believe how awesome Earth looks from up there! It's so big, so alive... moving even!"

"Proud of you, Springtime." Her dad said, his dark brown eyes twinkling, "Good job."

"Did you get to wear a space bubble helmet?" Her mom asked excitedly.

"No bubble helmets, that would be cute though! Thanks, but it was just a training flight. I mean, it's not the EFA." Spring stared down at her fuzzy robe, plucking at the fabric. "How is Hunter doing at EFA?" Earth Federation Academy was too much of a mouthful.

"Doing great so far, could call more often," her mom sat cross legged on the couch, surrounded by more books, "Oh! I almost forgot! Wesley called! We told him you were a going to the Moon. He wants you to call him. Such a nice boy, Spring. Why did you two break up? What did you do? Just kidding, hon!"

Ask his new fiancé. "Hmmm. Well, I'm tired, we have like, a million tests before graduation, better get some sleep...love you guys, night." Spring reached to turn off the call.

"Okay, honey, we'll see you at your graduation! Gran-Libby is so excited about that! Good night, baby, love ya!" Her mom blew her a kiss, hopping off the couch with a quick wave, returning to the books.

"Love you too, Springtime. Get some rest, night! See ya in a couple of months!"

"Night, Dad." Spring ended the Telocall with the image of her dad hurrying over to the smoking food replicator. Spring stood up stretching lazily, pulling the thick bath towel away from her hair, running her hands it. She glanced at the mirror, refusing to dwell on Wes. Her new life was just around the corner.

3

DANCING IN THE MOONLIGHT

TWO MONTHS LATER.

Spring resisted the urge to bend down and scratch her pantyhose clad leg as she stood outside the training building with her class, waiting to take their graduation photo. She shaded her eyes in the sun watching another class as they lined up on the entrance stairs, the mirrored glass windows reflecting the crisp cobalt blue uniforms and the bright green bushes and trees nearby. Five months of studying and worrying were gone, graduation day was just two days away. Spring cast a nervous look at her instructors, relieved that their backs were turned, then leaned down, scratching her right leg.

Spring loved the retro look of their Galactic uniforms. Her blazer was fitted, with 3/4 quarter sleeves, trimmed in white (along with a white collar), and pencil skirt. The cobalt blue shimmered with metallic threads, that sparkled with stardust magic under lights. Spring's favorite item had to be her new uniform pumps. A darker blue, they were given a space age feel with the outsole, shank, and sturdy low heel in a clear transparent blue. The guys wore a deeper shade of blue, with a shimmering tie that attached by a hidden magnet to the top button of their shirts. A very popular feature among Jorge and those that chose the suit option. The Airways side wore slate grey with navy trim. No clear Cinderella heels for them.

"Graduating class S26-79, please line up for your class photo please!" Evelyn, their chirpy facilitator called out, gesturing toward the steps leading to the main training building. A photographer with slicked back green hair, stood off to the side adjusting his equipment, a huge, old fashioned camera dangled from a strap around his neck. Spring, Pam, Jorge and the other twenty-two classmates were shepherded onto the steps by Evelyn, clucking after them like a mother hen. A mother hen wearing an Orion Galactic uniform and short spiky bright red hair. Spring made it on the first step along with the other vertically challenged trainees. Pam and Jorge stood in the back.

"Ok, guys, smile and say, 'Orion'!" called the photographer. "Great! Thanks! Congratulations, guys!"

"Class T26-79, line up please!" Another instructor yelled, as Spring's class stepped down, making way for the other class. Spring waved to a friend from the T class, before catching up with Pam and Jorge as they walked toward the shuttle bus back to the dorm building. They passed a few classmates waiting for the dorm shuttle, a silly five minute ride on such a beautiful April day. It was too beautiful to take a shuttle, even if it was still a little chilly. Spring smiled up at the brilliant blue sky squinting, blinded by the noonday sun. *I passed! No more exams! No more emergency drills! Graduation on Friday, here I come!* She did a little skip, swinging her purse.

It still amazed Spring that Orion Galactic's headquarters and training center were clustered together on a man made island off the coast of Long Island. Every building was identical, dark green mirrored glass, several stories tall, slanting roofs surrounded by manicured grounds. 'The Orion Island' was its own city with clear views of nearby JFK StarPort and off in the distance, the still operating ancient JFK airport. Spring went to sleep and woke up every morning to the sounds of StarShuttles taking off or landing.

"Kinda funny how all the classes are separated by our last names, huh? Glad I'm not an 'X'!" Spring joked, just an image of Wes popped into her head. She shook her head, "well, I'm Wesley's ex. Hey, what are we going to do tonight? We should celebrate passing the hardest exam on Earth!"

"Literally." Jorge added with a slight smile as they reached the entrance to their dorm building. They murmured hellos to a few brand new trainees sitting in the lobby studying, sprawled on the carpet and on the sofas. They stared openly at Spring's soon to be graduating class, a sea of cobalt blue uniforms.

"I can't believe that was us...like, five months ago!" Pam said in a loud whisper in front of the elevators.

Spring laughed, "Are you kidding? That WAS us studying our asses off for the final exam in the lobby last night! Tonight's the first night with no exams or door drills to do, let's go into the city!"

Pam shook her head, "I have a way better place ...how bout' old LaGuardia airport? I know a tastic place!" The elevator doors slid open

"LaGuardia?" Jorge frowned. "What's there? Isn't that some kind of museum?

Pam grinned widely, her eyes twinkling with mischief, "Ever hear of a little club called '747'?"

"Is that an old..." Spring started. The elevator doors opened and the trio dodged a few trainees dressed in pajamas carrying bulky training tablets. As usual the dorm hallway was lined with studying candidates, most of the doors to the dorms open, music blaring.

"Yep! An old 747 plane! It is so Absolute! You guys game? Wanna go?" Pam asked, leaping over a few legs in the hall.

"I'm in! When do we meet up?" Came a familiar voice. Spring looked over her shoulder at Gina sashaying down the hall after them.

* * *

An hour later, Spring and Pam were both dressed and ready to go. Pam in a deep, down to the navel V-neck dress made of shimmering shades of metallic gold. The kind of dress Spring always wanted to wear but was too busty for. Pam had used her ColorWand to temporarily change her red hair to bright cotton candy pink.

"Spring, can I borrow that magnif long pendant of yours? The one with the huge dangling teardrop crystal?" Pam asked, already making her way to Spring's crammed portable jewelry sleeve. "You know, the one with all the color? Tastic dress! Wanna use my wand to change your hair up? You should do silver to go with your dress!" Pam pulled out Spring's antique 1960's aurora borealis necklace, holding it up in triumph. Spring winced, biting her lip as Pam carelessly threw it over her head without unclasping it.

Spring inspected her reflection in the mirror. Her strapless silver mini dress with the tiny multicolored sparks of light, looked amazing with her brand new electric blue heels. The eight inch heels were a challenge, but she hoped she could pull them off and not walk like a drunken sailor. She touched her springy curls. "The color is just...well, it's not ...it'll go away before we graduate tomorrow?"

"Hells yeah!" Pam plopped down on her bed, shoving a pile of rejected club clothes onto the floor, uncovering the ColorWand. It looked like a long silver pen with minuscule lit up numbers dotting the side. "Here!" She threw it toward Spring, just as someone began banging on the door. Spring caught the wand, then ran for the door. A purple clad Jorge and an over the top Gina in a neon green dress entered.

"Hey there!" Spring waved them inside with the wand. Gina pointed to the wand, giggling.

"You're a brave one, changing your color before graduation!" Gina nodded at the wand. "What color?"

"Blond?" Pam said as she walked lopsided past them wearing one eight inch heel on one foot and a modest four inch heel on the other. The eight inch heels belonged to Spring of course.

"I like it the way it is now." Jorge winked at Spring.

Spring grabbed her hairbrush in one hand, the wand in another, smiling covertly. "You'll see!"

* * *

Thirty minutes later, Spring is crammed in the stuffy back seat of an AirTaxi, speeding dangerously, zipping in and out of traffic toward LaGuardia museum. Spring sat squeezed in the middle between Pam (who actually decide to wear her own shoes for once) and Gina. She blinked against the glare of the oncoming headlights bouncing off the taxi's windshield.

"Spring, you'll have to show me what numbers you used on the wand," Pam said. "I've had that thing for awhile, and I've never seen it do those colors before! Tastic!"

Spring glanced at her shadowy reflection in the rearview mirror, touching her hair lightly with her fingers. She barely recognized herself. Her black curls had morphed into sleek waves of metallic dark blue with wild streaks of bright blue, pink, purple and red. The numbers on the wand were so tiny, Spring was not sure exactly what numbers she pressed. She really did not want to keep everyone waiting, so she pressed numbers in a rush. She was not going to admit she was trying for one color...blond.

"I'm kinda not sure what I did!" she laughed nervously, "It, um, was not what I was going for...it's okay? I mean, not clownish? At least all the colors go together?"

"It's a stand out thing." Gina studied Spring's hair, "Unique, like, a 'what was she thinking' look."

"Thanks." Spring smiled sweetly at Gina, slowly taking in the blinking lights in Gina's hair to her gaudy green dress. "That's probably a comment you get all the time."

Gina angrily turned her attention to the window, ignoring Jorge's fit of coughing.

"We're here, gang! LaGuardia!" Pam pointed to a small brick, circular building with a rectangular, art deco style entrance. Spring could make out colorful airplane's against blue tile, bordering the top of the building. Their taxi flew lower, passing a few ancient airplanes parked behind the terminal. The planes varied in size, from a tiny propeller powered one, to what looked like a Boeing 757.

"This is LaGuardia?" Spring asked incredulously, "It's so small! Where's Club 747?"

"This is all that's left! All of those magnif high rises we passed? That used to be where the other terminals were. This Marine Air terminal place is all that's left...sad huh? Look! There's 747!"

Spring had seen images of old 747's online, but nothing compared to seeing one up close. Their AirTaxi glided gracefully to the ground on four wheels, driving toward the spectacle of an airplane turned into a nightclub. Club 747 sat on LaGuardia's old runway, half a mile from the old terminal, already surrounded by parked cars, hovering AirTaxi's and the longest line Spring had ever seen. The swirling kaleidoscope of lights in the old engines, bounced off the silver fuselage in a dazzling array of colors. A purplish glow lit up the glass ceiling/roof, giving a hint of what to expect once inside.

The tail itself sported thick, **747** in place of an emblem. All the original windows were intact. As they drove closer, Spring could see a bustle of activity. The wide, impossibly long wings were packed with partygoers dancing, chatting and leaning against the protective steel rails. One of the colorful engines had a group of people climbing up a ladder to have their pictures taken inside. Spring watched as five club kids squeezed inside the engine whirling with lights and booming music. The deep bass of club music shook the taxi windows. Their cab pulled up to the curb, close to the rear of what seemed like a mile long line of hopefuls.

"I got this!" Pam quickly leaned forward toward the fare keypad on the dashboard, pressing her thumb on the keypad to authorize payment. "Thanks, for the ride, Mister! Have a goodnight! Let's go, guys!" She opened her door, hopping onto the sidewalk.

"Ladies." Jorge helped Spring and Gina out, offering both his arms, following Pam. Pam immediately began walking toward the front of the line, totally oblivious to the glares from the people in line.

"Pam?" Spring stopped in her tracks, watching as Pam practically skipped to the velvet rope, before looking over her shoulder, beckoning excitedly to Spring and the others.

"Come on!" Gina yanked on Jorge's arm pulling him forward, jerking his other arm away from Spring's grasp. "Spring, you coming or what?" Gina glanced over her shoulder. Hundreds of angry eyes zeroed in on Spring. She bit her lip, hurrying toward Jorge and Gina, her eyes on the sidewalk, her cheeks burning.

Pam's tinkling laughter could be heard over the music as they drew closer to the front of the line. Two identical looking bouncers, (shiny bald heads, matching goatees, bronzed skin, tight shirts bulging with muscles), gazed at Pam with smiles that softened their rough faces. Pam stood between them, her arms linked with theirs, "Forget about my 747 fam? Never!" She said. "And here are my Orion favs! Gang, meet Vince and Theo, best door guys ever! Guys, meet my Orion peeps, Spring, Jorge and Gina! We're graduating tomorrow night!" Pam leaned forward, grabbing Spring. "Spring's from Virginia, can we help this chick celebrate New York style?"

Theo exchanged a look with Vince, before turning their attention to Spring. Spring held her breath, the club music pulsing throbbing in her ears. Without ceremony, Theo bent, unhooking the velvet rope, stepping aside with a wide grin. "Pam, you'll always be family at 747, your friends too! Go in, no cover!"

"Thanks, guys! I'll miss you!" Pam hugged both bouncers, before dragging Spring and Jorge toward the stairs. Gina brought up the rear.

"Good luck in space!" Vince called out, winking at Spring. She smiled, waving.

"Thanks!"

Pam led them straight to the whirling engine, where the four of them climbed up the ladder, posing inside for group and individual photos. Everything was 'on the house' for Pam.

"Pam, you know everyone!" Gina asked as they walked toward the blinking air-stairs at the boarding door. "Did you party here like, every night or something?"

"I used to work here! I was a hostess, like her!" Pam yelled over the music, pointing to the girl dressed as an old fashioned stewardess at the boarding door. The girl looked like something straight out of a history memo, micro mini with a pillbox hat, gloves and go-go boots.

The wind picked up, ruffling Spring's hair and dress. She blinked up at the full Moon shivering. A warm hand went around shoulder, giving her a gentle squeeze. "Cool, huh?" Jorge asked looking up.

"Cool and a little scary." Spring admitted. Five months ago, she would've mistaken the space station Pegasus I for another bright star, close to the Moon. She gazed up at Pegasus now, watching as two flashes of light shot away from the station like shooting stars. StarShips, headed who knows where. She shivered again, her eyes stinging. "It just seems like a dream...I can't believe I'm leaving Earth...even saying it sounds weird! Leaving Earth!"

"I know!" Pam chimed in as they reached the boarding door, "I used to dream of life on the Moon. I can't wait! See ya, Earth! Come on, girl!" Pam danced her way onto the plane.

Spring had never seen an airplane like 747. She blinked, her eyes trying to adjust to the surreal lighting that changed colors like a wave of light passing through the club. One second everyone was bathed in violet-blue lights, the next a wave of pink and purple would sweep along, in time to the pulsing music. Go-go dancers in stewardess and pilots uniforms (well, the 'pilots' in metallic shorts and tight shirts and pilot hats), danced high above in clear iridescent bubbles that flashed with video images. Famous faces were everywhere, on the dance floor, lounging on plush chairs, heading up the floating spiral staircase to the VIP section guarded by a burly looking 'pilot'.

"Is it always this packed?" Spring shouted into Pam's ear as they followed her through the crowd. Spring sidestepped a towering couple in tall headdresses that moved (and hissed), as they walked toward the dance floor. Spring glanced at the dance floor, nearly bumping into a woman in a dress that looked like it was made out of cascading water. Spring stared hard at the dance floor: holograms of long dead rock stars mingled with clubbers. She could've sworn she saw David Bowie. Madonna, and a few Beatles. A girl in a skintight sparkling mirror catsuit, brushed against Jorge, giving him a look under her lashes. Jorge muttered a hurried excuse, rushing after the catsuit girl.

"Oh, yeah!" Pam laughed, nodding to a scantily dressed gorgeous pilot carrying a tray of tall flutes. He headed toward them, making his way through the throng. "And this is a slow night! Fridays are insane!"

"May I offer you a beverage?" The Adonis of a pilot/waiter asked, offering a glittery gold beverage. Tiny balls of gold floated in the liquid. Pam snatched one up, giggling.

"Jet Fuel! This stuff is Absolute! Go on, try some!" Pam urged. Spring stared up into the waiter's eyes, they looked as golden as the Jet Fuel, he smiled at her. One of those sexy, disarming smiles.

"Thank you!" Spring smiled back shyly, accepting a tall flute. She raised her flute high, "To graduation tomorrow!"

"To the Moon!" Pam shouted over the music.

"And to rich Alien men!" Gina added, clinking her glass to theirs.

Jet Fuel was the perfect name for the stuff. It burned down Spring's throat, making her eyes tear up instantly. "Oh my god," she rasped, forgetting to look sophisticated around the waiter (who waited patiently for the empty flutes). "What's in this...real jet fuel, Pam?" She blindly handed her flute to the waiter. Gina was doing her best not to cough, despite a bright red face and watery eyes. Pam looked perfectly normal. Almost immediately, the Jet Fuel took effect, the room becoming more vivid as a feeling of weightlessness filled Spring. The club had a surreal, dreamlike quality to it now. Music emanated from her. She closed her eyes, grinning.

"Tastic, huh! Knew you'd love it!" Pam 's voice sounded far away. Spring opened her eyes, finding herself, on the dance floor, Pam helping a hacking, bareheaded Gina to a nearby chair. A guy walked through the crowd, wearing Gina's lit up headdress. Spring burst into laughter, tears rolling down her cheeks. She moved backwards on the dance floor, bumping into a broad chest.

"Oh! I'm so sor--" Spring turned, staring up at an incredibly tall man with the most beautiful pale eyes she had ever seen. He smiled down at her, a slow sensual smile that made his unusual eyes light up even more. *An Alien?*

"Dance with me." Spring whispered, her eyes locked on his, as she began to dance, giving herself to the music.

* * *

Spring rolled over on her side, staring at her offending dorm alarm clock, willing herself to move a few inches to turn it off. She blinked blearily at it, finally leaning forward to turn it off, then falling back against her pillow, gazing up at the ceiling. *What's happening today? Why am I up so early?* She eased herself up on her elbows, her eyes going directly to the closet. Her Orion Galactic uniform hung neatly.

"Graduation's today!" She shot up in bed, kicking the covers off, swinging her feet to the floor. "Mom and Dad are flying in this morning...

in an hour!" Spring yanked open her dresser, pulling out a random blouse and pair of jeans, before sprinting to the bathroom.

Ten minutes later, Spring stepped out of the shower, covered in a towel, wiping the steam off of the bathroom mirror. She smiled to herself as she cleared the mirror, *I get my gold wings today! And tomorrow, I'm off to the....* "Still have blue hair!" she squeaked, staring in wide eyed horror at her reflection.

"Oh." Spring leaned heavily against the counter, panic setting in, her chest tightening, she closed her eyes. "Breathe, breathe." She took a deep breath, before opening the door, running out into the coolness of her room. "Pam! Pam!" She ran to Pam's bed. Pam's feet lay on her pillow, while her head was obviously the blanketed lump at the end of the bed. Spring gave Pam's shoulder a hard shake, "Pam! Wake up!"

Pam groaned, peeling the blanket off, "Wha...what's wrong?" Pam blinked up at Spring, wincing at the morning sun. She blinked again, her eyes slowly focusing on Spring, widening in surprise, "Ooooh! Your hair is still ..."

"I know." Spring snapped. "How do I change it back? They won't let me graduate with blue hair streaked with ..." she glanced at the dresser mirror, "red, purple and pink!"

Pam sat up, fully awake. She pulled back the covers, sitting cross legged on her bed. She was still dressed in her 747 clothes. Pam's hair was back to strawberry blond. "Get the wand."

Spring retrieved it from the bathroom, silently handing it to Pam. She sat down on the edge of her bed, clutching her pillow, resting her chin against it. Pam studied the color wand carefully, her eyes scanning the numbers, her face suddenly going pale.

"What is it? What's wrong?" Spring asked. Pam looked up slowly, her eyes resting on Spring's hair.

"Do you realize," Pam said in a still voice, "that you set your color to last for..." she glanced at the wand again, "for forty-eight hours?"

Spring felt like the air was vacuumed from her lungs, "Forty-eight hours?" she gasped. "My hair will stay like this for, FORTY- EIGHT HOURS?" She fell backward on her bed, covering her eyes, "Great! My family lands in an hour, we graduate tonight, and I have blue, crazy, Martian hair. Great." Spring lifted one hand, peeking at Pam. "How long do you usually set it for?"

"Six hours, tops." Pam shrugged, fiddling with the wand. "Hey!" Pam looked up, smiling hopefully, "Maybe no one will notice? Okay, okay, don't look like that...at least its not forty-eight days, right?"

"Yeah, true." Spring got up, digging through her drawer for a scarf, tying it experimentally around her head. "At least the colors are semi patriotic! I better haul ass to the airport." She went back into the bathroom, shutting the door.

Do Martians really have Blue Hair?

4

DESTINATION MOON

Spring's wig itched. She felt like Cleopatra with the wig's shoulder length black bob and blunt bangs that skimmed her eyebrows. The new wig seemed to fit the occasion. Graduation. A new life in space. A new for Spring Stevens. She stood with the rest of her class on a set of portable bleachers flanking the small podium, with what looked like two hundred family and friends in fold out chairs, looking on. Graduation day. Spring had never seen the stuffy, Orion island look so festive, small white lights hung from every tree, mimicking the stars that were beginning to peep through the evening sky. Even the railing behind the podium and bleachers, were draped with lights that sparkled on the water. Waves lapped against the island, filling the air with the fresh salty breeze that reminded Spring of Virginia Beach.

She looked down at her brand new wings, gold plated with a shooting star in the middle holding a tiny crystal. 'S. Stevens' was engraved in black letters in a small rectangular box directly under the star. She gripped her brand new leather bound envelope containing her Orion diploma and extra set of wings, smiling to herself. Spring glanced up in time to see her CEO, Katherine Stewart, a stately woman with silver streaked hair approach the podium. Katherine had once been a flight attendant herself.

"Today, all of you have become members of the Orion Galactic family. Today and tomorrow you shall travel the stars as pioneers of space, as previous flight attendants before you traveled the skies. Flight attendants of old, including myself, flew among the clouds, and could only dream of life among the stars." She paused, glancing over at Spring's class, "Now ladies and gentlemen, it is your turn…to travel above the stars and beyond! To the Moon and beyond! Congratulations to you all, as CEO of Orion Galactic Airways, I salute you, and wish you great success in your travels throughout the galaxy! To the class of 2079!"

Loud, excited applause and cheers followed, accompanied by music from a live, old fashioned big band (dressed in Star Trek costumes of red, blue and gold), playing every 'Moon' related song ever made, starting with a jazzy 'Destination Moon'. Spring found herself twirling giddily with her classmates, singing slightly off key to the chorus. The evening sky with its shades of violet blue, already promising a clear view of a surprisingly big, glowing Moon and bright stars. Spring was glad the ceremony was held outside on the Orion grounds. The old Manhattan skyline was in the distance behind the podium, and their family and friends sat on bleachers on both sides, while her graduating class sat in the middle. All one-hundred and fifty of them. People began to circulate, moving toward the bleachers, snapping pictures, snacking at the refreshment tables (which included a giant, crescent moon shaped cheesecake) in the back. People were laughing, crying, hugging, doing silly little jigs to the music. Cameras flashing everywhere.

"Spring! We did it!" Pam launched herself into Spring, hugging her. Spring nodded, jumping excitedly with Pam.

"We totally did it! We survived training!" Spring laughed, waving at Jorge.

"No more tests, girls!" Jorge grabbed them both in a side hug, kissing the tops of their heads, "I don't even mind being based on Mars! Maybe I'll met some cute girl there." He cocked an eyebrow, "Use my half-human mystique on her!" Spring exchanged a smirk with Pam before bursting into laughter.

"Yeah right, Mr. Spock!" Spring gave him a playful jab, just as a stern looking man in full EF formal attire and woman in strangely designed full skirt came forward. The woman had a kind motherly face of deep burnished copper, and a slightly ridged forehead that gathered in a wide arrow design at the bridge of her nose. She also had Jorge's strange nose and reptile eyes. The man was human, curly hair, broad nose, thin lips. The woman grinned at them, displaying a small rotating beam of light that hovered a few inches above her gloved hand. "Picture time! Come now, gather yourselves close!"

"Mother..." Jorge looked sheepish. He put his arms around Spring and Pam's shoulders.

"Yeah! Kodak moment! Hold that! Perfect!" Spring's grandmother Libby examined her ultra thin camera, before looking up beaming, "Love your uniforms! They are so Awesome!" She turned to Jorge's parents, "Hey there! I'm Elizabeth Mattsson. Libby for short, Spring's gran!" She shook their hands excitedly, "I used to be a stew back in the day! Too old now... just turned a hundred! Born eons ago!"

"Hey baby, congratulations!" Spring's mom hugged her, enveloping her in a familiar cloud of perfume. "We're so proud of you! You look so pretty!" Her mother stood back, her hands going up to inspect Spring's hair. "Did you change your hair, hon? Summer, go stand beside your sister for a picture." Spring's mom literally shoved her kid sister forward. Summer stood red-faced beside Spring, smiling shyly at Jorge. Summer was at least three inches taller than her, her dark brown hair in a low ponytail. She looked like their mom, same cinnamon brown skin, hazel eyes. At least Spring had inherited her mom's dimpled smile. She reached up to give her wig a discreet scratch, hoping it was still straight.

"Gwen, wait!" Spring's dad handed her a bunch of sunflowers tied with a pink ribbon, planting a quick kiss on her forehead, before standing near Jorge's dad, giving him a firm handshake. "Marc Stevens. You're with the EF? Our son is at the academy right now. I'm retired Navy myself."

"My cheeks are going to burst!" Spring said through her smile. Pam assumed a faux glamorous look.

"One more, guys!"

"Yes, one more. Pamela, look this way," said a rail thin woman with icy blond hair cut in precise layers. An equally stiff looking man stood beside her, wearing an expensive suit, holding a small blue box with a white ribbon.

Pam's face lit up with surprise. "Drew! Hamilton! You made it? Tastic! Thanks!" Pam broke away, hugging the designer clad woman who patted Pam's shoulder awkwardly with an embarrassed smile. "Drew, Ham, meet my friends, Spring and Jorge, and their families too! Everyone, my big sister Drew and her hubby, Hamilton!" Drew and Hamilton nodded, Drew's cold green eyes widening a bit when she glanced at Jorge's mom.

"Of course we would be here, Pamela. You know that." The woman looked expectantly at the man, "Hamilton, the box please. Thank you. For you, Pamela." She handed the box to Pam. Spring could see the resemblance, despite the taut features and reserved demeanor. *So this is Pam's big sister Drew and her hubby.*

"Wow! Thanks!" Pam took the box eagerly, carefully avoiding contact with Hamilton's fingers, hugging her sister again, "This is so Absolute! Thank you! You know what? I'm going to open this on the Moon, on a Telecall! How about that? Little Madison and Everest will love that, huh? Are they here?" Pam looked behind her sister, before glancing back expectantly, "I mean, I leave for the Moon tomorrow...I'm their only aunt!" She laughed, her fingers plucking at the white ribbon of the box.

There was a short silence, before her sister answered, "You forget, we won't be home. You know we always go away around this time, and

Madison and Everest are away at school. Silly, Pamela! You never remember anything do you?" Pam's sister chuckled softly, shaking her cascade of hair.

"I guess not." Pam said in a small voice, "How stupid of me." She hugged the gift and her diploma folder close to her chest, staring down at her feet with a faint smile.

"Well!" Gran-Libby said smiling brightly clapping her hands, "Time to eat! I'm totally starving, and I wanna see more of this city!" She stepped closer to Pam, her back to Drew and Hamilton. "I used to be based here. Flew right out of JFK, lived in Kew Gardens!" She snickered, "Crew Gardens is what we used to call it!" She turned on her heel, "Come on kids, let's get some chow!" She marched through the crowd. Like a small group of baby ducklings, everyone trailed after Gran-Libby, headed toward the long buffet table, stocked with everything from light snacks to caviar.

"Your grandmother is so cool!" Pam said. She stared after Gran-Libby, then back at Spring, "Queens? She lived in Queens? That's all part of New, New York City now. Wonder what it was like in her day."

"Crowded! Do not get her started on life in Kew!" Spring laughed, watching as Gran-Libby 'worked' the crowd, dragging a blushing Orion executive out on the empty dance floor for 'Moondance'. She tried to see Gran-Libby through their eyes. A spunky, petite woman who looked half her age, wide hazel eyes that twinkled, an infectious grin. Warm caramel brown skin. A faint sprinkling of freckles on her nose. The only wrinkles she had were her 'smile lines', which she was proud of, and the way her pert nose crinkled when she laughed. Her chin length bob was snowy white. No matter what the weather, Gran-Libby lived in her collection of West Indian long embroidered tunics, loose pants and jeweled flip flop sandals. She had a gorgeous cherry red outfit with gold embroidery on now. She never left the house without, 'putting her landing lips on', cherry red lipstick.

"Think she would like 747?" Pam asked, as she tapped her fingers against the blue box absently in time to the music. A crowd began to gather on the dance floor, including Spring's parents.

"Are you kidding me? She'll probably close the place! She'll wear everyone out!" Spring caught a glimpse of Gina.

Gina walked between a couple that were obviously her parents. Despite the stiff new clothes they wore, Gina's parents looked like they had had a hard life. Both of their faces were heavily lined, her father stooped slightly. Her mother's eyebrows just mere lines drawn on, but she wore gold earrings and what appeared to be a Hermes scarf. Gina escorted them around, her arms linked protectively through theirs.

"You know," Jorge said eyeing Gina, "I don't think I believe Gina's tales about being raised on the Rivera or Swiss boarding schools."

"Well, at least it looks like she spends her money on someone besides herself. One gold star for her." Spring replied, digging into a slice of cake. She started humming to 'Dancing in the Moonlight'.

Pam put a slice of cake into Jorge's hand, "Guys, let's go to 747 tonight for old time's sake. We don't have to be at the StarPort till...um, 0600, and that's to deadhead up...sound like a plan?"

Jorge looked down at his feet, shuffling them awkwardly, meeting Pam's eyes briefly. "Pam, my parents came a long way....talking light years –long way. Want to take them to dinner or something."

"Same here, well, they flew in from Virginia, but ..." Spring trailed off, before grabbing Pam's arm excitedly, "Why don't you have dinner with us! I mean, you know if you're not hanging with your sister of course! *Shut up, shut up, shut up, making it worse! Bad enough her parents no showed.*

"Oh, you guys! Don't look so sad! I'm having dinner with Drew and Ham. Everything is magnif, promise!" Pam's voice had a strange note to it, "Just wanted to hang at 747 one last time, you know, say goodbye and all that. Probably better to get some shut eye!" She laughed. "See you two bright and early tomorrow! Bye!" She hugged them both, before disappearing in the crowd.

* * *

ONE MONTH LATER.

The crew customs line was long, typical for the Moons peak arrival period. The long line gave Spring the chance to check out the uniforms of the different carriers, as well as the always curious mix of passengers. She looked over at the long line of identical customs booths, trying to spot any of her passengers among the hundreds patiently lined up. The customs area had a mausoleum quality, with stark white walls, spindly white columns, dark tiled floors. Robotic (human) officers sat in levitating, swivel chairs in front of clear screens. Overhead, elevator music blared, and disc shaped lights made everyone look blue. Of course the people that were already blue, looked purple under the lights.

"When do you fly again?"

"Hmmm?" Spring turned her head, staring into the serious eyes of the youngest pilot on her crew. *Bill? Bob? Bowie! Yes, the quiet one!* "I have reserve days starting tomorrow," she said casually, moving forward as the last member of the Virgin Galactic crew cleared. "And you? Another trip back to Earth?"

Bowie smiled, his dark eyes lighting up, "No, have a few days off… was kinda wondering if you want to go to Century for pizza or uh, maybe to Area 51?" His cleared his throat, "Well, that's if they don't use you. I mean, if you want to go out tomorrow. Karaoke night at 51." He nodded toward the customs guy staring at them impatiently. "You're next."

"Hi!" Spring handed the sour looking customs guy her passport card, "Busy day?" The customs guy slanted a look at her, raising one thick, caterpillar eyebrow, before sliding her card through, flicking a quick glance at the screen, then a hard look at her. "Welcome back, Miss Stevens. NEXT!"

"Thanks!" Spring moved off to the side, watching Bowie. He was cute in a squeaky clean way, baby face and thick brown hair that flopped over one eye. Not very tall, but then neither was she.

He walked over to her, tucking his passport card into a front breast pocket, "Well, want to meet up tomorrow?" Spring nodded as they walked side by side toward the exit.

He walked her to the exit doors, lined on both sides with people holding banners and flowers. The eight o'clock train into the city pulled up outside, filling up quickly, as crew, locals and a handful of scared looking tourists piled on. "Take care, Spring, see ya tomorrow then?"

"Uh huh! Maybe!" Spring's feet quickened, her eyes on the full train. She looked over her shoulder, smiling brightly, "Great flying with you! Bye!" She maneuvered her way to a window seat at the back, falling into the seat just as the train lurched into motion, pulling away from the StarPort. The StarPort glittered, full of light, while a couple of StarShuttles took off behind it. Spring wedged her bag into the narrow space beside her legs, pulling out her music chip player, placing the wireless earring stud size buds into her ears. She leaned back in her seat, her head resting against the headrest. Classical music filled her ears as the train sped through the protective bubble tunnel. Spring's eyes shifted between the grey-brown rocky terrain outside the bubble, and the colorful, shifting hologram commercials on the seatbacks.

The train rocked gently, passing by several hotels and fast food restaurants, all encased in bubbles of their own. Her stomach growled as they passed a McDonald's, where a few of the newly approved 'scooter-cars' waited at the drive-thru. The scooter cars looked like an updated version of a golf cart, and were just as fast.

"Mom! Dad! Look! They have a Mickey D's! Can we go there!" exclaimed the boy sitting in front of her, as he breathed grape bubble gum breath against the window. His eyes wide with excitement. He wore an orange 'Gibson Family, Moon Tour 2079' T-shirt. "Maybe later, Tradd," Mr.

Gibson said, "Gotta list planned. Plus, we got McDonald's at home. Shoot! Look at the Earth! Damn! Now that is a sight!"

"Amazin', Harry!" Mrs. Gibson's chubby ringed hand touched the window, outlining Earth. "Oh, my stars! Look at the city! Like somethin' out of New Yawk Sitty, but on the Moon!"

Spring turned off her music, stowing it in her bag, as the train entered the city of Lunar Prime East, which did indeed look like a small New York City. Modest sized skyscrapers, stood clustered together under the dark, protective solar glass shield. The train glided through a boulevard lined with young trees. They passed a few joggers and a woman with a stroller, eliciting a few startled gasps from the Gibson's. The train raced past the lone shopping center and the dry cleaners, reminding Spring to pick up her uniforms. A few couples strolled outside the gelato shop, while a few read and had a few bites at the bookstore/sidewalk café on the corner.

"They have TREES? Trees on the Moon?" sputtered Tradd, as he pressed his nose against the window once more. Spring smiled. She was tempted to tell them about the climate controlled temperatures, and the scheduled rain, but she didn't want to interrupt. Spring still felt like a tourist herself, her eyes stayed glued to her own window. Another train whizzed by them, bound for the StarPort. She wondered if Pam was on it. Pam was on call today. *Maybe I have the place all to myself tonight!*

The train slowed to a crawl, coming to a gentle stop at Armstrong Circle, right in front of the Galactic Towers. Home sweet home. Spring stood up, yanking her bag, sending it right into her left shin. She winced, rubbing her right foot against her left ankle.

Mrs. Gibson tugged at her sleeve as she went past, "Miss! Do we get off here too? Harry, what was our stop again?" Harry scratched his head, leaving a few brown strands standing .

"Doesn't say. Just says Apollo Marriott hotel. Is that near here, Miss?" He asked. Beside him, Tradd blew a purple bubble. The train door was going to shut any minute, and her feet could not handle the twenty minute walk from the next stop in her concourse heels. Cute heels, but the cuteness expired after ten hours. Never again would she forget to pack her onboard flats.

"I think the Marriott's two stops away, on Sputnik Way! Um, have a good day!" She said hurriedly, stepping off just in time, as the doors slammed shut. From the window, Mr. and Mrs. Gibson waved, mouthing thanks, while their son flashed his purple tongue at her. She was tempted to flash hers back.

Spring limped across the street, casting a glance up at the top of the sky-dome, already filling up with soft, watery blue- grey clouds for the weekly scheduled rain. She could even 'smell' the generated rain in the air, mixing with the smell from the bakery across the street. Her building stood in the middle of four identical, round, towers made of black glass, rising ten stories, two were owned by Orion Galactic. A new tower was being built next door.

The other two towers remained illuminated mysteries. Spring had a feeling they were owned by another airline. She walked up to her building, scanning her entrance pass, before the wide double doors. The elevator opened as if on cue, letting a harassed looking flight attendant off. Spring stepped into the glass elevator with its view into tower one, leaning tiredly against the wall.

"Good evening, Miss Spring Stevens," the elevator said in a stilted voice, "do you request the ninth floor?" She mumbled yes, as the doors slid shut. Spring gazed at the building next door, noticing there was a party in full force on the fifth floor, while on the seventh a young father walked around his living room, holding a baby, while his wife dozed on the couch, wrapped in a cozy, plaid throw blanket.

Living on the ninth floor of a ten story building, was a big improvement over the thirty- fourth floor of the one-hundred floor building. It was a modest two bedroom, with a tiny galley kitchen, everything furnished by Orion. A hideous burnt orange couch and almond colored drapes in the living room and the towels in the linen closet were all company issued. Orion also provided two additional roommates and two unofficial commuter roommates that shared the tiny apartment with Spring and Pam. Spring had never met the commuters, she saw them as occasional blanket covered lumps on the bunk beds or as a smiling uniformed blur rushing out the door.

Spring walked into the living room, a delighted smile spreading over her face. She had the apartment to herself! Pam, Coco and Oslo (the other roommates) were not home. Spring walked down the short hallway to the second bedroom that contained the commuter bunk beds, sure enough, there was a suspiciously humanoid shape breathing deeply under a cocoon of blankets. Spring stared hard at the shape, trying to decipher if that was the 'guy' commuter or the 'girl'. Both were married to EF people based on space stations. The shape snored, so Spring assumed it was the 'guy' commuter. She gently closed the door, tiptoeing to her room .Actually, the room she shared with Pam, and Coco.

Spring stumbled into her room, kicking off her heels, flipping on the blinking televideo, while stepping out of her uniform, leaving it at a puddle at her feet. Hologram messages shifted on her nightstand., first her mom's slightly bleary image.

"Baby? It's mom honey, call when you get in, okay? Love ya, bye!"

"Hey, girlie!" Pam's face appeared in front of a large shifting crowd. "I'm next door at Building One, massive partaay! Come over to five…. uh…what was it again? Oh, thanks! Apartment 510 when you get in, kay? Bye Byeee!"

Spring stepped over her uniform, and into the coat closet sized bathroom, taking a quick shower, then sitting on her bed, combing the tangles out of her curls. She leaned her head against her headboard, relishing her freshly washed hair. Her eyes drifting lazily to her window, listening to the rain beating against the glass, and the soft rumble of generated thunder… or was it a StarShuttle? She thought of the pilot. Bill? Blair?

"Close my eyes for ten minutes," She said sluggishly, as she rested her cheek against the pillow, "Ten minutes, then go to ….party."

* * *

The buzzing of the televideo woke Spring. She blinked against the bright sunlight filling her room, her bedside lamp still on. Someone was making a racket in the kitchen. She gazed at the flashing televideo screen in the corner for a second, before pressing the 'answer' button on her night table. Immediately, the screen filled with a stressed looking man in a dark blue turtleneck, with the words 'Orion Scheduling' flashing on the screen along with his name. He looked around for a second, then his eyes seemed to zero in on her disheveled, frizzball hair. The time displayed on the screen read, three-thirty. P.M. .

"Hello, this is Michael, from Orion Scheduling. May I speak with Spring Stevens?"

"Speaking," she croaked. She leaned on one elbow, trying to blink the sleep out of her eyes.

"We have a trip for you. Pairing 1099, signs in at eighteen hundred."

Spring sat up straight, wide awake now, she saw his eyes glance down at her bright pink, moon and stars nightshirt. "But that's in like, less than four hours! What kind of trip is it? Where is it going?"

"It's a long haul," the scheduler said slowly. "To colony planet, Eden. Your room mate, Ms. Sloane has been assigned as well. She, uh, suggested you. We normally don't do favors, but…"

"It's just that…" Spring looked away. *I had a date! Well, maybe. Kinda.*

"Are you trying to refuse a trip?" The scheduler's voice had an ominous ring to it, his eyes narrowed slightly.

"To Eden? My first long haul and flying with a friend?" Spring grinned, throwing back her duvet, revealing a thick pair of matching pink socks, "No way! Where do I sign up!"

* * *

"Come on, Spring! We'll miss the train!" Pam barged into her room, already dressed in her uniform, her hair pulled back in a chignon. "Come on, old woman!"

"Well, pardon me for being space-lagged from an Earth two day." Spring snapped, as she threw as many clothes as she could into her suitcase, along with shoes, "What's the weather like on Eden anyway?"The Televideo buzzed again, and Spring ran to her table, jabbing the answer button, while she folded three extra uniforms. "Hello?" She said with her hairbrush in her mouth. She looked up into Gran-Libby's smiling face.

"Hey there! Did I call at a bad time, Spring Chick? Where are you rushing off to? Another trip to our blue marble?"

Spring ducked under her bed, dragging her favorite heels out, "No, not this time! I've been short called for a long haul, to a colony planet!"

"Whoo hoo! Awesome-sauce! How long is that trip, a few days? Weeks? Centuries? Eons? Does it involve wormholes or warp speed?"

"A month, I think. Jorge is the only one I know from my class that actually had one. I don't know what to pack, and I have like, ten minutes!" *Where is my new shampoo? If Pam 'borrowed' it...*

Gran-Libby leaned forward, sipping from a giant, daisy covered mug. "Well, always pack a good...no, a gorgeous, fabulous, sexy dress and some," she paused lowering her voice. "Fuck me heels!"

Spring dropped her makeup bag on the floor, staring up at her grandmother in shock. "Gran!"

Gran-Libby let out a soft, rusty laugh, "It's the truth, sweets! Oh pahleeze! Don't look at me like that! I may be over one hundred, but I still know about sex. Ha! Shocked you? Sex! Sex! Sex!"

"Grossing me out, Gran." Spring bent, collecting her makeup, "I don't want to know that!"

Gran Libby laughed harder, wiping a tear, "Have a great time, Spring. Why, I remember my first international like it was yesterday. God, I was so nervous! Almost spilled champagne on a guy in Business Class! Paris, Boeing 767, and with a crew of women older than my parents! I still have pictures too! When am I going to get to see my Spring Chick in action? We'll have to fly somewhere soon, love to see the Moon. Did I ever show you my picture albums? Why, I swear—hold on a sec..."

"Gotta go, Gran." Spring interrupted, closing her suitcase, glancing up at the screen, "wish me luck!"

Gran-Libby's eyes welled up for a moment, "Sure. Good luck, Spring, I'm proud of you! You're living my dream, Off-World! I never would've thought it would happen in my lifetime! Have fun, and don't be nervous!"

"I won't!" Spring considered, "I'll try not to be! Love you, Gran! Bye!" She reached up to disconnect the call.

"Spring, wait!" Gran-Libby said sharply.

"Yes?"

Gran-Libby's eyes shimmered with moisture, but her she smiled a Cheshire smile. "Don't forget to pack those heels! Call me when you get back, I want to hear all about it!" She winked.

"Deal. But, Gran, what were you calling about?"

Gran-Libby shrugged, sipping at what Spring knew was either Earl Grey tea or hot cocoa. "No big deal, totally forgot actually. Have a great time, Spring Chick, love you too. You better go before you miss your sign in."

Spring stared at her grandmother's face. She was certain Gran-Libby was hiding something, "Okay, bye, Gran-Libby, love ya!"

5

OFF-WORLD KINDA GIRL

The lounge was packed when Spring and Pam arrived. Peak sign in time, with flight attendants scurrying around, rushing to sign in, brief or hurry home. The lounge had a slight 'don't linger' vibe to it, despite the few, slanted windows, placed high in the walls. Icy blue walls decorated with shifting images of Orion crews from the 1940's all up to present day .Row after row of flight attendants stood at waist high counters made of polished steel, checking their schedules with holographic screens that popped up, displaying an array of information all at once. It took Spring awhile to get used to viewing her monthly schedule, along with her trip, the weather, and company news, in several, rotating, three dimensional images.

The rumble of StarShuttles could be heard overhead, as Spring and Pam entered the underground lounge. A few flight attendants glanced up from their screens curiously.

"Did someone burn popcorn again?" Pam wrinkled her nose, as she parked her bags along a wall of matching suitcases. She walked over to the sign in screens.

"Spring!" A familiar looking man with a made up face came up, air-kissing her on both cheeks. "Toots, are we flying to Earth together?"

"No, somewhere new and exciting!" Spring beamed, walking over to the sign in counter. "Off-World!"

"Mars? Titan? Surely, you are not talking about that Terraform-nightmare in progress, Europa?"

"No, none of those! We're headed to Eden!" Spring blurted loudly. A few people stopped and stared.

"Spring, girl," He took a dramatic step back, surveying her. "How did you two newbies, get that?"

* * *

"Ladies and gentlemen, we shall dock at space station Pegasus I in ten minutes. Please ensure your harness is fastened and your carry-on luggage is properly stowed, thank you."

Pam looked down at her harness, then at out the window, "I can see lights! And what looks like a giant Ferris wheel on its side…all lit up too. That must be the station! Tastic!"

"Can you see the ship?" Spring tried to see past Pam's head. "Guess the crew really is waiting for us? Hope they're nice. Didn't expect to dead-head out, did you?"

"Me too! Spring! There are so many ships parked at the end of the spoke thingys!" She glanced back at Spring with wide eyes, "They are big ones too, real StarShips! Here, take a look." She leaned back into her seat, sucking in her chin.

Spring leaned toward the window, stretching as far as her harness would allow. She could see how Pam saw the station as a Ferris wheel on its side. To Spring it looked like a brilliantly lit star or sunbeam, with long and short rays stretching outwards. The 'spokes' varied from long to short, all the way around. Thousands of tiny lights, made the station and its 'spokes' possess a polka dot look; as if they were wrapped over and over with twinkling Christmas lights. Twenty ships were docked around the circular station, they all dwarfed the small StarShuttle they were on. Their deadheading shuttle was small enough to use an interior docking port. Spring felt butterflies in her stomach as they flew closer, gliding by the silent, colossal StarShips and the equally large 'spokes'.

"Hey, do you think that's our ship?" Pam pointed to a sleek, incredibly large StarShip, ablaze with lights. It had a two tone chrome finish of a smooth 'battleship' grey on top; and a darker gunmetal grey on the bottom. The StarShuttles resembled airplanes, but the StarShip Spring was staring at looked more like a small scale cruise ship or large yacht. An obvious cousin to EF ships, down to the powerful, oblong shaped aft engines, with the glowing blue light. Very Star Trek.

It lacked the 'bloated look' of a cruise ship, but shared a similar shape with nine staggered levels, and hundreds of windows. Spring could just make out 'Orion Galactic' in bold black letters visible and intimidating against the fuselage. Even the shooting star emblem had a more subdued look to it, dark blue instead of a bright gold. Spring felt a serge of pride when the ships name and registry number came into view, under the star emblem, Excalibur-280/ ENC-23: EXPLORER.

"Look at the size of that thing! The mock up at the center was not even close!" Spring gaped at the StarShip, teetered to one of the longer spokes at the base.

Pam stowed her tray table, tightening her seat harness," Doesn't even look like it holds...what was it... two-hundred and fifty passengers? Twenty-eight flight attendants too!" she leaned forward, "It's a pretty ship...this is so awesome, Spring!" Pam bounced in her seat, clapping her hands.

"This is totally worth missing a date with the pilot from my last trip! Spring said as their shuttle flew past it, entering a hexagon shaped docking port tunnel, "Jorge said the designers of the Excalibur StarShips were Galtarrion, that's why it can travel so fast and only EF trained pilots can fly them."

"Maybe we'll find some cute pilots on our ship...there has to be at least one cutie in there! Excalibur 280, what a weird name for a fleet of ships."

"I know, right! Sounds like a cleaning product!" Spring said as their shuttle came to a stop. She glanced out the window just in time to see two massive docking doors, sliding shut.

"Or a toy!" Pam said slyly. Passengers were deplaning, stepping off onto a polished black platform, leading to wide stairs.

"Come on, girly, we have a StarShip to work!" Spring smiled brightly at the male flight leader by the boarding door, "Bye, thanks for the ride!" He winked at them.

Pegasus I was noisy, crowded and had the atmosphere of a mall on a Saturday afternoon. The sights and sounds of cranky children, fast food, and the drone of boarding announcements, added character to the formal looking floating rotunda. It had a warmer look to it(unlike the more sterile looking Lunar StarPort), luxurious, cream colored walls and tiered balconies, tiled floors in shades of terra cotta. A mall/airport in space, designed to make Earth passengers feel at home (and to make them forget being off-world). The station was larger than Spring expected, with eight tiered floors, open to a center atrium, with the standard mall fountain surrounded by plants. She craned her neck, staring up at the eight floors, recognizing a few of her favorite shops on the second floor. She spotted a few hotels and restaurants on the other floors.

"Look at this place! Can you imagine calling this place home? Those top floors must be apartments or something, right? Hundreds of people live here!" Pam stopped in her tracks on the platform, causing Spring to run right into her back, her suitcase crashing against her legs. Pam's bag slid out of her hands, rolling a few feet. All of this in the presence of three handsome businessmen who stood there watching with interest. Spring felt her cheeks burn. "How are we going to find our gate in this smorgasbord?" Pam asked, sitting down by the fountain, parking her bags.

Spring tapped the Orion issued rotation programmer on her wrist. It looked like an old fashioned wrist watch, except it was packed with trip and schedule related stuff and things required by the SAA like their onboard manuals. It also told time. "With this I hope!" she said, tapping the tiny face, watching a screen materialize, expanding above her wrist into a 3x5 inch, white screen displaying their rotation, gate information, map and weather. "There! Gate 12A! Let's go, I think they're probably waiting for us!" Spring began to weave her wave through the crowd. Gate 12 A was on the other side of the courtyard, on the second level. "Come on, Pam! The gate's over there." *With like, a million people waiting to board.*

"Paging Orion Galactic flight attendants, Spring Stevens and Pamela Sloane, please report to gate 12A." Announced a disembodied voice, that quickly repeated the page in five other languages, two of whom were Alien.

"Oh my god!" Pam hopped on the levitating escalator after Spring, "Think we're in trouble? They know we were short called right?"

"I…they should." Spring said her eyes on the crowd below, checking out crew uniforms of yellow, red, orange and every shade of blue, mixing with the travelers. All humans. Not a single Alien. "Wish we had more time here."

* * *

"We are so glad to see you guys! Good to see you! We thought we were going to go out short staffed tonight! I'm Luke." A handsome bald man with a intricate beard stepped away from the boarding door with a wide smile, that made Spring relax instantly. She could tell he was going to be a nice Purser. He was older, perhaps in his early forties, kind eyes, and a warm voice. Spring stumbled onto the main 'bridge', ignoring her suitcase falling sideways down her leg. She introduced herself in a soft whisper, while Pam mumbled something that sounded like 'Am'.

"They want to board any minute, so you'll have to meet the rest of the crew later, but then we'll have a month, right?" Luke joked as he lead them through the wide Galactic Elite boarding foyer; with its unique, recessed swirling crystal chandeliers and amazing mosaic tile work on the walls. They silently followed him through the GE departure cabin, filled with plush, airplane style seats, then into a golden beige circular hallway, stopping in front of an elevator that blended into the wall. Two flight attendants hurried past, nodding hello.

"That's Chandler and Wade, they're working GE with me." Luke explained, allowing them to enter the elevator. "You're both working Level C with Adiva. She's waiting for you guys. Sorry there's no time to brief you two, but if you have any questions ask Adiva, okay?" Luke paused, then added wryly, "or ask me if Adiva is being Adiva. Oh, you may want to store your bags in your dorm room, before we board. See ya in a bit! Deck C." He stepped away from the elevator.

"Deck Z." The elevator replied.

"Deck C." Luke repeated.

"Deck B." The elevator's calm female voice answered.

"DECK C!" Luke snapped. He shook his head at them, rolling his eyes. Spring bit down hard on her lip.

"Deck C." The elevator slid doors shut. As it jerked into motion, descending, Spring glanced at Pam before bursting into laughter, leaning against the wall for support.

"Deck Z!" Pam gasped, holding her stomach, "I was trying so hard to keep a straight face!"

"Me too!"

The elevator stopped, and the doors slid open revealing an another standard beige hallway, where boarding music blared overhead. "Let's find this Adiva girl, let her know we're here." Spring said, hopping off the elevator, studying the posted directions on the wall.

They walked down the wide, circular hallway, passing the dining room, bathrooms and what looked like an inviting observation deck. A flight attendant hurrying by pointed them in the right direction toward the Level C boarding door.

"Okay, we're boarding! Boarding positions please!" Luke's voice carried over the loud music.

A tall, thin woman in red stood by the boarding door. She slouched slightly, leaning impatiently against the open doorway. Her thin lips were pressed in a firm line that displayed puckering around her mouth. A smokers mouth. Her dark auburn hair was shoulder length, pulled away from her face with a thin headband, showcasing a long angular face with sharp cheekbones. Small close set eyes that narrowed slightly as they approached her. She stared at them, pursing her lips. "Well," she said flatly, "it's about time."

She impatiently waved off their introductions, zeroing in on their bags, glancing up at Spring and Pam. "You always work your trips dragging your bags? You do realize we are going to have passengers on here any second?"

"We're not ...not ... s...sure where we can put these?" Pam stammered. Her face was beet red.

"We're not sure what dorm we were assigned to, and besides," Spring heard the defensive edge creeping into her voice. "We thought we should introduce ourselves to you first, let you know we were here." She looked Adiva in the eye, watching as the older woman's eyes went from Spring to Pam, then back again. Sizing them up. At that moment, the first group of coach (Galactic Pioneer Class), started down the long jetway, another flight attendant came down the hall, her eyes on the door. She glanced at them curiously, then turned to Adiva. Something that looked like fear flashed through Adiva's eyes.

"Zavia, take uh, Spring and Cam to your dorm. You have that big room all to yourself, right?"

"Pam. It's Pam." Pam stressed. Zavia glanced at them with the palest eyes Spring had ever seen.

"I am supposed to board." Zavia said stubbornly to Adiva, just as a portly man stepped onto the ship.

"I'll do it. Just get these two out of here." She turned toward the man with an unsmiling face, "Hi, boarding pass?"

Zavia stared at her for a second, before turning, "Follow me." she said in a low voice. She lead them down another hallway to a smaller elevator with a security pad beside it. The screen lit up when she entered a code, and the doors slid open, "Deck two." The elevator obeyed, shooting up quickly. Zavia glanced over her shoulder, smiling faintly. She was tall, probably under six feet, with pale skin that had a faint blue tinge to it that brought out the blue tones in her black hair swept up into a French roll. Her long fingers tapped the wall in time to the boarding music that played loudly even in the crew elevator as she hummed along. Her features were humanoid, down to her classical profile and high cheekbones, but her eyes were so unnaturally pale. They were the color of a pale storm cloud, lined with a striking dark iris. Chrome.

"What is it? Is my hair out of place, standing on end? Why do you stare?" Zavia's pale colorless eyes were directed at Spring. The elevator slowed to a stop. Pam's mouth twitched.

"Oh, um…sorry. I uh, love your shoes!" *Are you an alien? Okay, stupid question.*

Zavia stepped off the elevator, digesting this, "thank you. This way."

They passed a rec area, gym, dining room and a large observation deck, before turning down another hallway with numbered doors. Their room was at the end of the hall. Zavia entered a code, and the door slid open, revealing a semi-spacious little dorm the size of an old hotel room. Four enclosed bed compartments were placed against two walls, a tiny plant in a bright yellow pot sat on a table under a round window in the middle. There was a standard bathroom to the right of the front door. One of the top bed pods was open, revealing a fluffy duvet, pillow, and a flickering monitor. A book lay on the neatly made up bed, along with a clear container that appeared to hold m&m's. Peanut m&m's. Spring's stomach growled.

"Just put your luggage down over there," Zavia gestured toward four mirrored closet compartments, "We have to get back to C." Spring took a quick peek at her herself, before following Zavia and Pam into the quiet hallway.

"This ship is amazing! How long have you been flying?" Pam's excited voice bounced off the walls, there was no boarding music in this area.

"Pam, the daytime crew is resting right now." Zavia said quietly. Zavia's voice had no accent at all. Even Jorge had an alien accent. Zavia swiped her card, and the elevator slid open, "Deck C-Level 5."

"I wish I was them." Spring said wistfully, "getting to sleep until later."

"I do not." Zavia answered as the doors slid open, revealing a steady stream of passengers, "We're the lucky ones. They will have their hands full while we are out! Of course, there is one advantage."

"What's that?" Spring asked.

Zavia looked at her sideways, "They don't have to work with Adiva. Their C-leader is nice."

"Adiva's not nice?" Pam asked glancing nervously at Spring.

"Put it this way," Zavia stopped at the beginning of another hallway, "I have met Octamarion dragon cats that were nicer than her, and that is saying a lot." Zavia smiled at a passing family. "See you two later." Zavia disappeared into the crowd. Pam turned toward Spring,

"What's an Octamarion Dragon Cat?"

* * *

Not knowing where else to go, Spring and Pam stood plastered to the curving wall leading to the boarding door, occasionally being bumped by passengers. A woman wielding a large bag rushed past Spring, the bag colliding with Spring's hip. The woman glanced back, before moving on, hitting others in her wake.

"I'm going to ask Adiva where I'm needed." Spring rubbed her hip. "I'm not going to stand here and be invisible AND black and blue... you coming?"

Pam looked in the direction of the boarding door, "No, I'll..um stay by the elevator leading to GE." Pam nodded toward the elevator leading to the Galactic Elite cabin. "Someone may come down by accident."

"Or try to go up there and sneak into Galactic Elite! That sounds more like it." Spring moved into the hallway traffic, dodging bags, passengers and children, swimming upstream until she reached Adiva. Adiva turned to stare at her. Adiva's thin lips were set in a half smirk that made her eyes smaller, pig like.

"What is it?" Adiva asked.

"I just want to know where to go during boarding, you know, my boarding position?" Spring looked away from Adiva, watching a very tall, well dressed man striding down the jetway. He was handsome in a sharp featured way, broad shouldered, nice build, late thirties. Adiva watched him approached too, her face going from indifferent to interested, her mouth curving into a smile. Adiva reached his nose.

"Welcome aboard!" Adiva said in an ultra cheery (but raspy) voice that was far from her flat, irritated tone a scant second before. "Level assignment, sir?"

Spring gazed up at the tall man as he stared at his hovering blue boarding screen floating above his wrist with a slight frown. His wide mouth was pressed in concentration, before he glanced at both of them, flashing a wide sheepish smile that lit up his blue eyes. His face reddened slightly, all the way up to his sandy brown hair. "I think I'm in the wrong section," he said in a pleasant, deep voice. "Level A? Cabin A-8?"

"Oh! Mr. uh...Williams? You're in Galactic Elite, just take the elevators down the hall, straight ahead. Enjoy your flight!" Adiva smiled up at him, like a cat that ate the canary. *She's at least ten years older than him...god Adiva laying it on thick are we?*

"Thanks, I hope so! Long flight." He nodded to Spring, then headed toward the elevator Pam stood attention by. Spring watched as Pam looked up, her face blossoming with a shy smile that matched the grin of the tall guy as he looked down at her. *Go for it, Pam! Work it, girl!*

"Uh…Adiva, never mind, I think someone is needed by the entrance to the passengers quarters…se ya!" Spring started down the hall, casting a look over her shoulder at Adiva. Adiva's gaze was glued to Pam and the passenger; her eyes narrowed slightly, her mouth in a thin line. Spring walked past Pam and the passenger as slowly as she could, her ears straining to hear above the boarding music and noisy hall.

"Totally! This starship is huge isn't it? It's my first time on it too." Pam was saying in a bubbly voice, "Here's your elevator, it was nice chatting with you!" Pam stepped aside as the doors slid open, her cheeks apple red.

"I enjoyed chatting with you too, thanks, Miss?"

"P…Pamela. I mean, Pam."

"Nice to meet you, Pam," His big hand swallowing up Pam's in a handshake, "I'm Guy. Guess I'll see you during the flight?" He asked as he stepped into the elevator. Pam waved as the doors slid shut.

"Hmm. I have a feeling someone may want to work up in Galactic Elite, wonder who that could be?" Spring teased as Pam turned toward her with a face as red as her hair.

"God, he was GQ cute wasn't he!" Pam replied."Welcome aboard!" She said cheerfully to a woman struggling with a shrieking toddler that was digging his heels into the carpet in one hand and a large bag in the other.

"Hmm, maybe you can swap positions. Ma'am, can I help you? Let me get that bag for you," Spring took the bag, grimacing under the weight with a strained smile, "I'll follow you, ma'am, where are you going?"

* * *

"On behalf of your ground staff at Pegasus I, we you wish you an enjoyable journey off-world, and thank you for selecting Orion Galactic Airways." Said the disembodied voice of a gate agent.

"Cabin crew, please assume all call positions," Luke said over the PA.

Spring circulated around the main passenger cabin, the only area that resembled a standard StarShuttle with row after row of passenger seats. Two wide aisles separated the passenger seats in sets of three. The passengers sitting in rows A-C, and F-H, were the lucky ones, sitting beside the large picture windows, with a clear unobstructed view. To Spring, the two hundred passengers, buckled in and ready to go, looked like a sea of bobbing heads. "Please fasten your harnesses," she said to a couple close to her age. Early twenties. Something about the guys buzzed cut brown hair and ruddy cheeks, and the girls bowed head; with he straight part in the middle, reminded Spring of home. They were dressed very conservatively for their age, the young woman clad in a brown turtleneck sweater dress. Her only item of jewelry appeared to be her plain wedding band, which she twisted around her finger nervously.

"Why can't we go to our pods?" The young woman asked. "Why do we have to sit in these here seats? Is it for the whole flight, ma'am?" Fear blanketed the girl's glossy eyes. The husband eagerly buckled his harness over a crisp button down shirt. He barely looked old enough to shave.

"Just until we break orbit." Spring answered, trying to sound professional. Two rows away, one of her crewmembers caught her eye and smiled encouragingly. She looked back at the couple, "As soon as we reach our cruising speed, you can go to your pods."

"Thank you, ma'am." The husband patted his wife's arm, "First time leavin' Earth. New life waitin' for us on Eden, right, honey?" The wife nodded, looking a little teary eyed. "First ones in our family. Our town too! Just got married last month!" He looked at his wife with such love and tenderness, that Spring's heart lurched painfully, thinking of Wesley. *He's getting married in a few months...but not to me.*

Spring felt her eyes sting despite her cheery smile, patting the woman on the shoulder, "This is my first time off-world too. I guess we're all ready for an amazing adventure huh? Where are you from?"

"Bluefield, West Virginia, ma'am," the husband said proudly. "Got myself hired on with Interstellar Construction. Building homes an' the like on these new colony planets. Martha here hopes to train as a registered nurse!" His wife smiled nervously, staring at her lap. She looked sixteen.

"Flight attendants, please take your seats for departure." Luke's voice blared over the PA.

"Well, that's my cue, enjoy the flight! Excuse me." Spring moved quickly down the aisle, the rest of the passengers just a blur of faces. She made it to the end of the main cabin, taking her seat beside her scary look-ing emergency door that was half the size of one of her bedroom walls on the Moon. Her eyes roamed over it as she fastened her harness, finally zeroing on the large, bright red cane sized handle. Her mouth went dry.

"Hey, at least we're not sitting by the emergency shuttle doors!" Spring looked across the cross-aisle at Terry, sitting casually in his jump-seat, a magazine under his thigh. He grinned at her, his slicked back hair and pointy goatee made him look a little devilish in the dimly lit cabin. "Relax, Spring, this thing is as smooth as buttah!"

"Oh, I'm not nervous!" Spring's voice came out high and squeaky. The ships shuddered delicately for a moment, before Spring felt the ship begin to move, the space station gliding away in her viewing porthole. She looked excitedly at Terry, "We're moving! It's so quiet!"

"Yeah, kid, sure are." Terry grabbed the special hand grips on his harness. "Captains about to punch it, so you may want to grab your handles and brace yourself. We really feel it back here. Hey, don't look so scared, it's really cool!"

"When will the captain...'Punch it' ?"

"Soon as we clear the station. What do you see? My window's facing space."

"The station's far away now." Spring reported, glancing at Terry, "like a tiny dollhouse."

"Count down to five. Ready? Five," Terry said.

"Four." Her heart was beating wildly in her chest. She squeezed her eyes shut. *Can I go back to the Moon?* Her nails dug into her palms as she clutched her jumpseat harness handles.

"Three." The starship began to turn slowly.

"T...two." Spring exhaled deeply, griping her handles until her knuckles were white.

The starship came to a shuddering stop. Then out of nowhere came a low hum that gradually increased as if the engines were charging themselves. Before Spring knew what was happening, she was sucked back into her seat, her body vibrating, feeling lightheaded. Her head felt like it was weighed down, glued to her headrest. Spring opened her eyes, biting down hard on her lower lip.

"One!" finished Terry.

Spring managed to turn her head slightly, glancing out the small porthole window; watching as the stars seemed to merge together, forming long white and multi-colored streaks that raced by the porthole. It reminded her of a downpour of rain. Sideways of course.

"Congratulations, Newbie!" Terry clapped silently. "You are now officially Off, Off-World!" Spring struggled to move her head, staring incredulously at Terry.

"To boldly go, baby, just like that!" He snapped his fingers, before crossing his arms with a smile and a wink.

* * *

Experience Colony Life on **Planet EDEN**

Live the good life on Earth's newest colony planet, luscious, tropical Eden. Beautifully TerraFormed planet with breathtaking Binary sunsets and two orbiting moons, Eden features four continents actively seeking colonists. With a year-round tropical climate, aqua blue oceans and beaches of warm sand, Eden truly lives up to its name!

The continents of Eden offer a diverse and unique experience, from the bright lights and city lifestyle, to a resort spa, there is room for everyone on Eden!

Not sure about re-locating? Tourists and visitors are always welcome! For those up for the challenge, here are some of the gems of Eden:

• Hike /Climb mountains taller than Everest

• White Water rafting down crystal clear rivers

• Tour the Rainforests

• Visit the majestic volcanoes or simply

• Relax and allow yourself to be pampered at one of our many resort spas

• Take a scenic cruise!

And many more!

Blink scan PLANET EDEN. for more information.

6

EARTH GIRLS ARE NOT EASY

FIVE HOURS LATER.

"The passengers should be waking up in a few minutes," Adiva walked into the dining hall, her eyes flicking over the rectangular tables and cheerful orange chairs. "Are you sure you have experience with the X-Pro food replicator?" She glanced at Spring dubiously.

"Uh huh! It was my favorite thing about the Excaliburs, and Pam can help if I get stuck, right Pam?"

"Sure, we had something like this back at 747." Pam said distractedly, running a finger along the polished galley counter, carefully avoiding Adiva's razor stare.

Adiva's eyes shifted from the two of them, narrowing. "It's only breakfast, so I guess you two have to learn sometime. Heat up fifty meals for starters. I can't imagine everyone waking up at once to eat. By then, Jackie and Jill will be up from crew rest... What? Did I say something funny, Patty?"

Pam giggled, "It's Pam, and yeah you did, Jackie and Jill!" Adiva looked at her as if she had grown two heads, "You know, like that old nursery rhyme...Jack and Jill? Jack an' Jill went up the hill to fetch—"

"I got it, I got it ...whatever. Anyway, fifty meals and don't burn them." Adiva snapped, giving them one final glare before leaving the dining hall. Spring turned toward the large freezer console, punching in the codes that retrieved the fifty meals. Behind her, Pam pulled out the 'china', sturdy plastic plates designed to look like porcelain china, down to the Orion emblem in 'gold' stamped in the middle.

"I don't get it," Pam was saying as she set the plates down on the counter beside a row of clear glasses.

"What? The meals?"

"No, not that. Why does Adiva have such a hard time remembering my name? It's not hard."

Spring grabbed a plate, placing a frozen, hockey puck sized disc on it, sliding it into one of the slots in the replicator, "Beats me. Maybe you should screw up her name, call her something like, Anna or Althea until she calls you Pam."

Pam frowned, shaking her head, plating the discs, "No, she'll probably think I'm really stupid. Glad we get to lie down soon. So tired!"

Spring put the last of the plates into the replicator, shutting the door, setting the computer for fifteen seconds. Almost immediately, the smell of eggs, potatoes and bacon, filled the air. "We're almost there. Hold on, girl! And I want to hear about that passenger in GE!" Spring opened the door, inhaling the food that was now spread out on the plates, puffy and 'real looking'.

Pam laughed, setting a pitcher of bright day glow orange juice down, pouring some of it into a few glasses. A couple of sleepy passengers wandered in wearing robes. "I'll fill you in don't worry! Good morning! Would you like some breakfast?" The passengers sat down by the large windows, watching the stars race by. Jackie walked in, blinking against the dining lights. Her magenta hair in a painful looking tight bun.

"Coffee please?" croaked a man.

Adiva's raspy voice boomed over the PA, announcing breakfast and that it would be necessary to vacate the sleeping pods.

"She always turns the lights in the pods up to full bright." Jackie muttered as she finished tying her smock. She moved swiftly behind the counter, pouring herself a cup of coffee. One side of her face still had the imprint of her crew rest pillow. She sipped at her coffee as a group of passengers stumbled in.

"You kids holding down the fort okay?" Jackie reminded Spring of what her grandmother must've been like. Spunky.

* * *

Zavia was already sprawled on her bed reading, when Spring and Pam dragged themselves into the dorm room. Zavia lay on her back, knees bent, her book balanced against her knees, her container of m&m's resting on her stomach. The screen at the end of her bed displayed an old movie, while music blasted from somewhere. Every light was on, even in their bunks.

"How was the Dining Hall?" Zavia asked, without looking at them. She grabbed her m&m's, swinging her arm out, coming within inches of Pam's nose, "m&ms?"

"Busy! My face feels like Crisco! Thanks, I love m&m's! What are you reading?" Spring asked over her shoulder as she pulled out her pajamas .

"Where were you, Zavia? We never saw you at all!" Pam had her arms full of her nighttime arsenal and her nightgown draped over her shoulder. She took one look at Spring, then the bathroom door; then back at Spring, before darting like a red-haired blur into the bathroom.

Spring put her PJ's and bathroom stuff on her bed, taking a handful of m&m's from Zavia.

"I was assigned to the Duty Free shop. Love it there. Nice and quiet, usually the most senior position too, but then so is the nighttime crew."

"You mean sleeping during the day is senior?" *Not that space had a 'day'.*

"Exactly." Zavia glanced at her with her strange eyes. Spring took an involuntary step back, instantly regretting it. A shadow passed over Zavia's eyes, before she turned away, "All of our passengers go to sleep, but during the day, everyone is up, up, up. Hold your ponies, don't get too excited, we switch on the way back."

"Oh," Spring sat on the edge of her bunk, swinging her legs, "How long have you been flying?"

"This is my third month. I only fly the ultra longs, language speaker."

"What language?"

"Palaqeon, but also Galtarrion, Etrueleon, and Germatalese in a tight spot. Hey, have you ever read this, it is extraordinary!" Zavia held up her book, 'Neverwhere'. "I'm trying to read all of your Human books. Our books are so different from yours..."

"On Palaq?" Spring stood up, moving to the bathroom door, rapping on the door, "Hey! Before I'm ninety!"

"On End—, yes, yes, Palaq," Spring glanced up at Zavia, just as the bathroom door burst open, and a Pam came out at last.

* * *

"I can't believe I'm meeting someone from Palaq! I mean, up until a few years ago, your solar system was called..." Pam chewed on some m&m's. They sat crosslegged on the floor. Their rest time had started an hour ago and they were still up. Debriefing.

"I remember! It was called RT-342X! Right?" Spring leaned her back against the table, "I always thought it was so silly, naming planets stuff like that. So anal. What did your people call our Earth?"

Zavia made a face as she opened a fresh bag of candy. The girl had a serious sweet tooth. "I think you do not want to know."

"Come on, tell us!' Pam said, helping herself to some candy.

"Can't be any worse than what our scientists called your place. I've always wondered what aliens called us." Spring admitted. "Even Jorge wouldn't tell us what the Etrueleon name for Earth used to be." She helped herself to plain m&m's, carefully picking only the green and yellow ones.

Zavia and Pam watched silently as Spring sandwiched the yellow m&m between two green ones, eating them at once. "Okay. If you must know, the Palaqeons named your solar system after the scientist that discovered it, so it used to be the Classitorie Cue'Par Star System."

"A mouthful." Spring giggled.

"What about Earth?" Pam went to the replicator in the wall, producing three glasses of water. She handed one to Zavia, then one to Spring, before sitting on the floor.

Zavia's face was carefully neutral, her eyes on the cover of her book, "Thanks, Pam. Since Cue-Par discovered your galaxy, the Palaqeons let him name the other stars, he uh.." Zavia wet her lips, before continuing, "had a sense of humor..." Zavia said slowly.

"So he gave Earth a funny name?" Spring asked sipping her water.

"He named the sun after his wife, and Mercury and Venus, after his sons and your planet Earth was named after his Octomezzorr."

"An Octo-what?" Spring asked, exchanging a look with Pam.

Zavia looked embarrassed, "His Octomezzorr. Earth was known as Zaap'Maz, until first contact."

"Was that his daughter?" Pam asked.

"Mistress? His Queen?" Spring glanced at Pam.

"Actually," Zavia's mouth twitched slightly, "Zaap'Maz was the family pet. An Octomezzorr, looks like a hairless cat with the wings of a bat."

"Earth was named after a bat-cat?" Spring sputtered, choking on the water. "How long were we called that?"

"Not very long, I'm not sure...I mean...uh...I think approximately a few thousand years. It's not a bad name, could've been worse." Zavia got up refilling her glass, "Imagine being known for all time as ... Reinazzoona."

"What does that mean?" Pam asked.

Zavia took a long sip of water, before training her strange eyes on them, her face expressionless. "Translated into Earth English it means," Her face darkened a few shades, "Face of an Ass."

There was a moment of silence, as Spring exchanged a look with Pam, before they both looked up at Zavia. Zavia was sipping her water thoughtfully, one hand on her hip. She slid a glance their way, making eye contact.

"Face of an Ass," Spring commented, "Now, that's one for the History books!"

The three of them burst into hysterical laughter.

* * *

Every time Spring entered the Crew Dining Hall (or Mess Hall as the pilots called it), she felt as if she was fourteen again, in the "Young Artist's" class her parents made her go to. That was Gran-Libby's idea, since physical schools no longer existed, and everyone was educated by far-away teachers via computer.

Today was Thursday. Pasta day. The dining Hall was swarming with crew from every part of the ship, including the engineers, hunched over in a corner by the aquarium wall. A few security guys sat near the cuter, 'Daytime' flight attendants, up for a midnight meal in jeans and full makeup. Spring liked the Dining Hall. It was the only brightly painted room in her favorite shade of butter yellow. It had six tall windows and one wall with a cheerful aquarium. Spring hurried over to the cafeteria line, inhaling the pasta made by an actual chef. That was another bonus, they had real food, just like the passengers on Level's A and B. Well, one meal was 'real' at least. Spring helped herself to a healthy portion of Fettuccine Boscaiola and a thick slice of garlic bread, along with a small salad. She looked around the room, trying to spot 'her peeps'. She felt shy and stupid standing there in the middle of the room. A few of the engineers stared at her curiously. Her cheeks burned.

"Spring! Over here!" Pam waved her napkin. Spring smiled, feeling some of the tension leave her as she moved confidently past a few tables, managing a shy smile at one engineer, before taking a seat by the window.

"You're just in time for the latest on Mr. Level A!" Squealed Tatum as she slid her grilled chicken over to make room for Spring's plate. Zavia and Terry exchanged matching smirks. "He's brought half the Duty Free shop, whenever Pam works down there."

"I mean, how many times can you accidentally get lost on Level C?" Terry added, biting into his pasta, "And only during the overnight hours, and only when you're around!"

"Are you going to see him on Eden?" Spring asked eagerly. Pam's face reddened, she looked down at her pasta, smiling, before looking up, her green eyes sparkling.

"I think so! He's wonderful, smart, funny…"

"Sexy?" Spring supplied wickedly.

"Is he moving to Eden, or is he coming back to Earth?" Zavia asked, saving Pam from bursting into flames.

"His company is sending him to Eden to head his department. He's excited about it, done a lot of research on planet Eden. He's not coming back to Earth."

"I guess you will have a tour guide there." Zavia winked. Terry and Tatum were the only other crewmembers who were not afraid of Zavia. It was if the others suspected she could read their minds. Zavia did have an ardent admirer in Rob, the youngest pilot on the Daytime crew.

"I hope so." Pam pushed her pasta around, grinning.

* * *

Spring sat in her bunk, hoping her voice was not disturbing Zavia or Pam. A quick glance out of the small viewing window in her closed pod revealed darkness with a sliver of light from the bathroom. Even with their individual bunk doors closed, Zavia hated having the room blanketed in darkness. They had four hours left before they relieved the Daytime crew. Gran-Libby's face flickered on the Televideo. Early morning sun filled the home studio behind Gran-Libby, showcasing her brightly colored paintings. Gran-Libby was decked out in her paint splattered, knee length tunic.

"Daytime crew? Nighttime crew? Wish we had something like that back in my day, but well, our flights were not long, I mean sixteen hours …." Gran-Libby paused, sipping from a mug with paint splattered hands.

"Yeah, we never really see the other crew, it's like they're invisible or…" Spring broke off as the ship suddenly made a sharp, brutal turn to the right, causing Spring to veer into the bunk wall. The ship shuttered violently, before jerking once more to the right, then a sharp left. Spring rocked in her bunk, steadying herself by grasping the handle on her pod door.

"Spring, what 's going on?" Gran-Libby's usual bohemian demeanor was replaced by a cool alertness Spring had never seen before. The ship shuddered once more, this time Spring bounced up a few inches. A red light began to flash above the televideo, and Gran-Libby's face abruptly disappeared, replaced by the message 'Crew Emergency Interruption ' and the image of the Daytime Captain, an ebony skinned woman with large sliver streaks in her hair. Immediately, Springs bunk lights went to full bright, and her pod door slid open, revealing a brightly lit dorm bathed in red light, with Zavia leaning out of her bunk, her eyes on the window. Below Spring, Pam poked her head out. An emergency chime sounded.

"All hands report to your stations." Announced the Daytime captain. "Await further instructions."

"What's happening? Are we being attacked?" Spring scrambled down, holding onto the side of the pod as she made her way to her closet.

Zavia and Pam were right behind her, pulling out their uniforms, changing quickly.

"Ladies and gentlemen," the Daytime Purser's voice was stern and professional, "Please fasten your harnesses wherever you are and remain seated. Thank you."

"Evil aliens?" Pam blurted before glancing at Zavia, "Sorry, Zavia, I didn't mean ..."

Zavia shook her head, running her long fingers through her black hair before heading to the door, "Don't worry, Pam, it's not evil aliens, and it's not an attack."

"Then what is it?" Spring bumped into Zavia's back as the ship made another sharp turn.

Zavia stepped into the hallway, filled with the same glowing red light. Loud chimes and a steady stream of Nighttime crew hurrying by. She moved out of the way of a passing engineer, her eyes darting toward Spring for a brief second, before replying in a matter of fact voice, "Asteroid Belt."

"We're going too fast for it, aren't we?" Spring asked anxiously, dodging another engineer.

Level C was virtually empty, barely a passenger in sight. Most had retired for the night and were inside their sleeping pods. Spring and Pam followed Zavia to the crew briefing room at the end of the main corridor. The room was crowded with Daytime and Nighttime crew, sitting by blank computer screens and leaning against the walls. A few looked exhausted, harassed. Adiva stood beside the Daytime C-leader, counting heads. The red light gave everyone an oddly flattering glow. Spring, Zavia and Pam slid into seats by their crew. It dawned on Spring that the Daytime and Nighttime crew did not mix.

"Stand By." Came the voice of captain, just as the starship stopped shuddering, and appeared to glide again. The chimes suddenly stopped, and the lighting returned to normal.

"Is the emergency over?" Spring whispered loudly, looking around the room, seeing grim faces.

"We have company." Someone by a window said, gesturing outside. "They're flying pretty close to us too, and it's not a commercial ship." People were on their feet, hurrying to the windows.

"EF?" Someone asked. Everyone was jammed by the windows, peering into the blackness at the unknown ship. It was slightly smaller, but looked powerful, full of sleek curves and sharp angles. It was barely visible, appearing to blend in with space. It glided along beside their ship with no sound.

"It's an Alien ship." The other C-leader's voice trembled slightly, he glanced at Adiva.

"Who are they?" Adiva asked. Even super bitch sounded scared.

"It's an Endarion ship." All eyes turned to a paler than usual Zavia, nodding gravely at the nearby ship. "A Warr'Takaar." She added, looking at Adiva and the other leader. "A warship." The room grew unnaturally quiet. Spring's stomach flipped nervously.

"Damn it all to hell," Jackie grumbled from a deserted table. "I knew I should've dropped this trip!"

"Cabin leaders, please report to Level A." Luke's voice came over the crew PA, just as the image of the two captains appeared on the overhead screens. Captain Taylor, the Daytime captain stood in front, behind her, Captain Songer, the Nighttime captain.

"Ladies and Gentlemen," Taylor began, "this is your captain speaking, thank you for your patience and for remaining in your cabins. We experienced a few minor scrapes making our way through an asteroid belt. We had to make a few evasive maneuvers that kept us from avoiding the larger asteroids, but as a result we have exited the asteroid belt off course…"

"Great." A Daytime crewmember shoved his hands into his smock pockets.

"The good news is an Endarion military ship has come to our aid. They will escort us to the closest space station, where we can make a few repairs before continuing to Eden." Taylor continued. "We apologize for the slight detour, but things like this occasionally happen in space, and we will get you to Eden as quickly and as safely as we can. Thank you."

Adiva and the other C leader returned, Adiva's face slightly sour. The emergency over, the Daytime crew went back to duty, filing out of the room, glancing at their watches, nodding to Spring's crew. Adiva faced them with crossed arms and a tired face. "Okay," she said once the Daytime crew was gone. "We have thirty minutes before we take over, so go back to your rooms and get ready, then report to your assigned duties."

"I could use another hour of sleep." yawned Terry as he left along with the others. Spring, Zavia, Tatum and Pam were at back of the line, passing Adiva on the way out. Adiva held up her hand, stopping them, her eyes roaming over them.

"Luke will need help in Galactic Elite tonight." Adiva said. "Looks like Captain Taylor has invited the Endarion leader onboard. I need three of you to volunteer."

"I'll go!" Pam piped up excitedly, raising her hand.

"Why do we have to go, what about the crew in Galactic Plus? What happened to Level A's crew?" Spring asked. Zavia was quiet, her face pale. She edged a few inches toward the door.

"Looks like a few of them had a small party during the rest," Adiva explained. "They're not legal yet."

"Legal for what?" Pam smirked.

"For work." Adiva 's eyes cut through Pam, focusing on Tatum. "Tatum, you, Zavia and Spring will need to go up there. Luke will tell you what to do." Pam looked shocked. Her eyes darting over to Adiva with disbelief.

"Pam wants to go." Spring stepped back, leaning against the wall, "You said you wanted 'volunteers', she volunteered."

"Polly is needed in C." Adiva 's voice held an edge of steel to it. "And anyway—"

"She can go in my place," Zavia spoke up loudly, interrupting Adiva. "I feel...ill. I'm going to lie down now, excuse me." Zavia may her way to the door, exiting without a backwards glance at an opened mouthed Adiva.

"Fine. Whatever. Patsy, you can go up to Level A." Adiva sighed.

"Thanks, Alfreda." Pam smiled her sweetest smile at a stunned Adiva, before turning on her heel.

Spring covered up her laugh with a cough, before smiling up at Adiva with watery eyes, "Later."

* * *

"I feel like a space waitress." Spring muttered to Pam as they stood to the side of hastily set up table of refreshments in the captain's ready room. Expertly carved fruits, and fragrant hors d' oeuvres were laid out on a snowy white tablecloth in front of a pair of wide windows. Spring, Pam and Tatum were dressed in their full uniform. No smocks up here.

"There's enough here for a wedding buffet." Tatum added in a low voice. "Is the entire ship coming over or what? Endarions. Men in uniform. Alien men at that!" She made a purring noise. "Yummy."

"I heard they were pretty blazin', so they must look magnif! Pam, it's a shame we're not actually in Galactic Elite." Spring glanced over at Pam as she stood poised with a tray of drinks by the door. Pam shrugged, smiling a secret smile.

"No biggie." Pam said. She took a few steps toward the open door, leaning out a little before jerking away, moving with wobbly flutes toward Spring, her eyes wide, "They're coming!" She said in a loud whisper. The sound of heavy boots and deep voices flowed down the hall, mixed with a stern female voice. Spring held her breath, planting a fixed smile on her face, trying to remember her lessons from 'Alien Etiquette 101'. *Did that class cover anything on Virile looking, Knight in Shining Chrome, Aliens from warships?*

A tall, broad shouldered man in uniform entered, walking beside Captain Taylor, looking down at her as she spoke. He was very tall, probably around six foot-six, with the presence of a leader, even though he appeared to be in his early thirties. Dusky blue skin. His closely cropped hair was jet black, revealing normal looking, slightly curved ears. *Okay, so he's not a Vulcan.*

Captain Taylor steered the Alien leader toward where Spring stood with a petrified looking Pam. "Commander Baldric, I would like you to meet some of our finest flight attendants." Captain Taylor smiled politely at them, "I'm sorry, ladies but I'm not familiar with the Nighttime crew, you are?"

"P…Pa…Pam Sloane. D…drink sir...uh….Mr. Commander?" Pam offered her rattling tray with a wide, manic smile. The Commander's mouth curved into a smile that briefly lit up his strangely familiar pale eyes. He reached out slowly, taking a flute from the tray with a large, gloved hand. Behind him, several equally tall men in the same snug looking eggplant colored uniforms stood patiently with Captain Songer. The Commander had black slashes by his high collar and on his right shoulder.

"Thank you, Miss Sloane." His voice was a rich, baritone, without a trace of an Alien accent. Smooth and flat. He turned his pale eyes toward Spring, and she froze for a second, swallowed up in his curious, slightly amused stare. *Alien Etiquette 101; Welcome, welcome, welcome! Smile dammit!*

"Hello…um, Welcome, Commander Baldric. My name is Spring…. Stevens." She wet her lips, staring into his bottomless pit eyes, drowning, "Welcome aboard, and thank you for helping us!"

Commander Baldric nodded, "Thank you. It was my pleasure." He smiled his faint smile again, ready to move down the line to Tatum. He was a beautiful man, and his pale eyes stood out among his pale, slightly bluish skin and chiseled features. Spring watched as he smiled down at Tatum, still holding his full flute.

"My dad is a retired Navy Chief on Earth!" Spring heard herself blurt. Commander Baldric paused, looking in her direction. Captain Taylor glanced over as well; Spring could tell the captains opinion of her rapidly deteriorated into that of the village half-wit. Spring felt the blood rush to her cheeks. Even the Commander's men stared at her. She felt like melting into the floor, *stupid, stupid, stupid.* She stared at the table, biting down hard on her lower lip.

"A Navy Chief on Earth." Commander Baldric's warm voice was suddenly very close. "How fascinating." Spring looked up slowly, staring up into the commander's face .He smiled openly at her, his opaque eyes bright. Spring shyly smiled back, and was rewarded by his wider smile, that made his strange eyes brighter. *Please say that's not a pity smile!*

7

UELAXION

"Ladies and Gentlemen, we shall dock at space station Velaxion in less than ten minutes. Please have your COE passport cards and other documents ready for inspection prior to disembarking. Please ensure your harnesses are securely fastened, thank you." Adiva's voice announced over the PA.

Spring breezed through the passengers sleeping quarters, checking to make sure each of the pods were empty and locked for landing. The pods were set into the walls, one on top of each other, with square shaped sliding doors that had a viewing window. Each pod was numbered, reaching up to the ceiling, assessable by an unusual forklift style elevator, that stopped at the desired pod. She felt sorry for the poor souls sleeping twenty feet off the ground in the top pods. That was a long way to the bathrooms.

"Spring! There you are!" Jackie caught up with her, her feet echoing down the empty hall. "Adiva sent me to round you up for docking. Pam too!"

"Why? Isn't Velaxion just like Pegasus I?" Spring asked, walking down the hall.

"No way!" Jackie chuckled, "Pegasus is our station. Velaxion is a REAL space station! Babycakles, everything , and everybody is at that place!"

"That place has been around since first contact. We're the Newbies there, even after twenty-something years!"

"We are?" Spring felt her stomach flip nervously.

"Damn kid, I scared you? Aw, sorry!" Jackie patted her arm, "Nothing to worry about, it's a tastic place. One of the biggest stations in the universe. Open 24/7. Take pics, the folks at home will need to see it!"

"And Adiva cares whether I see it or not?" Spring snorted.

"She's not that bad." Jackie slanted a look at Spring as they turned the corner past another hall of sleeping quarters. "I Just think seeing all you Newbies reminds her that it's close to her time to leave an' all. A shame they make us hang up our space shoes at 50. I don't mind going...hell, I can't wait till next year! People like Adiva are different." Jackie steered Spring down another hall. "She has nobody. She'll probably go back to Earth, transfer into the airways side, fly airplanes to Europe. It's hard to leave this when there's no one at home...know what I mean?"

"How long has Adiva been flying?"

"I've known her for close to twenty years, don't take it personal. Besides, every Newbie should see this station. It's kinda a blessing we went off course, cause' we woulda' passed this. Gone nowhere near it. On the corner of neutral space, not far from the Endarion and Galtarrion empires. Real nasty aliens, the Galtarrions, ya know."

"The Endarion Commander seemed nice." Spring said defensively. *Sexy and nice actually.*

"Sure he was," Jackie nodded to a passing passenger. "His people are our new allies." She stopped at the crew lounge, where Pam was seated by a large window. Beside her, Chris, another crewmember sat, his eyes fixed to the window. "Just take your jumpseat when you hear Adiva's final dock PA." Jackie waved to Pam, then left.

"Spring! Look at this! It is so absolute!"

From a distance, Velaxion looked like a massive sugar ice cream cone, broken up into pine cone or pineapple style tiers. Or like several Hershey Kisses staked on top of each other in varying sizes, twelve levels high. Like most of the structures in space, it had a silver, putty color, not too bright, but not so dark that a passing ship would mistake it for open space and fly into it.

It was truly a floating city, with the bottom two tiers covered with what seemed like hundreds of starship docking ports. As Explorer flew closer, Spring saw the Endarion escort ship dock, resembling a tiny speck among hundreds of illuminated specks. The docking ports formed a mass of unique, upside down 'V' designs that were lit up, forming a geometric pattern amid the black space. The other tiers of the station glittered with thousands of lights.

"I'm so glad I picked this trip up." Chris said in an awestruck voice, "I heard this place was a legend."

Spring kept her eyes on the Endarion ship, her mind playing back the commander's smile and his voice over and over. His strange eyes lit up with amusement. *Aliens.* She shivered, hugging herself.

"We have been cleared to dock at Velaxion. Flight attendants, take your seats."

* * *

Forty minutes later, the StarShip was virtually deserted. Most of the passengers had deplaned, wandering around the space station. The Explorer's engineers tinkered away, while large robotic arms worked on the outside.

"Come on you guys! We only have a few hours before we have to be back!" Pam stood by the door to their room arms crossed.

"Hold your horses! This place never closes, right, Zavia?" Spring did a once over of her reflection, hoping she didn't stick out in her new purple pleated leather skirt, fitted black sweater, and purple and black suede platform heels. Pam had thrown on a colorful printed dress with tights.

Spring looked behind her shoulder, glancing at Zavia, "Zavia, what are you wearing?" Zavia wore a thick, shimmering scarf over her head and a moss colored bodysuit with a wide tan belt and long gloves. A pair of large dark sunglasses completed her look.

"Why? Something wrong?" Zavia grinned, twirling around, modeling her outfit. Spring exchanged a sideways glance at a bewildered Pam, before being pushed aside by Zavia as she stepped into the hallway, "Come on, let's go!"

* * *

"Wow, this place is so huge! Look at everyone!" Spring stood backwards on the levitating 'escalator' step, watching the activity below her. People bustled about the station gates, races of every shape, color and size. Unusual chime and flute sounding music bounced off the rounded walls and tiered docking floors. As the floating steps rose higher, Spring noticed several 'Alien' flight crews, traveling in groups of six to twelve in identical uniforms.

"So many stews!" Pam nodded toward a group of flight attendants dressed in bright yellow, the shape of their heads and skin tone reminding Spring of upright hammerhead sharks. Another group dressed in sharply tailored suits went past them on the down escalator, their bodies rail thin, their heads the width of a tumbler glass. "Where are the shops? How many floors are there?"

Zavia shrugged, "I am not sure. We never stopped here... probably sixteen public floors?"

"We? You mean, Orion?" Spring asked as they left the 'StarPort' section, arriving at a brightly lit floor filled to its tiered rim with shops and a glowing upside down water fountain in the middle, that looked like a cascading chandelier. Aliens and humans circulated in an array of colorful to drab outfits carrying shopping bags. Zavia gracefully hopped off the still moving stair, Pam and Spring followed. Spring barely missing a collision with a mixed group of humanoid and octopus looking teens, racing by on mobile air scooters.

"My family." Zavia said, her long legs picking up speed, headed toward a large department store anchoring one end of the floor. "Orion never stops here. This is mostly a Non-Earthling place, but that's changing." She gestured to the Nordstrom coming soon sign.

"I love it here! I could totally live in a place like this!" Pam gushed a little loudly as they passed a group of intimidating, but handsome 'Alien' soldiers sitting by the fountain with takeout food. Spring glanced up at the different levels, noticing more soldiers, in varying races and uniforms on the tenth floor. She spotted two of the Daytime pilots on the tenth floor, mingling with stunning women and men.

"What's on the tenth floor, a nightclub?" Spring asked, sidestepping a female with a self guided stroller.

Zavia gazed up, "Oh that." She glanced at Pam and Spring, a wicked smile spreading over her lips, "Are you up for that, ladies? It is a Novo'Almarr. You know, a pleasure palace? Every fantasy granted, blah, blah, blah. There are a group of clubs on the ninth floor."

"My brother would love to visit a place like that." Spring gazed up, watching a pilot slide his arm around an ample shimmering woman. Her gaze moved to a couple of gorgeous Alien men by the railing on the ninth floor. She exchanged a quick look with a grinning Zavia.

"Your brother's at the EF academy, right? Thought he was brainy." Pam asked frowning.

"He is, but he's not dead!" Spring laughed, following Zavia toward the bustling department store.

"What about you, Spring?" Zavia threw over her shoulder, "Are you up for exploring that side of space?" Zavia stopped at the stores entrance, her fingers idly examining a dress that twinkled with intricate gems, her eyes slid over to them, filled with mischief, "Want to check it out, ladies? Want to play?"

"Would love too, but um…" Pam walked over to a dress that displayed all of its available colors in shifting hologram images, "I have a date with Guy!" She held up the dress, pressing the pause button, "What do you think? Red or green?"

"Jeans, cute top." Spring pulled out an embellished and embroidered top that changed patterns. "Like this."

"Too Human, way too Human." Zavia thrust a tunic dress into Pam's hands, "Jeans! What is the big deal? Do not look so, Earthy, show off what your mama, er,…gifted you! Well, Spring, want to check out floors nine and ten? I am game if you are."

"That's 'What my mama gave me', and Zavia, I am Human!" Pam added, "And Guy's Human too."

"Yeah, yeah, gifted, gave, same thing right? Well, Spring?"

Spring felt her stomach tighten with nerves, the neckline of the embellished top digging into her hands. She looked down at the top, conscious of the department store music and her friends silence.

"You've never been to one, Spring?" Pam asked hesitantly, "Don't they have them in Virginia?"

Spring felt her face burn, "They have them all right…it's just that I um, well…no. Plus, I had Wes…I mean, I had a boyfriend. Couples don't go to places like that, do they?" She hated how she sounded. So conservative. So unsophisticated. Of course couples went to pleasure palaces. She suddenly felt so rigid, and…so southern. Wes had been her first. Her only one so far. She hung up the top, looking up at Zavia and Pam, "Let's go up to the palace," she said with a small smile. *No one back home needs to know. I'm light years from Earth for god's sake, gotta leave the old Spring behind.*

"Are you sure, Spring?" Zavia asked, her mouth quivering, "I don't want to corrupt a poor innocent soul…especially a Human. You know, come off as some sort of sex crazed Alien girl and all that." Pam hid her face behind the tunic, her shoulders shaking. "I mean if you don't want to mungle with hands—"

"I'm going, I'm going!" Spring snapped, grabbing a two piece number in red. "And it's 'mingle.'"

"Vunda'klat!" Zavia squealed with excitement, strolling toward another set of dresses, picking up an iridescent number that shimmered like pale multi-colored icicles, "Aha! This has potential!"

"What does Vudda' klat mean?" Pam asked.

"Oh, Vunda'klat?" A shadow flickered over Zavia's face for a brief second, before she beamed at them, "It is like…wonderful or tastic. Now come on ladies, we have to get ready!"

* * *

Three hours later, Spring leaned against the railing on the ninth floor, letting the cool air wash over her skin, while the booming music of the nightclub blared behind her. She looked around the circular landing, watching as others cooled off by the rails, gazing down at the still open shops below and the distant star terminals. She had lost track of Zavia hours ago, among the crush of people (and creatures) inside. Spring closed her eyes, smiling, tapping her foot to the beat.

"Dreaming of me?" Spring's eyes flew open, staring at man with a webbed neck and greenish skin, leaning beside her, his easy smiled faded a bit, his skin turning a deeper green, "Bad pick up line, right? Sorry about that, names Oppru, can I buy you a drink?"

"Um, sure, I'm Spring," Spring smiled, holding out her hand. Oppru looked down at it, then shook it, his hand felt clammy and cold, like a wet frog.

"Spring! There you are! I have a surprise for you!" Zavia appeared out of nowhere, followed by a couple of studly male admirers, including one or two EF guys. Zavia glanced dismissively at Oppru, before stepping close to Spring, "Come on, time to see your surprise! Excuse us…Mr. uh?"

"Oppru." Oppru said in a disappointed voice, stepping aside, "Good journey, Spring."

"Bye!" Spring stumbled forward as Zavia dragged her toward a set of floating steps, the gaggle of men behind them, "Zavia! Where are we going?" she hissed to Zavia's barely there 'Bubble' dress. Spring felt her stomach flip as realization dawned on her, "We're going up to the …Pleasure Palace?" she squeaked. *What's the surprise, an orgy?*

"Uh huh!" Zavia stepped onto the landing, swaying a bit, "Ta dah! Here we are! Come on, no time to waste! Come!"

The landing was crowded with couples milling about the railing, chatting and sipping drinks, while waiters and waitresses circled around in strange circular, wire outfits. The light seemed overwhelmingly bright compared to the nightclubs below. Spring squinted, following Zavia into the foyer.

The inside was stark, surrounded by two levels of what looked like giant glass blocks with round doors cut into the middle of each one. The glass was opaque, with the soft glow of light coming out of each, shining down upon the smoky, black glass floor, lit up with the colorful lights from the club downstairs. Shimmering raindrop chandeliers hung from the high ceiling, their silver droplets vanishing before they touched the floor. A few couples strolled around, while a some traveled up the stairs. Spring caught up with Zavia, who stood by an extremely tall being dressed in a long silver robe with deep red skin.

"Beautiful is it not?" Zavia asked once Spring and the men were gathered around her.

"It's not what I expected," Spring said carefully, very aware of the men behind her. To her surprise, Zavia laughed.

"I know it is not! You were probably expecting something like red velvet everywhere, right?" Zavia laughed again, "Well, do you want to see your surprise?" Spring looked over her shoulder at the men, and once more Zavia collapsed into giggles, "No, not them! Well, unless that is your wish! This is Tutmoqar, a host here, and he will escort you to your Fantasy Chamber. You can dream up anything you want in there, and whomever you want." Zavia said in a low voice, "And you can have your red velvet!"

"But, how muc—"

Zavia shook her head violently, "It is a gift from me, so do not worry about the price! Just have fun, and perhaps tell me later? Or not!" Tutmoqar bowed low to Spring, gesturing to the stairs. Spring looked back at Zavia uncertainly. Zavia winked at her, grinning, "Go on now, I will meet you here in two hours, enjoy yourself, Earth girl! Come on guys, let us get our dancing legs going on!"

Spring followed the host up the stairs, until they stood outside one of the glass block rooms. It's round door was open, revealing a sheer white chamber. Gingerly, Spring stepped in, turning around in the large chamber, expecting the host to follow, but he simply leaned forward, craning his long neck.

"Welcome," the host said in an oddly metallic voice. "the Fantasy Prompter will appear shortly, simply tell it what you want and it will oblige."

"Everything? Anything?"

"Yes, madam. Down to the rooms theme and your partner or partners. If you need assistance of any kind, please call out. Good evening." The host stepped away, and the round door slid shut.

"Welcome, Spring," She jumped at the disembodied voice, "Please describe your fantasy environment."

"Um.." Spring was tongue tied, her first thought was of Wes and the oceanfront back home. But her mind suddenly filled with the Endarion commander, imagining his home world. She closed her eyes, picturing a world with multiple moons dotting a golden sky, while two binary suns began to set. An alien city of towering glass buildings and flying vehicles rose up in her mind; while she had a birds-eye view from an open terrace, looking down at the skyline. She imagined herself in a palace or villa, with carved pillars encrusted in jewels, tied with sheer drapes that rustled gently in the warm summer's breeze. Yes, a palace that floated in mid air, hovering over the bustling city, with a distant view of a shimmering ocean.

"Environment granted." The voice said.

"Wait! I didn't say anything...I thought ..." Spring trailed off as thousands of tiny blue vein -like lights stretched across the room, and the floor below her feet fell away, leaving only a small square under her feet. Spring gasped, staring down at a black abyss that slowly filled with the same blue lights, whirling rapidly, spinning up toward her.

"Um, sir, mister alien guy..." Spring stared helplessly at the door, now miles away, completely obscured by light. She felt panic setting in as she glanced down again, watching as the whirl of lights reached her feet.

The lights began to engulf her and the room in a spinning river of lights, Spring moved her arms with an effort, holding up a hand now covered in a beads of blue, while her club dress grew heavier and longer. Spring gazed at her hand in fascination as glittering rings appeared on her fingers, and a wide, filigree cuff spun its way onto her wrist. Through the haze of light, Spring could make out spiral pillars on a rounded terrace, gauzy curtains blowing softly. The soft sounds of a distant city filled her ears, while the room grew warmer.

Finally, the lights faded away, revealing the fantasy world she had imagined, down to the view of an active alien city. Spring stared down at herself, shocked to see her simple, one shoulder mini dress transformed into a seductive two piece dress of a sheer metallic gold silk. A harem girl outfit with a gem covered bra top, and a skirt that sat low upon her hips; held in place by a jeweled belt. Spring reached up, her fingers exploring her hair, touching a solid circlet with dangling links of chain cascading into her curls. She stared down at her feet, now bare except for twinkling anklets, she wiggled a foot, giggling. The marble floor under her feet felt smooth, and very real.

Spring slowly took in the round, circular room, the entire room supported by the tall marble pillars, exposing the room on all angles, soaring up to a domed ceiling of glass. It was like being inside a large, opulent floating gazebo. Spring felt her cheeks warm as her eyes fell upon the only real piece of furniture; a magnificent, mahogany four poster bed, intricately carved, covered with a snowy white duvet. She took a hesitant step toward the edge of the terrace, reaching out, wrapping her fingers around a pillar with one hand, pulling back the sheer drape with the other. Spring clutched the pillar tightly, staring down at the city from thousands of feet in the air.

"Next time, I should think about adding some railings to this floating thing," She moved closer to the sturdy support, leaning against it, watching as strange traffic raced miles below her. She looked up at the sky, making a note of the five moons of varying sizes, one was so close, Spring could see its craters.

"Please describe your lover," the wind whispered.

For a split second, she thought of her ex, Wes, but another image came to her mind; tall, broad shouldered, eyes the color of a summer storm cloud, a sensual, knowing smile. A liquid silver form appeared, molding into her dream lover. The liquid silver grew tall, developing before her eyes. Solid. Masculine. So real. So alive. His presence filled the room. He took her breath away.

"Image complete, madame?"

Spring smiled at the uniformed man standing before her. "Yes, thank you...you can uh...go now."

* * *

Zavia was waiting in the foyer two hours later, cooling her heels by the fountain. Her face lit up with a smile as Spring came toward her, "My, my, look at you! There is a spring in your step, Spring! How was it?" Zavia linked arms with her, as they headed toward the entrance.

"Amazing! Thank you! Did you have a great time too?"

"Always!" Zavia winked, before paling, stopping dead in her tracks. "I….I forgot something, be right back!" Zavia disappeared into the crowd of couples on the landing.

"Zavia, wait!" Spring whirled around, bumping into a broad, uniformed chest, "Oh! I'm sorry! Excuse me," She backed away, staring up into strange, familiar eyes. The pale eyes flickered with annoyance. The Endarion Commander. Color rushed to her face, as she saw recognition light up his eyes.

He stared at her for a moment, surprised, before nodding curtly at her, making his way through the crowd. Spring watched his retreating back, her heart beating wildly.

"Back! Sorry! Thought I left my…shawl, then realized I left that on the ship! Spring, what is wrong? Your face is as red as Pam's hair!" Zavia led her to the stairs, weaving their way through the crush of people.

"Nothing, just too hot up here I guess." Spring muttered, "We better head back to the ship, I guess."

"Yes, we should." Zavia said hurriedly, scanning the crowd, as they moved through it, "I cannot wait to hear about your adventure, and Pam's too!" Zavia forced a laugh as she nervously glanced around them, walking too fast, causing Spring to half run to keep up.

Spring glanced around too, hoping to spot the commander. The very image of her 'dream lover'.

8

EDEN

"Welcome back, ladies," Adiva greeted Spring and Zavia at the boarding door with crossed arms and her ever present smirk. "Hope you are ready to work in let's see, forty-five minutes?"

Spring exchanged a look with an expressionless Zavia, "I'm...I mean...we're so sorry Adiva! It's just that we, um, ah..." Spring bit her lip, her eyes focusing on the fasten harness placard above Adiva's head. Zavia was quiet. Spring felt her eyes sting. *Great. I'm still on new-hire probation... she'll probably write us up. I'll never get another long haul.* To her amazement, something that sounded like laughter came from Adiva. Spring's eyes darted to Adiva's face, now crinkled with amusement.

"Don't worry girls, I was a new hire too once." Adiva said "We'll let this slide and not happen again, deal?"

"I can agree to that." Zavia glanced at Spring, "Spring?"

"S...sure." Spring hurriedly stepped aside as a flight attendant from the daytime crew rushed by reeking of cologne. "And we are sorry Adiva. I mean, the station is so big..." Adiva held up her hand impatiently.

"Forget about it," Adiva jerked her head toward the crew elevator. "Passengers will be boarding in forty minutes, go get ready. We're leaving on the hour."

Spring waited until they were in the crew elevator before turning to Zavia, still calm as a cucumber, leaning casually against the wall. Spring felt a slight surge of annoyance, Zavia was still brand new too, why was she so blasé about being late? "You weren't worried at all? I mean, Adiva could've written us up, right?"

Zavia settled her eerie eyes in Spring's direction, shrugging, "Doubt it. Besides," Zavia stepped off the elevator yawning, "we were not that late. We still legally had ten minutes, that is why I was quiet."

"Oh." Spring felt stupid and thick headed. The floor of their room was strewn with Pam's discarded 'date' clothes/choices. Spring stumbled over a strappy sandal, kicking it aside, while stooping to remove her own. Zavia was already at the closed bathroom door, towel in hand. Pam's humming could be heard through the door. Zavia pressed her ear against the door just as it slid open, releasing humid steam, and a refreshed, uniformed Pam, beaming from ear to ear. Pam sailed by a bemused Zavia, still humming.

"Your date went well then I suppose?" Zavia asked. "Has he proposed yet? Name of your firstborn picked out?"

"It was magnif, tastic, vuddakatt!" Pam's voice was muffled as she pinned up her hair, "And why are you two so late? Adiva was kinda concerned and all."

"Vunda'klat." Zavia corrected over her shoulder, "You are not scared of Adiva anymore?"

Pam bristled slightly, "I wouldn't say 'scared'. She's kinda nice...I mean she saw Guy and I board, and she was friendly. She even chatted with us for awhile, and she called me Pam!"

"She was okay to us." Spring glanced worriedly at the clock set in the control panel by the door, "Still surprised at that. I totally expected her to yell at us."

"Like I said, Spring, do not distress about it. Besides, I saw Adiva at the club and she was anything but our 'C' leader." Zavia stepped into the bathroom, her eyes flicking down to the wet towel on the floor, before raising a disgusted eyebrow to Pam.

"Sorry! Geez! I meant to clean up." Pam slid the main door open, setting one foot into the hall. "See ya guys in a few!" She said brightly.

"Pam! Wait!" Zavia called out.

"Uh huh?"

"Be careful of Adiva. Do not trust her. Just watch what you say. Especially about Guy."

"Strange thing to say Zavia," Pam cocked her head to the side. "Sure you're not a mind reading Alien?"

Spring watched a coolness settle over Zavia's features, her eyes blanketed. "No, I am not a mind reading Alien," she snapped. "It does not take mind reading skills to see through people. Even a Human can do that." The bathroom door slid shut. Pam stood motionless in the entrance doorway, her hand preventing the door from sliding shut, staring blankly at the bathroom door for a moment. The door bumped noisily against her hand, sounding off an angry chime.

"The doors going to cut off your hand." Spring said lightly. Pam's eyes swiveled her way, wide and slightly troubled. "Don't worry about a dinosaur like Adiva, Pam. Guy likes you, not her. Who knows, maybe she met someone too." Spring shrugged, "Could be the reason she's in a good mood."

"Yeah, could be." Pam's expression lightened, she took a step into the hallway, nearly bumping into a passing pilot, "Hey, I want to hear about what you guys did, fill me in!"

"I'll give you a clue, Pleasure Palace!" Spring said hurriedly as the door started to slide shut, "Where are you working tonight?"

"With Adiva in the Observation room! See ya in a few, and don't leave any of the sordid details out!" The door slid shut, and Spring was left with the muffled voice of Zavia singing something in her native tongue. Spring got up, walking over to the potted plant, reaching out to touch one of the blue tulip shaped blossoms sprouting among green leaves.

"Doing well, Einstein." Spring gently stroked a velvety leaf, as the light of a departing vessel caught her attention. She leaned closer, pressing her nose against the window, watching as the ship pushed away slowly, before streaking off silently in a blaze of light. Was it the Endarion ship? *What was he doing on the tenth floor anyway? Probably thought the same thing of me. Oh god, what if Endarions can read minds? What if he knows, saw...oh god.* Spring pushed away from the table, "His eyes are just like Zavia's..."

"Yes?"

Spring jumped, turning around to find Zavia stepping out of the bathroom, fully dressed, her hair coiled into a braided bun. She was reading Jane Eyre now, so this was what Pam called Zavia's 'English Governess' phrase. Her next book was about twentieth century punk rock. Of course, Zavia's carefully lined eyes were very un-Jane Eyre. Spring found herself examining Zavia's chrome-storm cloud eyes. Zavia blinked, "Well?" She asked. She had Einstein's silver watering can in her hands.

"The Endarion commander has eyes like yours. And the same skin tone too. Are they related to your people?"

"Related?" Wariness crept into Zavia's voice as she turned toward the door.

"Like the Vulcans and the Romulans? You know, from Star Trek? It's a show that started –"

"I have heard of it." Zavia's voice was clipped. "And no, Endarions are not related to Palaqeons. I will see you upstairs." The entry door slid open.

"Zavia?"

Zavia turned back reluctantly, "Now what?"

"Einstein's watering can." Spring gestured toward Zavia's hand, still clutching the silver can with white knuckles. Zavia looked down, her face darkening a few shades as she marched back into the room, setting the can down hard beside the plant. She smoothed her hands over her uniform, heading to the door.

* * *

ONE WEEK LATER.

"Ladies and Gentlemen," boomed the captains voice, nearly causing Spring to drop the dirty plates she was carrying. She set them carefully into the dishwashing device. The machine scared her. It was a big, black, slot in the galley wall that gobbled up the dishes and a few times tried to eat flight attendant fingers, or at least their gloves. The glass doors would wait until the last plate was loaded then without warning, slam down like an old fashioned guillotine. Spring hated the dining hall. She strained to hear the captains announcement, but managed to catch Luke's.

"Ladies and gentlemen, we are within hailing range of Eden, which is now off to our right. It will be necessary at this time to leave your pods and take your landing seats in your respective cabins. Cabin service will be discontinued, so that your flight crew can prepare for docking at Eden 's port. We will be docking shortly. Thank you."

"You mean, we're not landing on Eden? I thought we flew there?" Spring asked another flight attendant, a guy named Rick. She couldn't help but stare at button beneath his tie straining to remain closed over his 'Santa' style beer belly. His long sideburns made him look like a relic from another century.

"We do, but the Ex is too big to land there, we have to dock at Eden's port." He replied, not looking up from the food he was storing.

"Oh. I thought I would get to see the planet." Spring tried to keep the disappointment out of her voice. Rick gave her a strange look, shaking his head.

"What are they teaching you guys in training now-a-days? Eden's Port is in the sky. A StarPort in the air, specially made for large ships like the EX. I think the governors of Eden want to keep their beaches and stuff looking pure and stuff, so we...you know...kinda hover in the air, like in orbit and all."

"And our passengers?"

"They take the domestic shuttles down, leave every, like, thirty minutes. You do know we have our own shuttle down, right?" He gave her a hard look. "Just sayin' so you don't try to board a passenger one. Ours takes us directly to the hotel. A lot of Newbies have gotten on the wrong shuttles." He shook his head, clucking his tongue as if in memory of the previous, clueless Newbies.

"Thanks, I'll follow you guys then." Spring washed her hands, removing her apron, folding it into a small square. She walked over to the large windows, where a few lingering passengers were staring in awe. She went over to the stand beside the couple from West Virginia, they smiled as she approached, moving to the side, sharing their window. Spring glanced out the window, nearly stumbling at the incredible sight before her. She stretched out her hand, touching the ice cold window, "Wow."

On the other side of the glass, sat Eden, a glowing orb of green and white swirls. They were far enough from the it to see the full planet, shimmering faintly with its protective atmosphere, surrounded by stars. Even at this distance, Spring could tell that Eden was a little smaller than Earth, about the size of Mars, but still impressive and so beautiful. So foreign. An occasional beam of light shot out of the planet, bursting into space light an extra bright star. Starships probably, headed to who knows where. The Explorer was approaching the sunny, 'daytime' side of the planet. Spring's fingers slowly outlined the oceans (which were bright green compared to

Earth's blue), and the snowy white clouds that every so often shifted, revealing the land beneath. Spring could not believe her eyes. She looked back at the couple, smiling at them. The young newlyweds from West Virginia. Toby and Martha. Toby grinned back.

"Look there, Miss," he said, "never ever thought I'd see a bona fide, real live, colony planet!" He squeezed his wife's shoulder, hugging her closer. "That is our new home, Martha," he said quietly."Our new life."

Spring felt her eyes mist as she watched the young husband staring tenderly at his wife; whose wide eyes were fixed on the approaching planet with something akin to fear. The young woman nodded in a jerky fashion, her hands nervously twisting her wedding ring. Slowly, a lone tear escaped, sliding down Martha's freckled face. Spring quickly averted her gaze, staring once more at planet Eden, feeling her own eyes begin to sting. As she watched the swirling mass of green and white of the planet, Spring could make out the reflection of the West Virginia couple. He planted a kiss on top of his wife's head.

"We'll do jus' fine, Martha," he said softly, "jus' fine. Don't you worry none."

At that moment, the chimes for final approach sounded, Spring and the couple both jumped slightly. The wife's eyes flew to Spring's in concern. "It's okay," Spring said reassuringly, "we're landing, that's all."

"Ladies and Gentlemen, we are making our final landing approach to planet Eden. It will be necessary at this time for all passengers to take their landing seats and fasten their harnesses. We will be docking within the next forty minutes, thank you."

Spring ushered the West Virginia couple and a few other stragglers out of the dining hall, before inspecting the area to make sure it was empty and secure. Rick, who was supposed to help her lock the dining hall down, had disappeared. She hurried from table to table, making sure the furniture was locked into place. She never realized how many tables there were.

At the tenth table, Spring glanced up, gazing out the window in horror. The face of the planet completely covered the windows now, they would be entering the atmosphere in minutes, and she still had ten more tables!

"Spring! There you are!" Pam and Zavia burst into the dining hall, "What are you doing in here? We're like, about to land!"

"I need to secure the tables and chairs or they'll slide, Help me?" She didn't mention she had spent initial approach at the windows. She looked worriedly over her shoulder at the fast approaching planet, then pleadingly at her friends. Tears blurred her vision. Zavia and Pam rushed into action, racing from table to table, the trio finishing just as the ship began to shudder slightly as it approached Eden's atmosphere.

"Flight attendants, take your seats now." Adiva's PA held a trace of annoyance in it.

"Th…thank you, guys!" Spring panted, leaning against a table, wiping her eyes. She felt so stupid.

"Come on, she means us." Pam said as they half ran, half walked to the door. Zavia and Pam waited in the hall for Spring, watching as she sealed the kitchen doors shut. The ship shuddered again, and they bumped into each other.

"We better take our seats, see you on Eden, Spring." Zavia said as turned down a hall, walking quickly to her jumpseat. Pam patted Spring's arm.

"See ya soon!" Pam ran down the hall. Spring bolted to her seat across form Terry, ignoring his astonished expression and his low 'close call' whistle. Her fingers were shaking so hard, she could barely fasten her harness as the ship began to vibrate and rock, bouncing as it fully entered Eden's atmosphere. She leaned back against her jumpseat, closing her eyes for a moment, feeling shaky and faint. Her heart would not stop pounding.

"You okay?" Terry asked. Spring forced her eyes open, sliding a sideways glance at Terry, managing a weak smile.

"Yeah, thanks."

* * *

"…And on behalf of your Moon based flight crew, we'd like to wish you a pleasant stay on Eden or wherever your journeys take you. Thank you, for selecting Orion Galactic Airways, have a good day."

Spring gazed out her window, watching as the starship approached what looked like an exact model of space station Pegasus I, only smaller, and with fewer ships. The station (or StarPort) hovered over a seemingly calm ocean, thousands of feet in the air. There were four or five ships parked at several spokes, and several smaller 'domestic' ships zipped downward, headed to ground based StarPorts. It surprised Spring that this was not the only hovering StarPort. From her limited view, Spring noticed two other massive ports lined up in a row next to theirs (with enough space between them).

Each of the StarPorts had a mirrored finish that reflected the ocean below, and the clear sky above, a very surreal vision. She could not see any land, and that was disappointing, but the sky was a gorgeous greenish-blue. A beautiful day.

As the Explorer sailed closer to the blinking white lights of the docking port, Spring could see figures moving about in the terminal, and she felt the urge to unbuckle her harness and run off and explore. She was really on another planet! She turned to Terry, who balanced a crossword puzzle on his lap.

"The floating StarPorts are..so weird! Why are there so many of them?"

Terry sighed, making Spring wonder how many times a 'newbie' had asked this. "Well, EDN is like how the old JFK airport used to look, it's broken up into separate terminals. We use terminal C."

* * *

Thirty minutes later. Spring stood in the small crew line up by the boarding door, saying goodbye beside Adiva and Jackie. On the other side of the door, the 'Daytime' leader and members of his crew said goodbye. Spring was surprised to see one of the pilots standing by the door too. Spring watched as each passenger made their way out onto the brightly lit tube shaped jetway, lined with a small group of Eden ground staff, each wearing neon bright vests of electric blue over their grey uniforms. They looked 'Human'. Spring inhaled deeply, trying to smell the moist foreign air, her first gulps of Eden air.

"What are you doing?" Adiva asked sharply, staring down at Spring.

"Just smelling the air." Spring felt the curious eyes of the others on her, "It smells different here, like, like...almonds and uh, a dash of cinnamon?" She caught the ground agents smiling at her.

Adiva stared at her for a second, her mouth deepening in a smirk as she shook her head, "Whatever. Smells like a typical jetway to me. Don't know what you're talking about." She nodded to the deplaning passengers, "Bye. Bye."

The West Virginia couple were the last in line to deplane, both rolling ancient, millennium era roll-a-boards that squeaked as they approached the boarding door. They stopped in front of Spring, reaching out to hug her, the wife stepped back smiling shyly.

"Thanks, fer all your help, miss." Martha said in a barely there voice. Toby grinned, patting Spring's arm.

"Y'all did mighty fine bringin' us here. Martha an' I sure are thankful. Y'all take care goin' back!"

Adiva tittered, covering it up with a cough. Spring ignored her, smiling warmly at the couple, feeling a little sad that she may never know what became of them. "Thanks, I hope you both like your new home, take care!" She watched them hesitantly step out onto the silvery jetway tunnel, slowly rolling their antique bags behind them. The rest of both the daytime and nighttime crews were bringing up the rear, bags in tow. Zavia held Einstein in one hand, while Pam had Spring's bag parked beside her own. The sight of the double 'C' crew was overwhelming to Spring. Were they all staying together? Traveling on the same shuttles?

"Y'all did mighty fine!" Adiva mimicked. "How did those country bumpkins get a job out here? Scraping the bottom of the barrel I guess." She shrugged off the frown the other 'C' leader gave her.

"No, Adiva," Spring looked Adiva squarely in the eye, "it takes a lot of guts to move this far from home, would you do it? No? Didn't think so."

* * *

The shuttle for Spring's crew was already filled, most of level A and B were already in prime seats beside the windows. Pam and Zavia squeezed themselves into the last forward facing window seats, fastening their harnesses. All that remained were the middle sideways seats. Spring walked slowly toward the seat closest to Pam and Zavia, her eyes looking over their heads out the window.

"Hey, this is your first time to Eden right?" Asked a pilot at a window seat. "Sit here. You don't want to miss this fly in." He got up, moving to sit across from Zavia, grinning widely as he sat down. Zavia glanced at him, a small smile on her face, before turning primly away. Spring looked at the salt and peppered pilot who winked at Zavia, grinning herself. *Well, well, well! Is that the real reason?*

"Thanks." Spring said as she slid into his vacated seat, fastening her harness. Luke stood up, counting heads, nodding with satisfaction at the young shuttle pilot.

"Alright." Luke says to the shuttle pilot, "Let's beat the Daytime crew to the mainland!" The shuttle lurched to life, zipping out of the shuttle bay and toward the glare of sunshine. Eden sunshine.

The shuttle burst out of the shuttle bay surrounded by overwhelming light. Spring squinted against the blinding light, straining to see Eden. She turned her head, staring at the line of StarPort terminals, then below at the aqua green ocean, glittering with light. Spring snapped her purse up from the floor, digging inside for her camera. She wanted a real camera, not the one on her wrist. *Gran-Libby would love to see this!*

The shuttle flew past barren golden brown rocky looking islands at first, then the shuttle began to turn right. Spring felt foolish tears sting her eyes. The mainland loomed ahead, a long stretch of smooth, pale brown shoreline, lined with vivid green plant life. The trees had spidery roots that rose up to cradle the leaves in a domed umbrella shape.

"Whoa! Look at that fella!" Spring exclaimed, pointing to a large yellow bird the size of a bald eagle with tipped feathers flying low along the coast. She followed the birds graceful path, resisting the urge to clap her hands.

She watched as it flew above the canopy tree tops, soaring up toward the green towering cliffs, becoming a bright speck of color among the green. The sterile looking grey of a large Earth Federation base sat upon the cliff, its dark blue flag blowing in the breeze as the bird flew by. Spring's eyes quickly scanned the vast base, filled with building after building and personnel housing beyond that. Her brother and sister could be based here one day, living on an base overlooking the city.

"Spring, look!" Pam shook her shoulder, "There's the city, see it! How Magnif is this, huh?"

The shuttle began to curve left, sailing over a brand new city not far from the sandy shoreline cradled by a series of gentle green mountains behind with the imposing EF base on the cliff overhead. The city stretched for miles, full of shiny, towering skyscrapers that reflected the sunlight. The buildings seemed to mimic the shape of the trees, willowy, with elegant twists and spirals. SkyCars zipped by in clear tube-shaped sky-highways, darting between the buildings. Little ant sized pedestrians walked along immaculate streets laid out in a geometric grid design. Everything looked so clean, so clear and crisp...so new. Vibrant and full of color.

Off in the distance, Spring could see raw soil and obvious construction, the skeletons of new buildings populated with construction crews and their airborne equipment. The shuttle continued past the large city, slowly descending, flying closer to what looked like a residential seaside area on the outskirts of the city. The city had a fan-shaped pattern that stretched to the lush looking mountains. Row after row of homes and small shopping centers of all sizes, some complete, others still under construction. Construction sites were everywhere.

"It's so clean! Look at the sky...the ground!" Spring gazed out her window as the shuttle flew lower, gliding over toward a large complex nestled on the outskirts of the city facing the ocean. The building was shaped like a large, silver ball, it's rounded front facing the ocean, reflected in the windows like a hundred times over. The aqua blue waters glistened invitingly with deeper shades of green. A few feet below the roof, etched in glossy, bold black letters were the words 'Mitte Hilton'.

The back side of the building held a large, steep slide that ended in a gigantic swimming pool surrounded by lounge chairs. A few tiny people were already relaxing by the pool as what appeared to be waiters in bright uniforms delivered drinks. It looked like the kind of place she could never afford as a 'real' person. Spring felt a silly smile tugging at her mouth, *It's not like I could afford to live off-world anyway!*

"What a tastic hotel! And right by the beach too! How absolute is that!" Pam bounced excitedly in her seat.

"Don't get too excited," Adiva's voice issued from the back of the shuttle, "We never get ocean side rooms, and the rooms are not great anyway. As old as the city by the looks of them."

"We're off-world, who cares what the rooms look like?" Spring shrugged as the shuttle glided up the long curved driveway lined with flowering shrubs. A uniformed doorman stood by the main doors, giving Spring a quick peek at the dazzling lobby chandelier and polished marble floor. The shuttle parked behind an identical shuttle, the Daytime crew had beat them after all! They were already standing at the rear of their shuttle, waiting for the luggage assistant to unload them. A few waved. Spring's crew were up and on their feet, shuffling toward the door. Spring was behind Adiva, her nose wrinkling slightly at the faint cigarette odor from Adiva's blazer. "Besides," Spring addressed Adiva's back, "who has time to waste in their rooms?"

* * *

Spring had an ocean view room. Everyone did. Each floor of the hotel rotated once every sixty minutes, allowing each guest an ocean view and a view of the mountains. One simply had to adjust to the hotel's slow rotation...especially after a few drinks. And her room was beautiful, modern, and clean.

Spring went to bed with her curtains wide open, forcing her drowsy eyes to stay open as long as possible; watching the strange star filled sky with its three moons. The largest moon held court over the ocean. The colorful striped gaseous giant was so close (closer than Earth's moon it seemed), it cast a small reflection on the calm ocean. Spring reached out unsteadily, her finger outlining its shape before her room gradually shifted away, giving her a glimpse of the illuminated city of Mitte. The skyline of Mitte was sprinkled with dozens of moving SkyCars going who knows where on a Thursday night. Two moons hovered over Mitte, one higher than the other, large and bright in the night sky. She had read that the two smaller moons were being Terraformed. She blinked sleepily at the moons, her fuzzy post crew dinner three glasses of wine mind trying to remember the names of the moons.

"Yes, 'member now," she slurred, "Hope and Forr being Terraformed, an' the big striped one is Oram." She smiled, waving at the two moons, letting her arm drop clumsily, knocking over the colorful brochure advertising a tour of the underwater caverns of Corsa. She sat up on her arms, biting her lip, looking down at the brochure on the wooden floor. She bent down, picking up the glossy booklet, reading the itinerary. 'Explore the

Labyrinth of CAVERNS OF CORSA made by Eden's EXTINCT Eelkeeln's! Journey deep under the Corsa ocean in COMFORT AND STYLE in our DELUXE sub-shuttles for an all day ADVENTURE!'

It was all Pam, Zavia and the crew could talk about during dinner at the hotel's rooftop restaurant. A surprisingly expensive restaurant, even with a twenty percent discount.

"Goodnight, moons." Spring placed the brochure back on the night table, carefully propping it up again.

* * *

Spring tried to blend in with the large potted plants in the lobby without success. Jackie grabbed her arm, dragging her out of her discreet hiding place, "There you are, hon! You didn't get up this early to miss our tour did you, kid? Found her! Here she is!" Spring planted a smile on her face as Jackie pushed her through the bustling lobby toward the small gathering of crewmembers, each dressed in their own versions of 'field trip' attire. Spring spotted a few 'Daytime' crewmembers in the mix. There was an air of excitement that made a lump form in Springs mouth.

"Spring!" Pam and Zavia strode toward her, followed by the salt and pepper pilot close on Zavia's heels. Pam sported a purple fedora hat, tank top and pink shorts; while Zavia wore a chic jumpsuit accented with a gorgeous embroidered belt. "We just called your room! Ready to go see some snake caves or what?"

"Well, um..." Spring glanced at the others, feeling her cheeks burn. Her eyes slid nervously to the pilot at Zavia's side, "I, um, I changed my mind. I think I'll just um...stick around here...you know, go to the mall? Maybe into the city." She glanced down at her yellow sundress and her brand new sunburst pendant, bought on Velaxion. She looked up, giving a helpless shrug, "I'm not dressed for a tour anyway, you guys go on and tell me about, okay?"

"Are you sure, Spring?" Zavia's eyes bore into hers as if she really could read minds. Spring bit her lip, taking a step back toward the elevators, instantly regretting it. Zavia flinched. Pam pulled her arm, steering her a few inches away. Zavia broke away from the pilot, following.

"What's up, doc? You were babbling away about this during dinner... why the sudden change?"

Spring fingered the necklace around her neck, staring down at her feet, "I...just feel like the mall. Maybe next time. I didn't really read the brochure until this morning. Didn't realize how long a day it was going to be." *Or how expensive. I would face six hours of listening to Gran-Libby's twenty-first century music than admit...*

Pam stared at her for a moment, then exchanged a look with Zavia. "Well, hold on a minute," Pam moved toward the elevators, "since you're headed to the mall, maybe you can return this for me? Be right back, don't leave without me!" Pam darted off into the elevator, leaving Spring and Zavia to stare after her. Zavia stared at Spring as if she wanted to ask her something.

Pam returned in a few minutes, her face flushed, thrusting a book in Spring's hands. "Thanks, Spring, you'll be doing me a huge favor by taking this!" Spring looked down at the little paperback book, noticing a bright pink envelope sticking out. "Gotta go, have fun at the mall. Alright, gang, let's roll!" Pam walked toward the group. Zavia stared sadly at Spring for a moment, then left.

"Pam!" Spring pulled out the pink envelope, surely Pam needed it. She took a closer look at the envelope, frowning. Her name was scrawled in Pam's large loopy handwriting in purple ink. With shaking fingers, Spring tore open the envelope, revealing a stack of Ceres dollars wrapped around a pink note. 'Spring, take it and hurry your ass up! I'm holding the shuttle for you! Hugs, Pam' .

Spring looked up with blurry vision, staring at the shuttle outside, loaded with her crew, most of them gabbing away at each other. Only Zavia and Pam's eyes were locked on the hotel's doors. Spring laughed a watery laugh, tasting a foolish tear, wiping it away with a trembling hand. Her feet moved slowly toward the main doors.

"Miss? Are you joining us for the tour?" Asked a guide in a garish safari style uniform. He tapped a clear clipboard impatiently. Spring looked beyond him, making eye contact with her friends who beamed at her, both beaconing excitedly. Even the salt and pepper pilot winked. "Miss? "he asked once more.

"Take me to your leader!" Spring quipped at the man. He stared blankly at her, "Yeah, yes, I'm going! Lead the way, kind sir! Oh...um, the water snakes are extinct, right? Sir?"

* * *

"Water snakes? Awesomeness! Did you see any? Are they edible?"

Spring laughed at the impish image of Gran Libby on the telecall. It was early morning on Earth, and the sun filled up Gran Libby's little art studio. Gran had a motley pile of fabric in crazy patterns sitting beside her ancient sewing machine. She was wielding a scary looking pair of scissors in one hand, and her ever present mug of tea in another. It was after five Saturday morning on Eden, while it was still Thursday on Earth. Spring yawned, stretching out on her stomach in her uniform, facing Gran Libby. Her crew had to be back on Explorer in two hours. The asteroid detour had shortened their layover from five days to two.

"No, not a single live snake! Just a few hologram ones thrown in ... you know, popping up beside the water shuttle. Not scary at all, kinda fake." *Practically wet my pants when that first one 'lunged' at us. The second had enough teeth to sharpen a Redwood tree! And were they really neon green?*

"Bummer! Sounds like you had an epic time! Underwater snake caves big enough for a submarine! Can't wait to see this for myself! Oh, and I want to hear about this commander guy! An alien right? Palaqeon?"

"He's Endarion, but my roommate Zavia is Palaqeon. Strange, but..."

"What?"

Spring looked away from the screen frowning. Outside the sun was beginning to rise over Mitte, and she thought of the nightclub she had left two hours before. "It's just strange how Zavia and the commander have the same silvery eyes. They're like looking into a mirror. Plus Zavia, well, yesterday after the tour, some of us met up with a crew from another airline and there was a Palaqeon guy."

"And they hooked up?" Gran-Libby asked eagerly.

Spring bit her lip, "She acted strange when he said something in their language. She got so pale. He like, he didn't have silver eyes. They didn't look the same at all, he was, kinda yellowish and Zavia is like, very pale in a bluish gray kinda way."

"Well," Gran Libby had a mouth full of pins, "look at us Earthlings, we're different colors and stuff. We used to be called, 'black'. Maybe he said something lame, like some cheesy pick up line."

Spring shook her head. The Palaqeon guy had been stocky, shorter than Zavia, with bulging eyes and a pug nose set in a narrow face. His fish eyes instantly narrowed when Jackie told his crew that Zavia was from Palaq. Spring remembered Zavia blanching when the Palaqeon shot off a rush of garbled words in an accusatory tone through a phony smile. Zavia had moved her frozen face into a smile, but her reply held a warning of some kind. Enough of a warning to make his fish eyes flicker with alarm, before he had stalked off muttering, ' imderkca'.

"No," Spring sat up, pulling the telecall monitor onto her lap, "his words didn't sound very nice or cheesy." She shrugged, "Probably reading too much into it I guess. Gran, I'm meeting my crew downstairs for break-fast, I better finish packing. Besides, I gotta hear how Pam's second date went with Guy."

"Is he an alien too?"

"Businessman from Earth. Human. Pam really likes him."

"Pam? Oh, that red haired girl! Is that leader of yours still being mean to her? Andrea...Antha..."

"Adiva." Spring slipped on her shoes, balancing the monitor, "She's nice to her now. She met Guy. She's even remembering Pam's name now, calling her 'girlfriend' too! What a one eighty!"

Gran Libby had pulled the pins out of her mouth, taking a long sip from her tea, "Pam better beware."

"Why?"

Gran Libby's set her mug down, "Sounds like a potential BBB. Backstabbing, Barracuda, Bitch. Don't laugh, Spring. Watch Pam's back." Gran Libby waved her scissors for extra effect.

Spring hid her smile, "Thanks, Gran," she said gravely. "I have Pam's back."

"Okay, Spring Chick. I love you, have a safe flight back so we can fly somewhere soon! Mwah!"

"Thanks, Gran, love ya too, bye!" The monitor went blank, and Spring carefully slid it into her suitcase, zipping it shut. The sky was now streaked with pink, yellow and orange over the ocean, in the distance Spring could just make out the StarPort terminals hovering over high above the water. On impulse she tapped her wrist, a small transparent screen popped up, hovering over her arm. The little screen displayed current events, weather, (local, the Moon, and Earth: Virginia Beach): and the current time. The screen was gradually filling with images Pam had taken from the tour, Spring tagged in each one. With her right hand, Spring made a sweeping move, clearing the screen until it was an illuminated blank slate.

"Translate please." She asked.

"Language?" The computer asked.

"Palaqeon, and the word...Imderkca into Earth English."

The screen flashed for a second, then the translation appeared, filling the small screen. Spring blinked twice, staring hard, her mind racing with questions. She read the screen once more, seeing the same word: Impostor.

9

IT'S ONLY A PAPER MOON

THREE WEEKS LATER.

The televideo buzzed loudly, blinking its red light furiously while Spring navigated her way past her suitcase and a few boxes in her new room. Her room. She loved those two words. No more sharing the tiny Orion apartment. Pam had her own room too. Thanks to Zavia, or rather Zavia and her insanely large, posh, apartment in the brand new Starry Towers. How a new hire like Zavia could afford a place in one of the Moon's most expensive areas was beyond her. Spring honestly did not want to think about it.

"I'm coming, I'm coming!" She snapped at the televideo, finally making it to the panel by her dresser (brand new, courtesy of IKEA). She flipped the 'call open' switch and her parent's three dimensional images jumped out at her. Her mom still dressed in a robe, and her dad wearing the Orion Galactic T-shirt she bought him with his plaid 'around the house' pj's. They smiled big, cheesy smiles at her.

"Hey, baby!" Her mom waved excitedly, her eyes already scanning Spring's new room, "What a nice room! So modern too! Is that a round window behind you? It's taking up the whole wall! Give us a tour, hon."

"Um, well," Spring looked around her room. She had just moved in with Pam three days ago, everything was still a mess. Reluctantly, she pulled the wafer thin viewing module off its stand, becoming a tour guide. She started off at her favorite spot, the floor to ceiling wall to wall, round window, with its actual view of real Moon terrain; not the generated blue sky. Beyond the grey sandy hills, Earth was visible, the best view in the world.. Her room was square, boxy, small, but larger than her old room. Big enough for a full size bed, dresser, and a plush low chair covered in a golden yellow velvet. The dark finish of her furniture matched the rich brown of the heavy sliding shoji screen doors and dark floor.

The apartment had a simple layout. Zavia had decorated it in a sparse, minimalist style that was saved from looking cold by Zavia's taste for bright primary colored accents; and her obsession with Earth products. Two large round windows flanked the living room, followed by a galley kitchen with pass through window. Pam's room was beside Spring's and identical, down to the tiny bathroom. Across the living room, Zavia had the master bedroom; larger with a full bath (including a real bathtub).

"My word, look at that bookcase!" Her mom's eyes popped at Zavia's living room bookcase bursting with not only books but knick knacks collected from Earth. It dominated the two dark grey couches, competing with the zebra accent rug and bright blue throw pillows. Green plants were everywhere.

"You girls have that bookcase secured to the wall right?" Her dad asked. Spring nodded staring at the slightly leaning bookcase, before propping the televideo on the coffee table, sitting on the couch cross legged.

"How much did you say this was, hon?" Her mom asked.

"It's not expensive, not with the three of us paying rent. Magnif huh?" Spring and Pam knew Zavia was charging them a ridiculously low amount for rent. They offered to pay more, but Zavia refused. They were the only airline people in the twelve floor building. Populated by executive types and the random celebrity. Even the pilots were envious of Starry Towers.

Her mom exchanged a quick look with her dad, "It's beautiful baby, it's just we want to make sure you're not over your head. It looks so expensive and you said—"

The televideo beeped, another call was coming through. Orion Galactic flashed over her parents face. Spring felt a wave of relief, "Mom, Dad, Orion is calling through, I gotta get this, could be another trip to Eden!"

"Love you guys, bye!" Her parents hurriedly said goodbye before Spring abruptly ended their call feeling a little guilty for cutting them off. The stern, familiar face of her supervisor, came into view. The woman's eyes zeroing in on Spring's pj's. Spring's mouth went dry. She smiled brightly. "Hi!"

"Orion Galactic. This is Odina Pat'Jor. Am I speaking with Spring Stevens?"

"Uh huh." *Breathe. Don't panic. It can smell fear.*

"Hi there, Spring. I'm calling about your recent trip to Eden…"

"Oh?" Spring's voice squeaked as images of the pleasure palace swam before her. Did Adiva report her after all?

"Orion would like you to deadhead down to Headquarters to join your crew in a press conference."

"A conference about the palace?" Spring blurted. *I did NOT just say that! Oh god, deliver me from stupidness.*

"Palace?" Her supervisor frowned, "What palace? This concerns your rescue by the Endarion ship following the asteroid incident. Commander Baldric will be on Earth, and we would like the entire crew on hand at Orion Headquarters to thank one of Earth's newest allies. You will leave for Earth tonight, and meet with Orion officials and Endarion representatives. In full uniform of course."

The Commander's face, eyes and smile filled her mind. She felt a giddy smile creeping at the corners of her mouth, followed by a thought of sheer panic, her eyes widened in horror. She remembered his expression at the palace, how surprised he was to see her there. Surprised and probably shocked. Disgusted. How could she face him now?

"And so it is already on your schedule…" Her supervisor was saying. Spring managed to nod absently, *Well, I need to have my hair, nails done. Do I have time for new shoes? May need a cute dress in case we have to go to dinner, um…*

"Spring? One more thing."

"Uh, yes, ma'am?"

"What did you mean by palace?"

* * *

EARTH. ONE DAY LATER.

"We're grateful for the assistance of our new allies in space, the Endarions of planet Endari. Without their help, the fate of our passengers and crew could've easily been one of tragedy. We owe our most sincere thanks to Commander Baldric and his crew for coming so swiftly to our aide. Humanity truly spans the universe!" The CEO of Orion Airways led the way in applause in the small bland, conference room surrounded by the flashing bulbs of press eagerly snapping away.

Commander Rexlen Baldric blinked uncomfortably at the constant assault of the flash bulbs, hoping his face did not betray the slight annoyance he felt. Standing beside two newly minted Endari ambassadors, in the windowless, brightly lit room; feeling like a uniformed prized animal. He was losing precious time on his real mission. His mouth twisted at the thought of why he was really on Earth.

Rexlen watched as Yountorr, one of the Endari ambassadors stepped up to the podium, droning on about peace and exploration between the two worlds. The ambassadors words slid into the background as Rexlen looked beyond him to the other side of the small stage, his eyes falling on the Orion crewmembers. They stood off to the side in a neat row, almost according to height, which made his mouth twist again with humor. His eyes skimmed over the two captains, and the pursers, finally resting upon someone who looked just as uncomfortable as he felt. Miss Spring Stevens.

She stood beside her red haired colleague, her eyes fixed with a polite but glazed stare at the Yountorr, her mouth fixed in a vacant smile. Her long tapering fingers were clasped primly in front, only her right index finger tapped impatiently over her left hand. Rexlen found himself drawn to this petite, dusky human who managed to yawn with a closed, slightly smiling mouth. Her hair was pulled up in a bun of sorts, different from the last time he saw her; at Velaxion with a mass of bouncy black curls, falling halfway down her back. Today, the glossy curls were restrained into primness with only a lone rebellious strand curling against her sculpted high cheekbone. Her dark hair complimented her brown skin, and black eyes. Her posture made her look taller than she actually was, her head held high and serene, even if her mouth quivered with what Rexlen thought was a hidden laugh. He studied her mouth, her top lip fuller than the bottom, painted a pleasing red shade with a moist sheen. He remembered her smile and how her cheeks deepened with small indentions. Her smile lit up her eyes, making her entire face glow with an inner light that warmed him. He wished she would smile now.

At that moment, she looked away from the podium, her eyes locking directly onto his, widening slightly. Rexlen felt his chest constrict as he watched her, wondering if she remembered their last, brief meeting at the station. She gazed at him with wide eyes, her teeth gently pulling on her lower lip as a slight rosy color filled her cheeks. She seemed to freeze. Rexlen moved his lips into a slow smile, giving the smallest of nods. Her answering smile was shy, but soon widened into a full smile, the power of it made Rexlen's own smile falter. How could she have such an effect on him? Why was his heart beating so against his chest? For the life of him, he could not tear his eyes away from hers. Nor did he want to.

The ambassador stepped down, the conference was over. Members of the press stood up, taking final shots of the ambassador, the Orion heads and Earth Federation brass. The room was suddenly noisy, filled with blinding flashbulbs and the sound of a band playing the Endarion anthem. Rexlen found himself face to face with a blustering Earth Federation general, posing stiffly for photographs. A quick glance her way confirmed she was still there, standing by her crew; waiting to shake hands with her CEO as she slowly made her way down the crew line. She met his eyes once more, before glancing looking away.

More EF brass surrounded him, introductions, photo ops, military prattle. Finally Rexlen had a chance to break away, find her, talk to her. He moved purposefully through the crowd, excusing himself among the cluster of press. The small room seemed to expand, and the journey to the other side felt like crossing an ocean. The line of crewmembers was no more, they were gone. She had vanished. Rexlen found himself staring stupidly at the blank wall, his heart still racing.

"Commander Baldric! Commander, may I have the pleasure of introducing you to…" a voice called from behind. Rexlen turned around, looking down at weaselly man wearing an Orion badge. Beside him stood the CEO of Orion Galactic, her chest puffed out proudly.

* * *

"Remind me to never wear my new Le Beau heels for stuff like this, talk about ouch!" Pam sat on a pier rail, rubbing one reddened foot. Spring, Pam and Tatum stood on the empty terrace of Orion Headquarters with the distant view of New York City. The tinny sound of music drifted from the conference room a few yards away. Spring leaned against the rail, savoring a rare, blue sky day, the crisp autumn air cooling her face. Her heart was still pounding.

"Pam, I don't think Spring gives a hoot about your heels!" Tatum smirked glancing in Spring's direction, "Did you see that blazin' commander checking her out? Those laser eyes were totally locked on her! I think he likes you, he wants to kiss you!" Tatum ended her sing song with squeals of laughter joined by Pam.

Spring shook her head, "He probably wasn't staring at me, I mean, why would he? He...he was probably checking us all out." Spring stuttered, feeling heat warm up her cheeks, "Not like I care. I mean, he's from another planet and all."

"Spring..." Pam said.

Spring ignored her, "I mean, it's not like I'll see him again. But, well, he was blazin' huh? I mean, he looked so ... I never thought an Alien could look so...non-Alien!"

"Spring..." Tatum said uneasily.

"I've always kinda liked a man in uniform," Spring mused dreamily, "so virile looking and delicious..."

"Spring!" both Tatum and Pam snapped, standing on either side of her, wedged shoulder to shoulder.

"I hope I am not intruding," A deep, rich voice said behind her. Spring stiffened.

"The commander?" She mouthed to Pam. Pam reached up, smoothing Spring's hair, giving a tiny nod, before hobbling away. Spring took a deep breath, slowly turning around, staring up into the commander's face.

"No, um, not at all!" She said breathlessly, managing a smile, "Hi... hello, Commander!"

His eyes shifted between the three of them, before resting on Spring's face, "Good afternoon, ladies." He bowed stiffly. He straightened, staring intently at her. Spring felt her cheeks burning under his penetrating stare.

"Hello, Commander, nice to see you!" Pam said in a rush of words, "Oh, uh,Tatum, we...ah...have to see our inflight rep about... something! Uh, have a good day, Commander, see ya, Spring! Come on, Tatum!"

Pam jerked a grinning Tatum away, limping as fast as her towering heels would allow.

Spring stood there staring at the commander with a dry mouth, and thudding heart. She had forgotten just how tall he was, and how striking he looked in his tailored uniform. She racked her mind, trying to think of something witty or funny, semi-intelligent. She half turned, gazing up at the moon, clearly visible as a milky colored globe in the blue sky. "I still can't believe I live up there."

"I used to stare it all the time before I flew." Spring said quietly, glancing briefly at the commander. "It's like it was beckoning me, inviting me to live there. Telling me anything was possible." She leaned against the railing, staring up at the sky, "Sometimes it was the only thing I could see, peeking out through the clouds, letting me know not to give up. Not to feel down." She looked down at her hands, smiling slightly, shaking her head, "I don't know why I'm telling you this. Silly, huh?"

The commander had moved closer, standing beside her. He looked up at the Moon, then back at her, his eyes intent on her face. "No," he said softly. "It is not 'silly'. It would be 'silly' to not follow your dream. Never go to the Moon. You followed your dream. That is admirable, not foolish. Now," He said in a business-like tone, "I have been on Earth for three days now, all of it with the Earth Federation. Do you know of a suitable tour guide, someone willing to accompany me to dinner? Preferably someone with firsthand knowledge of life on the Moon." He glanced sideways at Spring, his face serious except for the twinkle in his eyes, "Do you know anyone that fits the criteria, Miss Stevens?"

Spring tried to hide her smile, "Hmm," she stroked her chin thoughtfully, "such short notice. I have someone that fits the bill perfectly! Her name is Berthhugga and she's perfectly lovely! You'll love her! The only woman I know with a full beard and bald head ..."

"Berthhugga?" The commander looked stricken. "A full beard?"

"I'm just kidding!" Spring giggled, pressing a hand on his sleeve, "Pulling your leg!" Her humor faded at the flat look he gave her, "I'm sorry! That was an Earth joke. I,well...does the offer still stand for you know, dinner?" *Alien 101: No stupid Earth jokes!*

He looked away, his lips pressed in a thin line, that trembled slightly. Spring felt a heaviness in her stomach. She focused on her shoes. She peeked up at him through her lashes...he was grinning at her! She grinned back, letting out a breath she suddenly realized she was holding. "So, shall we have dinner, Miss Stevens?"

"Yes, that would be tas—wonderful! Only call me Spring, okay?"

"Good. Eight o' clock then? Where shall we meet? Pick a restaurant, Spring."

Spring's mind raced. "Uh, how about The Oasis?" She instantly regretted her choice. The Oasis, was one of those ultra cool, trendy restaurants where everyone sat on floor cushions in blue lighting with plates that glowed in the dark. It was very sophisticated and had a long waiting list. Pam's sister patronized it because it was one of THE places to eat in New York. "They're probably booked."

"I will make reservations." The commander said confidently. "I am sure the Earth Federation can arrange something for...out of town guests." He stood smiling down at her, "I will see you at eight, Miss, er, Spring. I look forward to hearing about Earth and the Moon." He bowed to her, then leaned forward whispering in her ear, "Perhaps, I should mention my mother is named Berthhugga."

Spring gasped in horror, jerking back to stare up at his face, only to find his eyes crinkled with amusement. He chuckled softly, "There. We are even. Pulling your leg, Spring. I look forward to tonight." He turned, walking away with long strides. Spring watched his retreating, broad shouldered figure, and sighed. Within minutes of the commander's departure, Pam and Tatum were half running, half-walking toward her in excitement. She had to admit, she liked hearing her name on his lips.

"Well?" Pam demanded, hands on her hips, cutting to the chase.

"Oh, only that I have a date at The Oasis!" Spring exclaimed. Pam and Tatum hugged her, the three jumped up and down squealing.

"Mamas, proud of you! Your first date with an Alien!" Pam said, linking arms with Spring, walking toward Orion's headquarters.

"A handsome uniformed Alien!" Tatum added.

"Wait till we tell Zavia! Hey! What are you gonna wear?" asked Pam. "This totally calls for a celebratory shopping trip in the city!"

* * *

Spring tried to lounge as gracefully as she could on the tufted floor pillow, conscious of all the chic New Yorkers around her. She hoped she fit in. Everyone was dressed in black. Everyone except for the commander,(still in uniform), and herself. She was going to wear an emerald green dress, but decided to don a slate grey sheath, paring it with 'stained glass' collar necklace of red, pink and purple. She thought it went very well with the commander's eggplant uniform.

Lars, their waiter came by their table (a slab of Lucite with a shattered mirror top), dropping off dessert, two chocolate confections in an artful design. Lars, and the other patrons did not bat an eye at the commander. With the Earth federation so near, Oasis was probably no stranger to Aliens, but then neither was New York. She murmured 'thanks' to Lars, and returned her attention to the Commander; digging into her dessert as daintily as she could.

"So how long are you going to be on Earth? I mean, when do you go home to Endari, Commander?" She asked.

The commander finished chewing his dessert, one bite left and it would be finished, "Please call me Rexlen. I still have a mission to accomplish here, so I expect to be here for a few months. I have to head up to the Moon in a few weeks..." He said, glancing at her with a faint smile.

"That's Vunda'klat! I can't wait to show you around, you'll love the Moon! Why I—" she stopped, the commander had paused mid bite, staring at her. Slowly, he put his fork down. "Did I say something?" Spring asked. *Do I have a ring of chocolate around my mouth?* She wiped at her mouth with her napkin.

"Vunda'klat. Where did you learn that word?"

"My roomie, Zavia. She's an Alien too." Spring shrugged, scooping up another bite, "she says it all the time! She was supposed to be at the conference today, but she didn't feel well." It was on the tip of her tongue to add how Zavia's eyes matched his, but she stopped, feeling uneasy under his intense stare.

"Is Zavia, Endarion?" He asked, his eyes bore into hers.

"No, she's… she's Palaqeon." Spring smiled brightly despite the wariness in her voice. "God, she has a sweet tooth! She's always baking cookies and stuff and as thin as a rail!" The commander was frowning slightly, his eyes narrowed as he read her face. Spring felt her cheeks warm. He was looking at her as if she was telling a lie. The room felt hot, and the weird, space age house music seemed to beat in time to her heart during the silence. The Palaqeon word 'Imderkca' floated around her mind. "Will you be here for Thanksgiving?" She blurted. Even to her own ears her voice sounded too high, thin. He looked blank. "It's an Earth holiday, I mean, an American holiday. It's in two weeks. Lots of food."

The commander shook his head, eating the last of his dessert. "Lots of food? Sounds enticing, but I have a few matters to attend with the EF. Perhaps we can meet up on the Moon? I find myself very curious about the world of Spring Stevens." He smiled again, his eyes warm and without the suspicion that had lingered there moments before.

10

BAD MOON RISING

THANKSGIVING.

"Dad's getting me one of those new HomeRobots for Christmas!" Spring's mom said cheerfully, sipping a glass of wine, "And not a scary metal type! Zavia dear, you don't need to help, you're our guest! Spring, what happened to your other roomie? I thought she was coming too? Summer, eat some of Spring's macaroni and cheese, she made it on the Moon you know!" Spring's sister sullenly submitted to a large dose of Spring's plastic looking mac-n-cheese, which fell onto her plate in one congealed clump of orange. Her brother Hunter snickered in a very immature, un Earth Federation cadet way. Her mom paused over Summer's plate, glaring at Hunter.

"Gwen, I'll take another helping, here, pile it on!" Her dad passed his plate down the table, patting his belly, "Hope I still have room for Miss Zavia's chocolate cake, never had an Alien cake before."

"It's not 'Alien', Dad." Spring said slowly, "it's a regular cake. I mean, a human…it's a cake!" Why did she always feel like a bumbling twelve year old at her parents house?

"It is okay." Zavia smiled politely. "I am an Alien, and it is my cake, so it is an Alien's cake! May I have some more…collard greens, please?" She passed her plate down to Hunter who gazed at her as if she was a goddess. He deposited a ladle full of greens without his eyes leaving her face. He was rewarded with a dazzling smile of thanks from Zavia and a gagging noise from Summer. Spring resisted the overwhelming urge to roll her eyes.

Hunter was home from the EF academy for the holiday, but insisted upon wearing his tan uniform. Spring had not seen him in months. His curly hair was cut in one of those severe military cuts, which managed to highlight his almond shaped eyes and dark bronzed skin. Of the three of them, Hunter's face showed the traces of their Japanese grandmother the most. With his full mouth, brown skin and Asian features, Spring could see why girls swooned over him. Well, just barely.

"You girls still on reserve?" Gran Libby asked. Spring tensed, sensing a 'back in the day' flight attendant story coming on, "Why, I remember I couldn't touch being off on Thanksgiving! Did I ever mention the time I spent Thanksgiving in Berlin? That trip was so senior, but I managed to fly with my friend Yul. He always called me his 'fag-hag' and whoa, did we have an epic time! We went to this S&M show at some club. I think it was called the Kit Kat club, or maybe Puss an'..."

"Mother!" Spring's mom said through clenched teeth bared in a smile, "Have some cake, Mom!"

"Gwen," Gran-Libby laughed, "I'm sure these girls have seen and done things I could never dream of!" Gran-Libby winked at Spring and Zavia. Spring froze, recalling a drunken telecall to Gran-Libby recounting the pleasure palace. "I wish I was eighty years younger, what an adventure...so cool!"

Zavia had taken an instant liking to Gran-Libby. They even dressed in colorful, sometimes elaborate clothes. Zavia had dressed up for the holiday, wearing a royal blue, square necked blouse trimmed with colorful embroidery and black skirt. Gran-Libby was decked out in her favorite burnt orange Indian tunic, complete with bangles, earrings and bright red lipstick. This was her annual, Thanksgiving outfit, but it seemed to hang on her this year. Gran's face was slimmer, her cheekbones more prominent.

Spring's V-neck brown sweater dress was saved from blah by the sparkling bib necklace she wore on her date with Rexlen. She touched it now and then, smiling remixing remembering how much he liked it on her. The past few weeks, Rexlen had made time to chat with her or send her a message every day. They had managed two holo-dates, and Spring was excited about seeing him on the Moon after her next trip.

"Are you Endarion?" Spring was jolted out of her thoughts by Hunter's blunt question, directed at a pale Zavia. Zavia slowly reached for her water glass, taking a careful sip, before meeting Hunter's eyes.

"No, I am Palaqeon." She smiled politely. She turned toward Gran-Libby, her smile widening, "You must have a lot of stories from your flying days. Did you keep all of your uniforms?"

Gran -Libby laughed, "Kept every scrap! I have a full—"

"We just studied Alien races at the EF, and you look and act like an Endarion." Hunter interrupted Gran-Libby. Zavia focused on him once more, her eyes glacial. "You look nothing like a Palaqeon."

"Hunter." Hunter ignored his mom's glare, pressing on,

"Palaqeons are short for one and—"

"I am Palaqeon." Zavia replied coldly. "Palaqeons are tall too."

"Well, from what I learned at the EF..."

"Hunter, drop it." Spring snapped.

"Could you be half-Endarion and not know it?"

"That's enough, young man." Spring heard the warning tone in her dad's voice.

Zavia simply stared at Hunter, her face unreadable, for a moment, then she smiled faintly, a trace of humor in her eyes, "Maybe I am the child of the milk farmer."

"Milkman." Summer corrected. Spring's little sister was eating this up, her eyes darting from Zavia to Hunter like a fan at Wimbledon. Hunter looked skeptical.

"Well, Hunter, poor Zavia comes over for her first Thanksgiving and is interrogated!" Gran-Libby quipped, placing her napkin on the table, rising slowly. "Sure you're not going into EF Intelligence, Hunter?"

"Compliments to the chefs and to the glorious OveCom that cooks a turkey in thirty minutes! Come on, time for some chilaxin time in the living room!" Gran-Libby gathered up her plate, heading toward the kitchen, "My belly is full from all that Thanksgiving deliciousness!"

"Kids," Spring's mom rose, grabbing the turkey platter, "grab something and follow me. Zavia, sweetie, you relax, you're the guest even if some of us," her mom looked meaningfully at Hunter, "have forgotten. We'll have cake in the living room."

* * *

By the time Spring and her siblings entered the living room with slices of Zavia's cake, Gran Libby held court on the couch, her large photo albums on her lap. Zavia sat beside her, gazing with interest at Gran's old flight attendant pictures. Summer took a seat on the floor, while Hunter sat in a chair by Zavia.

"Oh, here is when my crew and I had a reroute layover in Cocoa Beach! We caught a shuttle launch. God, that was like, so amazing! Course this was before NASA merged into EF..."

"Spring, is Pam flying over Thanksgiving?" Her mom asked, taking a seat beside Spring's dad. Zavia looked up, exchanging a look with Spring.

"Pam's on Eden with her boyfriend." Spring sat down on Gran Libby's other side, "I think her parents are somewhere on a yacht. They visited her last week though."

"Really?" Her mom sounded pleased, "On the Moon? Marc, we need to do that! I have some stuff for your new room, baby! What were they like?"

Snobs. Pam had just returned from a two day trip to Mars, when her parents called, giving her twenty minutes notice. Turns out her parents had been on the Moon for four days, visiting a friend. They had one hour before their flight back to Earth, and decided on a whim to call Pam. They had flown Delta.

Pam's mom looked like an older version of Pam, except her green eyes were frosty, and her face had that overdone pre-natal genetics altering, that was all the rage forty, fifty years ago. Her lashes were too long, her nose too pointed, her mouth too full. She was thin to the point of skeletal.

Her father had typical WASP, patricians features, complete with pale blond hair, and blank 'Barney Rubble' eyes. He patted Pam stiffly on the back, while her mom air kissed both of Pam's cheeks, stiffening when Pam impulsively hugged her. Her parents then turned their attention to Spring, Zavia and Zavia's date for the evening, looking down their noses at them before sitting on the couch.

Poor Pam ignored their disdainful looks, proudly showing them around, asking about their flight. The light in her smile faded when she realized she was home on call during the first two days of their visit. Her eyes took on a glossy sheen when her parents explained why they would not celebrate Thanksgiving. Spring felt a helpless anger as she watched Pam blink rapidly at the end of her parents brief, stilted visit. Pam walked them to the door, then hurried to her room, averting her face. Zavia and her date decided to stay in and order pizza, and the three of them were able to coax Pam into joining them.

It was during pizza and two bottles of wine, that Pam revealed her families lineage.

"You're so lucky, Spring," Pam had said, "I wish my grandparents were still alive, especially Mother's parents. They were so sweet. Grandmother

Vickleton always made rice crispy treats for me and Drew. She met my grandfather when they both worked at McDonald's you know."

"The french fries place?" Zavia was intrigued. She loved french fries.

"Uh huh. Grandfather started his company with money he won in the lottery when he was like, twenty. He and Grandmother got married, and then he started his startup company, made billions, blah, blah, blah." Pam let out a bitter chuckle, "Mother is pure Greenwich. Once she married into Father's family, she tried to forget she was ever, Victoria Vickleton. She doesn't like the McDonald's or lottery story to get around. Mother married into an old family and Father got millions. Match made on Wall Street."

Pam had smiled wistfully, "But I always loved visiting Grandfather and Grandmother. They had a huge house, but it was always cozy and warm. You know what I mean?"

"They were very glamorous." Spring said carefully, "Her mom is a Vickleton. Victoria Vickleton."

"A lot of V's," Gran -Libby smirked. "What's her middle name... Vivian? Violet?"

"How about Vicious." Zavia muttered under her breath.

* * *

A small ship hides within the protective shield of Ganymede, appearing like a tiny speck beside Jupiter. Inside, the small flight deck is quiet, the reddish glow of the controls and the occasional beeping of the navigation systems, the only companion of the woman at the controls. Her eyes shifted between the controls and the viewing screen, displaying the dark side of Jupiter's moon. She found herself slouching slightly, exhausted from three hard days of flying at top speed, only to take cover and hide from the Earth Federations scanners. The sound of hard footsteps make her sit upright quickly, suddenly alert once more, eyes on the viewing screen, just as her Captain entered. The captain rubbed his eyes, his clothes wrinkled from sleep. They wore no uniforms, they belonged to no one. Their ship flies unmarked, painted illegally in black.

"Esta," The captain acknowledged her, sliding into the chair to her right. This would normally belong to her first officer, but their crew is small, she is the only one at the controls in the cramped flight deck. "Have we heard word from the movement? Any reports from the human's Moon?" The captain asked.

"Yes, captain. A report was made an hour ago." She moved her chair toward a nearby screen, opening up the transmission, her eyes shifting to her captain. He was a tall muscular man, a Tobion. His features were handsome to some, too harsh for others. The grayish cast to his skin appeared murky, his brow ridge prominent with rippling along the brow continuing down his temples. His once dark hair was streaked with white. He was the only one that wore some semblance of a uniform. An exact replica of the long dead Tobion military; a bodysuit of dark blue, shimmering with the silver rank of captain .

She was a Mutavion, a race of beings that could never pass for humanoid operatives on the Moon. Her three-fingered hands and physical shape would give her away.

"The rumor is true then," The captain nodded toward the screen, "the BelFilia is hiding among the humans." Esta, glanced at the flickering image, her slit of a mouth, flattening in distaste at the image of a young woman dressed in opulent clothes. Esta's own outfit was crudely sewn, made of rough hewn fabric that covered the scars she still carried from her years as a slave. Her small button eyes, blinked in anger at the image; wearing a tall, fan-shaped, jewel encrusted headdress, the young woman's swan neck encased in a high necked gown also dripping in gems. The woman's face was unsmiling and stiff, the eyes serious and thoughtful.

"The BelFilia was spotted at space station Velaxion in neutral space, sir." Esta scanned the report, rubbing an old scar under her sleeve, "Her dwelling place has not been confirmed. It appears she has covered her tracks very well, Captain."

The captain smiled grimly, "So she thinks. She won't be able to hide for long, not from us or the others searching for her." He chuckled low in his throat, "We must find her first, and when we do, everything you ever wanted will be yours. You could retire, Esta, buy your own planet."

Esta looked doubtful. "You seem too confident, Captain. It may not be an easy task to catch the BelFilia." The captain gave her a hard stare, his jaw rigid. Esta had known him for close to twenty years, serving as his pilot for fifteen. His once boyishly soft face was scarred, as she watched, his mouth twisted into an ugly smile, "The BelFilia may have changed her name, but there is one thing she cannot hide...at least not for long," he made a mock bow at the glittering image of the woman, "her eyes will give her away. Set a course for this Earth's Moon."

"Yes sir."

11

SUSPICIOUS MINDS

Zavia kept staring at the huge Christmas tree Pam had set up in the corner of the living room. Christmas décor was all over the apartment. Pam insisted on placing small, 'baby' trees in each of their rooms, color coordinated to match each roomies personality. Spring's tree was a sunny yellow, and Zavia had a bright turquoise one. Pam naturally had a hot pink one, accented with a zebra tree skirt. Pam choose a traditional green tree for the living room, and oddly that was Zavia's favorite. Maybe it was because it reached the ceiling.

Christmas music blared from the hidden speakers as Pam hurried around, hair wrapped in a towel, "Zavia, I could use some elbow grease before the Christmas party! You're still baking your stuff right? Spring, bring that strappin' commander tonight, you just know we all want to drool over him! Don't roll your eyes! He's on the Moon in da flesh! I can't touch my hunk of burnin' love!"

Spring threw herself on the couch, examining her nails, (and for a second, imagining a ring), "Maybe. Pam, maybe Zavia will loan you one of her Earth boy toys." Zavia shot her a mock dirty look, Spring said. "We'll try to swing by Pam, but isn't this party just a little early? Christmas is like, weeks away!"

"We're all flying during Christmas, right, aren't we?" Pam said in a muffled voice with garland in her mouth. Her towel turban slipped, and a peek of fire engine red hair, streaked with green slipped out, "Anyway, you and Rexlen gotta come, Guy's not the only hologram guest tonight. Why is Rex so shy? Zavia keeps missing him." Zavia pretended to ignore that last comment, choosing this moment to sing along with Bing Crosby. She actually had a great voice, reminded Spring of Ella Fitzgerald. You could hear the smile and pleasure in her voice when she sang.

"Rexlen wants to meet you, Zavia, he keeps asking about you, fellow alien." Too much actually. Spring tried to ask him why he was so curious, but his expression quickly closed, his eyes unreadable. She got the same response when she asked about what he was doing on Earth and on the Moon. If he did answer, it was usually to say as little as possible. So, after seeing him for two months, she gave up. There were some things about her job she could not discuss. Gran-Libby loved the idea of Spring's non-human boyfriend, she bragged about it to everyone and anyone who would listen.

"He doesn't have a lot of time tonight. We're just having dinner and then he has to do some work stuff." Spring explained.

"Well, I guess that's why you brought those 'fuck me' heels and all that stuff at Lady Lace...work my ass! As your Gran-Libby says, 'no shame in your game', girl!" Pam grinned, passing Zavia who gave her a high five and grinned back.

"Yeah, Spring, just keep the whips and chains to a minimum, okay? I have an early sign in tomorrow!"

"Looks who talking!" Spring threw a pillow at Zavia, barely missing the tree. "You're still with that German guy, right? The one two floors up?"

"Behave, kids!" Pam picked up the pillow, and sent it Frisbee style onto the coffee table, "Don't mess up my tree, biatches."

"It is a beautiful tree, Pam." Zavia said softly, reaching out to tentatively touch an ornament. "Perhaps we can keep this one up all year? It reminds me of home...so magical."

"Vunda'klat!" Pam called out from the kitchen. Spring looked up, her eyes flying to Zavia's averted face. Zavia turned her face toward them, her eyes shining with emotion. She nodded smiling.

* * *

Rexlen stood in their doorway an amusing mixture of expressions crossing his face. The place was packed with live guests and hologram guests dancing, mingling. A few holograms had technical errors, appearing on the walls and upside down from the ceiling; but since everyone was pretty trashed at this point, maybe they meant to appear upside down. Even the elderly couple from two doors down were dancing away, the wife, grinding into her eighty year old husband. Jorge was there, wearing an illuminated Christmas sweater, dancing with his hologram pilot girlfriend. Pam sparkled in a emerald green dress that matched her hair. Guy hovered nearby, tapping his foot, snacking on party food. An old jazz tune was on, slow and sultry, making couples giddy and flirtatious.

Rexlen looked half amused, half baffled. Spring knew he loved music as much as she did, and she could tell the music was drawing him, especially the non-Christmas music. She shyly pulled him inside, her eyes roaming over his uniform in admiration. He paused, his eyes going over her in masculine appreciation, that made her tingle under his accessing gaze. She wore a new, cherry red dress with a modest v-neck. She fell in love with the high winged collar, trimmed on the inside with tiny red and black crystals in an elegant geometric design. She wore her down in thick, bouncy curls.

"Stunla'arr." Rexlen murmured low, bending to kiss her softly, "Beautiful." She loved when he spoke Endarion.

"Ostavti," She thanked him in Endarion. He smiled with approval. "Do you want to meet some of my friends? Jorge flew in from Mars, and Pam's boyfriend is here too…well, as a hologram. Even Zavia is here, she wants to meet you!"

That surprised him. He tore his eyes away from a hologram couple dancing through the Christmas tree, staring intently at her face, "Zavia is here? Where?" He looked around. Spring had the urge to lie, and tell him she just left. For some reason his interest in Zavia annoyed her. Zavia was by the window, dancing with her German flavor of the month. She was barely recognizable. Her black hair now platinum blond and wavy, her lips blood red. She wore a form fitting, deep green gown of satin with a black lace overlay. She looked like someone from another century. Jean Harlow meets Veronica Lake.

"I'll introduce you." Spring lead Rexlen through the crowd who parted, staring at Rexlen curiously. Zavia missed a beat of the song, stumbling, her eyes on Spring and Rexlen as they approached. She smiled brightly at them, a smile that did not warm her eyes. Her bright green eyes. Spring blinked in disbelief, but wiped the look off her face, feeling Rexlen's eyes on her.

"Rexlen, this is my roomie Zavia, she was on the Explorer too. Zavia, this is Rexlen." Spring looked meaningfully at Zavia's date, "And this is …"

"Commander, this is Wil," Zavia said smoothly, locking arms with the tall, handsome man who flashed a winning smile at Rexlen, extending his other hand, "Wil, this ez Commander Baldric, ah ze Endarion Empire." Zavia said in a strange accent.

Spring found herself gaping at Zavia. She slid a sideways glance at Rexlen. He was staring hard at Zavia, his eyes scanning her face, narrowed slightly. "I finally meet the elusive Palaqeon, Zavia." He said stiffly. "A pleasure."

"Ze pleasure ez ah mine, Commander." Zavia inclined her head. Rexlen's mouth was set in a grim line, while Zavia's eyes were frosty behind the bright green. The green did not work, her eyes seemed to shine behind the green, making the artificial color too bright. Spring shifted her feet, feeling an undercurrent of tension crackle in the air. *Do they know each other?* Spring's stomach felt uneasy. She bit her lip, managing a cheery smile.

"Well, we better be going!" Spring said brightly, tightening her grip on Rexlen's sleeve. "Have fun, Zavia. Tchuss, Wil!"

Spring struggled to keep up with Rexlen's long strides, waving to Pam and a few others as they made their way to the door. She didn't realize until they were standing in the hall, the music pounding from the other side, that she had been holding her breath. She let out a long sigh.

*   *   *

"This is a restaurant?" Rexlen 's voice held a trace of amazement.

"I know, it's kinda unusual," Spring said, "But the food is the best! Do you like it?"

It was still difficult to read Rexlen's expressions, he kept everything so controlled, it was hard to gauge his likes and dislikes. Standing in front of a life size, replica of a flying saucer was one of those examples. Area 51, was large, round two story restaurant. Blinking UFO lights of red, blue and green, circled the silver, chrome colored building. The round windows of the dining hall sat high upon the saucer, giving patrons a breathtaking view of Earth. The restaurant rotated, like a saucer preparing for flight. It had the atmosphere of a mom and pop place, with polished chrome tables, and shiny red booths.

She felt a slow warmth spread around her chest, as an easy smile spread across his face. A low rumble of laughter escaped him, "Area 51. How fitting. Finally a place that caters to a select, Alien clientele!" He offered his arm, "Shall we go in?" His strange eyes danced with amusement. The awkward meeting with Zavia seemed forgotten, Spring giggled, linking her arm with his.

A hostess in a black suit and tie, lead them to a quiet booth in the corner, Spring's favorite table. She winked at Spring. A waiter waved as he walked by.

"This must be a favorite of yours?" Rexlen asked after another waiter waved.

Spring looked around, smiling happily, "I love this place! Where else can you have a meal in a flying saucer?" Inside it looked like a vintage saucer from the 1950's. Shiny chrome walls with blinking lights, high booths with red leather seats and shiny chrome tables. Vintage framed art posters from old sci-fi movies and TV shows lined the walls, while mini silver saucer style lights hung over each booth.

Rexlen leaned forward, "As you would say, it is tastic. How old is it? Do you know?"

"A waiter told me it was built by one of the first colonists, back in the 40's. A real, former, 'Man in Black'. And that the restaurant is modeled after a real ship that was stored at the actual Area 51 on Earth." Spring lowered her voice, leaning closer with a secret smile,

"Some say that this was a real saucer, and the person in black flew it up here, can you believe that? What do you think? Does it look like it was an actual ship?" Rexlen opened his mouth, just as a waitress appeared. The wait staff dressed in shiny, silver suits, complete with a bubble style space helmet with a lone antenna sticking out of the top. The antenna had a tiny red light at the tip that blinked cheerfully. The waitress smiled. Rexlen seemed enchanted.

"Greetings and welcome to Area 51!" The waitresses voice sounded tin like and muffled through the helmet. "Would you like anything to drink? Are you ready to order?"

Rexlen glanced at his menu, his eyes widening with pleasure. He looked up expectantly at Spring, bowing slightly with his head, smiling faintly. Spring tore her eyes away from his with difficulty, focusing on her menu screen, aware of his eyes on her. She felt her cheeks flush with color.

In two months this was their fourth date 'date' in the same room. Two holo-gram dates did not count.

"I'll have a glass of Mercury Merlot." She smiled up at the waitress, then looked at Rexlen, "Are you ready to order?" She glanced at the illumi-nated, flying saucer hologram menu that hovered in orbit over the rocket shaped salt and pepper shakers.

Rexlen's eyes quickly went over the menu, his lips pressed in concen-tration, "Wine sounds good. Hmm, how about the…'Around the Earth', platter? Sounds delicious." He smiled a disarming smile at the waitress. The waitress blushed turning toward Spring, "An…and you miss, are you ready to order?"

Spring winked at Rexlen, "I'll have the 'Around the Earth' platter as well."

Rexlen and the waitress both stared at her with surprise, "Miss," the waitress said carefully. "that's a big meal, are you sure?"

"I think I can handle it, thanks!" Spring said. *How big could it be, right?*

The waitress needed the assistance of two waiters. Spring felt her stomach cramp at the sight of all the food. Around the Earth was a fitting name. Dishes from each of the continents filled the table, the best of each region, Europe, Asia, Middle East, Africa, the Americas, including some seafood. Spring blinked in disbelief. Every inch of the table was covered. Spring usually just ordered the Nebula potato skins.

"Is there anything I can get for you?" The waitress asked. Spring stared up at her speechless, she looked across the abyss of steaming dishes to Rexlen, who had his eyes locked on Spring,

"Spring, do you want anything else?" He asked. Spring could swear he was trying hard not to laugh.

You mean like, five other people to eat all of this? She smiled weakly at the waitress who gave her an infuriating, 'I told you so' look before leaving.

Well, she did try to warn me. Spring stared down at the curried dish in front of her.

"To the most beautiful woman in the galaxy," She looked up at Rexlen's words. He held up his wine glass, his easy smile, in contrast to his intense stare. Spring raised her glass, smiling back.

"Yes, to the most beautiful woman…where is she?" She asked innocently looking around, before gazing back at a laughing Rexlen, "And cheers to the best looking man in the universe."

* * *

The wine seemed to loosen Rexlen. Spring found herself intrigued by his homeworld, so different but so similar to Earth. In the past, Rexlen always avoided her questions, asking her about Earth instead. He knew all about her family. How her Grandpa Stevens met and fell in love with her Japanese grandma, when he was stationed in Japan. How Gran-Libby met Granddad Mattsson when he was a passenger traveling from Stockholm to New York. He knew that the Stevens were a military family, starting with Henry Stevens, a former slave turned Buffalo soldier. Rexlen knew Spring had applied, and was rejected by the Earth Federation Academy.

"Your winters last eight months! What does everyone do until spring?" she asked, eating her last bite of Thai Som Tam, a spicy papaya salad. Rexlen was already working on a delicacy from Germany.

A mischievous look crossed his face, "A lot of indoor activities," he said finally, with twinkling eyes. "My people are used to long winters, but then we have planet Tobi. That is like Earth, and it is warmer too."

"Was it Terraformed?' Spring sipped some of her wine. She looked up in time to see a shadow cross Rexlen's eyes. He glanced down at his uneaten Bratwurst, his face grim.

"No. We…acquired it." His voice sounded slightly cold. She knew he was preparing to close the topic, but Spring persisted. He glanced up at her with piercing eyes that held a trace of challenge in them. The room became unbearably hot and stuffy. Spring leaned back in her seat, cradling her wine glass in her hands.

"It was occupied then? Cool!" she said lightly, "What lived on it before? Creatures? Bigfoot?"

"Bigfoot?" Rexlen looked confused for a moment, before taking a sip of wine, "No, people lived there."

Spring stared down at an empty plate, before slowly meeting his eyes. His face was expressionless, his pale eyes wintry. "Wh…what happened to the people?" she heard herself ask.

Rexlen was silent for a long time. Probably no more than a few seconds, but it seemed like hours. The waitress came by, clearing the table during the awkward silence. Spring stared at hands. Finally he spoke, his voice devoid of emotion, "They were re-assigned." Spring's head shot up, her eyes flying to Rexlen's face. He gazed back, his mouth set in a firm line, his eyes intense.

A chill went through her. "Re…re-assigned? What does that mean? Did they stay on Tobi?"

"Some stayed, but most were sent where they were needed." He re-filled their wine glasses.

"Sent? As free people? Was it their choice to leave?"

"As servants to the empire." Rexlen said in a clipped voice. "We were at war with Tobi, Spring. The Tobians were fortunate to be assimilated into our world. A harsher victor would have killed them all. They became members of the empire."

Spring looked away, watching a family of tourists eating two tables away; swallowing the rising tide of anger. After their first date, Spring had looked up the Endarion solar system, (the only thing she had time to read before she was short called for a trip). Planet Tobi was the virtual twin of Earth, same size, 365 days a year, third planet from its sun. She wondered what the people were like. Wondered if they considered themselves 'fortunate'.

"Spring."

She glanced up, meeting his eyes, hating the way her heart fluttered. He didn't run the empire. It was not his fault. It was his leaders fault. Who knows, what happened on Tobi may have 'gone down' centuries before. Rexlen was right. The other option was wiping out the Tobians, and the Endarions did not do that. Maybe it was a good thing.

"Spring," Rexlen looked down at the table, "I should never have mentioned Tobi." He said heavily.

"No, I'm glad you did. Caught you off guard, huh?" She smiled faintly, "It's true. I'm glad I know. It helps me to understand your world better. And hey, it's not like Earth is a peaceful paradise. Stuff happened on my planet. My great, great grandmother Rachel, came to the U.S after World War II. She lost her whole family. I never knew her. Gran-Libby was just a kid when she...you know, died."

"Gran-Libby is the former flight attendant, right?"

Spring grinned, "She still is! I swear if Orion did not have an age limit, she would be flying through space right beside me!"

Rexlen smiled. "I hope I have the pleasure of meeting her one day."

Spring felt her heart leap at his words, "Be prepared for her endless tales of travel. When I was little, I would lay on her bed and listen to her old stories and look through her albums." She laughed to herself, twisting the stem of her wine glass, "God, I think I have every picture memorized!"

"She means a lot to you." he said softly.

"Yeah," Spring agreed, "She encouraged me to fly, rooted for me during training." She met his eyes," I thought...well, I was afraid to fail. I mean...my brother is at the EF, my sister is going there next year, and I was working at a department store. Gran Libby helped me practice for the interview...coached me on what to say. She..." Spring blinked away the wetness in her eyes, "she believed in me." She finished quietly. She looked away, staring at the blurry image of a toddler wrecking havoc a few tables away, "Sorry! I keep saying depressing stuff, don't I?" She said in a watery voice.

Rexlen pushed aside their wine glasses, his fingers closing around hers, "Gran Libby is a great lady, and so are you. Do not apologize. I am looking forward to meeting her and thanking her."

"Thanking her? Why?"

"Well," Rexlen's fingers tightened on hers. He looked down at their fingers then back into her face, "If she had not shoved you into becoming a flight attendant, we never would have met."

"Shoved me?" Spring arched a brow.

Rexlen shrugged, attempting to look innocent, "These Earth words, so confusing at times. I may need further lessons in Earth English, I am afraid. And not from anyone that goes by the name Berthugga."

"I'll see what I can do." She said sternly.

"Good." Rexlen winked, grinning. Spring laughed.

Ten minutes later, the plates were cleared, and Rexlen shook his head, impressed, "You are full of surprises, Spring Stevens! I did not think you could eat all of that ...amazing! Have room for dessert?"

"Are you?" She set her elbows on the table, leaning forward dramatically, "I challenge you to more food."

"Challenge accepted." He leaned forward looking into her eyes with something more than humor. Spring's breath caught at the stare. Her eyes drowning in his.

"May I offer dessert?" A voice spoke. Spring and Rexlen both jerked backwards in their seats. The waitress stood in front of them. With a tap of a button on her wrist, a dessert screen appeared before them.

"Yes, we'll have dessert, thank you." Rexlen said curtly. The waitress nodded, excusing herself.

* * * * * * * * * A R E A 5 1 * * * * * * * *

Celestial Treats & Other Desserts

Classified Crème Brule: delectable custard with caramel and tantalizing sugar ... $45 Ceres

Time Travel Tiramisu: Savioiardi dipped in fine Etrueleon chocolate espresso with luscious layers of whipped cream...$44 Ceres

Paper Moon Praline & Pecan Cheesecake: butterscotch cheesecake topped with pecans & pralines...$40 Ceres

Martian Strawberry Delight: fresh strawberries nestled in a rich strawberry glaze, topped with whipped cream on a cinnamon pie crust...$40 Ceres

Flying Saucer Sundaes: traditional earthling ice cream dessert 10 ice cream choices and over 12 toppings...$28 Ceres

UFO: house dessert of the day. Chefs specialty...$35 Ceres

**Out of this World Cocktails **

Little Green Mentarion Apple Martinis*** $20 Ceres

Lost Time Absinthe Tonic*** $30 Ceres

Roswell Rum Shakers*** $35 Ceres

Men in Black Triple Mystic*** $35 Ceres

Martian Mojito*** $35 Ceres

Lunar Martini*** $50 Ceres

Galaxy Glider*** $50 Ceres

Fire Nebula*** $60 Ceres

Beam Me Up*** $60 Ceres

Star Chaser*** $65 Ceres

Space Odyssey*** $65 Ceres

Starburst*** $65 Ceres

Saturn Martini*** $65 Ceres

Rexlen went with Spring's recommendation, ordering two slices of paper moon pie. She beamed with pleasure at his first bite, smiling as he closed his eyes for a second, before leveling a stare at her, his eyes filled with approval, "This is very good, delicious. I must admit, I had my doubts, considering the strange name, 'Paper Moon.'" He scooped another bite onto his fork.

"It's the title to an old song. Ooooh, no! Don't give me that look, I can't sing! Might scare small children! Zavia has the right voice for it... it's kinda of a jazzy song."

"Whisper a couple of lines." Rexlen coaxed with a smile, "Please?"

Spring glanced quickly around, leaning forward, softly singing a few lines to the centuries old song. Rexlen leaned forward, listening with a soft smile. Spring leaned back against her seat laughing, "there! That's all!"

"More?"

"Well, I don't want to ruin your ears with more!" She cut off a slice of pie with her fork, "Um...what's your family like? I mean...you know about Gran Libby, are your grandparents still alive?"

"My mother's parents are still alive." He allowed."They live on another planet, I seldom see them."

"And your father's family?" Spring asked casually, "Do they live on Endari?" Rexlen's face had become guarded, wary. Getting him to talk about himself was like pulling teeth.

"They live primarily on Endari, yes," He replied, "My father's mother is alive."

"Really? Do you call her grandmother? I mean...what is the Endarion word?"

Rexlen shook his head, his mouth in a crooked, humorless smile, "I don't believe we have such a word. Perhaps, Eck'Kara, that means, 'great mother'. My father's mother is quite unique. She rules over us all, you see."

"Ah, so she's a bossy granny!" Spring suggested with a mischievous grin, "A busybody right?"

Rexlen nodded, his eyes shifting to the approaching waitress, then back to her, "Yes," he said dryly, "Quite."

* * *

The after dinner walk home was slow and tranquil, just what Spring wanted, leading Rexlen the 'long way', savoring the stroll on Rexlen's arm. Their feet sounded loudly on the damp sidewalk, wet from a recent generated shower, the smell of rain still in the cool night air. The small lunar city seemed quiet and sleepy around them, the streets deserted, shops closed. The eleven fifteen shuttle to the StarPort raced by them half empty, it felt like they had the street to themselves. Spring smiled to herself; as she tightened her grip on Rexlen's arm, marveling at the firm, muscled strength under her fingers.

"What is that smile about?" He asked, staring down at her. He looked so handsome in his uniform.

"It's like we have the Moon to ourselves. Like we're the only people here." She felt her heart skip a beat as his lips curved into an answering smile. "I like it. It feels good." She said.

"So do I." He said smiling into her eyes.

The rest of the walk was in a comfortable silence. Spring leaned gently into Rexlen's side as they walked, breathing in the night air, gazing up at the clear, star-filled sky; watching as a few StarShips took off or landed, some dancing among the stars, going to places unknown. Earth loomed large ahead of them, crescent shaped, half of it cloaked in darkness. It was daytime back home, her family was just starting their day.

Starry Towers stood out among the apartments, most of its lights glittered. The lights were on in Spring's apartment. Together they crunched up the manicured walkway, wiping their feet on the large mat by wide double doors. Spring glanced at the security entrypad, then at Rexlen, wetting her lips, should she invite him up? "Do you want to come up? It's still early." She heard herself blurt.

Rexlen stood in front of her, his eyes on her lips, before slowing moving up, scanning her face, "I better get back to the EF base." He pulled Spring closer, enclosing her in his strong arms, wrapping them around her. Spring stared up into his face, her heart beating wildly as she gazed up into his pale eyes.

"Thanks for dinner," her voice sounded husky and thick, her hands grasping his upper arms in a smoothing motion. "Maybe a homemade meal next time? A meal on me? Well, I mean, I'll cook a homemade meal that is!" Her cheeks burned as he lowered his face, pulling her tighter. He kissed her, sending a shiver of pleasure through Spring. She leaned into the kiss, letting her tongue dart out to meet his, rewarded by Rexlen deepening the kiss. His hold on her tightening until she felt molded against him, her hips pressed against him, her feet on tip toe.

It felt like everything around them, the building, the possible nosy neighbors, even the stars in the sky, melted away, until it was just the two of them. Rexlen broke off the kiss, and Spring gazed up at him from beneath her lashes, her lips parted. He stared down at her with eyes that seemed brighter than normal, heated with an inner glow that excited her, rather than alarm her. He was breathing heavily, like her, as if they had finished running. He lowered his face again, then abruptly stopped, straightening, pushing her away slightly, "I think I should go now," he said, his face neutral except for the desire that still burned in his eyes, making them stand out in the dim entryway light. He stared at her for a long moment, before bowing, his eyes resting on her face once more, his mouth in a slight smile. "Goodnight, Spring, sleep well."

"N...night." Spring stammered as she stepped into the lobby. He waited a few seconds, until the elevator door slid open, then he waved at her, before striding down the walkway. Spring moved away from the elevator as it slid shut, taking a few short steps toward the entry doors, watching Rexlen's retreating back.

"Sleep well?" She remarked as he moved further down the sidewalk, finally disappearing around a curve, "How am I supposed to sleep well now?" She kicked her heels off, picking them up, tucking them under her arm, heading back toward the elevators. As the elevator slid open, Spring glanced over her shoulder at the empty walkway outside, "Sweet dreams, Rexlen." she whispered.

* * *

One week later, Spring stumbled into the apartment, dragging her luggage and two bulging grocery bags, fresh flowers, and two shopping bags from Earth. She actually had to ship four new pairs of shoes to the Moon because they had exceeded her allowed weight for the shuttle. She kicked the door shut with her foot, parking her suitcase, shoes, and shopping bags by the door. She hurried to the kitchen before she dropped the heavy bag with the three bottles of wine (she couldn't decide on just one). "Anybody home? Hello?" She called out, flexing her cramped fingers. Her eyes went to the door, noting that two pairs of suitcases were parked a few feet from hers. *Maybe they went shopping. No, Zavia flies tonight.*

"In here, Spring." Zavia's voice rang out in the direction of Pam's room. Spring glanced at her groceries, then in the direction of Pam's room. She hastily put the perishables away, then made her way to Pam's room, kicking her shoes off along the way. Pam's door was ajar, Spring hesitated, before tapping softly,

"Can I come in?" she asked. A pained looking Zavia, already dressed for work, pulled the door open; revealing Pam, sitting stiffly on the edge of her bed, still in uniform, her face red and blotchy. She blinked up at Spring with eyes swollen and red from crying.

"Pam! What's wrong? What happened?" She sat down on the bed beside Pam, wrapping an arm around her, feeling her own eyes begin to sting. Pam let out a long, shuddering breath, her eyes trained on her lap, her hands, restlessly plucking at a tissue. "Pam?" Spring said, glancing questioningly at Zavia. Zavia shook her head sadly.

"It's Guy." Pam whispered brokenly. "I think...I think he's..." Pam looked up, staring at Spring, her green eyes swimming with unshed tears, "I think he's seeing another flight attendant." Her face crumpled. "Adiva, I think." Pam said in a small voice.

"Oh, Pam." Spring pulled her gently toward her, letting Pam rest her head upon her shoulder. Zavia came forward slowly, hesitating, then sitting on the other side of Pam, leaning her head against Pam's, her hand patting Pam's back. Zavia hummed soothingly an unfamiliar but soothing tune. "Are you sure he's seeing her? Maybe you're wrong?" Spring said. *Adiva was old...almost forty!*

Pam shook her head, "No, it's true. Adiva...she told me herself!" Pam sat upright suddenly, jumping to her feet, facing them, "She thinks I'm stupid, telling me all of these hints...coincidences. Thinking I'm too stupid to figure it out, when everyone else knows! I thought she was becoming my friend!"

"What kind of coincidences?" Zavia asked.

Pam wiped angrily at her nose, clearing her throat, while tears continued to stream down her face. "She changed his name, but everything else is the same...height, the type of apartment he has. His age."

"What about Guy?" Spring asked gently. "How you asked him? What did he say?"

"He said it was not true." Pam said dully. "He denied it all, but whenever I fly with her...he, he suddenly can't see me. Makes excuses. Tells me to believe him. That he's telling me the truth."

"Do you?" Spring asked, "Do you believe him or do you believe Adiva?"

Pam shrugged helplessly, her eyes welling with new tears, "I don't know. I don't know. You warned me not to trust her didn't you, Zavia?" Pam whispered, "I should've listened."

"You are too trusting." Zavia, stood up, "You try too hard to see good in others, when it is not there. The galaxy is filled with Adivas. People will smile at you, befriend you, then stick you in the back."

"Stab you in the back." Pam said, blowing her nose.

"Right! Stab you in the back, and smile while they are doing it."

"Pam," Spring said slowly, "If you don't believe him, there is a way you can find out the truth."

Hope filled Pam's face, "There is? How?"

Spring glanced down at her clasped hands, letting out a long sigh, "Last year, I thought Wes was cheating so I ordered one of those, Deception Detection Devices."

"Did it work?" Pam asked.

Spring closed her eyes against the tears that threatened to spill. Painful memories filling her, making the room too stuffy, making it difficult to breathe. The anger was gone, but the hurt was still there. She opened her eyes, blinking rapidly, "Yes," she replied thickly, "It worked very well."

"Do you still have it? How does it work?" Pam sniffled. "Can I use it?"

Spring looked at the desperation in Pam's face, before staring at Zavia's face. Zavia stared back, her stranger eyes shimmering with concern. Silently, Zavia leaned forward, offering a tissue. Spring took it, nodding thanks, staring down at her hands. "I think I still have it. It's on Earth. It's going to take a few days. Gran-Libby knows where it is. I'll call her tonight." Her own voice sounded hollow and empty.

"I have an idea." Zavia gestured for Spring to come close. Spring stood up, allowing herself to be drawn into a hug /huddle. "I made some cookies this afternoon," Zavia pulled back, looking at both of them with a soft smile, "We will have hot cocoa, cookies, a fun movie! Does that sound okay? I will go make the cocoa...sound good?"

"Tastic." Pam said.

Zavia turned to give Pam a hug, "You are beautiful, and Guy should kiss the feet you walk on! Okay?" Pam smiled a watery smile at her, nodding. Zavia pulled Spring into her arms, hugging her,

"I am sorry the Lie machine worked 'very well', Spring," she said in a low voice. "But, you know, you are better off? Rexlen, is a good man...well, from what you have told me!" She turned to leave.

"Zavia?" Spring called out. Zavia stopped at the doorway, glancing over her shoulder.

"Thank you." Spring said.

12

REVELATIONS

Spring surveyed her dinner ingredients, lined up on the counter in two groups: dinner, dessert. Behind her, the oven beeped merrily, pre-heated and apparently excited Spring was using it instead of the faster OveCom. Zavia had gone out of her way, searching for an authentic, mid-century stove. She insisted they made cookies taste better. Zavia did make the best cookies, so Spring decided to overcome her fear of the intimidating relic from the past, and make peace with it. The turkey and phyllo pie was going to take twice as long to bake, as it would in the OveCom, but Rexlen's first meal at her house deserved to be special. It had taken her two hours to decide on her date outfit, silk wrap dress of her favorite colors, yellow and green. She hoped her new filigree earrings and cuff bracelet were not over-doing things. Spring had reluctantly decided against wearing her brand new Schon heels. She parked them at the entrance to the kitchen, so she could gaze at them. Perhaps she could talk Rexlen into a walk after dinner? *Of course he may be more interested in my new lace bra and panties!*

Spring unfolded her brand new, old fashioned apron (bought for the occasion), tying it around her waist, feeling quaint and housewifey. Some extra fabric in the back, and the red, white trimmed apron would make a tastic dress. Spring wiped the goofy smile off her face, pulling out a cutting board, grabbing the package of leeks.

A few minutes later, the leeks were in the skillet, sizzling with garlic and butter, when the telecall in the kitchen sounded. Her mom. Spring sighed, glancing at the recipe for a second, before, going to the sink, washing her hands. "Accept call," she called out, watching as her mom's face appeared on the screen.

"Hi, baby!" Her mom beamed, her eyes roaming over the kitchen. "Pretty kitchen! Is that an actual stove you're using? My Spring is cooking on an actual stove?" Her mom exclaimed, ignoring Spring's sour look. "Is this for the Endarion? Is he there now?" Her mom leaned forward, trying to get a better view of the kitchen. "Where are your roommates, hon?"

"Rexlen isn't here yet." Spring pulled some eggs out of the wall set refrigerator, she shut the door with her elbow. "He's coming in a few hours." She carried the eggs to counter, staring uncertainly at them, and Zavia's whisk, resting beside a mixing bowl. "Mom, do you know how to 'beat' eggs?"

Her mom let out a peel of laughter, "Baby, I doubt even Gran-Libby knows that, and those are kitchen tools from her era! Why did you buy all of those? And what's for din din? Are you making enough for your roomies? You did measure everything right, didn't you, Spring? Hope you don't screw this up, Baby. Remember when you tried to bake that cake?"

Spring bristled, cracking an egg too hard against the bowl, filling her hand with slimy yolk, and shell. "I was twelve. This is an easy recipe, Mom. Turkey and phyllo pie." She said patiently. "And I'm just making enough for two. Pam left this morning for Eden, and Zavia's coming home tonight, but she has a party to go to." Pam had left with high hopes, carrying the Deception Detection device. Gran-Libby had expressed shipped it the day before in a care package, which included paintings for each of their rooms.

Pam excitedly hung her painting up right away, gushing about it in a long telecall to Gran-Libby. Spring's painting still sat on the floor by her window. It had a mixture of her favorite colors, but Gran's abstract, splashy art was not her style. She'll hang it up later. Zavia's painting was placed on her bed, bright hues of varying shades of blue, Zavia's favorite color.

"Is Pam still dating George?"

"Guy. His name is Guy, and yeah, she's still with him." Spring rescued the leeks, scraping them into the bowl of eggs.

"That's good. Pam is so sweet." Her mom smiled, "Spring, I just hope you don't mess this good thing you have with the Alien." Her mom chuckled, "You know, that surprised me, you dating an Alien, and such an important one!"

Spring tensed, adding the bowl of spinach to the egg mixture in a jerky move. She glanced up at her mom's face. "Why are you surprised?" She asked tightly.

"Oh, Spring, honey, I didn't mean it like that!" Her mom looked distressed, reaching out impulsively with a hand, "Oh, honey,…I meant, I'm so proud of you! Okay, the Alien thing scares me and your Dad a teeny tiny bit, but, if you're happy, so are we! Anyway, I better let you finish your meal, just wanted to tell you, Dad and I sent you something."

"Really?" Spring said excitedly. "What is it?" *New shoes? A new necklace?*

Her mom grinned eagerly, "I saw it on QVC! I bought one for you and myself! Let me know if you like it… I know you will! Dad, kinda rolled his eyes, but he thinks it's cute too!" Her mom blew a kiss, "Have a good time honey, hope your meal comes out, love from Earth!"

"Love you, love to Dad," Spring waved goodbye with a spoon, "tell Summer 'hi', and Mom?"

"Yes, Baby?"

"Can you put Gran Libby on for a second?"

A flicker of emotion crossed her mother's face, her mom blinked it away with a bright smile, "Gran's taking a nap."

"Now?" Spring stared incredulously at the clock on the wall, displaying Lunar and Earth EST time. "It's four in the afternoon there, she never sleeps late!"

Her mom was quiet, looking down for a moment, before shrugging, smiling the wide smile Spring had inherited. Her mom's eyes looked glossy. "Well, Gran is old, Spring. I'm sure you're a take a couple of afternoon naps when you're over a hundred one day. No big deal. Nothing to worry about."

Spring scanned her mother's face, her scalp tingling with uneasiness. "Yeah, guess you're right. Give her a hug, when she wakes up...'kay?"

"Will do." Her mom said softly, "Goodnight, Baby. I love you, and I'm proud of you, Dad too!"

"Night. Bye." Spring said distractedly, her mind on Gran-Libby. She leaned against the counter, her hands in her apron pockets. Her mom was right. Gran-Libby was okay. Of course someone as old as Gran needed naps. Why Gran was one hundred...no...she just had a birthday in October, she was one hundred and one. Gran-Libby was born in 1978. Spring kicked her bare heel angrily against the dishwasher, how could she have forgotten Gran's birthday? It was a week after hers, and she didn't even think about it. She had non-reved to Velaxion for a shopping trip. She poured the turkey and spinach mixture into her carefully prepared phyllo crust, making a mental note to call Gran-Libby.

She folded the ends of the phyllo toward the center, standing back to marvel at the flower like design, before sliding the dish into the warm jaws of the oven. She stared at the pie through the window, feeling a sense of pride, glancing over her shoulder as the front door opened. She straightened up, smiling, Zavia was home! Wait until she saw Spring's oven experiment! Perfect timing. Maybe Spring could coax Zavia into helping with the apple pie? She quickly washed her hands.

"Hey, girl! How was your trip? "Spring stepped out of the kitchen, wiping her hands on a cloth, "Gran sent you some—" Spring trailed, off, her smile fading, her eyes going from a pale, subdued Zavia, to two other flight attendants, a man and a woman, their faces somber. They stood protectively on either side of Zavia. Zavia's face was thickly powdered, slightly swollen on one side, her scarf was wound tightly around her neck. She moved her face into a pained smile.

"Hi, Spring." She turned her neck stiffly, indicating the two grim faced crewmembers, "This is my Purser, Donna, and this is Eric. This is my roomie, Spring." The two nodded solemnly at Spring.

"What happened?" Spring demanded, her wide eyes shifting between the three of them, the towel clenched in her hand. "Well?"

"Nothing." Zavia said flatly, staring directly at the other two. "Nothing happened."

Donna pursed her lips, her eyes sliding to Spring. Donna was a 'young' senior mama, flying less than ten years. Her dark hair pulled expertly into a French roll, highlighting her kind, brown eyes which glittered now with suppressed anger. "Nothing?" she uttered, "Zavia, someone tried to abduct you on our layover…that," Donnas' voice shook with anger, "that is not 'nothing'! I'll need to report this!"

"Someone tried to kidnap you?" Spring looked alarmingly at Zavia. "Who? Why?"

"No one needs to report anything. It was nothing, really, Donna." Zavia warned, "It is not necessary."

"Not necessary?" Donna countered, turning angrily toward Zavia, hands on her hips, "A member of my crew was violently attacked, almost abducted!" She lowered her voice, her eyes filling with concern, "Zavia," she said in a low voice, "we need to report this."

Zavia shook her head violently, "No! Like I said, it was nothing. I am fine!"

"No, you're not." Eric said.

"Yes, I am!" Zavia snapped. "You Humans, are making a…mountain out of an ant hill!"

"Mole hill." Eric muttered, his eyes sparked with emotion, "If I, a 'human', had not been there, you would not be 'fine'. Zavia, that was no accident…they were after you." He glanced at Spring, his grey eyes clouded, his thin mouth, clasped in a firm line.

"We were at the Mars mall, near our hotel, the three of us split up to shop. I came out of J.Crew just in time to see two people, dragging, and," he added, shooting a stare at Zavia's averted face, "hitting Zavia. They were as tall as she was, taller even, and one was trying to inject something into her neck.

"Oh my god!" Spring stared at Zavia. Zavia's face was expression-less, her eyes, wide, unseeing. "Zavia," Spring said gently, "You need to report this."

"I said, no." Zavia's voice vibrated with anger. "There is no need. I am fine." Zavia walked over to the Christmas tree, her back toward them, her arms crossed, hugging herself. "Thank you," she said thickly, "thank you, for helping me and…for taking me home. Please, please Donna," she looked over her shoulder, her voice pleading, "Do nothing. Please."

Donna's hands went up in exasperation, "Fine. Zavia, fine. You call me if you need anything okay? I don't care what time, or if you wake up my kids at four in the morning, okay? Do we have a deal?" Zavia nodded mutely. Donna walked up to Zavia, giving her a quick, fierce, hug.

"I don't feel good about this, Zavia." Eric said gruffly, crossing his arms. Spring 's eyes went to his face, noticing for the first time, the slight redness around his jaw, and how one eye seemed smaller than the other. His eyes were locked on Zavia with emotion that was more than brotherly. She had a feeling he would sleep outside their door if necessary. "I'm here if you need me. Zavia, you got that?"

"Yes," Zavia turned around, meeting his eyes, "Thank you, Eric. I will be okay."

Donna and Eric stared at Zavia for a long time, then turned to Spring, nodding. Spring walked them to the door. "Thanks for looking out for her," she said to both of them. Zavia trusted few people, and half of inflight were afraid of her unusual eyes, and that she was not human. Spring was thankful two crewmembers cared about Zavia. It angered Spring that for all their advances, humans were prejudiced against Aliens.

"Watch out for her, will you?" Donna said at the door, before wheeling her bag down the hall. Eric followed reluctantly, casting one final look at Zavia, before striding out into the hallway. Spring shut the door, jumping at the sound of the oven timer going off. She glanced at Zavia, standing by the Christmas tree, Zavia turned toward the kitchen, her eyes going to the oven and then to Spring in surprise. She smiled slowly, wincing.

"Cooking with the oven? Vunda'—"

"Zavia, stop," Spring interrupted, watching the smile fade from Zavia's face, "we need to call the police!" Spring went into the kitchen, yanking on pot holders, pulling the oven door open gingerly, setting the fragrant smelling dish on a trivet. She turned to face Zavia, watching as Zavia slowly limped over to a plant, inspecting it. *Why would someone attack her? Was it some sort of Alien hate crime?* Spring walked over to Zavia, standing by one of the round dining room windows, staring down at the little green plant with unseeing eyes. Spring reached out, hugging Zavia, "Hot cocoa?" Zavia stepped away, holding the plant protectively against her chest, she shook her head, glancing down at the set table.

"No," Zavia's voice sounded drained, "I am so tired. When is your commander coming?"

Spring took a deep breath, walking into the living room, sitting on the arm of the sofa, "He'll be here in a couple of hours. Have dinner with us." *Who did that to you? Why?*

"No thanks." Zavia said dryly. "But if you do not mind, I am going to stay home tonight. I am not in the mood for a party. I will stay out of the way. You will never know I am here." Zavia went toward her suitcase, rolling it toward her room.

"Zavia?" Zavia paused, leaning against her suitcase handle, she stared at Spring, with wary eyes.

"Yes?"

"We really need to call the EF police." Spring stood up, heading for the call panel by the door, "This is bull, I'm sorry, but I'm calling them!"

"Stop!" Zavia had crossed the room in seconds, blocking the panel, she looked at Spring, her eyes flashing with anger and fear. Spring stared wide eyed at Zavia, backing away. She had never seen Zavia move so fast. "Calling the EF would make things worse! And besides, it happened on Mars, not here."

"Why? Are you an 'illegal'? Are you running from the law? Did you commit some horrible crime on your planet?"

Zavia stared at her, for a long time, then she let out a long, shaky sigh, "It is too long of a story."

Spring stared at her for a long moment, wringing her hands. Gran would know what to do. "Whenever you're ready to talk, okay? I'm here if you need anything. I just wish you would—"

Zavia glanced over her shoulder, her pale eyes moist, "Thank you. I'm ...okay."

* * *

Thirty minutes later, Spring emerged from her room, ready for Rexlen. She had added a few auburn highlights to her curly hair (using a color wand that was easier than Pam's), she hoped he noticed. The apple pie was baking, filling the entire apartment with a homey cinnamon, apple smell. An old classic, Rudolph the Red Nosed Reindeer, was playing cheerfully on Tv. Zavia had turned on the tree lights.

Zavia sat on the couch, bundled in her robe, her hair still wet from a bath, pulled into a loose bun. Zavia rarely wore it down. Her hair reached the top of her waist. Spring sat down on the other side of the couch, her eyes falling to the half eaten sandwich on the coffee table, and the still steaming cup of tea. She glanced up at Zavia's face, biting back a small gasp. The left side of Zavia's face was not only swollen, but bruised horribly, large blotches of purple mixed with blackish red, reaching from the corner of her eye, to her jaw. Her neck shared the same marks. Zavia 's eyes followed hers, she glanced down, pulling her robe higher, burrowing in its softness.

Zavia plucked at her robe, her eyes on the screen, "Did I tell you I now own a pair of jeans? I can't wait to wear them." She slanted a look at Spring, smiling faintly, "They were on sale."

"Who are you? Are you really Palaqeon?"

"No." Her voice was so low, Spring leaned forward. "I make a poor Palaqeon, I suppose." She glanced sideways at Spring, "Your brother was right, you know. I am a Endarion."

Realization dawned on Spring, "Is that why you didn't want to meet Rexlen? He gave me a funny look when I said, Vunda'klat on our first date. That's an Endarion word, right?"

Zavia nodded. "It slipped out. It is hard trying to live as a Palaqeon." Her mouth twisted with irony, "Should have tried another race, but I always liked the Palaqeons. They make the best chocolates!"

"Why? Why are you hiding? Is Zavia even your real name?"

Zavia bent forward, picking up her mug of tea with both hands, staring down into it. "Promise not to tell?" She asked, her eyes intense as she glanced at Spring. "Especially your Commander?"

Spring bit her lip, "Okay, I won't tell anyone." Zavia stared hard at her face, then nodded, apparently satisfied. Zavia sighed, her eyes glancing tiredly around the room, focusing on the lit up Christmas tree.

"My name is Savatareena Vashti Lurralina of the house of Snowendorrica. I am…a Daughter of the Blood. My mother," Zavia said in a strained voice, "My mother is BelReginar of Endari."

"BelReginar?"

"Sovereign. You know silly, what you would call an Empress or Queen. My mother is BelReginar.

"Are you a …." Spring struggled with the word, finding all of this hard to grasp, "a princess?"

Zavia nodded gravely, "My title is BelFilia, but yes, on your planet, I could be classified as a princess. Do not worry," Zavia said with a ghost of her former smile, "it is not contagious, you know."

Spring was embarrassed to admit she knew very little about the Endarion people. She had read everything relating to their solar system, but bits and pieces (touristy stuff) about the planet. She remembered glossing over something about a BelReginar, seeing a woman dressed in opulent clothes, and a high headdress that stretched out behind her head like peacock feathers. The BelReginar had pale eyes too, but they were a different shade. She remembered the climate being perpetually cold, and one part of the planet remained dark for a long time. She read as much as possible about the army.

"But, why did you leave? I mean, was it horrible there?" Spring asked.

Zavia took a small sip of her tea, before placing it down, tucking her legs under her on the couch. She turned to face Spring, "I wanted to be free. I wanted to live my life. See the galaxy! You know, be young. Nothing tying me down. No palaces. No rules. Be normal."

"You couldn't do that at home?"

"My life did not belong to me." She explained, she slanted look at Spring, arching an eyebrow, "You know, being a BelFilia, is more than just living in a palace and wearing clothes so heavy you lose weight walking around in them. Being surrounded by an army of courtiers, protocol this, protocol that, balls with the best looking officers in the empire. Trysts in the gardens…"

"And you hated all of that?" Spring asked incredulously.

Zavia gave her a deadpan look, "No, that was okay. It was the 'duty', BelReginar assigned to me."

"What was that?"

Zavia shifted on the couch, stretching out her legs, revealing a pair of bright blue polka dot socks, she rested her head against the arm of the couch, her eyes staring at the ceiling, "The role of Lady of Canaar." She said finally. "High priestess at temple Anla'Canaar. It is a stupid tradition. One child of the blood, is sent to Canaar, during every reign. It is always the youngest. Well, almost always, and BelReginar chose me. I am the youngest."

Spring made a face, "'children of the blood, 'daughter of the blood'. It sounds so …gory! You keep calling your mom, 'BelReginar', do you ever get to call her 'mom'?"

"It is not our way." Zavia answered frankly, "I have always called her that, for as long as I can remember." She looked thoughtful for a moment, a fond smile lighting her eyes, "I think my father was the only one that called her something other than BelReginar. Her given name I think."

Spring digested this, wondering what it would be like to address her parents as Chief Stevens and Mrs. Stevens. It felt very cold, and impersonal to her. She got up, walking into the kitchen, "What was wrong with being Lady of Canaar? Sounds kinda glamorous." Images of Grecian gowns and ruined temples popped into her head, along with visions of scantily clad muscular men feeding her grapes.

"Glamorous?" Zavia gave her a peculiar look. "Living celibate on the dark side of the planet for the rest of my life? Surrounded by over the top, pompous priests and priestesses so tightly wound, jewels are probably popping out of their backsides even as we speak. Not to mention the temple was as warm as the freezer. And," Zavia added gravely, "sweets of any kind are strictly forbidden."

"So you were at the temple before you left? Did they give you a tour or something?" Spring asked as she opened a bottle of wine. She set it beside the three other bottles she opened on the counter, before sitting down at the other end of the sofa from Zavia.

Zavia shivered, her eyes betraying fear for a moment, "I was there for two months." She said in a small voice, "Two months in the dark." She turned horror filled eyes toward Spring, "I had to sleep in a cold room with no lights. Everything was...so dark. The only thing that made me smile were the stars. They were always there. So many of them ...and the rings of Endari, sometimes shimmering with different colors." She laughed a mirthless laugh. "You know, the high priests and priestesses said I was rebellious, told me look to the stars for salvation. Well," Zavia smiled, "that is exactly what I did, the stars told me to runaway...so I did." Zavia glanced toward the kitchen, "Are you done with the oven? I think I will make some cookies."

"You can have a slice of apple pie number one!" Spring jumped up from the couch, padding into the kitchen, "I kinda screwed up on the first one, but I think it's edible." She reached into the fridge pulling out a carefully wrapped pie, the center caved in revealing chunks of apple. "Wanna try some?" She held it up hopefully. Zavia nodded, reaching for her mug, getting up from the couch, walking stiffly into the kitchen.

"How did you escape and become a flight attendant?" Spring sliced into the pie, haphazardly transferring a large misshapen slice onto a nearby plate. She looked over at Zavia busily pouring another cup of tea. "I mean, how did you leave your planet and stuff? Want some whipped cream? No?" Spring pulled two forks out of a nearby drawer, plopping one on the plate, while scooping up a sample of the defective pie for herself. "The EF is so anal about Alien Immigration...mmm, this is kinda good! Here."

Zavia accepted the plate, leaning against the counter with her mug of tea beside her, "Thanks." She took a cautious bite, before taking a sip of her tea. "It is delicious! Better than my cookies! May have to take a slice to my room later. "

"Zavia,"

"Hmm?"

"How did you escape? How did you pass for a Palaqeon?"

Zavia took another bite, chewing slowly, finally, her eyes slid over to Spring's, "I would rather not go into that right now." She said tonelessly, her face devoid of expression. "Besides, your commander is coming over in a few minutes, right?"

"What? Oh, yes! Here, have another slice." Spring slid another sloppy looking slice onto Zavia's plate, biting her tongue on more questions, "Rexlen will be here in like, thirty minutes!" She wiped some crumbs off the counter, glancing sideways at Zavia, her eyes flying to the bruises once more. "Are you sure you don't want to eat with us ? He's from your planet. Maybe he can help you?"

"Spring! I do not want him to know about this...about me! I do not need or want his help in this, okay?"

"Zavia, I don't understand why—"

"Leave it, Spring, please! Do not tell anyone. Especially him." Zavia 's eyes pleaded, "I am fine. Honestly. No one needs to know who I really am."

Spring crossed her arms, staring hard at Zavia, shaking her head, "I don't feel right about this, but," she bit her lower lip, "I won't tell anyone." She said reluctantly, watching as relief spread over Zavia's face. "But Zavia, if something happens again...your bag is stolen, anything ...I'm telling, got it?"

"A bargain! Thank you!" Zavia reached out, hugging her impulsively, before gathering her plate and mug of tea, limping off to her room. "Have a good time with your commander! Do not worry about me!"

Spring looked after Zavia, "Easier said than done." She muttered.

* * *

Spring gave the apartment a quick once over, before rushing to the door, smoothing her unruly curls with one hand, yanking the door open with the other, her heart thudding with anticipation. Rexlen was exactly on time, down to the minute. He stood smiling tenderly, wearing 'regular' clothes, Endarion clothes. Her eyes roamed over his dark blue tunic and pants, admiring how the plain, unadorned 'street clothes' (or 'civvies' as her dad would call them), suited his broad shoulders and athletic build. The only adornment appeared to be shimmering metallic trim around the low, mandarin collar. He still looked every inch the commander, especially with both hands clasped behind his back.

"Na'allo," Spring smiled shyly, watching the flicker of surprise and pleasure cross Rexlen's face, his eyes widening, Spring beamed happily.

"Na'allo," he answered back, his deep voice smooth and almost lyrical. "Very good Endarion. Not a trace of an Earth accent." He bent, planting a slow, gentle kiss on her mouth, straightening up, his eyes warm, "You have a talented tongue, my dear." He produced a bouquet of sunflowers from behind him, handing them to her. Her eyes widened with surprise, sunflowers were a rare and expensive treat on the Moon. "Your favorite Earth flower, right?" His eyes scanned her face, "Did I make an error?"

Spring accepted the flowers, gazing down at the bright orange-yellow leaves as they shook slightly. She tightened her grip on the stems, hoping her hands would stop shaking, "I love them, thanks! I mean, thank you!" She stepped back, "Come in!" He hesitated, his eyes roaming around the room quickly, then back at her. She grabbed his hand, leading him into the living room. He stopped abruptly in front of the Christmas tree, his face an amusing mixture of curiosity and amazement. He reached out, tentatively touching a dangling glass ornament, turning it gently, watching as the twinkling lights bounced off of it. Spring leaned against Rexlen, their fingers intertwined, his thumb gently caressing hers. Spring squeezed his fingers, relishing how strong they felt, how safe they made her feel.

She should be able to tell him anything. She wanted to tell him everything. She bit down hard on her lip, holding clutching the sunflowers against her chest with her free hand. She stared up at Rexlen, smiling at the childish delight that danced in his eyes as he gazed at the tree, touching the artificial branches, then a few of the tiny colored lights. Spring felt foolish tears rise as she watched him. He turned his eyes toward her, his delighted expression immediately transforming into concern. He pulled her closer, reaching up to touch a single tear that had managed to escape.

"Is something wrong?"

"Nothing's wrong." She shook her head, smiling weakly. "Just, you look so handsome in regular clothes..er, not that you don't look sexy in your uniform. I mean, you do...uh, let me put these in water!" Spring giggled nervously, her eyes sliding away from his, falling briefly in the direction of Zavia's room. Spring leaned on tip toe, kissing him, her fingers lightly framing his square jaw, sturdy chin. She tore herself away from Rexlen, leaving him standing by the tree. She felt his eyes on her as she walked over to the bookcase, plucking an empty vase off a shelf. "Zavia's here." She said lightly, placing the flowers in the vase, arranging them absently. "There." She placed the flowers on the coffee table, looking up at Rexlen's puzzled face with an overly bright smile. "Ready for a homemade Earth dinner?" She darted into the kitchen, "What do you want to drink? Wine, water?"

"Spring."

"Uh huh?"

Rexlen had moved over to the coffee table, the vase of sunflowers in his hand, the cut glass pattern of the vase, shimmered as he rotated it slowly in his hands. Her eyes lingered on his hands, strong, large, powerful. She raised her eyes to his face. Rexlen glanced at the vase in his hands, then at her with a half amused expression, "Do your Earth flowers thrive without water?"

"Huh? Oh!" Spring strode back into the living room, reaching for the vase. "I'm in space cadet mode! Here," Rexlen smiled faintly, shaking his head, striding confidently past her into the kitchen.

"It is okay, I got it." He said easily, angling the vase under the faucet. He looked so tall in the galley sized kitchen, bent over the faucet, filling the vase carefully. *Tell him. Tell him!* He straightened, holding up the vase with a slight smile, "Vunda'klat. I think the flowers are out of danger now." He moved past her, replacing the vase on the coffee table, then pulling her into his arms again for a quick, tight squeeze. He kissed her once more, a long, searing kiss, that made her lean into him, relaxing. He broke off the kiss, staring questioningly into her eyes.

"What is wrong, Spring? What is it?"

Spring looked down, her eyes focusing on the dark blue scroll pattern of his tunic, her fingers plucked at his sleeve. She glanced down the hall again, her eyes falling on the light shining underneath Zavia's door. Spring leaned her head against his chest, hearing the steady beat of his heart. She shook her head feeling miserable.

"Does it have anything to do with Zavia?" Rexlen asked in a carefully neutral voice. "Has something happened?"

"No," she blinked back the moisture in her eyes, before pulling away, standing on tip toe to gently kiss him once more. "Nothing's wrong. Just a long day, and…I'm glad you're here!" She managed a cheerful smile. Rexlen looked skeptical, his eyes locking onto hers with an intensity that made her cheeks burn.

"Are you sure?"

Tell him. "Yeah." She nodded, pulling him slowly toward the dining room table. "Everything's fine …I promise! Zavia's okay. She…um, had a hard day at work, but she's okay now. She's going to hide out in her room. She…it'll be like we're alone! I'm hungry, aren't you?"

Rexlen stared at her for a long moment, his eyes unreadable. Finally, he nodded stiffly, allowing Spring to lead him to a seat at the table.

13

ZAVIA.

The arrivals area of MLI bustled with manic, holiday crazy passengers, and crew. Christmas music blared loudly, interrupted every few minutes by robotic 'Welcome to the Moon' announcements. The usual sterile décor of the customs area, was decked out in metallic garland; and twinkling lights draped around every column and hanging from the ceilings like glowing jelly fish. Even the crew line was festive; the black booths lavishly covered with a small three dimensional snowman hovering above the booth with 'Happy Holidays' in red and green flashing across Frosty's belly.

"Welcome back to the Moon, Miss." The customs agent handed her passport card back, smiling. Spring looked at his shiny, brand new badge, crisp uniform, and fresh haircut. She grinned back. A newbie customs guy. It was on the tip of her tongue to ask, when she noticed her supervisor standing by the exit doors. The woman stood out in her pale, powder blue, inflight office uniform and white scarf, her hair in its trademark, painfully tight, top of the head bun. The exiting passengers, gave Spring's supervisor a wide berth, casting quick glances at the tall, reed thin, mature woman with the stern face.

"Thanks." Spring mumbled to the customs agent, hurriedly stuffing her passport card away in her purse. Her eyes trained on her supervisor as she moved forward.

"Well, well," one of Springs crewmember sided up beside her, tucking his passport card into his blazer, "Who let Odina Grimmer out of her cage?" He smirked, glancing at Spring, "Someone's in truubble. Wonder who she's out for now?"

Odina turned her hawk eyes in their direction, locking eyes on Spring, taking a few brisk steps forward. Spring felt her stomach flip, as her feet moved woodenly along. Spring took a deep breath, walking through the bustling arrivals area, watching as Odina moved toward her with long strides. Within minutes, Odina was staring down at Spring, her face set in a grim mask.

"Good afternoon, Spring." Odina's delicate, tin-like voice did not match her at all. "Would you join me in my office for a moment?"

Do I have a choice? "Sure!" Spring could feel her mouth pulling into a practiced smile; as she followed Odina's broad back through the arrivals hall and into the special company elevator partially hidden by a newsstand. Spring got in first, her eyes resting on Odina's severe bun, lacquered to an inch of its life, secured with a surprisingly girlish red and green ribbon. As the elevator zoomed upwards, playing an instrumental 'Silver Bells', Spring wondered how long (and how much product) it took to achieve Odina's bun.

The lounge was unnaturally quiet as Spring and Odina entered, only the electronic hum of the computers, and the gurgle of the built in beverage replicator could be heard. Spring felt her face flush as she followed Odina, biting her lip as conversations abruptly stopped as she walked past, all eyes on her. The supervisors hall was accessible only through the computer work area, the polished center aisle divided row after row of computers, occupied by curious flight attendants. Spring's heels clicked loudly behind

Odina, her luggage handle was slick under her hand. She planted a smile on her face.

"That's her." Someone whispered loudly from the sign in screens.

"Gurrrrl, I knew something like this would happen! Didn't I tell you?" Spring glanced over at Daisy Jones, (the base gossip), holding court in the last row of computers, shaking her head. Her listeners nodded in agreement. "Hey sweetie! You hang in there!" Daisy called out, smiling sympathetically as Spring passed by.

Odina's tiny office was crammed with official looking Orion representatives in dark, intimidating suits and stern faces. Spring felt the air leave her lungs as she spotted the two uniformed, armed StarPort guards standing in the corner, their flat, narrowed eyes fixed suspiciously on her. Odina waved a careless hand toward a plush orange chair in front of her desk.

"Have a seat, Spring." Odina said briskly as she sat down in her big desk chair, scooting it forward, "Spring, these are representatives from Corporate Security." she nodded to the suits. "They need to have a few words with you."

"W...w..words?" Spring sputtered, "Wh...what happened?" *Is this about the forty drinks I comped to the Trekkie tourists on my flight from Earth last week?* "Have I done something wrong?"

"No, Miss Stevens, you're not in trouble." One of the suits stepped forward, his eyes boring into hers, "This is about your roommate, Zavia."

"What about Zavia?" Spring felt a knot of dread form in her stomach. "Is she okay?"

"Zavia had a trip yesterday to Mars," Odina said, "she 'no showed' off of it. She has disappeared."

"Disappeared." Spring echoed, suddenly feeling faint. The room was unbearably stuffy. *Oh no.*

"Miss Stevens," A cat eyed woman in a severe suit stepped close to Springs chair, staring down at her, "We have reason to believe Zavia is not

Palaqeon. That she falsified documents. That she is an illegal Alien. Do you know anything about her?"

Like, that she's really an Endarion princess, who was attacked last week? "No, I...", Spring bit her lip hard, drawing blood, she felt the cold, assessing eyes analyzing her face, "I...um, don't know a lot about her. Maybe she's home, I'll check!" She began to rise from her seat.

"Spring," Odina leveled a hard stare at her, "Are you hiding something from us? Who is Zavia?"

"We know she was attacked recently, Miss Stevens." The suit said, "We do not advise hiding information from us. If you know anything at all, tell us now." Spring sat down again, her eyes on the suit.

"Um..." Spring shifted in her seat. "I need to use the bathroom, uh, do you mind? I'll be right back. I'll tell you what I know...okay?"

Odina sighed, exchanging a glance with one of the suits, "Okay, Spring, we'll wait right here."

Spring jumped to her feet. "Thanks! Be right back!" She backed into another suit standing behind her chair, "Oh! Sorry! Excuse me!"

Spring carefully closed Odina's door, hurrying down the hall; averting her face as she passed the rows of computers, walking as quickly as she could. At the lounge exit, she blended in with a group of flight attendants heading out the door, before bolting for the elevator.

"Spring! How are you? You look great! Wait up!" Spring glanced over her shoulder, watching as Tatum hurried forward, dragging her suitcase, "Hold the elevator!"

"Sorry, Tatum," Spring shrugged as the elevator doors slid shut. "Gotta run, good seeing you though, take care! Merry Christmas!"

As soon as the doors slid open, she made a mad dash for the shuttle, weaving her way through the crowd of passengers. She made it to the shuttle just as the doors slammed shut, and the shuttle lurched forward. She fell into a seat, ignoring the curious stares.

Spring ran up the walkway to Starry Towers, nearly colliding with a neighbor walking their dog. The neighbor glared at her as Spring raced past. "Sorry!" She yelled over her shoulder, as she hurriedly jabbed at the entrypad, before running inside.

"Please be home, Zavia." Spring leaned her forehead against the cool glass of the elevator.

Spring passed several EF officials and men in suits as she made her way to her apartment door. She practically fell into the living room as Pam swung the door open, staring down in surprise at Spring.

"Look what the cat dragged in...a backstabbing liar." Pam's face was bright pink, her eyes glittering.

"Pam, where's Zavia, have you seen her? She missed a trip!" Spring looked around the apartment, her eyes lighting on Rexlen standing by the windows in full uniform, arms crossed, his face dark.

"So much for all of us being friends." Pam stepped back. "Nice to find out in the lounge that one of my roommates was attacked and is a runaway princess!"

"Actually, she's called a..."

"A BelFilia, I know." Pam snapped. "Rexlen told me. She's not even a Palaqeon! Thanks you guys for letting me know...I mean, I thought we were all friends! Obviously not." Pam turned away, stalking angrily into the kitchen, throwing a half eaten salad into the refrigerator, slamming the door shut. Pam leaned against it, arms crossed, her face set. "Can't believe you didn't call the police after she was hurt."

"Pam, she swore me to secrecy! She didn't want anyone to know the truth!" Spring glanced at Rexlen, feeling heat rise in her cheeks, "She didn't even want Rexlen to know. I should've told you guys. Rexlen, I...should've told you the night you came over for dinner. That was right after she was attacked. She didn't want to report it. She insisted! What could I do? Drag her to corporate?"

"You're just another Adiva, aren't you?" Pam said stiffly. "Claim to be my friend. I mean, you knew Zavia was a princess all along? Thanks for trusting me. See ya, Commander. Find Zavia." Pam gave Spring a final withering look, before storming off to her room, sliding the door shut with a loud thud that rattled the glass. Spring glanced at Rexlen, cringing under the cold look he gave her.

"What else are you hiding Spring? Do you know where she is? Why did you keep her attack from me?"

Spring stared up into his face, feeling anger rise as his eyes narrowed with suspicion, "Tell me Spring, what else do you know?"

"I told you." Spring snapped, "I don't know! It's not like I knew all along, she told me the day you came over."

"Spring, if you are lying to me..." Rexlen warned, his voice low.

"Why would I lie?" She angrily kicked off her heels, tearing off her uniform blazer, as she made her way to her room, Rexlen followed behind, lingering in the doorway. "Do you think I'm psychic or something? Like, I know who took her?" She wiggled out of her skirt, leaving it in a crumpled heap on the floor,; snatching up her bathrobe, wrapping it hastily around her as she turned to face Rexlen,

"What are you hiding, Rexlen? Why were you always asking about her, huh? Are you two lovers? Is she the real reason you're here? Well?"

Rexlen stared at her long and hard, his mouth a firm line, his eyes glacial, "She is my aunt." He said tightly.

"Like, I'm supposed to believe that." Spring said acidly. "She's younger than you! Aunt! Right, what a coincidence that you managed to rescue the ship she was working on and that you start dating her roommate!"

"Coincidence or not, she is my aunt." Rexlen replied coolly. "I am not lying to you. I never have." He turned away, walking with long strides toward the door. Spring hurried after him, a few inches from him as he opened the door, turning around to look down at her. The anger had melted form his eyes, replaced by a complex mix of emotion that played across his face as he gazed at her.

He stared at her for a long moment, as if memorizing her face. A pained expression flashed through his pale eyes, before they became unreadable. Spring's heart ached as she blinked up at him, her throat closing with unshed tears. *Rexlen, oh, Rexlen.*

"And it was a coincidence that I met you Spring," he said softly. "A happy coincidence. Goodbye." Her heart lurched painfully as Rexlen strode through the door. She stepped out into the hallway, watching his retreating figure with blurry vision until he turned the corner and disappeared. Spring closed the door heavily behind her, pressing her forehead against it; before swiveling around slowly, finally getting a good look at the apartment.

There were a couple of new gifts under the Christmas tree, wrapped in bright blue and silver paper, bedecked with elaborate bows intertwined with glittering faux jewel garland. The same wrapping paper was spread out under a small box near the tree, a pair of scissors lay nearby, along with more ribbon. An untouched mug of hot chocolate sat on the coffee table beside a bowl of m&m cookies. Zavia. She did not practice what she termed an 'An Earth Religion', but she liked the idea of Christmas. *Zavia, where are you? I should've dragged your butt to corporate security or to the police. Why didn't I? I should've told Rexlen. None of this would've happened if only I had...*

A rush of emotion filled Spring, as she stared at the untouched cookies, "I'm not going to just stand here." Spring rushed to her room, throwing her extra suitcase on the bed, adding several dresses (warm and cold weather), five pairs of shoes (including some killer heels), and her favorite 'go to' jewelry. She also threw in her spare makeup bag with its six shades of lipstick, gloss and 'standby' lipstick. She also threw in her leave in conditioner and hair gel that her curls loved the most. Zipping the swollen suitcase shut, Spring changed quickly into a sweater and jeans, pulling her curly hair into a high ponytail.

Spring parked her bag by the door, her eyes on Pam's room. With a deep breath, Spring walked over to Pam's closed door, raising her fist to knock, then changing her mind, "Pam, I'm so sorry no one told you about Zavia. I wanted to...I really did! Anyway, I'm going to help find her, not sure Rexlen will let me, but, I'm gonna try. Just wanted to say sorry. Bye." Spring waited, but heard nothing. Sighing, she went back into her bedroom, picking up her winter coat. Her eyes landed on Gran Libby's painting still laying against the wall on the floor. Zavia hung hers up right away, taking endless pictures of it. Coat folded over her arm, Spring left her room; closing the door behind her, her eyes on the floor.

"Well, we better hurry if we want to catch up with your Commander."

Spring looked up in surprise. Pam stood by the front door, her equally bloated suitcase beside her. "We?" Spring asked.

"Yeah, is that a problem?" Pam said defensively. "She's my friend too, and besides, she needs us. There's no 'I' in team."

Spring felt a faint smile form on her lips, "Let's go then!" She joined Pam at the door, locking it behind them.

"Vunda'klat! Where is your man's ship parked...at MLI?" Pam asked as they made their way to the elevator.

"At the EF base, I think."

"Uh...Spring?"

Spring stepped into the elevator, turning around, "Yeah, what is it?"

"How do we get onto a EF base?"

"Easy! How hard could it be?"

* * *

"I'm sorry ma'am, but I cannot give you permission to enter the base." The intimidating EF guard handed her Orion I.D. back. He waved a large, cumbersome EF vehicle through the gates, saluting whomever was inside, before turning back to Spring and Pam, slightly annoyed they were still there. "I'm sorry, ma'am."

"But, I personally know the Endarion Commander! Commander Baldric?" Spring persisted, "Maybe you can let him know we're here?"

"He can vouch for us!" Pam piped in.

"Ma'am," The guard stressed through his teeth, his eyes filled with impatience, "Groupies, do not have clearance—"

"We're not groupies!" Spring lashed out. "Commander Baldric is my...my boyfriend, and ...his aunt is our friend!"

"Our roommate!" Pam added nodding.

"Ma'am, I don't care if you're his wife, you do not have clearance!" The guard snapped, his right hand hovering dangerously near his weapon, "Now, I advise you and your friend to turn around!"

"Is there a problem, Private?" Spring and Pam turned, watching as a tall, well built officer walked toward them. The vehicle that the guard had saluted belonged to him, now parked with the engine running a few feet inside the entrance. The officer was tall, over six feet, towering over the stocky gate guard, who quickly saluted. He was also very easy on the eyes in a rugged, chiseled way.

"No sir!" The guard answered, "Just two civilians, sir!"

"Oh?" Pam oozed sarcastically, "we're not 'groupies' now?"

Spring ignored the private, focusing on the officer. Lieutenant A. Kaplan. read his badge. He was a few years older than they were; his hazel eyes already crinkled at the corners as he looked with amusement at Pam. "Lieutenant, we are on an urgent mission." Spring explained.

"An urgent mission?" He glanced at Spring curiously, "What kind of mission?"

"Sir," Pam butt in, "We need to find the Endarion Commander Baldric! The life of our roommate, an Endarion princess is at stake! Perhaps the universe is in danger too! We must speak with the Commander at once!" Spring winced. The guard rolled his eyes. The Lieutenant looked intrigued. Spring was not sure if he was interested in their plight or Pam's green eyes and flushed face. He stared at Pam for a long moment.

"Let them in." He ordered the private/gate guard.

The private sputtered, "Sir, they do not have…"

"Let, them pass, Private." Lt. Kaplan said. "That's an order! I will escort them myself. Ladies."

"Thank you, Lieutenant." Spring said breathing a sigh of relief. She stepped onto EF territory, ignoring the sullen glare of the private as he stepped aside, letting them pass. She had the childish urge to stick her tongue at him, but resisted. He was doing his job after all.

"Yes, thank you Lieutenant." Pam smiled shyly up at him through her lashes. Kaplan blushed.

* * *

The ride through the enclosed base reminded Spring of the many Navy bases she had been on as a Navy Brat. The Lieutenants 'moon' car zoomed past sterile looking military buildings in grey, all laid out in a rigid grid pattern centered around immaculate grounds. Sharply manicured shrubs and a smattering of trees, added color to the base. The base was larger than she thought, seeming to stretch for miles.

Their car veered off to the left, passing a group of jogging soldiers in black EF sweatsuits, heading toward the outskirts of the bases protective dome. They rode in silence as the car passed large, imposing hangers; finally coming to a stop in affront of another checkpoint and a large, RESTRICTED AREA sign in red hanging overhead. Spring held her breath as two guards approached the car, one stopping to talk to the lieutenant, while the other walked around the car, peering into the windows, his gun in his hands. Spring exchanged an anxious look with Pam, who stared back with wide eyes.

The two guards returned to their post, and the car moved forward a few inches, stopping as a ray of neon green light washed over them, filling the inside of the car with a greenish glow.

"What is this?" Pam asked the lieutenant in a high voice.

"Just standard procedure, ma'am. We're being scanned." He replied. The green light vanished, and he drove onward, continuing to talk in his ear piece in military jargon, that went over both of their heads. The buildings in this area were newer, more modern, made of glass and steel, in low rounded shapes. The twinkling lights of starships landing and taking off were in the distance beyond the dome. Their car approached the largest of the buildings, strange, boxy shuttles were parked on one side of the building. Each shuttle had old fashioned 'tractor' wheels, most coated with Moon dust. The Lieutenant parked in front of the glass entrance. He hopped out, swinging the back door open, offering a hand to Pam and Spring as they jumped down.

"I'll escort you inside." He said leading them through the double doors. "The Endarion ship is too big to dock on the Moon, but I think their shuttle is still here. I apologize for not saying a lot during our drive ladies, I had to confer with the specialists here...let them know of your arrival. Good news is Commander Baldric is still here, finishing up a briefing with some EF brass." He lead them past a waxy looking receptionist, up to a cylindrical shaped, glass elevator. Immediately, a red light scanned his face, and the elevator doors slid open. He bowed to Pam and Spring, waiting for them to enter.

"Aren't you coming with us?" Pam asked as the lieutenant continued to stand on the other side.

"Sadly, no, I have to return to my duties but," He flashed a smile at Pam, "It has been a pleasure, Miss Sloane?"

Pam blushed, "Just Pam. And it was a pleasure meeting you too, thank you for your help!"

"Ah," His eyes lit up with interest, "Pam. Miss Stevens. Good luck and I hope we meet again, Pam."

"So do I." Pam stepped back as the doors slid shut, her grin matching the lieutenants.

"Well!" Spring smirked at Pam, "He'll definitely give Guy a run for his money!" She instantly regretted her words, watching as the light left Pam's eyes, replaced by pain. Spring reached out, patting her arm, "Sorry."

"It's okay," Pam turned her head away, focusing on the aerial shot of the base as the elevator soared up, "Guy's my friend ...and I'm happy with that."

"Sure?"

"Of course!" Pam 's eyes flicked her way before sliding away, "We're here! Look, Spring, we have a welcome party greeting us!"

The glass doors slid open revealing an irritated Rexlen and a few EF and Endarion men standing several feet behind him. He nodded absently to Pam before focusing his intense stare at Spring. Even when he was mad at her, Rexlen still made her heart flutter. He stood a good foot or two taller than the other men, and definitely the most handsome man in the room.

"Hi!" Spring stepped off the elevator, smiling brightly. Rexlen glowered back, his eyes as warm as chips of ice.

"What are you two doing here?" He asked calmly.

"We're coming with you to find Zavia." Spring answered.

"No, you are not." Rexlen shook his head, "It is too dangerous and to be honest Spring, you are not needed."

Spring flinched, and Rexlen's eyes widened, he took a step forward, moving close to Spring, grabbing her arm, pulling her aside. "I did not mean that the way it sounded," he said in a low voice, "It is just that my ship is not designed like your airliner ships. We do not carry guests. It may be a long journey and I assure you, it would not be comfortable."

Spring raised her chin, staring into his beautiful eyes, "Pam and I could care less if it's comfy or not. We just want to help find our Zavia. We'd be useless here anyway, we'd be too worried. Zavia would do this for us, Rexlen, please let us do this for her."

"What about Orion?" Rexlen asked, "What about your trips?"

"We'll work it out with them. Well?"

Rexlen considered for a moment, his gaze lingering on Spring. She held her breath."Okay. You may come along. Maybe your presence will help us find her."

Spring breathed a sigh of relief, throwing herself into his arms, "Thank you, thank you, thank you!" He stiffened slightly, pulling her away with an arched brow and a faint smile. He made a slight move of his head, Spring looked at the twenty pairs of amused eyes. Pam was applauding loudly. "Sorry!" She mouthed to Rexlen.

"The shuttle to my ship leaves in ten minutes, I will meet you both downstairs." Rexlen bowed toward the elevator, before turning toward an aide.

"Tastic!" Pam beamed.

14
STAR WARS

Spring and Pam had little time to gape over Rexlen's ship, before being led to their quarters two decks below the 'bridge'. Rexlen was right. The imperial warship, I.W.S. Gru'Ellar, was built for combat, not passengers. Least of all, human passengers.

"These rooms are usually reserved for dignitaries," Rexlen indicated, waving a careless hand toward two rooms side by side in a narrow, tube like, hallway. "I told my crew to make the rooms ready, the replicators have been re-programmed with a few 'Earth' food items." He leaned past Spring, pressing the wall, allowing one door to slide open, revealing a small, dimly lit chamber. "I will take my leave of you now. Stay down here and off the bridge." He glanced awkwardly at Pam, who quickly ducked into the open room, giving them privacy. She slid the door shut with a wink.

Rexlen waited a few seconds until the door clicked in the locked mode, before pulling Spring into his arms for a brief hug and a quick, hard kiss. Spring smiled dreamily up into Rexlen's serious eyes, "Stay below." he repeated, giving her one final squeeze, before heading down the hall.

Spring slid inside her new room, with its single bed with a neatly folded blanket and pillow, four dresser drawers set in the wall; a table with two chairs and a serviceable bathroom with the bare minimums. On the same wall as the dresser, a tele-screen and a replicator sat blinking; under the arrow slit style 'window'. What did surprise her was the large bouquet of sunflowers on the table. A knock sounded at the door.

"Yes?"

"Hey, I didn't get any flowers!" Pam waltzed in, going immediately to the vase. "How sweet of him! He's a keeper. This ship is magnif! Do we really have to stay below?"

"We'd get in their way, it's not the Enterprise, silly." It was an impressive size for such a sleek ship, but Spring could tell by the looks on his crew that they did not approve of new passengers. Besides, Spring felt a little out of place among so many Endarions. She had to admit, she would love to see Rexlen in action, commanding his ship on the bridge. *Maybe we can sneak up later, right now it's shower time. My skin is crawling! I haven't had a shower since…eighteen hours ago at the Mars Hilton!*

"Yeah, but it looks like you have your own 'Vulcan', um, Endarion!" Pam laughed, turning toward the doorway, "See ya in a few, Mr. Commander's woman!"

* * *

A half hour later, Spring stood by one of the arrow slit windows as Rexlen's ship broke orbit. The ship moved effortlessly, stealthily, none of the rumbling of an Orion StarShip. The vase of sunflowers barely moved, as the ship sped away from EF space. Spring watched the Moon become smaller and smaller, a white dot in front of the larger blue orb of Earth.

"Spring." Spring jumped at the sound of Rexlen's voice, bumping awkwardly into the table leg with her ankle. She just managed to save the flower vase from toppling, grabbing the vase in on hand, plopping down on the bed, rubbing her ankle with her other hand. She looked around the small room, trying to find the intercom.

"Rexlen?" She squeaked.

"Spring," Rexlen's voice seemed to boom from nowhere and everywhere in the room, "I need to speak with you and Pam in my Ready Chamber. I'm sending an escort in ten minutes."

Ten minutes later, Spring and Pam were ushered into Rexlen's sparse looking Ready Chamber. The long, narrow room held a large tele screen on one wall, off to the side of the screen was a large desk upon a slightly higher floor. The lighting was brighter in this chamber compared to the bridge, making the light grey walls and black floor feel more like an interrogation room. The only chair belonged to the large desk, apparently Rexlen's desk, since he stood beside it, staring at them with arms crossed. Spring stared at him, feeling a silly smile form as she took in his stiff 'Commander' stance. A look of amusement crossed Rexlen's face as he glanced down at Spring's outfit. Spring glanced down, realizing her embroidered red mini dress, sheer tights and knee high boots closely resembled a well known uniform from an ancient sci-fi show. She should've been more discreet, like Pam in her head to toe black.

"We have a lead." Rexlen said abruptly, stepping off down to the main floor, walking toward them, his eyes on Spring. "An illegally unmarked merchant ship broke orbit the same day The BelFilia disappeared."

"And Zavia is on it?" Pam asked. She exchanged a worried look with Spring.

"Is Zavia okay? I mean, this means she was kidnapped, right?" Spring blurted, impulsively grabbing Rexlen's sleeve. Rexlen closed his hand over hers, giving it a slight squeeze.

"We believe The BelFilia is onboard." Rexlen's voice was grim. "And that she is a captive."

"BelFilia. Rexlen, she's your aunt. Stop calling her by that cold title!"

"They're related?" Pam squinted at Rexlen with new eyes. "Ah, yeah, same eyes totally."

"The merchant ship is two days away, on the fringe of Bentaz space." Rexlen ignored Spring's comment, "We will intercept it. This may turn into a skirmish…"

"Really? A real space fight! Cool!" Pam squealed. Rexlen glared at her.

"You mean, like, lasers and stuff?" Visions of every space movie Spring had ever seen raced through her head. She stared at Rexlen, imagining him decked out all in black, light saber in hand. She smiled.

"Yes, it may be intense…" Rexlen said staring at her with a strange expression, "We will pass a neutral space station in six hours, we can stop there if you like."

"To shop?" Pam said incredulously.

"You want to off load us, right?" Spring crossed her arms, feeling her heart sink .

"It could be dangerous, Spring." Rexlen paused, before adding gruffly, "I do not want you endangered."

"Wow, I feel like chopped liver." Pam remarked, "Guess it's okay if I'm endangered."

"I meant both of you." Rexlen snapped.

"Well," Spring exchanged a look with Pam, "I think we'll stay put. I mean, Zavia is on that ship…"

"And we can be the 'welcome committee' when we rescue her!" Pam added.

"We?" Rexlen echoed.

* * *

A few hours later, Spring entered Rexlen's private chambers, feeling like a child on a field trip, nervous and excited. The spicy, exotic aroma of dinner greeted her the moment she stepped over the threshold. Rexlen greeted her at the door, taking her hands into his, leading her into the main room.

"I will return in a moment." he gave her a quick distracted kiss, "Have an unexpected communication from Endari, should be just a few minutes." His eyes went over her red dress, "You look...very enticing."

He turned, walking into a small office-like chamber off to the side, the door sliding behind him. Spring sighed, smoothing her hands over her Star Trek style dress. She had planned on wearing something else, but Rexlen asked her to wear the mini to dinner. She glanced at the closed office door, a covert smile spreading as she turned her gaze toward his room.

His chambers were bigger than hers, but still pretty compact. The main room held a strange, low couch protruding from the wall, along with a dining room table covered with steaming dishes and a decanter of a golden liquid, that made her dry mouth water with interest. The walls of the main room were bare, except for a large, imperial emblem surrounded by a row of replicators.

She tip toed into his bedroom, her high heeled boots sinking into the surprisingly soft carpet, as she ventured further into the dimly lit room. Everything was pristine and in order, down to his full size bed, which felt cool under her finger tips as she ran her hands across the top sheet. She sat down on the bed, bending low to rest her cheek against his pillow, inhaling his scent. Memories of her night at the pleasure palace, sent a tremor of excitement through her. It was like being Goldilocks, finding the bed that was just right. Across from his bed, a small, built in encased bookcase was crowded with books, their spines adding a shock of color in the overly masculine room.

Curious little knick knacks were placed between some of the books. Spring got up, peering closer at the bookcase, rocks of every color, shape and size; were on every shelf, some sparkled with dazzling color, others were as grey and lumpy as a moon rock. Tentatively, Spring picked up one, examining the unusual purple crystals that shot out prisms of color in the room. She cradled the rock against her, her eyes lingering on a tiny colorful doll, half hidden between two books. Gently, Spring reached between the books, pulling the child size doll dressed in a miniature uniform out. It was the kind of toy a toddler would have, big black eyes, simple half moon mouth, brightly colored hair. It was worn with age, one leg had survived 'doll surgery', and the eggplant uniform had been mended. Rexlen's?

"It was my favorite toy." Rexlen's amused voice startled her. Guiltily, she turned around. Rexlen was smiling fondly, his eyes distant, lost in time, before advancing toward her. He took the small toy into his own hand, it looked like a toy ship in the vast ocean of his large hand. He stared down at it with a forgotten, boyish smile.

"What was its name?" She asked, stepping close, leaning her head against his chest, as his other arm wrapped around her waist, drawing her closer. She nestled her cheek against the stiff fabric of his uniform, hearing the steady thud of his human sounding heart. "Does it always travel with you?"

Rexlen let out a low rumble of laughter, "No, actually I just discovered it again when I was last at my mother's home. Thought I would..ah, take it on the adventures I ...used to imagine when I was small. Quicoo was its name .'Q' for short."

She peeked up at his slightly darker face, "I wish I had known you as a child," she said softly. "I bet you and Q traveled all over the universe."

"Well," Rexlen sounded embarrassed, carefully placing the toy back on the shelf, while his other arm tightened around her waist, holding her close, "That was a long time ago." He gazed down at her, "Hungry? I had an Earth meal prepared, come."

"I was hoping for some Endarion grub." Spring teased, moving away, placing the large rock back on the shelf, glancing up at Rexlen, "You collect rocks too? These are so pretty, are they from Endari?"

Rexlen stared at the rocks for a moment, a shadow crossing his eyes for a brief moment, "No." His eyes moved over the neatly arranged row of rocks. "They are mementos from other planets. You would say, souvenirs."

"Magnif! You have so many, do you have one from Earth yet?"

"Not yet." He said briskly, leading her out of the bedroom with long strides.

"Hmm, maybe I can help." Spring slid into the seat he pulled out for her, "You know, help you pick out a really nice one?"

He sat down across from her, his eyes locking onto hers with a strange intensity that quickly faded into amusement, "Would you? Thank you, I may need your help." He held up the decanter of golden liquid, "Orvallion wine? It is made from flowers that bloom in the Endari mountains every five years."

"Finally something Endarion!" Spring held out her glass, "To Rexlen's new rocks! Cheers!"

"Yes, to new rocks, and new planets. Cheers."

* * *

"Those are Endarion warships alright." Doric nodded grimly toward the flickering screen, then back at his pilot, Esta, "Didn't expect them to pick us up so fast, especially not Baldric's ship."

Esta shrugged, her prong-like fingers skimming over controls, "I hope your plan works, Captain. I'm not so sure having the imperial fleet on our trail is a good idea. They will vaporize us before we have a chance to negotiate."

"Not with The BelFilia onboard." Doric, turned around, his eyes focusing on the tall gaunt figure of his one and only security officer. "Sujit, bring our..." his mouth curved into a twisted smile, "'guest' to the bridge ."

Moments later, Sujit shoved The BelFilia forward. Doric looked her up and down slowly, insolently, noting how her pale eyes flashed with anger. Her blue black hair lay in tangled clumps upon her shoulders, her body clad in snug fitting 'Earth' clothes, an electric blue sweater and a pair of 'jeans' that clung provocatively to her hips and thighs. His eyes lingered on her hips, before meeting her eyes.

"I never thought I would see an imperial BelFilia dressed like a common whore." He said, leaning forward to caress her curved bottom. "Living with humans has brought you to their level. Intriguing."

The BelFilia made a noise in her throat, before dispatching a large spray of spittle into Doric's face. She smiled coldly. Doric wasted no time, pulling his hand back and delivering a blow that sent the BelFilia slamming against the wall behind her, landing in a sprawled heap.

Slowly, Doric wiped his face with the back of his sleeve, staring down at The BelFilia. One side of her face was already swelling up, the imprint of his blow a blotch of color in her pale face, "You'll pay for that." She said in a still voice, her pale eyes glittering. Doric stooped closer, his eyes locked onto hers, he allowed his mouth to curve into a smile .

"Yes, I will be paid." He said, watching the fear dance in her eyes before they became expressionless. She leaned against the wall, meeting his eyes, her chin raised defiantly. "I believe the empire will pay dearly for you, BelFilia." He sneered, "Or perhaps I can trade you …"

"Trade me?"

"Yes, trade you." Doric explained with a cold smile, taking a seat in a chair beside Esta. He motioned for Sujit to haul the BelFilia to her feet. His eyes falling on her restrained hands, already turning a soft purple from too tight clasps. "For something that was stolen from me long ago. It appears I will not have too long to wait." He nodded toward the flickering screen beside Esta, "A warship docked by the your human's moon is a day or so behind us. Carrying two humans signatures no less."

"Two humans signatures…" A flicker of surprise crossed The BelFilia's impassive face. She glanced at the screen, then back at Doric, "Two humans on are board an Endarion ship? No surprise there. EF perhaps."

"My dear BelFilia, you know who the humans are." Doric said. "The EF has their own ships and their own problems. The two humans are female. Civilians. I believe they are, acquainted with you? Spring and Pam. Such strange, common sounding names…don't you think?"

"How did you…"

"Know who they were? Know their names?" Doric chuckled softly sliding a glance toward a smirking Esta. "There are rebel operatives every-where, BelFilia, even as far as the humans space. It was easy you know, breaching the human's primitive Moon, blending in with the other visitors."

"Our operatives followed you and the humans to a shopping center." Doric shook his head. "A place my sister would've enjoyed. I don't under-stand them, but I think she would've liked your humans."

"Where is your sister?" The BelFilia asked politely. "On Endari? Tobi? You are Tobion, correct?"

"How observant you are BelFilia," Doric replied. "Yes, I am Tobion, but that does not matter to your empire, does it? Esta here is Mutavion, as you may have noticed. One of the best pilots I know."

"I thought Mutavions were…" The BelFilia paused, "extinct."

Esta swiveled around in her chair, her dark, pin prick eyes locked on The BelFilia; her mouth set in a firm line, "I am not extinct, my lady." Esta said proudly.

"Esta and her people work the mines on Styop." Doric stared hard at The BelFilia, feeling his anger rise the longer he looked at her aristo-cratic face and her wide, pale eyes, "The empire sent them to mine the jewels you and your kind wear." He curled his lip, "Don't look so shocked, BelFilia, you knew this. You knew what the empire did to the Mutavions and Tobians. I would not be surprised if you had something in mind for the gullible, trusting humans."

"Earth is a new ally." The BelFilia said acidly. "We do not betray alli-ances. Mutav and Tobi were—"

"Were what, BelFilia?" Doric stood up, standing close to the BelFilia. "Go on, say it, BelFilia, they were what? Say it."

She remained silent, staring icily back at him. His fingers itched to strike her, strike that proud, defiant look off her face. Tear her human clothes off her back and sear her imperial back the way his was. Inflict everything the empire did to him, on her. Doric looked over her shoulder at Sujit, "Take her below." He said wearily. "Use the Retainer Beams to keep her in her room. And remove those hand restraints…we do not want damaged goods. Go!"

Sujit put a large, beefy hand on The BelFilia's shoulder, turning her around gently. Sujit's rocky, textured face seemed to deepen in color as he glanced quickly at The BelFilia.

"BelFilia?" Doric called out, watching as she looked over her shoulder expectantly, "You asked about my sister? Her whereabouts?" The BelFilia jerked her head in a stiff nod. "Ah, ever the polite royal! The BelReginar would be impressed by your manners, BelFilia!"

"Perhaps you should ask your mother, The BelReginar," Doric said coldly. "My sister Ula is a slave somewhere in the empire. Ask the empire where she is. Sujit, get her out of my sight."

15
SEEDS OF THE PAST

Spring looked over the Endarion telecall device in her bedroom wall, chewing her lip. The small device was more advanced than any she had used before. For one thing, there were no buttons to push, just a glossy black screen, in the middle of blinking replicators and ship interphones. She tentatively reached out a finger, touching the smooth screen.

"Testing, one, two, three…" She said loudly. "Hello? Spring calling home? Space Operator?"

Nothing.

She stood back, wishing she had paid more attention to Rexlen when he had helped place a call to Orion Scheduling, a few hours ago. Of course at the time, Spring was too obsessed with his handsome, noble profile, and how the back of his black hair was beginning to curl ever so slightly on the top of his high collar. She had been sorely tempted to run her fingers along his collar, perhaps plant a kiss there. They were 'behaving' themselves on his ship, nothing stronger than a hug or kiss, which Spring was finding difficult to abide by. He seemed so in control, and she felt like some kind of wanton human.

She tapped the screen again, "Um, calling Earth. Uh, anyone there? Operator?" She glanced at the ships intercom system, (something she mastered on day one) her eyes focusing on the Endarion word for 'Bridge'. *I can't keep bugging him over silly stuff like this! His crew will think I'm some kind of idiot* .

She moved away from the telecall wall, bending down by the bed, pulling out the low drawer underneath, dragging out her purse, "I'll use my phone." she muttered to herself. *Roaming charges from hell, here I come …*

"Miss Stevens," announced a voice from overhead, "An incoming call from Earth, via Earth Federation, …shall I extend the call to you?"

Spring glanced at her wrist phone, still 'searching' for a signal, then at the now illuminated telecall screen. Breathing a sigh of relief. "Yes, thank you, please put it…um, extend the call!"

Immediately, Gran-Libby's face filled the screen, beaming at her with a cheery smile and a wave, "Wassup, Spring Chick!" Gran -Libby grinned, before continuing in a robotic voice, "Greetings from planet Earth!"

"Hi, Gran!" Spring squinted at the screen, Gran Libby was sitting on her bed, dressed in a kimono robe that made her look tiny and frail. Her face seemed thinner, her cheekbones like sharp pointy angles in her face."What time is it on Earth? What day is it?"

Gran-Libby considered for a moment, "It's almost dinner time, eight-ish. What, they don't have some kind of universe clock? You know, so you can tell time anywhere?"

"They do, I can't figure it out yet." Spring admitted, looking sheepish. "Maybe I'll ask Rexlen later. Gran, what are you doing still in bed? Everything okay? I mean, with you an' all?"

"Just chill- laxin', nothing to worry about, everything's all good! I'm a double digit, let's me indulge in some lazy fabulous- ishness!" Gran-Libby's tone became serious, "Any news on your roomie, Zavia? You guys are all over the news. All this stuff about your roomie being a princess, empress! And she baked us a Thanksgiving cake! I'm praying she's okay, Spring Chick. Her poor family must be close to the edge about all of this!"

Spring looked down at her hands, feeling guilty for lusting after Rexlen while on a rescue mission for Zavia. "Yeah, I wish I was on Rexlen's ship for another reason, but hey," she added brightly, "Rexlen has a lead, a ship left the Moon on the day she vanished, we're chasing after it now."

"Awesome! Can his ship go invisible? You know, de-cloak and stuff?"

"Don't know." Spring sighed, looking around the room, "This ship is so...well, 'alien', it's not like the movies or your old TV shows. Pam and I have to stay down below, out of the way. I feel so human here! I mean, the replicator has some 'Earth' food, but it doesn't taste right, look right, and I can't read anything! Nothings in English!"

"Like a novel?"

"I mean, programs and things."

"Hmm," Gran -Libby sat back against her pillows, tucking her blanket around her waist, "Looks like Rex will have to teach you, like your granddad Sven taught me." Gran -Libby grinned, "the best Swedish lessons I ever had!"

"Granddad Sven was still human."

"Yeah, but he had a different culture, way of doing things, just like your hunk of burning, Endarion love." Gran- Libby countered. "Hey, when am I gonna met this specimen of Endarion deliciousness?"

Spring laughed, "He would love to hear you say that! As soon as we rescue Zavia. She's his aunt."

"His aunt? For realsies? So ol' Rex is a prince? Woo hoo!"

"I'm not sure...he, well, he kinda keeps stuff to himself. Family stuff."

"You're telling me the guy you're dating may be a prince and you don't know?" Gran-Libby asked incredulously, "Spring..."

"Oh, Gran," Spring tapped the screen, causing the picture to jump, "looks like the signal is breaking up...gotta go!"

Gran Libby smiled knowingly, "Gotcha. Interrogation ova! Hope you guys find Zavia safe and sound, and tell your prince, hello!"

"Will do, Gran."

"Oh, and Spring?"

"Uh huh?"

"Don't forget, you owe me a ride to space! I'm a good non-rev! Okay, you don't have to plant that clueless look on your face! You know what I mean, willing and able to travel and not ring the call light!"

"Soon, Gran, we'll fly together somewhere soon." Spring promised, standing up, stretching her legs, "And you'll meet Rexlen too!"

" Cool! I can see beautiful, off-world, great grandchildren around the corner!"

"Don't get too excited, Gran." Spring said dryly, just as her mom's curious face came into view carrying a tray of food; setting it down on Gran-Libby's lap. "Hi, mom! I'm on Rexlen's ship!"

"Hi, baby." Spring's mom sat down on the edge of Gran-Libby's bed. "On his ship? That's nice, hon. Just don't embarrass yourself…you know, do anything, rash or…stupid on the ship. I mean, these alien races may…" Her mom sounded tired, her face drawn as tightly as her ponytail.

"Mom," Spring gritted her teeth, "I don't think you need to worry about me doing anything stupid…"

"Gwen, the girl's doing fine!" Gran-Libby interrupted, "Not like she's planning on holding an orgy on his bridge, or parading around naked and stuff!"

"Mother!" Spring's mom threw a backward glance at a chuckling Gran, before turning back to Spring,

"Spring, baby," her mom sighed, "I didn't mean my words to sound like that. I don't want you to…you know, screw things up like you did with Wesley. And these alien men, well…who knows what they're really like, right? This commander sounds like an exciting novelty but…"

"He's not a novelty, Mom."

"Okay, okay, fine." Her mom stood up, smoothing her hands down her pants. "Good luck finding your friend, she was so sweet …for an alien I mean. Well, you know. Dad says 'hi', he's over at the EF, touring with Summer, while I keep Gran company. Coming home for Christmas? It's in six days you know."

"Not sure yet." Spring watched Gran-Libby's thin arms slide the tray closer, her usually ageless fingers looked bony and gnarled, as they folded around a spoon. "I'll let you guys know. I was supposed to fly during Christmas anyway. Gotta go now, love ya guys!" She put on a wide smile, waving to the screen. Gran-Libby raised her spoon, waving in her best royal wave, twirling her wrist.

"I love you, Spring Chick!" Gran Libby called out, "Do whatever makes you and your hunk of Endarion deliciousness happy …and satisfied!" She winked.

"Love you, baby!" Her mom blew a kiss, "not sure I agree with this old woman behind me," she looked over her shoulder just in time to see Gran stick out her tongue, "But, you're an adult, so..uh, I'll leave it there."

"Thanks! Bye!" Spring leaned forward, searching awkwardly for the 'end call' switch along the sleek, black screen. *Damn, where is it ? Do they control stuff with their minds?*

Finally the screen went blank, flashing words in Endarion that could only mean 'Transmission Ended', or perhaps 'Call Dropped'.

* * *

Doric surveyed the dinner table carefully, frowning. "Robi, you are sure this is what they eat? The replicator did not make a mistake?" He eyes settled on the mushy looking, yellow dish in a silver bowl, parked beside a platter of browned meat in small, palm shaped discs enclosed between puffy slices of bread. A few inches from the discs, a tall pitcher of opaque liquid, swirled with sliced, yellow fruit and chips of ice. Little Joli, Robi's daughter carefully set a small shallow plate, holding large bits of bright red fruit, swimming in a red syrup, encased in a golden brown pastry crust along the edges.

"It is what was observed, Captain." Robi placed a bowl of small, wafer thin, golden brown discs beside the pitcher, "It is very strange looking."

"I'm sure The BelFilia will be used to eating this." Doric looked up at Sujit, "Bring her in."

"Can I stay and see The BelFilia?" Joli tugged at his sleeve, turning hopeful eyes toward the doorway.

Doric gazed down at Joli, noting the contrast between her mother Robi, and Sujit her father. Robi's half Endarion blood showed itself in Joli's dark hair, and luminous onyx eyes, while her skin was as rocky and ruddy as Sujit's. Her solemn eyes blinked at him curiously, and Doric smiled in spite of himself, "We'll see Joli, we'll see."

At that moment, Sujit led The BelFilia into the dining chamber. She had attempted to braid her tangled hair into a long side braid, a few wisps hovered around her face. Her eyes widened in surprise at the table, before turning a wary face in his direction.

"Surprise! It's for you!" Joli squealed, clapping her tiny hands.

Doric watched The BelFilia look down at Joli, as if shocked to see a child onboard, then back at the table before returning her attention to the little girl. "Yes, it is a surprise." The BelFilia smiled faintly, nodding.

"I can serve you, BelFilia!" Joli moved eagerly toward the table before her mother could stop her.

"Away from the table, Joli!" Doric's voice sounded harsher than he intended, he instantly regretted it. The little girl spun around, her eyes huge. "The BelFilia will serve herself. No one is a servant here." He finished in a softer voice. He gestured toward a chair, "Sit down, BelFilia."

The BelFilia moved cautiously toward the chair, her hands resting on the chairs back, she stared down at the table; before wetting her chapped lips, raising her eyes to meet his, "Why have you made this? What is the reason?"

Doric took a seat across from her, "I thought you would enjoy 'Earth Food' BelFilia, no reason. Sit down, it's not poisoned."

The BelFilia sat down slowly, tentatively grabbing a nearby plate, "But, how did you know? I mean, how did you know about this food?"

Doric shrugged, "You were observed along with the human signatures eating this exact food at a gathering on Mars. A strange gathering, with artificial bursts of colorful stars in the air. What kind of event was that?" Doric helped himself to the mushy, golden dish, "And what is this?"

"Potato salad." The BelFilia fingers went around the rim of her plate, "You must be talking about the Fourth of July party, a barbecue. They call the colorful stars fireworks...like our 'firzarsarrs' that we send up." Fizarsarr's were more elaborate than fireworks, they covered the entire sky on cascades of flowing light.

"Ah, I see. This potato salad is good. Eat, BelFilia."

The BelFilia paused for a moment, glancing at a beaming Joli standing beside her mother, before scooping a small serving of potato salad. Doric followed her lead, watching as she took a handful of the golden wafers (potato chips), and the brown meat discs (hamburgers), before pouring a frosty glass of 'lemonade'.

As they ate, The BelFilia slowly relaxed, telling him about Earth and her human friends. "Of course, it makes no sense why they celebrate the Fourth of July on Mars. But as Pam would say, 'Any excuse for a party is fine by her!'" The BelFilia helped herself to the 'strawberry pie' slicing a smaller slice for Joli who had drifted closer to the table, her eyes like saucers on the desert. The BelFilia winked at her, and Joli giggled, hurrying back to her mother, holding her plate carefully.

"Ula would have loved to have met your human friends." Doric bit into his slice of pie. "My sister was always curious about people. She would have enjoyed seeing planet Earth."

"Is your sister younger than you?"

Doric looked down at his plate. "My parents always called her a gift, because she was born ten years after me. She was my shadow, following me around the farm until I left for service on a space station." His mouth twisted, "that was before the final war with Endari of course."

"How old were you when you left?"

"Nineteen. Ula was about to turn ten." Doric smiled. "She wanted a Helleium bead necklace because it was 'off-world' and no Tobion girls she knew had one yet."

"Helleium? That's an expensive stone! Pretty, but expensive."

Doric nodded, "It was expensive, but I saved three months salary for two. One for my mother, and one for Ula. The necklaces were probably not up to your caliber, BelFilia, but they were...are beautiful."

The BelFilia smiled politely, "did they like the necklaces?"

Doric stared hard at the BelFilia, watching as her smile faded. "No, they did not get their necklaces, BelFilia."

Doric felt the old anger mixed with pain, rising up, his eyes seeing another place and time, "I came home, BelFilia, home to find my planet swallowed up by your empire. My father's farm was destroyed. Nothing remained. My parents..." Doric paused, closing his eyes for a moment, "their bodies were...dishonored. I searched everywhere for my sister, then I heard, she was taken along with the other children. Servants of the empire. I was captured as well, but I escaped."

"Your sister is the prize you wish to trade me for." The BelFilia said.

"She is the only family I have." Doric answered. He reached into his chest pocket, pulling out a small, black pouch. "You see, BelFilia, I still have a promise to keep." He opened the pouch, letting a small strand of iridescent beads pool in his hand. "I still have her necklace. She'll have her necklace and her freedom."

"Even if you die in the process?"

"As long as she is free, I do not care what becomes of me." Doric said flatly. "She's been a servant to the empire for thirty years, she deserves to be free. See Earth if she wants."

"What if she's dead?" The BelFilia asked in a low voice.

Doric closed his fist around the necklace, his cold eyes meeting hers. The BelFilia's face paled, her eyes widened. "If my sister is dead," Doric said calmly, "then so are you."

16

PROMISES,PROMISES

Spring stood outside of the bridge entrance, her eyes trained on the two double doors with the ominous dark red stripe in the middle. She wet her lips, looking over her shoulder at Pam facing the empty corridor like a quarterback, "Pam, we can't just sneak onto Rexlen's bridge like this!" She hissed.

"Spring, come on, don't back out now! We finally caught up to that ship Zavia's on, and you want to hide downstairs? Rexlen won't mind, he's your man! Besides, what action are we gonna witness in those broom closet, dignitary rooms!" Pam moved forward, her eyes scanning the black panel by the door, "Now, we just have to figure out how to open this thingy...why is this ship so hard!"

"Pam, shhh!" Spring pushed her out of the way, studying the panel, "Can't be that difficult. Pam, move your big ass head please, I can't see the rest of the—"

"Evening ladies." Rexlen's voice made Spring bump heads painfully with Pam. Rexlen stood in the open doorway, the dim lighting of the bridge flooding into the hall. He surveyed them with barely concealed annoyance. Spring rubbed her forehead, smiling brightly.

"Na'allo! Um, Pam and I were just...um, strolling by! You know, ah…"

"Can we come in? We'll be so quiet! You won't know we're there!" Pam blurted.

"Like how quiet you two were out here?" Rexlen crossed his arms, arching a brow. "The bridge is no place for guests, especially not now." Rexlen turned around, stepping into the darkened bridge, "This is not your starliner, Spring."

"I know that!" Spring hastily stepped through the doorway, following Rexlen. Pam ran into her back, "I never said it was, Rex, er, Commander! It's just that—"

"Commander, we are within hailing range of the corsair ship." Rexlen's man ignored Spring and Pam, staring directly at Rexlen. The man sat in front of a large, rectangular shaped window, ahead of them, surrounded by stars, a small ship stood in their path. It looked like a small toy compared to Rexlen's ship. *Zavia was on that?*

Rexlen slid a glance in Spring's direction, before stepping away, "All stop!" Rexlen barked, taking his seat in his commander's chair in the middle of the strange, octagon shaped room. His bridge crew of six basically ignored them, busy doing whatever they did at their illuminated panels. "Hail them."

"Tastic," Pam breathed. "Just like all those sci-fi shows!" She allowed Spring to tug her toward a semi-empty spot off to the corner which still provided a good shot of Rexlen, his crew and the tiny ship outside. Spring could barely take her eyes off of Rexlen. Spring tore her eyes away from Rexlen, watching as a large square screen materialized above the 'window'. The screen was blank for a few seconds, before an image took shape, showing a human looking man standing behind a strange, squid-like creature. The man leaned forward, closer to the screen, partially obscuring the squid-being.

"Commander Baldric." The man drawled in Endarion. "What do I owe the pleasure?"

"He's kinda cute, in a scary, mangled, bad guy kinda way." Pam whispered loudly. "Too much muscle for me, his necks as thick as my waist! A little too WWE if you know what I mean."

"Pam!" Spring hissed, giving her a warning look.

"You know what we are here for, Doric." Rexlen said smoothly,

"Oh, are you referring to my guest, Baldric? The BelFilia?" The man smiled, his eyes glittering. "Or did you just signal us to say 'na'allo'?"

"Where is The Belfilia?" Rexlen asked coldly.

"Cutting to the chase, eh, Baldric?" Doric gestured with his hand to someone out of view, "No introductions to the human females? Maybe I can include them in my bargain."

"Leave them out of this, Doric." Rexlen's jaw twitched angrily, despite his carefully controlled voice.

"Fine, it's The BelFilia you asked for, here she is. My guest." Doric reached out of the screens frame, and Spring could hear, someone being shoved forward. Doric reappeared, his fingers clasped hard on Zavia's shoulders. Zavia's hair was in a tangled side ponytail, her face haughty and proud. She shook Doric's hands off her shoulders with a shrug.

"Zavia!" Spring and Pam blurted, in unison. "Zavia, it's us! Zavia!" Zavia peered closer into the screen, her eyes suddenly shining with an inner light that made them glisten slightly. She smiled a lopsided smile.

"Hi, girls." Zavia said calmly in Earth English. "Hello, Commander, it's about time you showed up."

"Very amusing, BelFilia." Rexlen answered back, "Perhaps you should stay on board Doric's ship after all." One of Rexlen's officers caught his attention, nodding silently at Rexlen, who nodded curtly.

"On the contrary, Commander." Doric said, "I have no desire to play nursemaid to The BelFilia. The empire has something I want to trade." Doric paused, listening to something the squid creature said, before returning his attention to the screen, "I see we're not alone, Commander.

I'm surprised half the Endarion fleet is now surrounding my humble little ship. Don't you warships have anything better to do? Perhaps, befriend another gullible planet with resources, then conquer them? That's what the empire is all about, isn't it? Why waste all of this manpower over recovering a wayward BelFilia?"

"What are they saying?" Pam asked, "I wish they would talk in English!"

"I kinda like the sound of Endarion." Spring mused. "Sounds sexy, intense. Hey, look, other ships are out there now! Looks like the Endarion Calvary."

Pam snorted, causing Rexlen to glare over his shoulder at them, "That's because your commander speaks it. Who knows what they're saying. Yeah, must've called in the cavalry."

Spring watched as the expression on Rexlen's face darkened, "Not very wise of you, Doric. Daring to insult the empire, surrounded by armed imperial ships. Not the best way to resolve or negotiate ..." Something about Rexlen's words in Endarion sent a chill down Spring's spine, it was like seeing a new side to Rexlen .

"Commander, incoming hail from Commodore Yantai of the Anatarr." An officer looked at Rexlen for instructions. Rexlen held up his hand, his gaze focusing once more on the flat eyes of Zavia's kidnapper.

"I advise you to rethink your approach, Doric." Rexlen said coolly, before signaling an officer to end the hail. The screen went black for a second, before suddenly filling with life, and the stern looking face of an intimidating Endarion, decked out in a more elaborate version of Rexlen's commander uniform. The man onscreen sported a higher collar that nearly reached his chin, while his eggplant shoulders had bold slashes of gold, instead of Rexlen's silver.

The man regarded Rexlen with a narrow face devoid of emotion, his eyes were a pale, murky brown, light, but nothing like Rexlen's or Zavia's. It appeared Rexlen and Zavia were the only Endarions she had met with those strange eyes. Maybe it was a family trait. One thing the Endarions seemed to share was their pitch black hair.

"That guy must be an admiral or something." Pam nodded at the screen.

"Thought I heard 'Commodore,'" Spring whispered back.

"Baldric," The Commodore said in a gravelly voice, "Command code one, eighty-two. Standby and await my order."

"Code one, eighty-two. Acknowledged, Commodore." Rexlen replied, "Standing by."

The screen disappeared. The window below it displayed what appeared to be five or six ships, identical in size to Rexlen's. The ships surrounded the kidnappers smaller ship, their powerful looking engines glowing bright. The small ship looked like prey…like an ambush. *Were the other ships there all along, invisible? How did they pop up so fast and so quietly?*

"Standby on weapons. One, eighty-two." Rexlen ordered.

"Standing by," replied an officer behind Spring. "On your command, sir,"

"Good." Rexlen turned, looking over his shoulder, somewhat startled to see Spring and Pam still standing there. He sighed, standing up, approaching them in two quick strides, "it is time you both went downstairs." He glanced at a young, junior looking officer, "Motqar, escort our guests below and out of harm's way."

"You're dismissing us? Just like that?" Spring asked.

"Yes," Rexlen's voice was clipped, his face grim, "It will be safer below."

"No! We're staying put!"

"Spring?" Pam looked at Rexlen's dark expression, then fearfully at Spring, "Uh, maybe we should sit this one out? I mean, this is totally magnif…but it looks kinda serious?"

"Spring," Rexlen's eyes were hard, impatient, "leave the bridge…now. That's an order."

"Okay, fine." Spring grabbed Pam's arm, "I'm sorry, we'll get below, out of your hair. Come on, Pam." Spring walked toward the bridge door, chin up, feeling Rexlen's eyes boring into the back of her head.

"He looked pretty pissed." Pam said as soon as their escort had left. Pam took a seat beside Spring's vase of sunflowers, drumming her fingers, while Spring paced in front of her, "How are they going to get Zavia? That guy looked …"

"Rough, I know." Spring said absentmindedly. "Wish we were back up there. Something's about to go down and I don't want to miss it."

"It's a little scary, Spring. I mean, this is real! This ship…its weapons are real!" Pam shuddered. "Go back to the bridge now? No thanks! Pass!" She slanted a look at Spring, "I'll stay right here. Well, unless you want to go."

Spring hesitated, "no, we better stay put…I don't want to screw up Zavia's rescue and my thing with Rexlen." She walked over to the table, taking a seat, her eyes staring off into space, watching the gathered ships, "Yeah, it is scary. This is not Star Trek." She looked at Pam with wide eyes, "Pam, I—don't know if I can handle all of this."

"You mean, the space battle?"

Spring looked down at her lap, then back out the window, shaking her head, "No, Rexlen…Aliens…space is so big." She shrugged, "This is going to sound totally stupid, but, Earth seems so simple now…there's way too much drama up here!"

"I'll drink to that."

* * *

Doric smiled with satisfaction as the grainy image of Commodore Yantai appeared, "Hello, Commodore, have you come to hear our demands?"

The commodore's serious face creased into a slow, calculated smile, "Of course, Doric. The empire does not seek bloodshed. I'm quite sure we can conclude this matter. You have the BelFilia?"

Doric slanted a look at the BelFilia, "yes, she's here. You know what I demand Yantai. My sister for the BelFilia. Do we have an understanding?"

"We do." The commodore replied.

"Is my sister onboard? Have you found her?"

The commodore paused, steeple-ling his fingers in thought, "No, locating and freeing a slave will take some time, Doric. We believe we have located her. On Gentor. Any further demands?"

"This is too easy, Captain," Esta murmured. Doric ignored her.

"What do you offer?"

The commodore made a careless wave of his hands, "Anything your crew desires, Doric. Name it and you shall have it."

Doric felt the hair on the back of his neck prickle, he glanced once more at the BelFilia. Surprised to see her eyes on him, her expression strange, her pale eyes unnerving him. "Anything." He echoed.

"Return the BelFilia now, and we will let your ship go." The commodore's voice was smooth, oily, "safe passage to the next space station. Of course we do not have your sister on our ships, but she will be delivered to you. We have jewels and money on board right now, Doric. Enough riches to last you and your crew. Your family's farm on Tobi can be made available to you, just deliver the BelFilia to my ship, now."

"We should wait, sir." Esta looked at him, "Wait until we actually see your sister, then send the Bel---"

"Silence." Doric snapped, he looked back at the screen. "What planet did you say she was on?"

The commodore chuckled, "Do you think I lie, Doric? Gentor. She is on Gentor. Now, do we have an understanding Doric?"

"Money, land, my sister's freedom, and no retribution?"

"As you wish, Doric." The commodore replied, "Now, I ask again, do we have an understanding?"

Doric swallowed, his eyes flicking over Esta who stared back with concern. He glanced at the BelFilia's expressionless face. Finally he turned back to the screen, "We have a deal, Commodore."

"Very good. Very wise of you, Doric." The commodore looked over his shoulder, nodding once, before turning back to the screen, "We are prepared to receive the BelFilia now. Lower your shields."

Esta shook her head frantically, "Captain, we should wait!"

"Lower your shields, Doric." The commodore repeated, "We have money ready to transport the moment The BelFilia is onboard."

"What about your shields?"

"Lowered. This is a business transaction, Doric. Well?"

Doric jerked his head toward Sujit, "Prepare to send the BelFilia aboard the Commodores ship."

"Wait!" The BelFilia blurted, "Yantai, I want to go to Baldric's ship."

The commodore paused, staring at The BelFilia, his eyes going over the fading bruises on her neck and cheek, finally he nodded. "Granted, my lady. I will relay the request to Baldric's ship." The commodore glanced over his shoulder, then back, "It is arranged, my lady."

Doric stared at The BelFilia, "Take her to the transport bay." He ordered Sujit. "The BelFilia will be aboard Baldric's ship in five minutes." Sujit led her away.

"Very good." The commodore ended the transmission, the screen going black.

"You just sealed all of our death warrants," Esta said flatly. "You of all people know never to trust the empire!"

"I died a long time ago, Esta. Tired of running." Doric looked down at the panel, "She's onboard now—time to see if the empire has honor—keeps to their word."

* * *

"Okay," Spring stood up, throwing up her hands, "I can't stand the suspense! I'm going back to the bridge, you coming?"

Pam blew a puff of hair out of her face, slanting a look at Spring, "um, okay?"

"Tastic! Come on!" Spring's bedroom door slid open, she stepped out into the hall, looking both ways before signaling Pam to follow. Pam tip toed out.

"If we die, do I still have to return your Venus pumps and new earrings?" Pam asked as they crept along the hall, flattening themselves against the wall when a crewman passed. They slowly made their way to the fork in hallway, a few yards from the lift.

"Who knows, Pam, maybe I'll make you maid of honor one day!"

"Goodie, I always wanted to wear a poofy—"

"Sshh!" Spring held up a finger to her lips, "Someone's coming down the other hall!" She jerked Pam's arm, pulling her around the corner, crouching. Spring peeked, her heart thudding like a drum in her ears, as the heavy sound of footsteps grew closer.

"My lady, it is not advisable to access the bridge, surely you wish to rest from your ordeal." Came a slightly out of breath male voice, "A chamber has been prepared—"

"That can wait, I need to see Baldric." answered a voice they knew too well. Spring exchanged a look with Pam.

"It's Zavia! She's here!" Spring scrambled to her feet, bursting into the hall, almost colliding with a harassed looking officer, "Zavia! It's really you! How did you get here? What…"

"Hey there. No time to explain, I need to speak to Baldric, excuse me!" Zavia pushed the baffled officer out of the way, sprinting down the hall.

Spring darted a quick look at Pam before bolting down the hall after Zavia, "Wait up! We're coming too!"

"Yeah! We have your back girl!" Pam said. "Oh, those jeans are magnif!"

They reached the bridge just in time to see the room awash with a blinding flash, followed by a soft shudder of the ship. Spring's eyes automatically shot toward the large viewing window.

Spring gasped, her eyes flying to Rexlen's face in horror. Zavia had moved close to the window.

"No!" Zavia's hand went to her mouth, turning to face Rexlen, shaking her head "No."

"The ship—the little ship is..." Pam's eyes grew wide, "that was the explosion? The light show?"

"Rexlen..." Spring took a step toward him, he stood stiffly by his command chair, his eyes on the screen.

"There was a child on there, Baldric." Zavia's voice trembled with anger, "A child! Commodore Yantai made a deal...safe passage!"

"Rexlen," Spring touched his sleeve. Slowly, he looked down at her, his face terrible, his eyes dark, clouded. He stared at her with unseeing eyes, his mouth grim.

"All lies, right,Baldric?" Zavia advanced, arms crossed, "Lies. Yantai was never going to let him go, was he? He just wanted to free his sister!"

"Take leave of my bridge, my lady." Rexlen said coldly, staring at Zavia before nodding to two guards that had materialized near Zavia, "Escort the BelFilia and our guests to their chambers."

Zavia locked eyes with him for a long moment, before waving away the guards, storming off the bridge. Pam hesitated for a second, glancing worriedly at Spring, before leaving. Spring turned to face Rexlen, annoyed to find him looking away from her, taking his seat. She moved in front of his chair, blocking his view, her back rigid.

"How could you?" She seethed, "You blew up a tiny ship like that, with a little kid on it! How could you do that? What kind of blood runs in your veins ...ice?"

Before she knew it, Rexlen was on his feet, pulling her into a side room off the bridge, his grip iron clad on her arm. It was a conference room of some type, Rexlen seemed to take up the whole room, facing her with wintry eyes.

"You dare to speak to me like that ...on my bridge?" He said in a chillingly calm voice,

"Yes!" Spring raised her chin, staring up at him, "Yes, I dare! Why did they have to die? Hasn't your empire heard of negotiating? Why? Earth would never do this!"

"Of course they would not." Rexlen sneered, "that is why your planet is riddled with crime. Countries warring between each other ...like savages! Your people are no saints."

"I never said they were!" Spring shot back, "but they don't blow up ships! Well, not unless we have a good reason! We negotiate first!"

"We do not negotiate with pirates." He said. "We do not reward bad behavior that would encourage others. That ship has been linked to terrorizing and robbing starships across the galaxy ...including a human starship. Killing six people. They were no innocents."

"Except the child."

A glimmer of pain flashed in Rexlen's eyes, "I was not aware of the child." He said heavily. He moved toward the windows, rubbing his eyes as if he was tired. "I followed my orders as I have always done."

Spring followed him, standing by his side, "If you had known, would you have obeyed the order? Would you have fired?" *Please say no, Rexlen.*

Please. He gazed down at her, then turned away, facing a window full of stars.

He sighed, slowly he turned, his eyes meeting hers, he looked weary. "No," he said simply, "I would not."

Spring moved closer, finding herself in his arms, resting her cheek against his chest. Rexlen's body slowly relaxed, his arms going around her waist, his cheek resting against the top of her head. "We'll talk later." he said into her hair, releasing her. She nodded. Silently, Rexlen strode toward the door, it slid open, revealing a silent bridge. He stood by the doorway, staring at her expectantly. Spring felt her cheeks burn as she walked out, Rexlen close behind. She moved quickly toward the bridge doors, her vision blurred.

"Set a course for Endari." She heard Rexlen say as the bridge doors shut.

17

ENDARI

TWO DAYS LATER.

"Spring, can I come in, please?" Pam's voice sounded muffled through the thick sliding door. Spring lay on her side, a hand shielding her eyes. She moved her head a little on the pillow, giving a half-hearted peek through her fingers. "Spring? You there? Still part of this world, uh, universe?"

Despite herself, Spring felt a tiny smile tug at the corner of her mouth. She pushed herself upright, feeling slightly lightheaded from the sudden movement. She always felt this way if she had not eaten for awhile. "Come in," She said sluggishly, running a hand over her stiff, tangled curls, grimacing. It felt like a bushy, wild, afro. Heaven knows what kind of nightmare it looked like. Her whole body felt drained, her teeth fuzzy, she looked down at her nightshirt, tempted to change, but too tired. She tucked her legs back under the covers, pulling her no doubt ashy knees up to her chest, leaning against her pillow, "Come in!" she said louder this time.

"About time!" Pam breezed in, stopping dead in her tracks as she took in the darkened room, and Spring huddled on the bed. "It's like a tomb in here!" Pam marched over to the window, expertly pressing the automatic shade up. "First Zavia, now you? Zavia is all secretive and won't let me in...even when I replicated some cookies!" Pam snorted, picking up the vase of dying sunflowers. "Left them at her door, and hid around the corner…her door slid open and her hand shot out and grabbed those bad boys!"

"Put those down!" Spring said sharply, her eyes on the vase. Pam looked down at the vase in surprise, her nose wrinkling.

"You're joking right? They're like, dying!"

"But, Rexlen gave them to me."

"He'll give you more flowers, Spring." Pam said gently, putting the vase down, taking a seat at the table. She chewed her lip thoughtfully, before smiling brightly, "want some cookies? They're some Endarion recipe, but Zavia ate hers so they gotta be yummy! Here, I'll whip us up a batch and some tea, or vodka, or whatever…" Pam hopped up, poking at the replicator. Within seconds the sweet aroma of cookies filled the air.

"How did you learn about Endarion cookies? And the replicator?"

"Your commander, told me about them yesterday." Pam smiled, glancing her way, "Hold up! Don't give me that look, I'm not pulling a Adiva on you! He's all yours! Ta dah…cookies!" Pam opened up the replicator, producing a plate of large, palm sized, colorful, yellow and pink cookies. "The color was my idea. Thought it would look, you know, cheery. Have one!" She offered the plate to Spring.

"You spoke to him?" Spring tried to sound casual, "how is he?"

"He looks better than you do." Pam came over with two steaming cups of tea. "Kinda ran into him in the hall, near Zavia's. Think he was talking to her. He stopped me …asked about you."

"He did?" Spring sat up straighter, almost spilling her tea.

"I get the feeling he thinks, you're mad at him for all the stuff that went down with Zavia's rescue. Are you? I mean, you can't hide in here forever. You know we're a few hours from Endari, right?"

"I thought we were headed back to the Moon." She nibbled on a pink cookie. It was good.

"No, Zavia's headed home. Think that's why he was near her room, telling her about going home. I don't think she's happy about that. He didn't seem happy either, but that could be because of you."

Spring shrugged, "I don't blame her. Her mom wants her to live in a cold temple, as a priestess on the dark side of the planet. Their winter is like, eight or nine months long, they have two seasons, winter and spring... that's it. And I'm not mad at Rexlen, just...I don't know it was disturbing... you know?"

"I know, but, isn't your dad a military man? Your grandfather's? They had to follow orders, do stuff they didn't want to, right? Is it different because he's not one of us...Human?" Pam asked.

"No, you're right," she smiled into her cup. "I thought he was mad at me, we both said some ugly things."

"Well, you need to wash all that negative stuff away, and," Pam glanced out the window, "and soon, because we're supposed to be really close to Endari." Pam grinned mischievously, "I was just talking to one of Rexlen's men, he told me we'll orbit soon. Your commander may stop by, so you may want to ..."

"What?" Spring said a little shrilly, her right hand flying up to her hair.

"He may stop by." Pam repeated, "things have slowed down upstairs I guess, so he has free time." Pam stood up, gathering her tea cup and one last cookie. "But I have a feeling, he would make time to see you, even if he was busy ...unlike a human man I know whom shall remain nameless."

"Have you talked to him lately, heard from him?" Spring said softly.

Pam shrugged, letting out a small mirthless laugh, "We keep in touch, but I know he's seeing Adiva. Little things slip out in conversations, then he tries to lie, backtrack. He's a horrible liar ...but hey," Pam jabbed her cup in Spring's direction, "get dressed, you! Do you want Rexlen to come knocking on that door, seeing you like that? Do you really want the poor man to be traumatized?"

"Thanks!" Spring laughed, reaching behind her back for a spare pillow, raising it high above her head .

An hour later, Spring was ready, when the chime on her door sounded. She gave herself the once over in the mirror, glad she had packed her favorite burgundy, empire waist wrap dress that clung delicately to her curves. The deep V-neck perfectly complimented the vintage peacock pendant (on permanent loan from Gran-Libby). She loved how her favorite colors of red, green, and yellow enameled detail of the spread feathers, went with anything she wore. Her hair was 'behaving', in loose, thick, curls down her back. The dead sunflowers were gone, save for one, pressed between the pages of a book (borrowed from Zavia's bookcase), under the pillow.

"Come in!" She sat down hurriedly by the window, then got up, leaning casually against the wall, before moving hurriedly to the table again, just as the door slid open. She tried to look aloof, but the moment she saw Rexlen's face, she started smiling widely, like the village idiot. Rexlen's slow relieved smile, made her heart feel as if it was beating so hard, it was making her dress bounce. She jumped up to her feet, forgetting to act aloof and worldly, meeting him at the doorway.

"Na'allo, "she murmured shyly.

"Hello," Rexlen said softly. "You look beautiful, "his eyes moved over her in appreciation. He looked handsome as ever in his uniform, holding a small bouquet of strange looking bright yellow flowers that resembled tiger lilies with the center filaments stems in bright blue. They smelled surprisingly fresh, their scent reminded her of jasmine and of lazy summer days on Earth.

"I am afraid I had to improvise," Rexlen handed her the flowers, his fingers brushing hers. "Our replicators, do not recognize sunflowers... cannot go back to the Moon to get any. I...I thought these would please you...they are the closest thing to your flower that we have. I have always liked them."

"I love them!" She reached up on tip toe, delivering a quick kiss, "thank you." A passing crewman glanced curiously their way, Spring felt her cheeks burn. "What are they called?" Spring stepped back, pulling Rexlen inside, moving toward the empty vase. As soon as she placed the flowers inside, water instantly appeared, she cast a startled look at Rexlen.

"It is a growing vase." he explained, moving closer, tapping the bottom of the vase. "It holds a reserve amount of water it collects when you clean it. The flowers are called Meslons, they bloom in the spring."

"Tastic, learn something new every day!" Spring gazed up at him, "Rexlen, I…"

"No, do not say it. You were right to be…upset over the outcome." Rexlen paused, searching for words, "Things are done differently in my world, and to be honest, I do not always agree, but that is how my world works." He took hold of her hand, caressing it in his with his thumb.

"Maybe you should change how things work." Spring said, staring down at their entwined fingers. "We can change things together. It can start with us. Your grandmother is BelReginar, she'll listen to her grandson, right? And what about your dad, he's the future BelReginar…you're his son."

"My connection is—complex." Rexlen said guardedly. She could see his face closing up again. It stung to see his unreadable expression, but she held his gaze, squeezing his fingers. "Hard to explain. No matter," he exhaled harshly, pulling her into his arms. "My world collided with yours, and you are all that matters to me." He lowered his mouth to hers, kissing her chastely at first, but quickly deepening the kiss into one of longing, desire, and hope. Spring lost herself in the kiss, every nerve in her body tingling with erotic sensation, as she pressed herself closer, molding her body to his. Craving his touch and the thickening hardness of his desire. He made a low sound in his throat, as she rubbed hips against him.

"Commander, we are approaching Endari," came a voice from out of nowhere. Rexlen groaned, breaking off the kiss reluctantly, giving her one tight squeeze, before slowly releasing her. He gazed down at her, his eyes hot with lust. She was mesmerized, her eyes locked intently on his gleaming ones.

"Commander?" the disembodied voice, broke their trance. He moved toward the doorway, pulling her along by the hand he paused in the hall, gazing down at her.

"The only place to see Endari is from the bridge, will you join me?" he asked.

"I would love to."

"Can I come up too?" Spring looked over her shoulder at Pam, sticking her head out of her chamber door. Rexlen offered his other arm.

"Care to join us?" He asked politely. Pam bounced out of her room, grinning.

"Vunda'klat!" Pam beamed. Spring's steps slowed by Zavia's door, casting an uncertain glance at Rexlen and Pam, before tentatively knocking.

"Zavia? Do you want to hang out with us on the bridge?" Spring waited, holding her breath, *Is she mad at me for telling Rexlen? Sending all these warships on her tail?* There was no reply. Gently, Rexlen pulled her away from the door.

"Give her time." Rexlen said as he led them down the hall toward a lift, "Endari is different than the Moon. Come, let me show you my home."

Spring felt awkward and shy, stepping onto the dimly lit bridge, while Pam bounded forward confidently, nodding to a few officers, who smiled back. Pam took a corner spot by the large window, waving her over excitedly. Pam wore a black sweater dress, paired with thick black and white vertical striped tights and white bangles. Spring stood close to Rexlen, her fingers playing restlessly with her pendant.

"You better grab a good spot, or Pam will block your view," Rexlen said, leading her halfway to the window. Spring's eyes were glued on the screen before her, her heart beating wildly, she let out a thin giggle. *How many light years were they from home? A million? Will I meet his parents? Will they like me?*

"Breathe, Spring," Rexlen murmured low in her ear, "Breathe." She took a deep breath, looking up into his face, nodding mutely in case another 'giggle' sneaked out. Rexlen gave her arm a small reassuring squeeze.

Pam was kneeling by the window, half reclining with her legs tucked under her. Spring sat down carefully beside her, grabbing hold of Pam's hand in excitement and a little bit of fear.

For several minutes, Spring and Pam gazed at a blackened star filled sky, that reminded them of home, then as they drew closer to a brilliant star, they both gasped. The star took shape, resembling a twin version of Earth, down to the white swirling clouds and light blue-green seas, mixed with green and brown.

"Endari looks like Earth!" Spring exclaimed excitedly.

"That is planet Tobi," Rexlen said form behind them, as the ship sped by planet Tobi. "You could call it your planets twin, I suppose. The days of the year and climate are the same as your Earth."

"Wow, it really looks like home," Spring felt an unexpected tug of home sickness. She wondered what life was like on Tobi. Tobi was some distance from their ship, surrounded by six tiny moons, like little grey balls or pebbles, smaller than the moon back home. "Tobi's the third planet from your sun isn't it?" She looked back at Rexlen, pleased she remembered that little detail.

"Yes, it is." He said a little stiffly, eyes on the screen before glancing at her, his eyes warming a bit. "Endari is next. Look, there it is, see it?"

Spring turned back toward the window, as the ship moved away from Tobi, gliding effortlessly toward another, more brilliant planet. They were still some distance from it, but she could feel the excitement bubbling in her. Endari. She had seen countless pictures of it, but nothing compared to actually seeing it..

"It's ringed like our Saturn! How tastic is that!" Pam said.

Endari seemed to expand as they drew closer, and it did indeed look like Saturn, tilted slightly, with a thin wispy halo of rings. The planet itself resembled Earth, but the blue water was darker, almost purple in color, mixing with long white streaks of clouds, that looked as if an artist had taken a brush and used rapid downward strokes. The planet moved softly underneath the almost invisible rings, that shimmered in colors of gray, and varying shades of blue, from pale to almost black. The rings seemed to rotate as well, sparkling as they caught the light. Up close, Endari looked bigger than Tobi, almost the size of Jupiter, but Spring knew it was just slightly larger than Earth. The atmosphere around the planet gave it a slight purple ultramarine glow. They were still some distance away. It felt so strange staring at a completely alien world, full of people that were not human...not like her. *We're definitely not in Kansas anymore!* She found herself trying to memorize every detail, from the white icy caps on top of the planet, to the magical purplish water and streaks of white clouds; that contrasted against the blackness of space.

"It's beautiful," she heard herself murmur. She refused to blink, she did not want to miss a second, her eyes glued to the window, as they slowly flew closer. One side of the planet was cradled in darkness.

"Command Base Hecate One, is hailing us sir." One of Rexlen's officers said just as Spring noticed the large, intimidating looking, stationary starbase hovering near one of Endari's moons. Several small lights blinked around the oddly shaped base that to Spring reminded her of an upright tube, lit up with vertical lights from top to bottom. Ships were parked around every level of the long vertical lights, and a few more jutted off of the nearby moon. Spring watched as a miniature black dot raced away from the base, contrasting with the white clouds of Endari as it raced toward it.

Spring listened to Rexlen give orders in Endarion, loving the sound of his deep voice, even though she had no clue what he was saying. The

Endarion sounded smooth and easy on his tongue, some words guttural, while others had a musical lilt to them.

"We're not flying into Endari?" Pam sounded so disappointed, that Spring laughed, forgetting the nervous flip of her stomach as Rexlen's ship drew closer to a the base. A metal docking arm half the size of the ship stretched forward like a snake, silent and graceful, it's 'mouth' filled with row after row of lights. The 'mouth' latched onto the ship with a soft mechanical shudder, the ship jerked slightly, rocking into place. Spring's heart pounded loudly in her ears, staring at another warship parked several yards ahead of them. Suddenly, the image of a twentieth century style carhop popped into her head, and she let out a giggle, imagining a carhop in a space suit, floating by offering food. Pam glanced at her, then back out the window, looking back at Spring, confused.

"What is it? What's so funny?" Pam asked.

Spring shook her head, swallowing another giggle, "Nothing, just a little slap happy." She looked over her shoulder at Rexlen. He was jabbering away to one of his officers in Endarion, Spring turned back to Pam, lowering her voice to a whisper, "Are you scared?" She asked.

Pam nodded slightly, shifting her legs once more, smoothing her hands down her lap, "yeah, a little. I wonder if all of the warships have nice people on them…I mean, there are so many! But, isn't it tastic to be here? This is way better than some stupid, Earth two day, and hey," Pam smiled wickedly. "You'll get to meet his family and stuff!"

"Yeah." Spring glanced over her shoulder at Rexlen, just as his eyes locked onto hers, he smiled faintly, before turning a professional face to his crew, "And Zavia's family too. Royalty. So hard to believe. Hope I packed right."

* * *

Spring adjusted her silk dress, stretching the fabric, hoping to make it drape closer to her knees, and more modest. She tugged her short bolero style green sweater under the shuttle harness, carefully draping Gran Libby's peacock necklace over the bulky harness buckle, ignoring the stares of Pam and Zavia. She was thankful Rexlen was in the front of the shuttle, sitting beside an officer, while she sat in cramped passenger area, facing her two roomies.

"Your other outfit looked fine Spring, why the quicko change-o?" Pam was still dressed in her black dress and crazy tights. Zavia was in her sweater and jeans, her arms crossed defiantly, her gaze turned toward the narrow rectangular shuttle windows.

"I like this," Spring glanced down at her golden yellow silk dress. True, it was a light weight, 'summery' dress, but she loved the dark blue and green art nouveau style flowers that rose a few inches from the hem. Zavia looked over at Spring, her eyes moving to Spring's strappy dress sandals, before returning her gaze out the window.

"You're going to freeze," Zavia sighed. It was the longest sentence she had uttered since the day of her rescue.

Spring shivered unconsciously as the compact shuttle enters the atmosphere, rapidly approaching the main city of Beltarria. The sky was white with puffy grayish clouds, blocking out the violet blue sky, hovering over the city with a somber air wintry air. They flew over a vast ocean, filled with that beautiful deep purple-blue water rippling with white caps and small waves. A few large boats, zipped by below, surprising Spring. *They had boats here? Of course, they do stupid!* She looked over at Rexlen, he was watching her tenderly for a moment, then got up from his seat, giving the pilot a pat on the shoulder before moving toward Spring. He took the seat beside her, not bothering to buckle in, as he faced her with excited eyes,

"Allow me to be your tour guide," he said with a twinkle in his eye. He glanced at Zavia, "Unless the BelFilia ..."

"Go ahead, Commander." Zavia said abruptly, her eyes on the window, her face pale. "I have been away for a long time ...you will do a better job." Zavia managed a small smile, her eyes moist .

"What's the name of the ocean?" Pam asked as they neared the coastline of a grand city flanked by mountains in the distance.

"That is the Selta ocean." Rexlen answered, "And here is our capital city, Beltarria."

The city was a cluster of old and new buildings, some of them right on the coastline, surrounded by immaculate grounds. Not a speck of sand in sight. This was not a resort city, but a manicured, cultural mecca, with well placed trees, and parks.

The sun peeked through the clouds offering tiny glimpses of a vivid indigo sky; illuminating the city, highlighting the ornate, arched bridges that curved over what seemed like dozens of canals lined with naked, winter trees, stark and without leaves. Their shuttle flew low, allowing Spring to witness the seemingly sleepy, royal city. It felt like a Sunday morning, the streets were virtually deserted, only a few pedestrians strolled across the long bridges. Spring found herself staring hard at a well dressed couple walking hand in hand down a tree lined boulevard, both dressed in thick luxurious winter coats that reached their knees. Their wide fur trimmed hats reminded Spring of Russia.

It surprised her how much the city looked like home, down to a bakery on the corner with its red and gold striped awning. Spring felt a little embarrassed, she had expected strange, 'Alien' architecture, instead she found a quietly regal city, with all the old world charm of Berlin or Paris. There were a few 'funky' structures, dizzyingly tall skyscrapers of twisting spires and curves of glass, but most buildings were modest (but lavish). Still it felt 'alien' to her, there was a pristine, orderly coldness about it. Everything appeared rigid, tightly controlled. The few AirCars were highly polished, their occupants well dressed and restrained as they zipped past them.

"We are approaching the palace." Rexlen said as their shuttle turned down a lane lined on both sides by palatial homes. Spring gazed down at a little boy and girl playing in one of the large front yards, a uniformed servant standing guard. Spring looked up just in time to see the palace, slowly coming into view.

"Wow, Zavia," breathed Spring. "That's your home?"

Their shuttle swept over the palace, painted a striking dark blue that seemed to mimic the indigo sky. It was long, stretching out like a strangely slanting rectangle. The slant reminded Spring of an Egyptian pyramid, as if the building was designed to allow each of its many white trimmed windows direct access to the sky above. Spring gazed down in awe at the sheer size of the palace, the slanting rectangular wings forming four large wings encasing an inner courtyard of four large gardens, each separated by unique wings. The wings came together in the center, tapering to narrow points, surrounding a curious square building with a high domed roof. It was the only domed roof in the complex.

"It is the oldest part of the palace," Rexlen spoke up, reading her mind. "It is the temple of Canaar." "Canaar." Spring repeated, slanting a quick look at Zavia's profile. Zavia's face held a peculiar expression, sadness mixed with happiness as she looked down at the palace. She suddenly looked up at Spring with moist eyes and a small smile.

Finally, the shuttle came to a vast, garden laid out in a geometric design, complete with a large fountain, spraying white frothing water, that made Spring shiver. The shuttle made a low turn over the garden, facing the palace and a wide terrace, coming to a smooth landing in front of what looked like fifty steep stairs. A double row of guards dressed in black and gold, stood on both sides of the stairs, their faces as blank as the rows of sparkling windows above them. A man in long, almost gaudy robes of silver stood at the top of the stairs.

Frigid, bone chilling air greeted them as the shuttle doors slid open. Spring pulled her little cardigan tighter, *Okay, maybe the silk dress was not such a good idea…geez! It feels like snow weather!* She shivered again.

"Allow me." Rexlen reached down, opening a small compartment, removing a bulky but warm looking military jacket. A tall man's jacket.

Spring looked at the eggplant jacket, then down at her dress, then back at Rexlen's slightly amused stare, "Spring, do you want to freeze? This is our winter."

"Ah, it looks like a short walk ...I mean, how bad can it be?" Spring willed her body to stop shivering, smiling bravely at a skeptical Rexlen, ignoring the smirks of her roomies, "I'm not really cold anyway...see?" She stood up, inhaling deeply, feeling her lungs ice over and the cold ripping through her dress. She smiled down at Rexlen, "why, I can barely feel the cold!" Her breath frosted in front of her. Pam snickered. Zavia coughed loudly. She glared at them over her shoulder.

"Fine." Rexlen sighed, standing up, just as the robed man approached the doorway, bowing deeply.

"My lady, BelFilia," the man groveled in an oily voice that matched his long narrow face. "Welcome." The man straightened, his small eyes moving toward Rexlen, "Commander Baldric." his eyes flicked over Spring and Pam with undisguised displeasure, merely nodding at them.

Zavia moved forward, ignoring Oily Man's offered hand, hopping down onto the ground with a loud plop. Rexlen thanked his pilot, then stepped down onto the lawn, turning around, offering his hand. Spring gestured for Pam to go ahead. Spring wanted to savor the heated shuttle as much as possible. With a deep breath, Spring took Rexlen's warm hand, jumping down as gracefully as she could. She did not want to slip in front of horrible, Oily Man. The familiar wintry smell of firewood almost made her feel at home...almost. The damp morning dew of the grass tickled her toes. Her heels immediately sank into the grass.

Together, they all crunched up the stairs in silence, Spring walking beside Rexlen, Zavia and Oily Man in front, and Pam bringing up the rear. Behind them the fountain sounded like a small waterfall, the noise magnified in the quiet garden. Spring stared up at the many windows, that seemed empty but not empty. It was hard to tell with the slant of the building and the way the morning sun flashed against them, displaying the reflection of the cloudy sky. She felt the hair standing up on the back of her neck, she could not shake the sensation of thousands of eyes watching them.

"I love your home, Zavia!" Pam gushed as they reached a pair of ridiculously tall gilded double doors, "I wish I had a fountain in my front yard!"

Zavia glanced over her shoulder, "This is the back entrance. We are being sneaked in the back door." She said dryly.

"Oh," Pam took a second look around the garden behind her, before grinning back. "Well, it's a tastic backyard then!"

"Who mows the lawn?" Spring heard herself say before bursting into a peel of nervous laughter joined by Pam. They were still giggling as the huge doors swung open, revealing a darkened interior. Spring rubbed her eyes, squinting, letting her eyes adjust.

The soft morning light barely illuminated the room, giving it a lazy quiet atmosphere. The casual air contrasted sharply with the oval shaped ornate room, opulent even in the early morning sun. Spring's eyes were drawn to the high ceiling; it's slight domed shape covered in thousands of geometric patterns of muted black, brown, gold and red that glittered and winked around a large crystal fixture that resembled a chandelier. She marveled at the light fixture, wondering how the fluid swirls and curves looked illuminated.

Flowers stood in small recessed alcoves in the walls, but Spring could not smell them. Instead, the room had an almost musty, unused quality to it, the air had a ghost of a chill to it. The tall windows were framed by heavy looking embroidered drapes of reddish black, pulled back exposing the brownish green of a garden in winter. Despite the coldness of the room, the glass windows were slightly frosted against the cold temperature outside. Spring half expected the few chairs lining the walls to be covered in sheets of a thin layer of dust. This room was not 'lived' in, but rather like a room in one of those historic homes open to the public.

Smiling she blinked rapidly, staring at Zavia's suddenly rigid back, watching as Oily Man bowed deeply. She felt Rexlen stiffen beside her. She looked up him, his face was expressionless, but his eyes held a hint of surprise. He was staring straight ahead at something (or someone). Abruptly, Rexlen bowed, a graceful, reverent bow unlike Oily Man's subservient one. He straightened, his eyes masked. Slowly, with her heart pounding hard, Spring followed his gaze. Behind them, Pam let out a soft gasp.

The BelReginar and a small group of official looking people stood a few feet away. No one had to tell Spring that the imposing confident looking woman standing in the middle was Zavia's mom. She was tall, but not as tall as Zavia or some of the dour looking officials standing behind her. Her dark hair, so much like Zavia's was pulled back from her face, piled high upon her head secured with glittering combs that were dressy and casual at once. It was hard to believe she was Rexlen's grandmother.

She had a youthful face, smooth and unlined, rounder than Zavia's. Her large eyes were darker, the coppery color of new pennies. They were locked on Zavia with an icy intensity.

The BelReginar's somewhat understated, high necked gown of deep orange sparkled here and there with tiny beads. Around her waist she wore a low slung tasseled belt of a braided gold with small gems. Oddly, the women in her group were lavishly, gaudily attired in tall boxy headdresses of red, their eyes lowered discreetly. Their red robes were thick and heavy looking fanning out, making them look wider than they probably were. The men were decked out in formal very tailored uniforms, resplendent in thick braid, high necks and stiff demeanors.

Spring managed to tear her eyes away from Zavia's mom, staring at the man standing closest to the BelReginar. The tallest man among the group, his mature handsome face was stern, confident. His eyes were the same exact color as Zavia's and Rexlen's, and the way he stood so close to the BelReginar (when the others were respectfully a few inches from her, made him appear a member of Zavia's family.

"You have returned." The BelReginar's cold voice rang out in the large, hollow chamber. Spring's eyes flew to The BelReginar's face. The woman's voice had been clear, but her eyes glistened and shone with moisture as she gazed at Zavia from head to toe. Spring had hoped Zavia's mom would've rushed forward to hug her; but the woman stood stiffly, her arms crossed, her hands hiding in the large bell sleeves of her long, high necked gown.

Zavia gave a small shrug, "Yes," she answered in Endarion. "Thought I would cut my vacation short. It was time. Hello, brother." Zavia inclined her head toward the tall man beside her mother.

The tall man beside Zavia's mom cracked a familiar wry smile, his eyes lighting with amusement. Spring gasped, staring harder at the man, taking in his square jaw, and the same, familiar twist of his mouth. Rexlen's dad! There was a faint resemblance, although Rexlen's father had a broader hook nose, and thinner lips, the eyes and smile were identical. "Welcome home, Savatareena," Rexlen's father said, before looking past Zavia toward Rexlen. "Commander Baldric …well done."

Rexlen bowed again, "Thank you, my lord, BelFilius," he replied formally. Spring watched the stiff father, son exchange with slight annoyance. *Was it too much for them to use 'son' or 'dad'? Even Darth Vader called Luke his son!*

The BelReginar's eyes flicked over Spring, landing on Rexlen, "I am pleased you have found and returned the BelFilia safely, Commander Baldric. We were," The BelReginar's voice quivered slightly and she pressed her mouth into a tight line. "Most concerned for her and her whereabouts." The BelReginar turned her attention to Zavia, she took a half step forward, her eyes scanning Zavia's slightly bruised face, "I see she has been— harmed." She took another step forward until she was a few inches from Zavia, her gown rustling softly on the floor.

"'She is fine." Zavia answered, shocking her mother, before adding gently, "I am okay now …BelReginar. Do not—do not worry, it does not hurt anymore." Zavia's eyes glistened, catching the faint light of the room as she tried to smile reassuringly at her mom.

Raw emotion played across The BelReginar's face, her eyes shimmering as she continued to gaze at Zavia. Spring felt her own eyes well up as she watched Zavia's mom struggle to regain her composure, schooling her features into an impassive mask once more, "Very well then," The BelReginar said sternly. "You must be quite fatigued from your ordeal. Your rooms have been prepared. Go now, we shall discuss this incident after you have rested. Rest now."

With a slight move of her head, The BelReginar summoned two virile looking guards that materialized out of nowhere, while another set stood by two double doors, opened and revealing the warm, golden light of a hallway. The faint sound of music drifted in as did the enticing aroma of breakfast and distant chatter. Spring stared down at her feet, her shoes blurring with the floor. *It's Christmas now, I wonder what mom and dad are doing right now? Don't cry in front of Zavia and Rexlen's family and... friends?*

Spring looked up to find The BelReginar's laser-like stare trained on her. Spring shifted uncomfortably under the gaze, unconsciously stepping closer to Rexlen. Her hand resisted the urge to twist the chain of Gran Libby's peacock pendant. She wondered now if wearing the large gold enameled pendant with the outstretched feathers was such a good idea. The BelReginar's eyes went from Spring to Rexlen, widening slightly.

"Commander, you shall meet me in the East room to discuss your mission," The BelReginar said, nodding as Rexlen bowed once more. With another nod of her head, an adviser dressed similarly as Oily Man, but with a kinder face, stepped forward, standing a few feet from the BelReginar. The man (close in age to Rexlen's dad), made a short bow toward Spring.

"The BelReginar bids you welcome." the man said in a stilted voice, his eyes on the floor, "You are most invited to stay and rest at Snowendorrica as honored guests and friends of our Lady BelFilia."

Spring curtsied toward the BelReginar, smiling directly into her face, "Thank you...your majesty." Her face felt hot from all the stares directed at her. *Nice of Zavia's mom to invite us to stay. I have a feeling there are no Holiday Inn's around here.*

The BelReginar inclined her head, before walking briskly toward the open doors, her entourage close behind. A rustle of skirts and the loud chomp of boots sounded in the hall. Rexlen's father lingered behind for a moment, glancing at Spring and Pam with curiosity. Zavia joined her escorts at the door, turning to wink once at Spring and Pam before disappearing. The large room was suddenly empty, two lone guards stood by the doorway, staring blankly ahead. Obviously escorts to their new rooms.

Rexlen looked tenderly at Spring, "I will see you soon then…" he leaned close to her ear, "Sweet dreams." He straightened, moving his head a little toward the waiting escorts. He looked at Spring expectantly.

"Oh! Sweet dreams or and uh, happy talk with your grandma…uh, BelReginar! Come on, Pam!" Pam stumbled forward, smiling up at the guards. Spring followed her, stopping at the doorway, glancing back at Rexlen. *Why can't you escort us to our rooms? What if we are invited to stay in the dungeon? Do they have dungeons in Alien palaces? Where are your rooms? Are you going home after your talk? Take me with you!*

"See you soon." Spring whispered. She felt foolish tears sting her eyes. She looked away from Rexlen, staring up at the ceiling instead. There was no way, she was going to walk out into the hallway crying like a baby. She heard Rexlen's boots approach her, felt his solid warmth beside her. She turned her head slowly, staring up into his eyes, surprised to see her feelings mirrored back. She wanted to walk into his arms, but the guards were there …what would they think?

"Rest well, my dear." Rexlen said, his eyes boring into hers, "sleep well."

Spring willed her feet over the threshold, turning away from Rexlen's serious face, focusing on the broad back of the guard in front of her.

18

SUNDAY DINNER, IMPERIAL STYLE

Spring wasn't prepared for the few curious courtiers and guards lining the vast hallway. Once again her eyes had to adjust to her surroundings. The hallway 's long ceiling was made up of a rectangular skylight that stretched from one end to the other, bathing everything in light. The atrium hallway itself felt like a 'room', with arches and columns of thick stone soaring up toward the higher floors, curving toward the ceiling. A few faces peered over the arched railings above, staring down at them with twinkling head-dresses and shimmering uniforms.

All the earlier noisy chatter stopped, only a few loud whispers filled the great atrium. Down the hall, the clash of dishes could be heard from an open doorway. *Is that where they all ate breakfast?*

The guards lead them silently down the long hall, lined with busts of Zavia's family in alcoves and a few gilt chairs and vases. Spring 's heels sounded clunky on the polished floor.

"Humans." Someone whispered as they passed a group of handsome men in uniform.

"Earthlings," whispered another. Spring felt the back of her neck prickle, but she forced her best 'Calm & In Control' flight attendant look.

The courtiers close to them stared boldly, clustered in small groups by several columns, looking over their shoulders as Spring and Pam walked by. They all looked so human to Spring, even their elaborate clothes reminded her of stuff she saw in history books. A few merely glanced at them with disdain, while others smiled, nodding before diving back into their groups whispering. Spring felt her cheeks flush as they approached a particular trio of women by the wide double staircase.

This group was dressed more lavishly, especially the one in the middle with the green fan shaped headdress and high necked encrusted dress. The obvious 'queen bee' crossed her arms, staring down her long nose with distaste, her mouth curving slightly. Her eyes were a striking pale liquid green and she would've been pretty if it were not for the hard set of her jaw. Spring felt her steps falter as they neared the ornate double stairs, seemingly the 'turf' of the catty clique. She had the urge to hide behind the broad back of the guard, but resisted, holding her chin up; smiling cordially as they came within inches of the trio. Spring noticed that the other two women also wore shades of green too.

The trio gave Spring and Pam the insolent, bitchy, outfit once over assessment, before gliding slowly away from the stairs. The leader seemed gratified as the guards bowed low to her before climbing the stairs. Spring locked eyes for a second with the queen bee before following the guard up the stairs.

"Wonder who that was? Zavia's sister?" Pam asked when they were halfway up the stairs out of earshot. "She had 'Bitch' written all over her."

"I know." Spring said as they reached the landing, glancing over her shoulder at the trio (who had the gall to stare up at them), "She doesn't look like Zavia." *Please do not let THAT be Rexlen's mom!*

* * *

The BelReginar was already seated when Rexlen entered the East Room. He walked slowly toward the BelReginar sitting under the large wide window, with her small arsenal of advisors surrounding her with dour faces and clasped hands.

Rexlen had always hated this room. The BelReginar always selected it for her meetings with him, ever since he was a child. He could memorize every detail of the room with his eyes closed. The smooth polished floor was slightly uneven. The towering heavy golden drapes with the black diamond pattern were the same curtains he had stared at when his mother brought him to the palace for the first time. He was three years old then, nervous and excited to be at court. Excited to meet the BelReginar.

His mouth twisted in irony as his eyes swept the room. It seemed smaller now, the gaudy, heavily patterned walls glinting in dull golds, blacks, and faded reds. The heavy, dangerous looking chandelier that dwarfed the ceiling was always lit. Even now in the late afternoon. The BelReginar's ladies in waiting sat off to the side in their hard looking, cushion less chairs, their feet carefully avoiding the ancient mosaic tile floor, each valiantly trying ward off the cold chill by folding their hands deep in their sleeves. The room was perpetually frigid, despite the four glowing 'warming 'orbs hovering over thick carved stands.

"You smile, Baldric." The BelReginar's voice jolted him out of his thoughts. "Does something amuse you?"

Rexlen stopped in front of the BelReginar, bowing "No, My BelReginar." He straightened, clasping his hands behind his back as he stared directly at the BelReginar. Her eyes narrowed slightly, her mouth set in a thin line.

"Wise answer." She said, tapping her hands against her arm chair, the tips of her nails colliding in a grating rhythm against the inlaid gems in the chair. "What is your progress, Baldric? Have you accomplished your other mission yet?"

"No, My BelReginar. The rescue mission of the BelFilia diverted my attention. I will need more time to set all plans in place."

"More time?" The BelReginar echoed coldly. "How much time could you possibly need? They want a protective planetary grid for Earth, and we want an Endarion station in their system. A simple arrangement, Baldric."

"It is not as simple as you may think, My BelReginar." he said stiffly, hearing the anger in his voice. "They are already suspicious of our alliance with the Galtarrions. They do not trust us completely. It will take time to fully gain that."

"So, they do not trust us, and yet they are greedy enough to accept our technology." The BelReginar let out a low chuckle, leaning back in her chair, tapping her hands rapidly. "There is a price to pay for our help, Baldric. Set the plans in effect, let them decide which path to choose. Which price they prefer. It would take so little to topple their meager defenses. I've read your reports. They would fall easily."

"They have other allies, My BelReginar."

"Indeed they do." Rexlen watched as the BelReginar's mouth curved into a wintry smile, "But none of them would dare stand up against us. Earth has nothing to contribute to the universe…nothing except itself, and into the hands of an empire ready to enfold it. Protect it. How much time, Baldric?"

"Why Earth, My BelReginar?"

The BelReginar sighed lazily, "Why not? Tell me, Baldric, would you rather have it fall into Galtarrion hands?" She chuckled again, her eyes glittering softly. "Ah! Your warrior mask slips! How disturbed you looked a second ago! Not a pretty thought is it? How much time?"

"A few months. No more than that."

"Good. Very good. Do not delay it further or we'll be at war with the Galtarrions over it. There are three ships ready to enter Earth's territory— our ships of course. Well done, Baldric, you may go."

Rexlen bowed once more, turning sharply, striding toward the closed doors.

"Baldric!" The BelReginar called out. Rexlen stopped, looking over his shoulder before turning around, facing her once more. She leaned forward in her chair, her hands like jeweled claws, "Tell me, do they suspect anything?" A few ladies in waiting looked over at him.

"No." He said simply, "Not at all."

* * *

Spring shifted uncomfortably on the edge of massive, prickly, throne-like chair, pulling her borrowed robe closer. She had been sitting in that position for close to an hour now, still a little awestruck by her suite in the palace. Maybe awestruck was not the right word. Shocked. Terrified to break anything perhaps.

Her fingers plucked at the rich, thick brocade material of her robe, absently tracing the path of flowers, as her eyes lingered on the strange warming orb floating before her. The maid that had drawn her bath, explained that the glowing, shifting ball of fire was normal; kind of like a portable heater. Orange, red, and yellow flames leaped and swirled. Her very own, toasty sun-fireplace. The cheery orb did little to warm up the large mausoleum style room though.

The ceilings were impossibly high, and like the walls were layered in geometric tiles of dark primary colors in what was apparently supposed to be relaxing floral designs against muted gold mosaic. Dangling overhead, an unusual chandelier made up of dozens of colorful tear dropped crystals set off a faint glow. The heavy looking drapes, stretched up to the ceiling. Her two windows overlooked a narrow (one foot wide), Juliette balcony with a 'lean on it if you dare' delicate filigree railing. Down below was an inviting garden with a couple of book reading stone benches.

Even with the two mile long drapes pulled back, the room was still dark. The corners of the room remained in shadows. Spring did not dare explore the bedroom area: It's double doors were open, revealing a sunken room filled with more museum quality, hard furniture. An equally hard looking bed wide enough for five people, piled high with a thick coverlet gleamed in semi darkness. The bed was turned down, revealing a stark white sheet and a long unibrow pillow. At least the bathroom was bright and sunny with a small bathtub that could easily moonlight as a mini swimming pool. She had stayed in the bath until her skin wrinkled and the water cooled, her eyes looking into the dim sitting room.

She knew she should nap, but she could not seem to relax in her room. Maybe it was all of the gilt and mosaics. Spring shifted gingerly in her seat, sliding back cautiously, drawing her feet up, tucking them under her robe, wishing she had a pair of socks, just as a soft knock sounded.

"Uh…yes…I mean, Na'allo?" She sat up quickly, crossing her feet at the ankles. Her eyes went up to the tall double doors covered in filigree and looking like they each weighed at least sixty pounds. "Hello?" she stood up, moving toward the door, her bare feet stepping off the rug and onto a cold floor. *Should I open it myself?* She stared helplessly at the doors, "Come in?" The doors did not budge. "Come in!" She shouted.

Finally the doors swung open, smoothly and easily, revealing an abundance of light, a kind looking imperial guard and Pam clad in a similar high necked robe. "Hey there! About time! Me and the guard were about to bust the door in." Pam nodded thanks to the guard before following Spring into the room. "Didn't you hear me? These rooms are so magnif!" Spring smiled at the guard, gesturing for the doors to be left open.

"It's kinda too big…I'm a little afraid to touch anything!" Spring waved a hand around the room, "I like the little floating sun, keep wanting to touch it, I wonder…" feeling brave, Spring approached the orb, reaching out tentatively, she slanted a glance at Pam.

"I dare you!" Pam moved closer, to the orb gazing down at it. "Wonder if it burns?"

"Together then?" Spring held out a finger, Pam hesitated, then held out a finger, "Okay. Ready, one two, three!"

"Stop." Called a voice from the doorway.

Spring and Pam froze, looking over their shoulders with wide eyes at Zavia. She grinned at them, shaking her head as she stepped into the room. "You know, that will just give your hands sunburn. You'll have a bright red hand for dinner…not a pretty sight." Zavia was dressed in a soft flowing gown with a delicate, lacy high collar. Her hair piled in a bun. Her eyes painted like the other ladies of the court.

"Dinner?" Pam uttered, exchanging an excited look with Spring, "Tastic!"

"Will Rexlen be there too?" Spring asked hopefully.

"I think so." Zavia winked, falling gracefully into one of the prickly throne chairs in front of the orb, "Some 'layover hotel' huh? Home sweet home. What do you think?"

"It's has that um, old world charm…very lavish." Spring ran her hand against the wall wincing when her fingers collided with a rough mosaic, "Opulent." *If you're going for that homey, cold museum look.*

"Magnif!" Pam sat down cross legged on the floor, revealing warm looking slippers.

"Tacky, old and drafty." Zavia said shrugging, "I hate it here."

"But, all of this history…I mean, these must be heirlooms!" Spring argued, "Everything is so …"

"Ugly." Zavia finished, she glanced at Pam, "It is okay…laugh. It is ugly and dark here. Everyone hates it."

"Why not change it then?" Spring asked. "Can't your mom do that? It's her palace, right?"

Zavia shook her head slowly, "She cannot. None of us can. It's been like this for centuries and it has to stay that way. My ancestor, built it and made some idiotic law prohibiting any change to the interior." She swept her arms wide, "Everything you see is from his era…and that was thousands of years ago. See that bed," she pointed to Spring's bed. "Hundreds of people have slept and died in it."

"Gee, thanks, Zavia," Spring gave her a dry look. "I'll sleep well tonight."

"Zavia," Pam hesitated, "Are you...are you okay? The whole rescue thing..."

Zavia blinked, a brief shadow filling her eyes, before she nodded curtly, "Of course. I better go and get ready for dinner now. Just a small family affair." She turned towards the door, picking up the hem of her gown. "Cannot wait to see how you two like our clothes!" She laughed, waving at the doorway, "See ya, ladies!"

As if on cue, four maids entered, weighed down with fabrics and carved boxes. They halted a few feet inside, heads bowed discreetly. Spring could not get over their Shriner hat headdresses.

"I better go, I bet my peeps are waiting for me next door. Can't wait to try on their headdresses!" Pam turned in the doorway, glancing at the maids before looking back at Spring with a sly grin, "Maybe you can slip Rexlen in here! Byeeee!"

* * *

This is a small affair? Spring's eyes roamed around the BelReginar's private receiving hall, silently counting up to ten people lingering about, dressed as if for a state ball. The BelReginar was nowhere in sight. Spring had already spotted Rexlen's dad across the room. Rexlen's dad, along with half of the gathered men, was dressed in full dress uniforms, the medals flashing in the light. The woman wore their heavy jewel and embroidery laden gowns easily, navigating perfectly with their high, half moon headdresses. All of them were absorbed in their conversations. Spring and Pam were virtually invisible.

Spring reached up with one hand, cautiously touching her own headdress, her fingers running over the line of tiny gems and braided trim. Her headdress was smaller, more like a rounded diadem off velvety fabric, sitting a few inches above her head. It reminded her of the ancient images of Anne Boleyn's 'French Hood' garment. Her hair had been brushed into submission, falling into gently curling black waves, free of restriction, and on its best frizz free behavior.

The only part of her that was not restricted it seems. It had taken the maids an hour to dress her from start to finish. Her deep cranberry red dress was gorgeous, trimmed with a generous amount of gold and dark blue embroidered wines and leaves, accented with a sprinkling of gems. Her wide gold filigree belt was placed high over her natural waist, cinching her in, making it look tiny. Her red dress was cut low and square, revealing the high necked, golden lace under dress with its exposed billowing sleeves. Her shoes were surprisingly comfy, soft platform wedges with criss crossing straps in the same velvety fabric as her hat.

"I love their headdresses! I wanted a tall disc one!" Pam nodded toward a familiar looking lady in green in a fan shaped headdress that added a foot to her height. "My maids said only the royals wore the big things like that." Pam was decked out in stunning burnt orange and gold.

"That thing must weigh a ton!" Spring winced, watching as the green ladies headdress wobbled slightly as she talk animatedly to a woman wearing a frightfully high purple one. "Maybe you have to build up a resistance to the big ones…maybe ours are like training wheels. Oh, thank you!" Spring smiled, accepting a tall flute from a servant passing by.

"Yeah, probably," Pam took a flute, delicately sniffing at the clear liquid. "But it would've made a Tastic profile picture! Cheers!" She clinked her glass loudly against Spring's.

"Profile picture? In that case, I will arrange for a Ontebla for you …easy!" Zavia had materialized beside them, almost unrecognizable in a turquoise blue fan shaped headdress that had scalloped silver tipped edges. Her dress was the same turquoise blue color. Her over dress was split open in the middle (right under her multi colored jeweled belt), revealing her metallic silver lace under dress. Instead of a high lace collar, Zavia's long neck was swathed in a spectacular multi stone necklace that covered her shoulders, ending just below her chin.

"Hey, Girl!" Spring said, her eyes glued to the dazzling necklace. "You look amazing! Can I borrow your necklace?"

"Yeah, like a real princess...er, BelFilia!" Pam agreed, laughing as Zavia did a quick spin for them. "What's an...Ontable?"

"Ontebla." Zavia corrected, leading them deeper into the room, toward Rexlen's father. "The tall headdresses you like? They're Onteblas. And they only look heavy," she paused, her eyes lighting with mischief. "No training wheels required." She stopped in front of her brother, gently touching his arm, he looked at them curiously. "Javarr, may I introduce my roomies? Miss Spring Raine Stevens and Miss Pamela Olivia Sloane of Earth."

"A pleasure." Javarr's voice sounded exactly like Rexlen's, deep, rich and kind. He smiled warmly at them, bowing his head politely, "What lovely but unusual names to go with such beautiful—"

"Earth beings." The lady in green interrupted, standing close to Javarr, placing a possessive hand on his sleeve. She smiled widely, baring her teeth. "Savatareena, aren't you going to introduce me as well?"

Zavia bristled slightly, her eyes frosting a little, "Of course," she said stiffly. "Spring, Pam, may I introduce you to Onaldi...Javarr's wife."

"And Crown BelFilia." Onaldi added preening.

"Oh, yes, that too ...what she just said." Zavia smiled sweetly. "My brother's consort when he becomes BelReginar."

"Sava..." Javarr said in a warning tone that did not match his eyes. Zavia shrugged, sipping on a thin goblet of orange, swirling stuff.

"That's so strange hearing your real name, Zavia. I mean, Savatareena." Spring said.

"Does this mean we should call you, Savatareena now?" Pam asked. "That's a mouthful."

"Of course you should." Onaldi answered for Zavia. "That is her name. As commoners, she is BelFilia to you." Onaldi looked at Zavia, her eyes glittering, "My dear, Savatareena, wherever did you come up with such an…amusing alias?"

"Zavia was the name of a pet of mine when I was little." Zavia explained staring into her glass, before glancing at Spring and Pam. "She was a Catli bird …a gift from my father."

"I remember that bird." Javarr nodded fondly, "That was your fifth birth year, right?" He said to Spring and Pam, "That bird had the brightest blue feathers you have ever seen! And it sung too!"

"Oh, how marvelous, Savatareena! I did not know." Onaldi replied.

"My brother Hunter and I had a bird too. Dino." Spring supplied. "Zavia, I mean, Savatareena…"

"BelFilia." Onaldi supplied.

"Spring," Zavia smiled, "it is okay. You can still call me, 'Zavia'. Or if you want, you and Pam can call me, Sava. My friends and family do." Zavia pointedly looked at a frowning Onaldi.

"Spring!" Pam nudged her shoulder, jerking her slightly toward the wide doorway, "Look who just arrived!"

Rexlen strode into the room, looking effortlessly handsome in his dark eggplant, formal uniform with the high collar lined in black. His jaw was rigid for a moment as he surveyed the room, then he spotted her, his face visibly relaxing, his eyes lighting up with pleasure. He slowly made his way toward them, stopping every few inches to say hello to a few guests along the way. He stopped a few inches from Spring, bowing deeply. "My ladies, BelFilia, my lord, BelFilius. Misses Stevens and Sloane, good evening." He straightened, his eyes going over Spring in masculine approval. Spring blushed.

"A surprise seeing you here, Commander." Onaldi said grandly, offering her hand. Rexlen took it, giving it a respectful but quick peck before releasing it. "Excuse me please, the air is so stiff!"

"Well done, Baldric." Javarr said gruffly, barely acknowledging Onaldi's departure. "I hear your mission on Earth is progressing smoothly. Earth sounds like a fascinating place. What is it like?" He glanced at Spring and Pam once more, his mirror eyes (so much like Rexlen's), twinkling. "Are all humans like these two wonderful specimens? I must say ladies, I am very impressed you traveled so far on behalf of my adventurous little sister. Very brave of you."

"Brave and beautiful." Rexlen said staring at Spring with a faint smile. Spring felt heat rise to her face. She stared up into his face feeling breathless and faint.

"And loyal." Zavia said in an oddly thick voice. "I do not think I thanked you both. I...I cannot imagine anyone else on the Moon or at Orion doing that for me." She looked over at her brother, "my eyes scare them a little bit, I think!" She laughed again, wiggling her eyebrows. "I suppose Alien colleagues are still new for a lot of Humans."

All conversation stopped as men and women sank immediately into bows and curtseys. The BelReginar, followed by a small entourage entered. Moving slowly, and regally into the room.

"It is dinnertime." Zavia said under her breath, bowing her head as her mom approached.

Spring stood rooted to the spot, staring at The BelReginar with wide eyes. Zavia's mom (whether she planned to or not) was wearing a gown in a shade of turquoise slightly darker than Zavia's. While Zavia's dress was trimmed in silver, The BelReginar's dress had gold with canary yellow stones. Her skirt was wider, swinging out in a soft, farthingale bell shape. The BelReginar swayed to a gentle stop, her eyes locked on Spring expectantly with mild annoyance.

Belatedly, Spring gazed around, everyone (but herself), were curt-
seying, bowing or both, all eyes were averted and staring at the floor. Even
Pam had managed a sweeping 'debutante ' curtsey. Petrified, Spring's eyes
slid back toward The BelReginar. *Is she waiting for me?*

Spring wet her lips, swallowing hard. Taking a deep breath, she
raised one hand, holding tight to her headdress before executing a somewhat wobbly, but passable curtsey. She forgot to avert her eyes of course.

Seemingly satisfied, The BelReginar inclined her head, before slowing walk past, her gown swooshing noisily in the silent room, followed by
the boots and rustling of her entourage. One by one, courtiers rose smoothing their uniforms and gowns, lining up, ready to follow in the BelReginar's
wake. This time they all glanced toward Javarr and Zavia. Onaldi had mag-
ically appeared at her husband's side, chin high, a proud smile on her face.
Javarr offered Onaldi one arm, while offering Zavia the other, escorting
them both behind The BelReginar.

Rexlen turned to Spring and Pam, bowing, offering his escort, "Shall
we?" he asked winking

* * *

Spring watched silently, stomach full as her last dessert dish was cleared
away. Her eyes meet Rexlen's blushing as his mouth curved into an covert
smile. She picked up her goblet of slightly sweet Yuctari wine, raising it in
mock salute toward him, grinning. *To surviving my first Alien formal dinner!*

When Spring realized they would be dining on the wide terrace, all
she could think about was the frigid cold air that cut through her when
they arrived. But now, sitting under a glowing wave of heat that hovered
over the table, stretching the entire length in flowing stream of red, orange
and yellow; she was toasty and happy. The food was very Earth-like, dishes
in heavy sauces, roasted meat (which she a had a few daring bites), colorful
dishes of vegetables and fruits. She did however, feel sorry for the dancers
and musicians, dancing in the garden before them, their breaths frosting

in the air. The musicians were at least dressed warmly, while the dancers cavorted in light costumes of muted browns and greens, decorated with little balls of light.

The other 'guests' were actual members of Zavia's family. The BelReginar's entourage included Zavia's older sister Isaduirra, a stern, cold looking virtual twin of The BelReginar. Spring saw a hint of Zavia when a servant delivered a plate of Tobion chocolate pie, warranting a beaming, radiant smile from Isaduirra that greatly amused her portly husband. The others were' Barnacle' relatives, distant cousins two or three times removed. Some were obviously annoyed that Pam and Spring were seated ahead of them at the table, out of rank, but no one dared to complain. Spring and Pam sat a few seats away from The BelReginar, Javarr and Zavia. Rexlen was across from Spring.

Spring sipped her wine, smiling dreamily, listening to the soft strings of the musicians and the lilting sound of Endarion. Rexlen was speaking to his neighbor, while every now and then glancing at her. She wished he would stay in her room. Pam seemed absorbed in a detailed conversation of one of Zavia's handsome 'cousins'. The man rattled away in Endarion, while Pam nodded and smiled excitedly. Spring glanced at her neighbor, an elderly woman, softly dozing, her chin resting against her stiff ruffled collar. Spring smiled at the old woman, thinking about Gran-Libby. She turned away, staring down the table at Zavia and The BelReginar, talking furiously in Endarion.

"Then it's only fair we speak in Earth English," Zavia leaned back in her seat, her face dark with emotion. "My friends have a right to know what you think of them!" The table grew quiet. Spring exchanged a look with Rexlen, and Pam. "The moon is my home, I am not staying here!"

"Earth English then? As you wish, my child." The BelReginar said in a chilling voice, her eyes glinting angrily. "No daughter of my flesh is going to bow down and serve anyone, let alone some diseased, idiotic, inferior, Humans! You will not return to the moon. You will *not* live among heathens. And finally, you will *not* disgrace your lineage! You are Lady Canaar of the temple, that is your duty!"

"That is not what I want to do, My lady Bel—"Zavia broke off, glancing at Spring and Pam, before turning back to The BelReginar, "Mother … Mom." Isaduirra gasped, casting frightened eyes at The BelReginar. The BelReginar stared disbelievingly at Zavia, her face tense with anger, Zavia continued, raising her voice, "Yes, Mother—it is an Earth term, and I like it, and it fits. Mom, my life is my own, the moon is my life! I love traveling through space…it is …it's," Zavia paused for words, "it's Tastic!"

"Tastic?" The BelReginar echoed icily, "what is so…tastic about being a servant to others? People that are far beneath you? Travel through space? Fine, perhaps we can arrange for you to serve a sabbatical on a research vessel. You are not returning to Earth or its decrepit little moon."

"Why not?" Zavia challenged, refusing a slice of chocolate pie, waving it away.

"Because I have spoken." The BelReginar replied coolly. "Now the subject is closed …"

Zavia stood up, shoving her chair away, "No it is NOT ! You cannot make me stay here!"

"Sit down, Sava."

"No! I am not going back to the temple," Zavia's voice shook. "I hate it there! I would rather die. The moon is my home. Mom…mother, I have friends there …real friends! They could care less if I am of the blood! Please," she lowered her voice, pleading, "let me go back home."

"No." The BelReginar said simply.

"Why? If you hate the Humans so much why—"

"Because they cannot protect you." The BelReginar's voice quivered with more than anger. "You could have been killed! They cannot guarantee your safety. I will not allow you to risk your life and live so far from home and our protection in a world new to space." The BelReginar said tiredly, "I will not have it, and if your father were by my side, neither would he. The matter is settled."

An awkward silence filled the air. Zavia blinked rapidly, taking shallow breaths, struggling to reign in her emotions. Finally, she said in an emotionless voice, "My lady, BelReginar, I wish to be excused."

"You may go." The BelReginar gestured, and two guards appeared behind Zavia. Without another word, Zavia turned on her heel, storming blindly off the terrace, followed by her escorts. Spring put her napkin on the table, exchanging a look with Pam. Rexlen stood up, clearing his throat.

"My lady, BelReginar, if I may come in defense of Earth and its moon..."

The BelReginar turned her attention to Rexlen, snapping something in Endarion that made his jaw go rigid, hurt and anger flashing in his eyes. Spring looked over at Javarr, noticing how he gazed at Rexlen with a pained, troubled expression. Onaldi seemed to gloat, smiling gleefully as she took a large lazy sip of wine, keeping her eyes trained on Rexlen. Rexlen waited for The BelReginar to finish, then he bowed stiffly.

Spring didn't realize she was already on her feet. She was so angry. She glanced at Rexlen finishing his bow, his face neutral. He said something low and respectful to The BelReginar. His face proud and coldly handsome. Javarr looked away, his eyes sad. Onaldi smirked. Within seconds, Onaldi was soaked with Yuctari wine, sputtering in shock and indignation, staring dagger eyes at Spring. Spring looked down in shock, Pam was prying a goblet out of her hands, setting it carefully on the table. Spring looked in bewildered shock from Pam to Onaldi to Rexlen. She did not dare look at the BelReginar. The room was suddenly too hot, she looked dimly at Rexlen again, watching as disbelief and then concern filled his face as he quickly darted out of view. She heard Pam, shouting from far away, an iron grip clamped around her waist, pressing her against the warm solid wall of Rexlen's chest just as the room grew dim.

"Sorry." She whispered, before everything went black.

19

MOON RIVER

Spring slowly opened to her eyes to a darkened room feeling disoriented for a moment, staring up at the inside of tall half canopy draped in soft fabric. She blinked adjusting to the soft light, her eyes going at once to Rexlen sitting in a chair by the bed. She watched him for a moment, lost in thought, staring off into the shadows, his brow furrowed, holding her little headdress, absently turning it over and over in his hands. His attention zoomed to her at once, when she moved to sit up on her elbows, leaning against the pillows.

"How long have I been out?" Spring said with a raspy voice. Her head felt heavy. She was still dressed, her wide belt had been removed. She could breathe again.

"Just a few minutes. Here," Rexlen reached toward the bedside table, pouring a refreshing looking glass of what looked like water from a small silver pitcher. He offered her the glass, "drink this."

It was water. Cool, soothing and so familiar. She was so far from home, and yet water still tasted like water. Dinner came flooding back, Zavia's fight with her mom. Onaldi being the queen of bitches. Rexlen's eyes filled with pain. Onaldi drenched with wine. She set the glass on her lap, staring down at it.

"Some impression I made," she said softly. "I'm sorry I…no," she looked up into Rexlen's face, her eyes locking on his."She deserved it, but I'm sorry—I didn't mean to. I just could not stand that look on her face!" Rexlen moved closer, sitting on the edge of her bed "It's over with, Spring, nothing to be sorry about. Although," he said with a ghost of a smile, "I have never had a beautiful woman champion me…especially with two hundred year old wine."

A discreet knock sounded on her open bedroom door, Pam stood in the shadows, "Can I come in?" She tip toed in still wearing her gown and headdress. "You okay, Spring?"

I would be okay if you wouldn't barge in when Rexlen is with me! Spring hid her annoyance with a small smile. "Yeah. How you guys checked on Zavia?" Spring looked at Pam and Rexlen, "Maybe we should all have dinner outside the palace tomorrow."

"Dinner will have to be on the ship." Rexlen abruptly. "We are leaving tomorrow morning."

"Leaving? We just got here!" Spring cast a horrified glance at Rexlen's set face, "Is this because of dinner?"

Rexlen shook his head, "no, The BelFilia has been brought home, it is time I finished my mission on the Moon."

"Zavia's not coming with us, is she?" Spring asked, "She's going back to the temple to finish her life sentence…right?"

"Yes, I believe so." Rexlen was gazing at her intensely, "I should go," he said suddenly. "Get some rest,. We leave at sunrise. He leaned closer, his lips brushed hers, "sleep well, sweet warrior." He planted a gentle kiss, before standing up, nodding to Pam as he passed her.

Spring stared after him, feeling hopeless. "We just got here. It feels like we're being kicked out, doesn't it?" She looked over at Pam, leaning against a column. "How is Zavia?"

Pam shrugged, "I wish I knew." She said evenly, "I'm not allowed to see 'The BelFilia'. They act like we're not her friends! I better go too, just wanted to check in on ya, see you in a few hours. Night." Pam waved, closing the door behind her.

"Night." Spring said to the closed door.

* * *

Spring leaned against the window, pressing her fingers against the cold glass, watching her breath fog it up. The early morning sky was already turning a soft rosy pink, the puffy clouds outlined in a halo of white morning sunlight. She could just make out the faint rings in the sky. *Just like home . Well, minus the rings. Of course it's sunny on the day we get kicked off the planet.* She smiled ruefully, buttoning her sweater over her yellow summer dress. She woke in the morning surprised to see her comfortable Earth clothes laid out on a chaise in the dressing chamber, clean and pressed. A warm, floor length Endarion cloak of emerald green trimmed with delicate black embroidered flowers hung nearby.

Thirty minutes later, Spring was back in her Earth clothes, the heavy cloak, falling in perfect folds at her feet. She wondered who thought of it. Zavia? Rexlen? Zavia's mom? A brisk knock sounded at the door behind her, startling her out of her thoughts. Hugging herself, Spring looked over her shoulder, her eyes sweeping over the virtually untouched, pristine suite. The doors to her bedroom were open, the bed bathed in a cascade of light, showcasing Spring's attempt at making it up neatly. The knock came again, this time louder, with more force.

"Coming! I mean, come in?"

An escort guard opened the door, bowing humbly, "I am to escort you to the commander's shuttle." He said tonelessly, staring at a space above her head.

"Can I say goodbye to The BelFilia first?" Spring asked. "What about Pam? Miss Sloane?"

The guard hesitated, frowning slightly, as if translating her words, finally he shook his head, "Not possible …Miss Stevens." He stepped outside into the hall, clearing the doorway, bowing formally, "Please follow me, Miss Stevens. Miss. Sloane has already departed."

"Oh, okay." Spring wrapped the Endarion cloak around her, fastening the jeweled clasp. She cast a final glance around the room. "Coming."

She followed the escort down a maze of hallways, empty and still except for a few servants carrying fresh flowers, linens and pushing silver domed breakfast trolleys, that left a fragrant smell in their wake. As they went past the many elaborate closed doors, Spring wondered if couples were snuggled under warm covers wrapped in each others arms. She wondered which room belonged to Rexlen, what it looked like inside. *Did he have a rock collection set up here? Was his room with the rest of the royals?*

She haltingly followed the escort down the stone staircase, her eyes on the army of servants that busily moved around the first floor, getting the vast atrium ready for the courtiers. She barely kept her eyes trained on her escort, watching as the palace servants polished the jeweled columns. A few inches away, a servant girl no older than ten, polished a table to a high sheen under the portrait of a stunning woman with striking pale violet eyes and caramel colored hair set in sausage curls. The painting was as tall as Spring, encased in heavy frame. The woman seemed to gaze dreamily off into the distance, a small thoughtful smile on her lips. She wore a simple gold circlet high on her forehead, so Spring assumed she was a relative of Zavia's; especially in her rich gown of deep purple. She looked vaguely familiar. Spring tore her eyes away, hurrying to catch up with her escort (already halfway down the hall…the big alien oaf), her Earth heels snapping loudly.

Spring caught up with her guard just as he stood in front of an open doorway, he stared at the top of Spring's head, bowing, his left hand extended, indicating she should go in. "Thanks…uh, have a good day!" Spring caught herself saying automatically as she stepped into the room.

"I thought you were going to add 'thank you for flying Orion'!" Pam laughed, sending an echo in the room. She was back in her black dress and striped tights, an Endarion Imperial guardsmen coat draped over her shoulders. "Morning, chica! Your commander is out there." Pam pointed to the waiting shuttle. "The shuttle thing just landed. Rexlen will be right back. He said stay put."

Spring swallowed the nagging tug of jealousy, managing a tight smile. "I swear you spend more time with him than I do!" she joked, trying to sound light, even though memories of Wes swam in her mind. She gazed around the room curiously, "Been here long? Nice coat, Pam."

She recognized the room at once. It was the same room they had entered the day before, still dimly lit, two guards stood at the set of doors leading outside. The garden looked bleak and stark through the glass doors. She could make out the bulky shape of their shuttle with two of Rexlen's men standing beside it.

Pam shrugged, "Uh, probably a few minutes before you. Got here just as the shuttle landed and Rexlen was heading out the door." Pam looked down at the coat, pulling it closer. It hung close to her knees, she gave Spring a covert smile, "And the coat? This old thing? Thanks! My cloak was way too long. I almost tripped on the stairs! My guard gave me his coat. Cool, huh?" Pam took one hand out from under the coat, smoothing it down on of the sleeves covered in gold braid. "Awesome souvenir!"

"Working on your own Endarion, are we?" Spring said, smiling widely as Rexlen came marching up the terrace steps, followed by two of his men. The palace guards opened the terrace doors, inviting a cold blast of winter air inside that was thankfully blocked by her new cloak. Rexlen strode over to where she stood by the door, his face lighting up. He stopped, staring down at her, his hands reaching out to pull her cloak tighter. He smelled of fresh lawn, and a masculine musk that was pleasing, but still took Spring a moment to grow accustomed to. Spring beamed up at him, a fierce tide of love washing over her.

"Sleep well? He murmured, gazing down at her. She lifted her eyes, smiling into his. He looked so handsome in his uniform.

"A little bit," She looked around the room dramatically, "Where's the farewell committee? No parting gifts?"

"We better go." Rexlen's hands gripped her shoulders, steering her toward the frigid open doors. "We plan to break orbit in an hour."

As their small group trudged across the grass still damp with morning dew, Spring felt sadness slow her steps, her feet dragging in the grass. She raised her eyes, scanning Rexlen's expressionless face, he stared stonily ahead, his mind wrapped in thoughts. Spring's fingers brushed against his gloved ones as they walked in silence. Pam had stopped her chatter, her face tight and drawn, her eyes downcast.

"We should've tried," Spring spoke up as they reached the open shuttle doors.

"Tried what?" Rexlen frowned down at her.

Spring was gazing back at the palace, her eyes roaming over the hollow looking windows, now bright with the rising sun's reflection, "We should've helped her escape." She looked back at Rexlen, "Told that dragon BelReginar, Zavia belonged on the Moon. She escaped once didn't she?"

"Spring," she felt Rexlen's arm wrap around her shoulder, drawing her close to his side, turning her slowly until she faced him. "Spring, you came a long way to support her, find her…but she belongs here. If she returned to the Moon, she would be in constant jeopardy from other infidels upset with the empire. She is safe here. Come, we have to go." He guided her toward the shuttles doors.

Spring nodded mutely, moving sluggishly forward. Pam lingered behind, staring at the palace, "Bye Zavia," she said softly. "We'll miss you." Pam turned toward the shuttle, trailing Spring and Rexlen.

At the doors, Rexlen, hopped in front of Spring, climbing into the shuttle easily, leaning forward to hoist Spring up. Spring reached up, gripping Rexlen's sleeves.

"Wait! Hold on! Stop!" shouted a voice from the direction of the palace. Spring and Rexlen both froze, looking at each other in surprise. Rexlen looked up, staring in disbelief over Spring's head. His grip on her loosened, lowering her gently to the ground, sitting back on his haunches with a small smile. Spring whirled around, squinting at the cloaked figure running toward them. Behind it, two uniformed specters, carrying bulky bags struggled to keep up.

"Zavia!" Spring and Pam both cried, racing through the grass toward a bare headed Zavia, sprinting toward them with her skirts in one hand.

Zavia came to a halt, panting, reaching out to hug both of them, before stepping back, hugging her tightly belted waist. "Our dresses are ....not...made...for ....running!" She let out a winded laugh.

"You're coming home after all!" Spring exclaimed. She jumped up and down excitedly with Pam.

"We'll have to throw an epic, 'welcome home' party when we get home!" Pam piped in.

Zavia's smile faded. "Oh, I am not coming with you. I...I just wanted to...say goodbye. A send off."

"Oh." Spring said glancing at the luggage. "Are you—I mean, you have luggage with you..." she exchanged a puzzled look with Pam. "We—thought you were coming home."

"I guess I am home." Zavia replied. "But I have some gifts for you and cookies too! Here!" The servants stepped forward, handing Spring and Pam two tall, bulky packages, heavily wrapped, but lightweight. The third servant went past Spring and Pam, handing a large, sweet smelling box to Rexlen, who accepted it, staring at it with interest.

"Thanks! What's in here?" Pam turned her large gift over and over.

"Let's just say it will make a tastic profile picture," Zavia said in a mysterious voice. "Send me pictures!"

"Thanks, Zavia." Spring hugged Zavia again, careful not to crush her gift. "What about Orion? What should we tell them?"

Zavia waved a hand, "That will be arranged. Do not worry! Just wanted to thank you both. Sorry you had to leave so soon...I heard about dinner." She hid a smile. Pam slid a look at Spring.

"The wine went very well with her green dress," Spring said innocently. "Very Christmas like." The three of them laughed. Rexlen came up, standing beside Spring.

"Morning, BelFilia," He offered a quick bow, he looked down at Spring, "I am sorry, but we have to go." He glanced at Zavia again, "Good day, my lady."

"Safe journey to you all!" Zavia stared hard at them, her pale eyes unnerving, "Come back and visit ...okay? We have some modern cities here too!"

"We will. We'll miss you, take care!" Spring stood there for a moment, her gift held close to her chest. "Sure, you can't sneak on the ship?" she asked under her breath, glancing nervously at the guards.

Zavia shook her head, smiling sadly, "My little adventures are over... but at least I have a pair of jeans, huh? Safe travels back to the Moon. I will miss you both, goodbye."

Reluctantly, Spring and Pam turned away, feeling Zavia's eyes on them as Rexlen hoisted them up, one at a time.

"The apartment is paid for, so do not worry about rent!" Zavia shouted as the doors were sliding shut. "Feed my plants, please! That's if they are still alive!" She waved as the doors latched shut.

Rexlen leaned over Spring as she buckled herself in, she looked up into his worried face, "Ready." she said in a trembling voice, buckling her harness. He stared at her for a long moment, then moved away, taking his

seat beside the pilot. Spring cradled her package in her lap, the paper crin-
kling noisily under her hands. She slid a glance at Pam. Pam's grip on her
package was tight, her knuckles as white and strained as her face.

* * *

It felt strange being back on the ship, seemed like they had been on-world
for more than a day. The crew of Rexlen's ship were busily preparing to
break orbit. Rexlen practically hit the ground running as soon as their shuttle parked in the shuttle bay. He did stop and help both up the steep platform steps in the darkened bay, illuminated only by tracking lights of blue
against shiny black walls. The small hexagon shaped room with the low
ceiling was not how Spring always imagined a shuttle bay to look, she felt
blind as a bat. Rexlen's second in command, Ordon, stood granite faced on
the docking platform beside a crewman (in this case a woman actually, but
hard to tell in the dim chamber). Two security officers stood by the doors
into the ships interior. Spring had met Ordon once, when they boarded on
the Moon. If anyone had the Vulcan-like personality of Spock, it was Lt.
Ordon. All he needed was a pair of thick, blunt bangs and pointed ears.

"I hope you will excuse me," Rexlen had said as he led out of the
shuttle bay and into a curved hallway. He sent Ordon off down the left side
of the hall, while the two security guards hung back. Rexlen glanced down
the hall, watching as Ordon turned a corner, before gazing down at Spring,
"I am needed on the bridge, we'll speak later." He looked behind her, direct-
ing his gaze at the guards, "Escort the Misses Stevens and Sloane to their
chambers. He gave Spring a final look, his lips parting, then clamping shut
grimly, before heading down the hall that Ordon had used. Spring stared
after him for a moment. *Was he about to kiss me or say something?* One of
the guards cleared his throat, inclining his head, offering a hand toward
Spring's gift from Zavia. Spring clutched it for a moment, then handed it
over, a little relieved of the weight. She smiled in thanks, wiggling her wrist.

"Naw, I'm okay, but thanks, I got it." Pam shifted her gift from her
right arm to her left, hoisting it on her hip like a baby. "We should try to

form some type of escape for Zavia." Pam panted, quickening her steps to keep up with Spring. "We can't just…leave her there."

"I don't know," Spring stepped into lift, moving to the rear with Pam as Rexlen's security guys squeezed in. They stood shoulder to head as the lift climbed slowly, "She seemed …okay. Besides, I've already made a bad impression …I don't feel like adding kidnapper too."

They walked in silence the rest of the way, the security guys walking them to their familiar rooms, before departing. Pam followed Spring into her room, outside, planet Endari filled up the entire window, its faint rings sparkling with pixie dust. Spring took a seat at the little table, placing her gift in front of her. Pam sat down as well, already tearing into her package, letting the wrappings fall to the floor.

"This is so Absolute …look at this!" Pam held the eye popping head-dress a few inches away, twisting it here and there to make it sparkle more. Every shade of red, pink and purple was represented in the jewels that covered a double fan shaped hat. Spring's head hurt just looking at it.

"Try yours on!" Pam stood up, moving toward the mirror, headdress crushing her hair, as she grasped it with one hand, "Wanna post this, like, right now." She cast a look back at Spring, "But you're right you know."

"About what?' Spring gingerly pulled her dazzling yellow and green headdress out, it too was fan shaped but made of a triple row of golden fili-gree lace covered in gems. It looked like a giant, lace tiara/halo. Immediately she had an idea of wearing it (and nothing else), showing it off to Rexlen.

"About helping Zavia escape," Pam said preening in front of the mir-ror. "Guess it's better that she's home. I can't imagine life on another world."

"Not even if it's with Guy?" Spring asked, daring to look at Pam. Pam took off her headdress, staring down at it, smoothing her fingers over the faceted stones.

"Yeah, right." Pam said stiffly, "three's a crowd. I'm not sharing him…I don't want to become some kind of polygamist! She can have him."

"Sorry, Pam."

Pam shrugged, staring at her feet, her headdress dangling. "Not in the cards. Maybe I should hook up with an Alien man like you...I saw a few that had...massive potential!"

Spring arranged the flower vase for the second time, finally moving the vase of Endarion flowers to a shelf beside the replicator. Speaking of the replicator, it clinked softly behind her, churning out what smelled like roasted turkey with herb stuffing. Her small table by the window was already straining with mashed potatoes and green bean casserole. Actually they were green Jackara beans, big, shiny gumball sized Endarion beans that were as transparent as wet gummy bears. At least the casserole 'smelled' like a regular one from home. Pam was somewhere on the ship enjoying dinner with the Spock-look-alike.

Outside the stars zipped by in white, sideways streaks. They were two days out of Endari and Spring had managed to see Rexlen only three times. Her little dinner tonight would be the longest time she had spent alone with him since they broke orbit. It was still so surreal, leaving Zavia back on Endari. She glanced at her Ontebla on a small recessed shelf by her bed. Even with no natural light, it sent prisms of color throughout the room. It's a shame Zavia didn't include a lightweight gown. That's if they even wore anything that did not weigh twenty pounds and have ten yards of fabric. She went over to the headdress, picking it up carefully, turning to face the mirror as she held it above her head.

"Well, it doesn't look too bad," She scrutinized her reflection. "It kinda looks good with jeans and a sweater. I look like I'm wearing a Christmas tree topper..." Spring paused, her eyes widening, "Christmas!" Her eyes went to the blank televideo screen .

Spring had to resort to asking one of Rexlen's communication officers for help placing a call to Earth. She didn't realize Alien calls went through so many steps and operators. She was totally convinced the last

Earth Federation operator was still on, listening in, when her dad's surprised face filled the screen.

"Springtime! Calling from a starship! Happy New Year!" Her dad tipped an imaginary hat to her. Behind him, the Christmas tree was still up, a green blur with lights, she could hear the TV blaring in the background. "Gwen! Spring's calling from a ship!"

Spring felt her heart sink, "I missed Christmas *and* New Year's?" *God, I feel like Spring Rip Van Winkle. Have we really been gone so long?*

"New Years by one hour, Happy 2080!" Her dad let out one of his belly laughs. Her mom appeared in the screen, waving, grinning. Both of her parents were dressed in their robes.

"Happy New, 2080, baby! Where are you?" Her mom looked a bit tipsy. All it took was one glass.

"Rexlen's ship. Did you guys just stay home and watch the ball drop? Where's everybody?" She cringed, "Did I wake you guys?"

"Don't worry, Springtime, we were already up. Your mom had a feeling you'd call." Her dad said giving her mom' s shoulder a squeeze.

"And you know we always stay put Spring," her mom added with a sniff. "There's no way I'm heading out with all those AirCars zipping around at high speeds. Summer's at a party with her guy. Hunter's still at the academy. Oh! I should show you my new HomeRobot, Dad gave me!"

"How's Gran-Libby? Is she up?" Spring watched her parents exchange a quick look, before her mom shook her head.

"She's asleep, baby, sorry." Her mom looked down at her lap.

"But…but…she always celebrates New Years!" Spring protested, "she's the biggest night owl." Spring pulled out her headdress, "I wanted to show her this."

"Well, she did dress up. She fell asleep right after midnight, still glammed up!" Her dad's cheerfulness sounded forced, despite his loud laugh. Her mom looked at her dad, the corner of her lips turning up, gradually widening into a smile again. "Wow!" Her dad exclaimed, "what is that? Did you win a space pageant?"

"She's old, Baby," Her mom said slowly. "She needs her rest. She was around for 1980, you know! That is a beautiful hat, show it to Gran when you come home. Are you near the Moon now? Is your friend, the princess okay?" Her mom paused, "How is your Alien boyfriend?"

Spring put on the headdress, "This is an Ontebla. It's what the royal women like Zavia wear. Thought Gran-Libby would get a kick out of it." Spring reached up, taking the headdress off, holding it in front of her, "We just left Endari. I think it'll take a while to visit Earth …I mean, I'm sure Orion has a lot to say to me and Pam on the Moon. Zavia had to stay behind on Endari… and my boyfriend," a defiant tone kept into Spring's voice, "Rexlen, is fine."

"Planet Endari," her dad whistled. "Strange hearing you say that. Can't wait to meet your —Commander is it? Maybe I can talk military stuff with him." Her dad winked. The chime on her door sounded, Rexlen stepped inside his eyes on the telescreen with interest that shifted to wariness. He walked toward her, standing beside her, seeming impossibly tall, and very much the 'commander'. He looked down at Spring expectantly. She swallowed, wetting her lips, pasting a smile on her face, despite her heart beating in her feet.

"Rexlen, these are my parents…ah, Mom, Dad, this is Rexlen …" She looked up at Rexlen, suddenly feeling shy, "my boyfriend."

"Chief Stevens, Mrs. Stevens," Rexlen said bowing with a warm smile, "It is an honor to finally meet you, even if it is via televideo." Her dad's chest puffed out proudly when Rexlen addressed him as 'Chief'. Her mom just stared with saucer eyes at Rexlen, a dazed smile on her lips. Rexlen turned to Spring, "I did not realize you were in the middle of a call, I will return later."

"Oh, no, that's alright!" Her mom said hurriedly, "It's almost two, we better go anyway. Bye, baby, love you! We have your gifts, and we're going to open them when you come home! Nice meeting you, Commander." Her mom blew a kiss, waving again.

"Yeah, we're keeping the tree up too…and you know how that drives your mom nuts! Love ya, Springtime, stay safe in space. Great meeting you, Commander, keep our little girl safe out there. Happy New Year!"

"Goodnight, and the pleasure was all mine." Rexlen bowed again, making her mom stare in stupefied fascination. "Happy New Year."

"Happy …" Spring felt so weird saying it, "Happy New…2080. Love you guys, give Gran-Libby a kiss!" Spring returned her mom's wave. The screen went black, returning to the imperial emblem.

"Speaking of kisses," Spring teased as she stood on tip toe, giggling as Rexlen pulled her close. Rexlen's gentle kiss, quickly deepened into one of possession, his tongue exploring her in a sensuous rhythm Spring eagerly answered, her hands in his hair, drawing him closer, deeper.

"Commander," Came a disembodied voice. Both Spring and Rexlen jerked. A bucket of cold water could not have been more effective.

"Yes, what is it?" Rexlen snapped. He held Spring in his arms, glaring up at the ceiling.

"Your attention is required on the bridge, sir." The voice replied.

Rexlen reluctantly pulled away from Spring, straightening his uniform. Spring rubbed her arms, glancing at the set table. She never pulled the food out of the replicator. "I'll stay and reheat the food." She said, moving toward the replicator.

"No, come up with me," Rexlen grabbed her arm, pulling her forward, "This will not take long."

* * *

All eyes turned toward Rexlen and Spring as they entered the bridge. Spring fought the overwhelming urge to hide behind Rexlen's bulk, deciding to do a 'Zavia' and stand beside him, chin up. She wished she was wearing her headdress. Rexlen strode toward his seat, casting a dark stare at his officer, third in command, Lt. Erictor. Erictor was one of the few women on the ship, she reminded Spring of a bald eagle with her beak nose and razor eyes over thick slanted brows. Her severe bob, curving sharply toward her cheekbones made her face looked permanently pinched. She could pass as a Vulcan too. Or a Romulan.

"Well?" Rexlen asked impatiently.

"Another ship is hailing us sir," Erictor said in a flat monotone, "The Octseptar. It has a passenger onboard requesting transport to our ship, sir."

"Erictor, this is not a passenger ship. We have a mission to attend to. Who is this passenger?"

Erictor turned her intense stare onto Rexlen, "Perhaps you should advise the passenger in question yourself, Commander. Shall we hail them?"

"Hail them." Rexlen ordered, crossing his arms. Spring stood close to his chair, she took a few steps back at the look Erictor gave her.

The image of a ship vanished, transforming into Zavia's beaming face. Behind Zavia, a harassed looking Commander looked on.

"Zavia?" Spring blurted.

"Na'allo, Commander Baldric," Zavia smiled widely, "Hi, Spring! Do I have permission to come aboard?"

"Is this another escape of yours, BelFilia?" Rexlen asked bluntly.

Zavia looked innocent, "No, not at all. I am quite free to return to the Moon...by order of The BelReginar. So, may I come aboard...nephew?" She winked.

Rexlen's face darkened a few shades, "Permission granted." he looked sideways at Spring, then back at the screen, "Aunt." he said so low, only Spring heard him.

20
MOONAGE DAYDREAM

For once Spring was grateful she had over calculated the replicator serving portions. Dinner was moved to a formal room down the hallway from Zavia's. Spring was a little put out that she had never been inside the larger room, big enough for four narrow windows, and an oval shaped table of a dark green stone. It was the largest room (beside the bridge) that Spring had seen on Rexlen's ship.

"So, your mom let you go? Why?" Pam asked as she used a knife to cut her mashed potato. Spring looked down at her plate, her mashed potatoes seemed to stare back, taunting her. At least the Alien bean casserole had not transformed into edible concrete. Rexlen sat to Spring's left, his plate clean except for a few crumbs. *It may have taken him awhile to chew each piece, but at least he didn't use a knife on my potatoes. Love that man.*

Zavia poured a healthy dose of gravy onto her turkey, keeping her eyes on the cookies in front of her, "The BelReginar and I came to a compromise. I can return to the Moon but..."

"But?" Spring prompted.

"I have to return once Commander Baldric...I mean," Zavia glanced at Rexlen, "Rexlen finishes his assignment. I...I told her I would not continue to fly."

"What? You're going to quit Orion?" Pam sputtered, practically choking on her mashed potato. She grabbed her goblet, taking a gulp, "What are you going to do then?"

"You mean you'll have to leave as soon as Rexlen finishes?" Spring's eyes flew to Rexlen in shock, "You're not staying? What's going to happen to...to..." *To us ?* She felt dizzy and faint, blood rushing to her toes as she stared into his expressionless eyes. He blinked, looking away, choosing to gaze at her fingers near his. Zavia and Pam's chatter seemed far away ...a babble.

"Well, I suppose I could read all of my books. We will see." Zavia was saying, finally reaching for a cookie. "Endari is so far away from the Moon ...maybe I can fly a trip or two, who is going to tootle tale on me?" Zavia cast a meaningful stare at Rexlen.

"It's Tattle tale!" Pam laughed.

"And I have a message from Comm—, I mean Rexlen's mother." Rexlen looked up, startled. "She arrived at court the same day you left. She missed seeing you by hours."

"She never comes to Endari anymore." Rexlen's face a peculiar expression, he turned his intense eyes onto Zavia, "why was I not informed she was en route to Endari? How long did she stay? Is everything all right? Was she okay?"

"She looked stunning as ever." Zavia turned to Spring. "Lady Dreux'Jalio, is so pretty she is ...what do you call it, Pam?"

"Bitch pretty." Pam answered sliding the rest of her potatoes under her napkin.

"Uh,...yes," Zavia continued, "It was believed she would have been consort instead of Placagearine."

"Pla..what?" Spring looked questioningly at Rexlen. His face was hard, his jaw clenched.

"It is a tradition. Time honored…reserved only for the noble women. His mother, Lady Dreux'Jalio is from the ----"

"Bentorr class." Rexlen finished, his face flushed a deep color, his eyes on Spring's. "Landed, old families with distant royal blood. My mother's grandmother was a princess."

"A cousin of Zavia's?" Pam asked, munching on a cookie.

"She is not related to the current house, no." He looked deeply uncomfortable with the subject, his cookie lay half eaten on his plate. "Were my brothers and sisters present? Lord Dreux'Jalio?"

Zavia shook her head, "Just Lord Dreux'Jalio." Zavia grinned. "He tried to buy your mother's portrait again. Javarr refused of course. You should have seen Onaldi's face when the whole court started fawning over your mother! Even Javarr himself !"

"Wish I could've met her." Spring said quietly.

"Her portrait is the biggest picture in the palace." Zavia slid three more cookies onto her plate, "She has light hair and violet colored eyes… all the Bentorr's do. They come from the northern part of Endari. They don't stick out like the rest of us. A lot of Endarion intelligence are Bentorr, right, Rexlen?"

"I thought your mom lived on another planet?" Spring asked.

"She does. She left Endari when she married. She lives on Kelti now with my stepfather." He slanted a look at Spring, "Perhaps you'll meet her. I…I told her about you." He said with a slight smile. Spring's mouth parted.

"Ah ha!" Pam squealed. "She was on a mission! Typical mom!"

"The portrait of the lady in purple?" Spring sat up straight, "That's your mom?"

Rexlen nodded once.

"Learn something new every day." Pam said matter factually. "More cookies, anyone?"

* * *

"You have quite a…talent for the replicator," Rexlen said into her ear, pulling her closer, drawing his long legs up around her in the curving chair. Spring snuggled against his chest, her eek pressed close to his heart, tapping her fingers gently in time to his beats. It was just the two of them now, in his private chambers, snuggling in his curved 'figure eight' shaped chair. Rexlen had moved it, placing it by the window so they could see the multicolored space. For once Rexlen was in civvies, wearing loose pants and a tunic with the same soft sheen as his eyes. He rocked her gently between his knees, his fingers smoothing over the silk of her robe.

"You're joking, right?" Spring peeked up at him with a skeptical look, "Yeah, a talent for managing to turn replicator food into stones only a three legged troll would eat."

Rexlen let out a ripple of laughter, his eyes lighting up mischievously, "Which troll? A Mactofollese water troll? Or perhaps you mean the humble Captovimona forest troll? How about the agile, Nocturnarean mountain troll? And you must not forget the underground trolls of Caliguarr …"

"Trolls?" Spring pulled her head away, staring up at him, incredulous, "Trolls…really exist? Three legged? Do they…um, live under bridges? You've seen these things in person?"

"Just the three legged kind," Rexlen replied, straight faced. "Bridges? No, maybe I will tell you about trolls. The three legged kind of course, although I would not want to waste your delicious food on them."

Spring shivered, letting out a nervous laugh, snuggling closer, "No, thanks! I'll take my Alien 101 lessons one Alien at a time!" She bit her tongue as soon as the words slipped out. "I meant …"

"Spring." Rexlen said softly. Spring raised her face, staring into his liquid silver eyes. She felt her heart quicken, she lowered her gaze to his wide, sensual mouth. She reached out with her finger, tracing his lips lightly, her eyes on his, watching as the color gradually deepened, warming with a light from within. She wet her lips, his eyes followed the motion, before returning to her eyes with a burning intensity that excited her. She turned around slowly, tantalizingly in his lap, pressing her body to his, molding herself against the length of him, her breasts full and tender against him. Her hips undulating.

She relished how hard and firm his body felt, a hot shifting wall of muscle and arousal. Hers. With a low groan in his throat, he pressed her harder into him; his mouth closing on hers, claiming her as his legs locked her between them. His hands running down her back sending tiny sparks of sensation that made her whimper, her nipples grow taut and swollen, sending a throbbing heat down, down. Her fingers in his hair, lowering her right hand to the base of his neck, the tree branch shaped arousal veins were pronounced, raised, pulsating under her hand, giving off heat. Spring ran her fingers lightly over the arousal veins, rewarded by his sharp gasp. He broke off the kiss, moving out from under her, and onto his feet. He stood there for a moment breathing hard, staring down at her with a penetrating gaze, she stared back, lips parted. He moved suddenly, leaning down, scooping her up into his arms, Spring grasped his shoulders, her fingers inches away from the arousal veins on his left.

"Maybe we shouldn't," Her voice came out husky, her eyes locked on his. "What if you're called to the bridge? They seemed to have a knack for paging when we're alone. And the—"

"We'll worry about that later," Rexlen silenced her with a searing kiss, hugging her close. He broke off the kiss, gazing down at her, his eyes hot, burning, "Well, my lady?" he asked thickly.

"Yes...jatah," She whispered in Endarion.

Wordlessly, he carried her across the room, his bedchamber door sliding open, before sliding shut.

Three days later.

Spring, Zavia and Pam stood with their faces pressed against the small, waist high observation window in the hall by the lifts. Outside, the

Moon gleamed like a grey boulder with scattered lights, domes and tiny craters. It looked so barren compared to Endari's ultramarine blue water and cotton candy clouds. Still, it was so loved…so the Moon. Solid, grey, reliable Moon. Lurking behind, Earth dwarfed the Moon, rotating slowly, half of it cloaked in shadow, the other half glorious blue and milky white against stark black. It looked much closer to the Moon than it really was.

"Home sweet home." Spring mused.

"Which one, Earth or the Moon?" Pam joked, her eyes glued to the window.

"I don't know." Spring answered, watching as the Moon grew bigger, closer. Soon they would go into orbit, and shuttle down to the EF base. She cast a confused stare at her friends, "That's funny …Earth is home, but then so is the Moon."

"Maybe you will add Endari too," Zavia winked. "You shall be Rexlen's wife, my aunt! Duchess of Baldric! Three homeworlds!"

"Don't get too excited, Zavia." Spring said grinning. Rexlen's wife. *I kinda like the sound of that*

* * *

The EF base looked like a ground based cluster of stars as their shuttle approached. Bright lights were everywhere, from the landing lights to the hangers. A few tiny pops of light rippled on the ground like a tidal wave of fireflies .

"Paparazzi." Spring eyed the small horde of flashes as their shuttle landed, taxiing to close to the open hanger ablaze with stark light and officials. Their shuttle came to a stop in front of a lined carpet walkway. The carpet was far from being red, but dark blue with the Earth Federation emblem on it. Armed guards were everywhere. Spring swallowed hard, her stomach cramping, "What a crowd!"

"Like we're rockstars." Pam said, her green eyes wide, her voice tinged with fear. "So many. My hair must look like—why didn't I pack my color wand!" She hastily yanked her hair out of its ponytail, digging into her purse, brushing it out.

Zavia glanced at Rexlen, watching his stern profile as he sat beside one of his officers at the controls. He glanced outside, the harsh base lights illuminating his profile, bouncing off his eyes, making them glow strangely. His hair black, stark against skin which looked bluish grey under the harsh glare .Her eyes fell toward the back of his neck. His arousal veins, or Pleauxurra were flat and as pale as his skin, half hidden by his uniform collar. He looked very 'alien' in that moment. Memories of the past few nights, made heat rise to her face, and desire course through her. She tore her eyes away from him, chagrined to find Zavia staring at her knowingly in the semi dark shuttle.

As soon as the shuttle stopped, Rexlen removed his harness, making his way toward where Spring, Zavia and Pam sat. He shook his head at his young looking officer by the door, before taking a seat beside Spring. Her hands froze on her harness buckle, staring up at him expectantly.

"Is your harness jammed, Miss Stevens?" He asked pleasantly, ignoring the fit of coughing from Pam and Zavia, Allow me to assist you." He leaned forward, his hands moving over hers, his forehead almost touching hers, "Dinner tonight? Area 51?" He said in a low voice. Spring smiled, nodding her head. "Good." He said as he unbuckled her harness, moving away, standing up, he looked over at Zavia. The laughter had vanished from Zavia's face, now ashen and tense. She was already unfastened, her hands clasped in her lap. Pam was busily applying gloss beside her. Spring's gloss. Spring bit her tongue. *No biggie. Hope I haven't licked all my lipstick off. Too late now.* She took a quick peek with the polished silver of her harness buckle, before looking back at Rexlen.

"Ready, my lady?" Rexlen asked, offering his hand. Without a word, Zavia slid her hand in his rising. For the briefest of seconds, Spring saw The BelFilia in her friend. Regal. Haughty. Alien.

"Of course." Zavia said coolly, with a slight smile, releasing his hand, "Last one out is a rotten melon."

"Rotten egg." Pam unbuckled her harness, standing up, shaking one of her legs. "Last one out is a rotten egg." Rexlen looked at Pam as if she were a certifiable nutcase, before signaling his officer to open the shuttles doors.

The shuttle was awash in a stark, blue white light, with flashes everywhere. Spring squinted, barely making out Rexlen stepping forward, followed by two accompanying officers, that assisted Zavia as she hopped down onto the blue carpet. EF soldiers stood close to the shuttle, their visors down. *At least someone's eyes will not be fried by the 1,000 watt lights.* Spring stumbled toward the shuttles doors, refusing to grope like a blind woman. A strong, firm hand clamped down on her right hand, then another one griped her waist, gently lifting her down. Spring shielded her eyes, staring up. Rexlen. She grinned. *My knight in shining space lights.*

"Hey! Can someone please help me down?" Pam called out, "I can't see the ground!"

* * *

The meeting with the EF and Orion Corporate security ate up half the 'day'. It took Spring a few minutes to adjust to Moon life again and the lack of day and night. Especially since the EF base refused to use the generated 'blue' sky that hung over Lunar East and the rest of the cities on the Moon.

After the short walk down the blue carpet, Rexlen had disappeared, glancing over his shoulder at her, before walking off with a group of EF men and a few unfamiliar Endarions in plain clothes. The paparazzi were mostly holograms and droids, the holograms flickered and shifted, shouting questions, while the droids (actually small metal spheres with cameras) bobbed and floated around snapping pictures. Spring was fascinated by the droid spheres, making out the companies they represented: USA TODAY, BERLINER MORGENPOST, THE NEW YORK TIMES, HERALD TRIBUNE, PEOPLE MAGAZINE, EDEN DAILY PLANET.

After what seemed like an eternity, Orion corporate loaded Zavia, Spring, and Pam into a company space rover; taking them to the StarPort, finally leaving EF headquarters. At the StarPort, they went over things all over again, this time for Inflight heads and what looked like every nosy supervisor on duty. The ones not crammed into the conference room, patrolled the hallway, sailing by the closed glass doors regularly, their steps slowing to a crawl as they passed. At least InFlight headquarters was away from the general flight attendant population. Spring had never ventured this far into the lounge, not even during her visit with her supervisor after Zavia was kidnapped. The headquarters was one floor up from the 'real' lounge, sterile, glass walls and doors, full of the supervisors of flight attendants supervisors. Everything was silver and white up there, walls, furniture, lights. No plants. The supervisors wore their own clothes up here. Grey of course.

"So glad that's over," Spring sighed as they headed down stairs toward the lounge. "Can't wait to take a nice, relaxing shower." *And see Rexlen tonight. Maybe I can talk him into some classic Star Trek?*

"And some fresh out of the oven m&m cookies!" Zavia added.

"Yeah, no more sonic showers for me!" Pam said as they walked toward the lounge entrance. It looked the same, flight attendants hurrying in and out of the two sliding sets of doors, dragging their luggage behind them. Spring watched as one group of ten babbled their way out the doors, looking fresh and ready to go, while another group walked quickly and purposefully toward the lounge. The group heading toward them had that 'Space Lag' look, tired but eager to get inside. Walking past the lounge was the only way to get outside to the shuttle area. "1730 shuttle should be here any min if we hurry! I bet—" Pam stopped in her tracks, staring hard at the approaching crew, the color draining from her face.

"Pam? What is it?" Spring asked in alarm, her hand on Pam's arm, "What's wrong?"

"Adiva." Pam said in a hollow voice, "That's Adiva's crew. The Eden crew." Pam nodded her head toward the group, now a few feet away, Adiva heading up the rear. She was busy chatting to one of her crew, ignoring Pam, Zavia and Spring as she followed her crewmembers inside at the same time as a large group exited.

"Adiva and Guy?" Zavia turned bewildered eyes on Pam. "It is just a rumor, right?"

"True." Pam says tightly, glancing at Zavia and Spring, staring at the lounge doors, "Girls, I…need to do something in the lounge." Pam looked toward them, her expression strange, "I'll take the next shuttle."

Spring didn't like the strange calm on Pam's face, "Pam…are you sure you want to do this now? "

"It's time. I need to take care of it now." Pam took a few steps toward the doors, side stepping a few exiting flight attendants, before stopping to loom over her shoulder, "Don't worry guys," she said with a trace of her usual smile. "I'm not going to do a Vulcan neck pinch or anything! Just say what I should've said awhile ago."

'Well, we are coming too then," Zavia caught up with Pam just as the doors slid open. Spring hurried forward, nearly tripping over someone's suitcase.

"Sorry!" Spring called out over her shoulder to the owner of the suitcase. "Pam! I'll hold your earrings!"

The lounge was always overwhelming, but 'Rush Hour' was worse. Add 'Bid Award Day' and it was a nightmare of hurried F/A's lined up at computer stations, rows of halo images of schedules, hovering in front of the feverish, flushed faces. Small groups of flight attendants leaned against the walls, near the sign in portals and by the help desk, gossiping, complaining. Black luggage lined the walls still decorated with virtual signs that shifted from red and green 'Happy Holidays' to the festive multicolored 'Happy New Year'. Holiday music still blared from overhead speakers interrupted occasionally by announcements.

Pam stood a few feet from the entrance, her eyes scanning the crowd. Zavia and Spring stood behind her. A guy raced by them, nearly knocking them over with his suitcase, a waft of cologne behind him.

"Sorry 'bout that!" he called out, looking over his shoulder, his eyes widening with recognition. He was so busy staring at them, he slammed into a 'senior mama' flight attendant. She glared at him, before huffing off toward the restrooms.

"It's them!" He said out loud to no one. "It's the princess! The Alien princess!" He said loudly, pointing. The room grew quiet. Spring looked uneasily around them. All eyes were on them, each face full of varying expressions. Most were staring at Zavia.

"A real princess?" Someone whispered. "Which one is the Alien?"

"Come on," Pam ignored the small group forming around them, "Let's find Adiva."

"Looking for Adiva?" A mature looking, purser in red asked. "She's in the snack room."

"Thanks." Pam weaved her way through the crowd. Zavia and Spring followed. Spring was a little annoyed by the spectators that trailed behind them, following them into the break room. Spring had always liked this room. It had a peaceful, library feel, with couches and armchairs and a real fish aquarium that gurgled right along with the snack machines to the right. The walls were still painted grey, like the rest of the lounge, but the dark red sofas warmed it up a bit. As usual, the room reeked of burnt popcorn and coffee. Adiva was seated between the wall TV and the bookcase filled with donated books. She had a small group of cronies sitting near her, all of them leaning forward, listening to whatever she was saying. Pam walked briskly past a few curious onlookers, glancing up from their devices and computers, stopping a few feet from Adiva. Adiva's group quieted, turning to stare up at Pam and what looked like the entire Luna base behind her. She paused in the middle of her story, looking up at Pam, her mouth stretching into a smile.

"Pam! Zavia! Spring!" Adiva exclaimed, rising from her seat, her made up eyes gleaming, "Welcome back!" She glanced at Zavia, "I was so worried about you all." She oozed.

"Thank you." Zavia says stiffly, turning away from Adiva. Adiva looked back at Pam, her smile becoming smug.

"You know, Pam, I was just telling Gu—uh, Tom…"

Spring felt anger flood her cheeks as she watched Pam's face drain of color, her eyes filling with pain. Zavia saw it too, turning pale flashing eyes on Adiva, who flinched under Zavia's direct stare. "Adiva, you —" Zavia began.

"Zavia, it's all right," Pam placed a hand on Zavia's arm, shaking her head, "I ..I think I can handle this."

"Are you sure Pam?" Spring asked, her eyes flicking to Adiva's tight smile, and crossed arms, her group of friends standing behind her. Spring had the overwhelming urge to wipe that patronizing smile off Adiva's overly made up face.

"Yeah," Pam's voice quivered slightly, her eyes locked on Adiva. "I think it's time to get it all out in the air, wouldn't you agree?"

The crowd was silent, forming a wide 'fight' circle around the two women. Only the sound of scheduling paging a standby flight attendant, broke the tension that was slowly building. Adiva shrugged her narrow shoulders, a look of mock innocence filling her eyes, "What are you talking about?"

"About Guy."

"Who?" Adiva's face was blank for a moment, before recognition, "Oh…him!" Her voice was carefully controlled, upbeat, while her face had hardened into a mask, her eyes watchful, "What about him?"

"He was mine! You claimed to be my friend …I trusted you, confided in you." Pam paused, before continuing, her voice firmer, stronger, "The you went behind my back, stole Guy away …"

"Pam," Adiva took a small step back, rolling her eyes at the gathered crowd. "I don't know what you're talking about. Really!"

"Cut the lies." Spring snapped. "We know the truth."

"Why, Adiva? What did I ever do to you?" Pam said, her voice vibrating with anger, "I mean, did you think I was that stupid? That I could not see through the bull?"

Adiva was quiet. Her blue eyes hostile, her lips pressed together in a hard line. She stared back at Pam, her arms crossed, tapping one of her feet.

"I guess you're just a liar, huh?" Pam said in a still voice, "What else have you lied about? Did you poison his mind with lies like you poisoned mine? Were you that afraid of me?"

"I'm not afraid of you," Adiva shot in a low voice, barely moving her lips, "He's mine. Not yours. Get over it already."

"Why not tell the truth, why continue with the charade?" Zavia asked.

Adiva shrugged her shoulders casually. "Seeing him was none of her business," she said in a bored voice.

"But you made it her business." Spring pressed, "you told Pam about him every chance you got. What kind of creature are you?"

"Spring," Pam glanced at her. "Please let me, I need to do this."

"Oh, please! Spare me!" Adiva turned around, ready to walk away. The crowd of spectators blocked her path, "Parties over people, move!" She barked angrily. No one budged.

"Adiva." Pam called. Adiva looked over her shoulders, her eyes two dark, hostile slits. "I feel sorry for you." Pam said softly, moving closer, "I don't know what made you into the thing you are, but I hope to god, I never end up like you."

"What does that mean?"

"You're a cruel person." Pam answered calmly, "You hate the passengers, and you feel like you have to stab people in the back...poison the minds of others. You cheat…you don't play fair." Pam smiled, "I'm glad I'm not like you."

"Give yourself a few years in this job, and you'll be exactly like me." Adiva shot back.

Pam shook her head, a look of pity in her eyes, "No, I will never be like you. I will never prey on friends. Steal their happiness. Be a bitter old bitch like you."

"Bitch?" Adiva said shrilly.

"You may have him now," Pam said coldly. "But not for long. You'll never trust him, will you?" Pam smiled a radiant smile, "You see, that's the best revenge. You are both liars. You'll never fully trust his words."

"Well, he's never going back to you."

"How do you know? I was with him last month." Doubt crept into Adiva's face.

"You're a liar." Adiva snapped.

"No," Pam said evenly, "I'm afraid that title goes to you."

Adiva stood there for a moment, before pushing through the crowd, stalking off like an angry scarecrow. The audience stared after her, a few glancing back at Pam with astonished faces. Someone made a loud cat 'meow ' hissing sound. Slowly the crowd dispersed, a few patting Pam on the back, smiling at her.

"Good for you!" Someone said in the crowd, clapping .

Spring moved forward, giving Pam a quick hug, "Way to go, girl!" Spring said proudly.

"Vunda'klat!" Zavia grinned, clapping along with the others.

Spring stepped back, watching Pam. Pam smiled, tears standing in her eyes, "Pam, you okay?"

Pam looked down at her hands, then up at Spring, smiling a watery smile, "A hard lesson learned." She shrugged, managing a shaky laugh. "Oh well, huh? Wish I could go back in time."

"What would you change?" Zavia asked, supplying a tissue.

Pam sighed, wiping her eyes, "Being so trusting...so stupid. Didn't realize people were like that. You would think I'd know better—I live in New York! I...I miss him. I know, I know, but it's true. He's a good guy, he really is. A good friend. He's like your Wesley...a wonderful person, friend."

Spring enveloped her in a fierce hug. "So are you, Pam. Never forget that, okay?" She pulled back, "His loss, right? If he wants to end up with a fake tart like her..."

Zavia slid her arm in Pam's leading her out of the break room, "Come to Endari again. I will introduce you to the most handsome men in the universe! Princes, dukes! Why, they will make Guy look like, uh..."

"Chopped liver?" Pam supplied.

"Exactly!" Zavia grinned. "Chopped liver!"

"Um, Zavia?" Spring asked as they headed down the hall toward the exit, "Why are you not with one of these handsome Endarions?"

"Simple," Zavia replied as the fresh air greeted them, "I am related to most of them. You are dating my nephew, and besides," Zavia said with a wicked smile, "I am partial to human men. My new passion!"

The shuttle to Lunar East, was parked a few yards away already filling up with passengers and crew. Spring, Zavia, and Pam, ran across the small walkway, sliding into seats just as the shuttle doors slid shut.

"Ah ha...the real reason she came back to the Moon!" Pam laughed.

* * *

TWO MONTHS LATER.

Spring sat on her jumpseat in the forward galley, her standard crew tray of chicken breast, veggies, and salad, and appetizer of seared tuna balanced on her lap. It was a miniature replica of one of their business class meal, all pre arranged in a slotted crew tray. Spring poked at her crew meal, stabbing at the dry chicken with distaste. She wondered how the passengers could stomach the cardboard food, even if it did look enticing in its separated tray, neatly divided. Her stomach grumbled, her mind thinking of her upcoming dinner and movie date with Rexlen. Homemade dinner. Rexlen was now addicted to 20th – 21st century sci-fi movies. They were slowly making their way down a long list. They had finally reached the 1980's. Spring smiled ruefully at her food. *Homemade pizza please.*

"How's the chicken?" Stacey, her purser waltzed by, opening one of the ovens, quickly plucking a cooked entrée out with her bare hands, setting it on the counter. Stacey was one year senior, and already a purser holding Earth to Moon trips. Spring stared at the sensible, serious looking girl with awe. The only other person she knew whose parents did not genetically erase her curly hair.

"It's okay," Spring stood up, stepping into the galley, stooping to open a storage bin, sliding her unfinished meal inside, along with the other dirty meals. "Think I'll do a walk through, grab some hot cocoa, see what they have leftover in economy. Do you need anything?"

"Naw, go ahead." Stacey leaned against the counter, slicing into her meal, "I'll give the steak a try." Stacey lowered her voice, glancing out into the darkened cabin, "That old lady at 4B is like, the only one still awake. She kinda creeps me out…the way she keeps staring at all of us."

"I'll check her out. She's been nice to me." Spring carefully made her way into the aisle her eyes roaming over the sleeping passengers, most harnessed snugly in their seats. Outside, nothing but stars, they still had three or four hours left before they reached the Moon. There was only one reading light on in Business, the old lady, Ms. Grant sat reading quietly in 4B.

She glanced up at Spring, smiling as Spring went by. Spring smiled back, the woman reminded Spring of Gran-Libby with her snowy white hair falling in shoulder length waves. Her lean, unlined face, carefully made up with a young looking bright pink lipstick, and carefully arched eyebrows. She looked 90- ish,with keen intelligence in her warm eyes. Spring stopped by her seat, leaning over discreetly.

"May I get you anything, Ms. Grant?"

Ms. Grant looked up from her book with an inviting smile, "I'm okay, but thanks for asking, sweetie. You know," she put her book down beside her, looking excitely at Spring. "I used to do this a long time ago. Well," she chuckled, "not in space...although it seemed out of this world sometimes!"

"You were a flight attendant?" Spring asked intrigued. "What airline and from when to when?"

"Orion." Ms. Grant said. "For over forty years! I never made it to number one in the base ...retired as the fifth most senior out of like, twenty thousand flight attendants."

"Twenty thousand?" *Wow. We only have around eight hundred on the Galactic side.*

"Oh, yeah," Ms. Grant continued. "I take it the Airways side is smaller now? Did everyone switch over to Galactic? I know I would."

"I'm not sure about the Airways side," Spring said. "We call it the domestic part. We...we don't mix."

"Ah, I see."

"Ms. Grant..."

"Call me, Erica. I may be old, but I still feel 30!"

"Ms... Erica, did you know my grandmother? Libby...I mean, Elizabeth Mattsson? She was Elizabeth Raine before she married my grandfather."

Ms. Grant's eyes widened. "You're Libby's grandchild? Are you...are you kidding me? Really?"

Spring gave a hesitant nod.

"Oh my goodness! I can see it now...small world!" Ms. Grant grinned. "What's your name, precious?"

"Spring. Spring Raine Stevens."

"Hilarious!" Ms. Grant mused, with a gentle shake of her head, "Libby used to joke about her future children's names! Bet she talked your parents into naming you that! Libby's grandchild! I shared a crashpad with your grandma, back in Kew Gardens!"

"You...you did?" Spring whispered, trying to keep her voice down.

"Sure did! Back in 2011 to 2013. God, there were ten of us in that place! Bunkbeds, luggage racks ...I have some pictures somewhere." Ms. Grant reached down, pulling her purse out, digging through it, finally producing a small, ancient screen album pad. The square palm sized device lit up, Ms. Grant bent over it, "I bet I still have pics from the crashpad ... how is Libby?"

"She's fine." Spring lied. Lately, Gran slept a lot. She had not painted in months.

"That's good. Ah! Here, have a look." Spring kneeled down beside Ms. Grant's chair, squinting at the still images, surprised at how recent they looked. They had to be at least sixty years old. "Here's one of all of us at Kew, that's your grandmother there on the couch."

A much younger Gran-Libby sat on the couch, her legs tucked under her, wearing a backwards looking robe with long wide sleeves, an open Apple laptop sat perched on her lap. She grinned at the camera, while someone beside her made a face. Spring was taken aback by how much she looked like Gran-Libby.

"Your Grandmother was always on Skype." Ms. Grant looked up at Spring. "Talking on Skype to her Swede."

"Granddad Sven." Spring smiled fondly.

"That's right! She was commuting back and forth to Stockholm then. Think I even met him once…how is he? He was so tall and handsome. They were so striking together. Ebony and Ivory." Spring winced.

"He passed away two years ago," Spring felt her heart tug painfully, her eyes misting. She focused on the smiling image of Gran-Libby, young and in her thirties. "He was …103."

"Sorry to hear that." Ms. Grant looked down at her lap, turning the screen off, before smiling brightly at Spring. "You know, Spring, all of us dreamed about this …traveling to space. Here you are doing it! I blew half my retirement for this and it makes me smile."

"It does?"

"Yep. I mean, when I flew…well, when I started….people didn't dress up. They …" Ms. Grant's face looked sad and cynical for a moment, "they didn't respect us. It was nothing like the days when all the old dinosaurs were called 'stewardesses' and wore girdles and pillbox hats. People would come on half naked and they never listened to us. It's so different now." Ms. Grant leaned back in her seat, gazing out the star filled window, then back at Spring. "Everyone on here is dressed up, looking good, traveling to the Moon! This is what it must've been like during the golden age of airplane travel. I totally envy you guys. You're pioneers. Libby must be so proud of you."

"Yes," Spring said softly. "She is."

21
LIBBY

"Oh, I remember her," Gran-Libby let out a raspy laugh. "Erica Grant, eh? One sloppy ass chick and she liked to 'borrow' food!" Gran-Libby laughed again, "But she was cool though. She cooked up some lasagna awesomeness with homemade garlic bread. We had a blast at that place…good peeps."

Spring leaned forward at the dining room table, resting her elbows, her half eaten breakfast beside her. She smiled up at Gran-Libby's image on the tele-screen. "She seemed nice." Spring said, trying to ignore how frail Gran-Libby looked with her blankets going up to her chin, making Gran-Libby look like a brown baby bird. Spring was lucky to catch her awake, even if she was still in bed at seventeen hundred. Gran looked older, her face more drawn, but her eyes still sparked with energy.

"Kew days seem like a century ago," Gran-Libby mused. "Flying back and forth to Stockholm…seeing your grandpapa. His birthdays coming up in a few days. Will you …are you coming to our blue marble for a visit?"

Spring looked away from the screen, gazing out the window, "no, I have a trip to Mars today. I'll visit next month, I hope."

"Cool." Gran-Libby sighed, sinking deeper against her pillows. "Bring that hunk of alien studlyness, will you? How's your painting holding up? Where did you hang it? Like it?"

"The paintings above my bed," Spring lied, feeling guilty. Gran's painting was still on the floor, propped against the wall by the door to her room. Love it, thanks!"

"Awesome! You know it's named after my favorite song? Drops of Jupiter? Played that song to death, back in the day. Better let ya go get ready for your trip to Mars. See ya soon, Spring Chick, bring your man with you when you visit. Wanna learn more about these pleasure veins I read about."

"Gran!" Spring felt herself blushing furiously, "Where did you learn about those?"

A slow Cheshire smile creased Gran-Libby's face, warming her eyes, "looked them up! Still know how to go online! See you soon, I love you, Spring Chick!" Spring looked over at the front door, someone was turning the knob. A few seconds later, the door swung open, revealing a rosy cheeked Pam and a handsome EF officer.

"Bye, Gran! Ditto, see ya soon!" Spring said hastily, ending the call. Her attention drawn to the vaguely familiar looking officer, whose arms were bursting with groceries. He dutifully followed Pam into the kitchen. Spring leaned out of her chair, her eyes following Pam and the handsome stranger with interest.

"Morning, Spring! Thought you were flying today." Pam came out of the kitchen, officer in tow. "Is Zavia home too?" Pam looked around, her forced smile held a slight trace of roomie annoyance.

"Morning," Spring said casually. "Zavia's on a trip, and I sign in, in a couple of hours. So I won't be here for breakfast or even for tomorrows breakfast!" She grinned. "Morning, Lieutenant?"

Pam reddened, "Oh! Spring, this is Adam, Adam my roomie, Spring. Spring, you remember him from the EF base right? He helped us get on base that night ...took us to Rexlen's ship?"

"I thought you looked familiar!" Spring stared at Adam with new eyes, "Thanks for helping us that night ...that seemed like a million years ago!"

Adam chuckled, "sounds like you two had an adventure!" He glanced at a blushing Pam, "More glamorous than my office job. Warships. I haven't even set foot off, off world yet!"

"Have buddy passes will travel," Pam laughed, grabbing hold of his arm, steering him back into the kitchen. "Come on you, I need your help in the kitchen! Pop tarts are my only specialty, so I'm going to need help with pancakes! Have a good, long trip Spring! Sorry you have to sign in so soon...bye!"

"I better get dressed (*for my sign in four hours from now*), nice meeting you Adam, later Pam!" Spring rose from the table, missing Rexlen, feeling a little jealous. She went into her room shutting the door on giggles from the kitchen. *Get this trip over with, and I'll see Rexlen. He'll be back from Titan by then.*

* * *

Spring stood beside her Purser, watching as the ground staff operated the forward boarding door. The door slid up from the floor slowly, rising up into the ceiling, revealing bit by bit several pairs of polished black shoes and heels. Two men, and three women. "Are there normally so many agents for Mars?" Spring asked her purser under her breath, her eyes going from one somber looking agent to another. Only two wore the dark grey uniforms under bright green vests, the other three wore plain suits.

"Not normally." Spring's purser glanced at her quickly, a strange expression in his eyes, before he moved toward the door, handing the nearest agent their entry computer sheets. One of the suits stepped up, speaking low in her pursers ear. The purser nodded curtly, sliding a look toward Spring. Spring stared back, her mouth going dry, her stomach tightening into a ball. *Rexlen? Zavia? Did something happen to Rexlen, Zavia or Pam?*

She swallowed hard, just as the pilots stepped out of the flight deck, joining her, their faces carefully neutral.

The purser moved away from the door, standing beside the captain, while the suits and agents lined the jetway, blending in with the walls as the passengers filed past. Spring slid a look to her purser, "What was that all about? What are the suits here for?" She asked anxiously between good-byes. He did not answer, bidding the passengers farewell in a hollow voice, his wide smile not reaching his eyes. Spring blinked, forcing her mouth to stretch into a wide smile, mouthing 'goodbye' because the words refused to come. She kept catching the pilots and the purser staring at her between passengers. She clutched her hands tightly behind her back, squeezing them so hard, the fingers on her left hand began to tingle under her right hand. Her eyes shifted back to the jetway anxiously.

Finally, the last passengers were trickling off, only a small family were left, taking their time gathering their belongings at the back of the cabin. Spring glanced back at the suits, one of the women stepped forward, close to the boarding door. She was smaller than the rest, her asymmetrical hair cut did not fit her freshly scrubbed face, revealing slight ridges on her forehead. Half Falariese. Her eyes were kind, her slight smile gentle. "Miss Stevens? Hello, my name is Suzy, I'm with Mars InFlight."

"Y..Yes?" Spring rasped. She could barely breathe, black spots were beginning to block her vision.

"Would you mind following us, dear?" Suzy said, her voice sounding faint, miles away. Spring looked over at her purser and pilots. They met her gaze with sympathetic eyes. Dread seemed to squeeze the air out of her lungs. *What's going on?*

"Go on, Spring," her purser said. "Don't worry about your stuff, we'll get it."

"Su..sure …okay." Spring said, willing her legs forward.

Numbly, Spring followed Suzy down the long jetway, ignoring her first glimpses of Mars and its sunrise. Instead, Spring focused on the women's shoes, how the back of her right heel was scuffed on the inside, showing white streaks. The other two suits are close behind her, their shoes slapping loudly on the tile floor. As they led her through customs, then down an elevator; Spring seemed vaguely aware that Mars's JTK StarPort was not as luxurious as the Moon. Lower ceilings and long wide corridors with glass walls lined with large potted plants and the occasional leather tufted bench. Even the carpeted floor was in a soft muted color of beige and rust brown. Spring glanced outside, half expecting to see dry red soil, but dully registering a terraformed blue sky, half obscured by golden clouds. Directly outside, were the manicured trees and bushes surrounding the StarPort. The bushes were flowering in bright pink flowers, like azaleas. Spring stopped to stare, watching the activity in the 'parking lot' of the StarPort. Gazing as small two -seater compact cars slowed by the curb, picking up passengers, dropping them off, people hugging hello or good-bye, dragging luggage. In the distance, she could just make out the largest city on Mars, its skyscrapers as tall as those on Earth. AirCars buzzing around like tiny gnats, with trains whizzing by into the suburbs. Mars was a real colony. No protective domes or generated rain here. A replica of Earth.

"Miss Stevens?" The woman prodded gently, tapping her arm. "The lounge is just around the corner." Spring willed her feet forward, turning down another glass walled hallway. The lounge was at the end of the hall, a tiny, L-shaped room, with break area; computer area rolled into one large room with orange furniture, and a toast colored carpet. A couple of flight attendants glanced up from the row of halo-computers against the wall, as Spring followed the suits down a brightly lit yellow hall lined with Orion posters and parked bags.

"In here, Miss Stevens." Suzy held a door open, revealing a room painted in bright yellow. A small box, big enough for a corner shaped desk, an extra chair, and a small bookshelf. The two windows behind the desk overlooked the runway area. Spring stumbled forward, sitting down in the chair facing the desk, while the woman went around the desk, sitting across from Spring.

"Am I in some kind of trouble?" Spring asked in a thin voice. "Has... has something happened?"

Suzy looked down at her hands, then up at Spring, her eyes full of compassion. "Spring, we received a message from Earth," Suzy began. Spring could barely hear her, her heart seemed to echo noisily in her ears. She stared hard at the woman's mouth, while the room closed in, choking her, making her uniform feel too tight across the chest. Spring pulled at her collar.

"What...what message?" Spring asked in a shaky voice.

"Spring," Suzy began again, "I'm so sorry to tell you this, we received a message from your parents. Spring, your grandmother has passed away."

"Passed away." Spring said numbly. The words did not make sense. "Passed away? Gran-Libby?" Spring blinked at the supervisor in disbelief, "I...I just spoke to—passed...away? There must be some kind of miscommunication...that's a mistake."

"I'm so sorry, Spring. We have a member of the Employee Assistance Program on the way, she should be here shortly." Suzy was saying, reaching out to pat Spring's hand, "I'm so sorry, dear. Is there anything I can do?"

"I need to call home." Spring's throat felt tight, "I need to call home." She bit her lip hard, staring out the window, watching as a StarShuttle took off. "I need to call." she repeated.

"Of course." Suzy said solemnly, tapping into her clear screen, swiveling it around to face Spring. The large CALL IN PROGRESS, PLEASE STAND BY, flashed over Spring's reflection. Spring stared at dumbly at the screen. Suzy stood up, smoothing her uniform, clearing her throat, moving around the desk, going toward the door. "I'll just step out for a moment, okay, Spring? I'll just see what's keeping the EAP rep, be right back." Spring didn't answer, just stared at the screen. Suzy paused at the door for a few seconds, then opened it, closing it quietly behind her with a soft click.

"Hello?" Spring's mom filled the tele screen, her face bewildered for a moment, before recognition popped into her eyes. Her mom looked tired, her mouth drawn downward, her eyes puffy."Hi," Her mom whispered.

"Mom," Spring, paused, swallowing hard, twisting her hands in her lap. "Mom, is Gran…?" She couldn't finish, she just stared at her mom's face; her vision blurring as her blinked rapidly, looking away from the screen.

"Yes. She's…she's gone, baby."

"Gone? When? How did this…?" *I just spoke with her.*

"In her sleep. Last night."

Spring shook her head, taking a deep breath, "Gone." she repeated. "But I just spoke to her! Mom…she was fine…what happened?"

Her mom looked down, biting her lip like Spring. Minutes seemed to pass before her mom sighed deeply. "She was sick for awhile, baby, she …"

"Sick?" Spring said sharply, blinking the threatening tears away as she stared hard at her mom's face, "I didn't know she was sick. Why didn't anyone tell me?"

"Spring, she wanted us to keep it a secret from you. She…she didn't…"

"Why would she keep it a secret from me? Why did you and Dad… everybody," Spring felt anger and resentment washing over the pain, "Did Hunter and Summer know she was sick? Was I the only one in the dark?"

Her mom didn't reply. She looked helplessly off screen, her gaze focusing on someone, her mouth quivering. A moment later, Spring's dad popped in view, sitting beside her mom. His face filled with concern as he gazed at her mom. She leaned against him, keeping her eyes down, chewing on her lip. Her dad cleared his throat, his somber eyes meeting Spring's. Spring stared at her mom, feeling horrible. *Mom, just lost her own mother, and here I am giving her the third degree…what's wrong with me?*

"Your grandmother didn't want us to tell you, Springtime…she made us promise we wouldn't ."

"Why?" Spring asked in a raw whisper.

Her dad glanced at her mom, giving her a squeeze. "She wanted you to have a good time flying."

Her mom looked up, her eyes glossy, "She didn't want you to worry, Spring. She knew if you were told…you would come home right away or quit. She didn't want that. She wanted you to enjoy yourself. Baby, we're so sorry we didn't tell you."

Spring nodded silently, feeling the hot tears spill down her cheeks. "When …when is the …" the word *funeral* refused to come out, her throat seemed to close up around it .

"We're worry about that when you get home." Her dad was saying, "One thing at a time, okay, Springtime? We'll wait until you make it home, okay?"

"Kay. Mom?" Spring's mom glanced up, her eyes swimming with tears. "Mom, I'm so sorry about Gran." Spring said, tasting salty tears in her mouth, "I'm sorry about your mom." Her mom nodded, smiling sadly. Her dad cleared his throat, pulling her mom closer to his side, his arm tight around her shoulder.

"Alright then," her dad's voice had taken on a brisk, military tone that soothed her. "Let us know when you'll be back on Earth, ASAP." he looked at her mom again, "We're going to rest now…been a long day, especially for your mom, but call anytime to let us know when you arrive, will you?"

Spring nodded again, sniffling, "I will, Dad."

"Good." her dad said gruffly, "We'll see you soon then. Have a safe flight."

"Okay." She leaned forward, reaching out with a shaky hand to end transmission.

"And Spring?" her dad said suddenly. She looked down at the screen.

"Yeah?"

"We love you, Springtime."

"Love you both too." Spring stared down at the screen, watching as the image of her parents vanished, replaced by the large blocky, END TRANSMISSION, words. She stared at the screen for a long time, listening to the distant roar of a StarShuttle. The screen changed, the Orion Galactic emblem filling the screen as Spring continued to sit there. Minutes passed. A discreet knock sounded at the door, Spring moved her head slightly toward the door.

"Come in." She croaked.

Suzy and another kind looking supervisor walked in. Suzy's companion was older, his hair and mustache sprinkled with grey. He smiled gently, his deep brown eyes shining with warmth and understanding. He was more casually dressed, wearing jeans and a white shirt under his formal looking dark blue blazer. Spring's eyes flicked to his large badge hanging from a lanyard; it had the large letters EAP above a picture of his face, followed by his name : Ron.

"Spring, this is Ron," Suzy moved toward Spring carefully. "Ron is with EAP."

"Hi, Spring." Ron's voice was a calm as a running brook.

"We have booked you on a flight to Earth," Suzy said as she slid into her seat on the other side of the desk. Ron remained by the door, his hands clasped in front of him. "You're scheduled to deadhead to Pegasus I, then change shuttles for your deadhead back to Earth. You'll land in New York by 1700 tomorrow, and Norfolk by 1930. That's a mainline flight…Orion Airways." Suzy was saying in a slow deliberate voice. "Your flight leaves in an hour, hope that's alright?"

Spring managed a small smile, "Yes, thank you. I should let my parents know, thanks."

"Do you want to call them now?" Suzy asked, her fingers poised on the telecall keyboard.

"No, it's late there, I'll wait till Pegasus." Spring stood up, her legs feeling rubbery. She swayed slightly, waving off the assistance of Ron and Suzy. "Thanks again, Suzy. I…I guess I should get my bags."

Ron stepped forward, opening the door, "I'll come with you, Spring, if you don't mind an old grizzled dinosaur tagging along?"

Spring let out a watery laugh. "Thanks. No, I don't mind."

Ron accompanied her out into the hallway, leading back through the maze lounge. At the entrance to the lounge, Spring came to a startled stop, staring at a suitcase similar to hers, down to the small brass star tag attached to the handle. Behind the suitcase, stood her purser and the captain of her flight, both staring at her with slight smiles. Spring felt foolish tears rise up, blinking them furiously away as she strode toward her crewmembers.

"You guys shouldn't be here," Spring frowned, trying to sound angry. "You're on your layover! You've missed an hour of it, you didn't need to wait."

Her purser held up a hand, "We wanted to wait, Spring. It's okay, we wanted to make sure you were fine. I'm so sorry, is there anything I can do?" He asked in a soothing voice, wheeling her bag toward her. The captain handed her shopping bag from Pegasus, giving her shoulder an awkward pat, before stepping back.

"They're sending you to Earth?" The captain asked, his brow furrowed, his thick eyebrows drawn together sternly.

"Yeah, in about an hour." Spring held her shopping bag with a limp hand. "Thanks for waiting you guys." She looked around the lounge, focusing on the two flight attendants, obviously eavesdropping by the computers. "I guess they'll replace me…h…have a safe trip." Her voice caught, she looked down at her shoes. "Tell the rest of the crew—I'll see them. Thanks for bringing my bags."

Her purser reached out, giving her a hug, enveloping her in strong cologne, "Great flying with you, Spring." he stood back, grabbing his suitcase, "I'll be thinking about you and your family, take care. See you around."

The captain reached out, patting her shoulder again, "Have a safe journey back, Spring. I'm so sorry about your grandmother. Take care."

"Thanks," Spring clutched her bags tighter. "She's 101, she's used to be a flight attendant." Spring blurted, "I mean, she...she was 101. Her birthdays in October. She's a Libra." *Shut up, shut up.*

"Then she had a fine life." The captain said, "Take care, Spring."

She watched as her purser and the captain went through the double doors, their suitcases behind them.

"Ready, Spring?" Ron came up, gently taking her suitcase handle and her shopping bag from her hands.

No, I'm not ready. I wasn't ready.I didn't even get to say 'goodbye'. Spring nodded, dry eyed. "Yes, sure."

* * *

"Ladies and gentlemen, we have begun our initial descent into Earth's atmosphere, please recheck the security of your harnesses..."

Spring stared with unseeing eyes out the window, her harness buckled tightly over her chest. It seemed to help her, keep her tears at bay. She felt numb. Not even the thrill of deadheading in Galactic Elite on the Boeing 807 phased her. Her Galactic duvet, pillow and purse sized amenity kit, sat unopened and untouched beside her. Spring had practically froze for most of the flight. She didn't have the energy to open her duvet's plastic package, so she sat in one position, never unbuckling her harness.

"Can I get you anything, kid?" A vaguely familiar flight attendant leaned over, a silver tray of water in her hand. Something about her magenta colored bun...

"No, I'm fine." Spring rasped, scanning the older woman's face in the dim light. "Jackie, right? Eden flight?" The woman looked blank. Spring added, "we ran into an asteroid field?"

"Oh, yeah! Gawd, that was almost a year ago! Good memory, kid!" Jackie grinned. "How are ya doin', goin' home?"

"Yeah."

"Well then," Jackie said hefting her tray up. "Welcome home, kid."

"Thanks." Spring turned back to her window.

22

DROPS OF JUPITER

Virginia Beach. Spring sat in the back seat of her parents car, blinking up at the out of place, cheery blue sky, watching as AirCars flew in clear traffic tubes over head. There were more AirCars in the air compared to last year, making the old fashioned interstate a virtual ghost town of LandCars.

The ride from Norfolk International was quiet. Spring rolled her window down, gulping in the smell of pine, earth and firewood in the air as the scenery slowly changed from sparse tree lined interstate, to towering glass buildings. Row after towering row, some twinkling with lights, Spring could just make out the dark blue-green of the ocean as they finally made it onto Shore Drive. Gran-Libby always complained about how Shore Drive had changed from modest sized condos and private homes to what it was now, full of high rise condos and office buildings. The 'resort' area was further along Shore Drive 's winding curve, most of the hotels and landmarks from Gran's day were long gone. Everything was glass and metal, soaring higher than the next building. Only the beautiful, historic, Y-shaped Cavalier hotel sat majestically on its hill. Her parents building stood near the Cavalier, shrouding it and the cottages and bungalows next to it in a perpetual dusk. A tiny one hundred fifty-three year old 'dollhouse' on a hill.

As they drove past the green Cavalier hillside, with its name planted in large green shrubbery on the slope; Spring tried to crane her neck upwards, hoping to spot her parents 34th floor apartment. Gran-Libby's room faced the old hotel. The sun glinted off of the polished glass, Spring looked away abruptly, rubbing the black dots out of her eyes as her dad drove into the underground parking garage.

In the long elevator ride up, Spring glanced at her parents. Her mom kept her gaze locked on the floor, her arms folded in front of her; fingers tapping against one of the large shiny buttons of her coat. Her dad's trench coat and polished black shoes made him look so military, even in his civilian clothes, but his shoulders slouched slightly, his face drawn.

"Good evening, may I take your coat?" Asked a strange looking man in an old fashioned morning suit with an ascot tie and tails. His smooth unlined face held an empty smile, his glassy eyes focused on Spring as he held out a gloved hand, bowing slightly.

"This is Miles," Her dad said behind her as he helped her mother out of her coat, before peeling his own off, handing it to 'Miles'. "Your moms Christmas gift." Her dad strode past Miles.

"He's a HomeRobot." Her mom added with a glimmer of excitement in her voice. "A Droid."

Spring halted in mid action, her fingers freezing over the buttons of her uniform coat, staring at the bland face of Miles as he waited patiently; hand outstretched, her parents coats folded over his other arm. She looked at him closely, from the top of his wavy molded hair to his somewhat shiny plastic uniform. He was also on the short side, almost nose to nose with Spring. "Miles?" Spring looked over at her parents. She had seen Droids on the Moon, working out on the ramp, handling luggage, but they did not look as lifelike as 'Miles'. Fortunately he did not resemble the scarily realistic 'Stepford' Companion Droids she had glimpsed on flights and at the StarPorts. He could pass for a human at first glance. Even if his face was a bit on the waxy side.

"Gran-Libby named him." Mom said from the couch, slipping off her shoes, curling up under a soft throw. Flowers were everywhere. Bright cheerful lilies and roses, along with sensible green plants, piled on the coffee table and the floor. Her mom sighed tiredly, she looked like she had not slept in days.

"Just checked the message com," her dad walked over to her mom, sitting down beside her, gently moving the edge of the throw out of the way. "Hunter's inbound, he'll land at Oceana in two hours."

Spring handed her coat to Miles, absently thanking him, walking slowly through the living room. The living room drapes were pulled back, revealing the ocean in the distance; the sun beginning to set, turning the sky yellow and red, outlining the clouds. Her feet carried her down the hallway, dragging her suitcase.

Spring stopped by her room, leaving her suitcase in the hall, making her way to the closed door at the end of the hall. She stood in front of the closed door for a long time, her right hand resting against the firm painted wood. She tapped lightly. "Gran?" She whispered, "Gran?" Her hand dropped to the door handle, closing on the cold metal, opening the door a crack, "Gran-Libby?" She swung the door wide.

Everything looked the same. The neatly made up bed with its silk Indian sari duvet cover, the Moroccan night table, the warm saffron colored walls covered with Gran's art. The wooden blinds were drawn up, letting in the last traces of sunlight. The setting sun highlighted Gran-Libby's low bookcase crammed with actual books and framed pictures. Gran's perfume lingered in the room, faint and warm. Spring went over to the bed, staring down at it, before lightly smoothing her hands along the embroidered silk, her eyes moving to the night stand. A worn old fashioned paperback (one she knew Gran-Libby re-read at least once a year), competed with a jumbled mix of jewelry. Three narrow medicine bottles stood out among the color, their white caps stark and prominent. A silver framed picture of Grandfather Sven and Gran-Libby as a young couple smiling at a café somewhere in Sweden. Pictures of Spring's mom as a little girl, along side a photo of Gran's parents. Gran's favorite butterfly ring resting on the edge.

Spring reached out, touching the ring with her finger, as salty tears ran into her mouth. "Gran."

* * *

Gran's memorial service was larger than Spring expected. So many of Gran's old friends and coworkers came out to pay their respects. Most were as ancient as Gran was, over a hundred, some spry, but most were fragile, a few in wheelchairs. It touched Spring to see how many had squeezed into their old flight attendant and pilot uniforms. Their vintage wings flashing dully against sharp navy blue, crisp white shirts, swollen feet crammed into polished black pumps. What really surprised Spring were the somewhat young fifty-ish crewmembers. Her parents held the wake and memorial at the Cavalier next door. It was what Gran had wanted. It was where she and grandfather Sven had had their U.S. wedding reception, and where they celebrated their 50th and 60th anniversaries. There were even a few geriatric colleagues of Grandfather Sven's days at NASA Langley, milling about.

"She was so nice to me on my first trip fresh out of training." A mature matron in her sixties said after the service. The woman still had a girlish voice, despite her soccer mom bob and tight face. "I started in 2042, right out of college. I was on standby at JFK, and they gave me Prague! Your Gran was the Purser. She was so sweet and funny!" The woman laughed. "I try to be like her with my crews today ...well, at least until I retire next year!" she looked at her husband, winking, "or maybe I'll fly until I'm number one in the base."

"We were in the same training class, back in '09!" A reed thin woman piped up, standing beside an equally old but dignified man, both wearing flight attendant uniforms. The woman's cheeks were heavily rouged, matching her raccoon like eyes, dyed blue-black goth hair. The man 's hair was silver, contrasting with his deep tan and sparkling eyes, "Congrats to you new brand of stews! Flights to space! Never thought I'd see the day!"

"Thanks." Spring said politely, excusing herself. She glanced over at her parents, chatting in subdued tones and then at her brother and sister sitting awkwardly at a round table, staring at the gathered crowd.

With the exception of the uniforms, and everyone in black, it felt like a party to Spring. Overhead, chandeliers glittered, casting everyone in flattering light. There was a healthy line at the buffet table, complete with an ice sculpture of an old fashioned jet airplane with a winged couple sitting on one of the wings, like two angels. Gran had specified a D.J., so music from her era played softly but respectfully, a few boogied on the small dance floor; some having kicked off their shoes long ago. Mourners mingled from table to table, hugging, laughing, snapping photos. A few old ladies in uniform waved away the waiters, preferring to circulate around the tables, serving champagne and wine themselves, pretending they were still flying. Of course they were a little tipsy, helping themselves from their own silver trays, while posing for pictures. Spring and her brother and sister were the only 'young ones' in the room.

Spring joined Hunter and Summer, sitting down by the dance floor, watching as a centurion couple danced wildly to some tune from the early 21st century in stocking feet. The jovial atmosphere angered Spring. She plucked a flower from the table arrangement, twirling it in her hand, conscious of her long sleeved, black dress. The same dress she wore when Grandfather Sven died.

"Trust Gran-Libby to go out like this," Summer remarked dryly, making a face. "How embarrassing! She was always so off."

Hunter glared at Summer. "Show respect, Summer. This is what she wanted. She didn't want anyone to be sad."

"But why did she have to do this? It's so…stupid! Look at all of these old…" Summer waved her arms.

"Shut up." Spring leaned forward, jerking her sisters arms down. "When you're one hundred and the last of your family, you can plan whatever funeral you want, but don't make fun of Gran. Leave her alone! At least you got to say goodbye to her." Spring scraped her chair back, snatching up the lone flower. She looked at Hunter, so handsome in his grey E.F. cadet uniform. "Tell Mom and Dad I'm walking home."

* * *

Spring went straight to Gran-Libby's room, curling up in Gran's reading chair by the window, tucking her legs under her skirt, hugging herself. She wished Rexlen was there. Her eyes fell on Gran- Libby's bed.

"I'm sorry, Gran," Spring murmured, staring up at the ceiling. "Sorry I never took you flying up to the Moon. I...I always thought I had more time..." Spring trailed off tasting tears, "Why didn't you tell me you were sick? I would've come home!" Spring looked out the window, resting her head on her knees, gazing at the blurry afternoon clouds. Her eyeliner ran into her eyes, making them sting. "I didn't get to say goodbye, Gran. I didn't...get...to say goodbye. I didn't tell you I loved you."

* * *

A gentle hand shook Spring's shoulder, waking her. For a moment, she thought it was Gran-Libby, smiling down at her in the dim, evening sunlight. Spring rubbed her eyes, blinking up at her mom's face, her mom's hands smoothed her hair, something she used to do when Spring was little.

"Hey there, baby," Her mother's eyes were swollen, despite the slight smile. "Hungry?"

Spring shook her head, unwinding her legs, her neck stiff. She stood up, hugging her mom. "I'm sorry, Mom." Her mom gave her a fierce hug back, stepping back, with Gran's smile.

"She's happy, Spring. She's with your grandpapa Sven now. She missed him so much, now she's up there with him, probably exploring space. Boring the angels with airline stories."

Spring let out a watery laugh, "yeah, I guess. But, she—"

Her mom patted her arm, gently steering her away from the window. "She lived a long time, Spring. A long time. She was ready to go." Her mom sat down on Gran's bed, patting the space beside her. Spring hesitated, then sat down beside her mom. Watching curiously as her mom pulled an old shoebox out from its hiding place behind the pillows. The box was covered over with bright green sari fabric and faux jewels glued onto the cover in a starburst pattern. Spring's mom looked down at the box for a moment, before holding it out to Spring.

"This is for you." She said, offering it to Spring. "Mom wanted you to have this."

Spring sat the box on her lap, staring down at it, "What's in it?" She asked in a small voice.

Her mom shrugged. "Open it, when you're ready." Her mom stood up, leaning forward to hug her again. "Brought a plate back for you, it's in the fridge if you're hungry, come out and join us when you're ready, we're going to watch a movie."

"A movie? Tonight?"

"I know," her mom shrugged again. "It was on Gran's list. Just family, no strangers, well," her mom smiled ruefully, "well, Aunt Paige's strange surfer boyfriend." She lowered her voice, "He's twenty years younger than her! So come on out, we have popcorn!"

Spring gave a small hesitant smile, "okay, just a minute."

Her mom closed the door behind her, leaving it slightly ajar. Spring could smell the buttery aroma of popcorn, followed by her dad's loud laugh. She looked down at the box, tracing the gems with her finger, finally popping the lid with a shaky sigh.

Inside, a small, leather photo album, engraved with gold letters read: Elizabeth Autumn Raine, 2010. Below Gran-Libby's name, the embossed image of a golden airplane circling a globe. Spring flipped open the cover, reading the faded inscription from Gran-Libby's parents:

Libby, Congratulations on your first year of flying, we are so proud of you! Love Mom and Dad

Spring ran her fingers over the words. Her great-grandparents had died long before she was born. They had been born in the 1950's, almost one hundred-thirty years ago.

Spring carefully thumbed through the album, filled with pictures of Gran-Libby during flight attendant training and her first year of fly-ing. She found herself smiling over the pictures of Gran-Libby; clowning around, posing inside an open overhead bin and standing inside the enor-mous engine of the Boeing 747. Gran had inserted Spring's own picture beside her own, posing almost a year ago at Club 747, standing inside the lit up engine.

Another box sat inside the shoebox, it was smaller, a department store costume jewelry box, spray painted silver with a pair of old kiddie wings glued on top. Spring placed the album back inside, opening the lit-tle box, guessing what was inside. Neatly displayed on gauzy tissue, Gran-Libby's six pairs of wings, along with tiny gem accented replica service wings, each commemorating milestones. There were even two half wings for her uniform hats. They all gleamed as if they were worn only yesterday.

Spring picked up one of the wings, feeling the raised molded feathers on the cold metal. Her fingers traced Gran's engraved name: E. Raine, in black letters etched in gold below the enameled emblem of Orion Airways. The other wings had the Mattsson surname. The later wings varying in size and color, from gold outstretched eagle wings; to a more streamlined pair of silver that looked vaguely like a flying saucer.

Spring smiled, placing the wings back in the box beside the album. She reached for the lid of the shoebox, examining it in her hand a moment, watching as the overhead light made the starburst sparkle. Her fingers brushed against something taped on the other side. Spring frowned, flipping the cover over, revealing a folded letter taped to the lid. Spring's name was written in the middle. Spring laid the lid on the bed beside her, carefully peeling the letter off the back, trying not to rip it. Wetting her lips, she unfolded the paper, gazing at Gran-Libby's slanted cursive that rose slightly, making all of the sentences climb toward the right corner, in small, impatient strokes. Spring read, finding herself grinning, swinging her legs softly against the side of Gran-Libby's bed.

Hello Spring Chick!

If you're reading this, then I guess I am finally up in heaven, having EPIC adventures with your Grandpapa Sven. I have had a LONG, wonderful, very happy life, and I'm happy to be with my Sven again. You know, he was once a Registered Alien?

Anyway, when I was little, I would look at that beautiful Moon, and wonder what life would be like on it. I never thought I would one day have a beautiful, brave, fearless, granddaughter, who would live on the Moon. That she would explore space the way I always wanted to!

Star light, star bright,

The first star I see tonight,

I wish I may, I wish I might,

Have the wish I make tonight,

Spring, my wish for you is happiness and love.
Do not stop your epic adventures and follow your heart!

You are and have always been my very own, Shooting Star. Shine bright always.

 Love & ((Hugs))

 Gran-Libby

P.S. I included my favorite song in here, cuz I'm cool like that!

At the bottom of the page, Gran-Libby had attached one of those old fashioned, mid twenty-first century song tacks to the letter. The words, 'Train's Drops of Jupiter', were written above the small penny sized music tack that looked like a green raised button. Spring bit her lip, reaching out to tap the button. It lit up instantly, glowing a soft green as the song began to play. Spring stood up, walking over to the window, leaning against the frame, staring up at the early springtime night sky. The Moon was just a sliver of bright white. Home. The smell of Gran-Libby's perfume seemed to fill the room as the song played. Spring gazed out the window, tapping her foot, smiling faintly.

* * *

TWO DAYS LATER.

Spring stood staring down at her suitcase, on her old bed, trying to find a secure spot for the popcorn balls her mother had made and for Gran's box. It always felt so strange being back in Virginia Beach, back in her old room. Filled with her parents taste, pale Scandinavian furniture and white walls. It had the sterile look of a guest room now. Her dresser and nightstand empty except for lamps and a bright yellow flower vase. The vase matched her old bright yellow duvet, the only real punches of color in the room. Sighing, she carved out a corner by her folded up uniform, closing the suitcase just as someone knocked on her door. Spring looked up at the open doorway, raising an eyebrow in surprise at her sister, standing shyly by the door.

"Hey." Spring said.

"Hey." Summer glanced at the suitcase, then ambled into Spring's old bedroom. Summer casually leaned against Spring's old dresser, resting both hands behind her, staring at the floor. "Leaving today?"

"Yeah." *Obviously.* Spring resisted rolling her eyes, pulling her suitcase off the bed, setting it down on the floor. "Aren't you heading back to EF with Hunter?"

"No," Her sister looked up, "not until June. Hey...I...I just wanted..."

Spring waited, looking at her sister expectantly. Her sister chewed on her lip for a moment, before meeting Spring's eyes once more. "I didn't mean what I said about Gran-Libby. You know, how she planned her funeral an' all?" Her sister paused, looking troubled. "You don't think she heard me, did you?"

Spring gave her head a slight shake, "No, and if she did, she'll probably agree with you and laugh. It was a magnif way to go, huh?"

Her sister nodded, looking relieved. Her serious dark eyes lighting with humor, "yeah. Maybe that's how I'll go when I'm her age." Her sister glanced at her bag again. "Do you like living on the Moon? Are you scared to be...you know, traveling through space, so far from home?"

Spring stared at her little sister. She still looked like a child, not like someone about to enter The Earth Federation Academy. Summer leaned hard against the dresser, rocking the flowers in the vase.

"I love it." Spring said simply. "You will too. It's so awesome, seeing Earth from space, and all the stars! I can't believe I'm paid to travel through space...it's amazing.

"But, are you afraid? What about your Alien? Will you move away and marry him? Live on his planet? Can you live on his world? With his people? Would you? Do they like black people?"

Spring looked down at the floor, frowning slightly. Images of Rexlen filled Spring's mind and her heart skipped painfully. She missed him. Life on Endari scared her. She turned to Summer, forcing a bright smile as she released the handle on her suitcase, "I don't know yet. Maybe you'll beat me to that and marry your own Alien!" Summer's face turned red. Spring laughed, joined by Summer.

"And Hunter will marry a green woman!" Summer grinned, "can you see that?"

"Oooh yeah!" Spring made a face that cracked Summer up. Summer wiped the tears from her eyes, following Spring out into the hall.

"Can I ride with you to the airport? That okay?" Summer asked.

"Sure." Spring said.

23

SHOOTING STAR

Spring wanted to do an about face when she spotted Daisy Jones at the boarding door, greeting the Moon bound passengers. Daisy, with her loud, pink lipstick and orange hair. *Great. The last person I would want to run into.* Spring slowly made her way closer to the door, slumping a bit, trying to hide behind the bulky businessman in front of her; hoping to blend in with his brown trench coat. *Maybe she won't see me.* Spring regretted taking her sunglasses off. Her eyes were still red and swollen from crying on the Orion Airways mainline flight from Norfolk.

Spring stepped onto the shuttle, thankful that Daisy had chosen that moment to make a boarding PA, nodding absently to the stream of boarding passengers; while examining her bright red nails at the same time. Spring hurried down the aisle, sliding into her seat by the window, listening to Daisy drone on about the flight. She leaned back in her wide, business seat, staring out the window, sighing.

"Good evening," Spring jumped. An unfamiliar flight attendant said, flourishing a silver tray filled with sparking flutes of champagne and orange juice. "Would you like a refreshment before we depart, Miss?"

"No thanks." Spring smiled tiredly, turning back toward the window. She gazed up at the blue black night sky, staring up at the crescent Moon, just a white sliver in the sky.

"Spring! I thought that was you! Toots, are you deadheading?" Spring looked up at Daisy's shrill voice. Daisy grinned down at her, one arm casually placed on the seat back in front of Spring. Spring glanced at the Daisy's long, pointy talons then up at Daisy.

"No," Spring said in a still voice. "My grandmother died."

Daisy's eyes widened, her mouth forming an 'O'. "I'm so sorry, Sweetie," Daisy reached out, patting Spring's shoulder, "I'm so sorry! You need anything, you holler, 'kay? Want some champagne?"

"No, I'm okay," Spring was surprised at the compassion in Daisy's eyes. She felt a little ashamed now, for not liking Daisy. "Thanks, Daisy."

"No problem." Daisy smiled. "Anytime." Daisy turned away, navigating her way up the single aisle, back toward the boarding door.

* * *

"Ladies and gentlemen, planet Earth is on your lefthand side and righthand side. Please sit back relax and enjoy your flight to the Moon." Daisy's voice could barely be heard above the clapping; as the luminous view of Earth loomed large in every window. The dim cabin seemed to glow a faint blue. Cameras snapped. People sniffled, blowing their noses.

Spring unbuckled her harness, leaning forward, reaching for her purse. Gingerly, Spring felt around inside, grimacing as an opened bag of M&M's overturned, scattering in her purse. Finally her fingers closed tightly over Gran-Libby's box of wings. She pulled them out, snapping her purse shut, dropping it at her feet, kicking under the seat in front. She opened the box, pulling out the oldest pair of wings, Gran's silver first year wings, the E. RAINE, rubbed smooth, the black letters almost invisible.

Spring stared down at the wings, twisting them in the bluish light of Earth, watching as the silver wings twinkled under the light. Taking on a blue tinge of their own. Spring glanced at the empty seat beside her, then at the wings, before turning her gaze toward the swirling mass of Earth outside her window .

She blinked the burning tears away; rubbing furiously with her hand, clutching the cold wings in her other hand, the pointed edges cutting into her hand. Spring opened her hand, gazing down at the wings. Slowly, she removed the two old fashioned pin backings, placing them in her lap as she reached up to pin the wings to her thick sweater. Holding the wings in place, she fastened the backings one by one, securing the wings. She pulled her sweater down, stretching it out, examining the old wings, shining with the light of Earth. She touched them, running a finger over Gran Libby's name; before staring outside, watching the Earth surrounded by its atmosphere. Spring smiled tentatively.

"Gran, welcome to outer space."

* * *

It felt like years had passed since she walked though her first Moon jetway, forgetting to take a picture of Earth. She still had the photo of her shoes. Spring's feet moved sluggishly toward customs, her eyes smarting at the ultra bright, white lights that reflected off of everything. Everyone seemed to move so fast compared to her, tourists, customs agents, crewmembers hurrying to the crew line. She felt like she was several minutes behind the rest of the StarPort. Not really existing among them at all. They all seemed so happy, full of energy. At least her eyes were no longer puffy.

She even managed to wave to a few friends as they zipped by. Spring shuffled along in the regular customs line, resisting the urge to sneak through the crewline. Of course she picked the line with the anal agent. He was thoroughly going over the tourist couple in front of her for ten minutes. Finally, he finished with them, impatiently waving Spring forward. Spring moved forward, managing a small smile. She was rewarded by a hard look and a grunt from the beefy officer. His hair was a perfectly

299

shaped flat square on top, one of those severe military looks. He scanned her card, handing it back with stubby red fingers.

"Welcome home, Miss Stevens." He grumbled, already turning to wave on his next victim.

"Thanks." Spring walked away, temporarily feeling lost for a moment. She was so used to clearing customs in the crew line, it took her a few moments to find her bearings in the bustling crowd of the arrivals area. She rescued her suitcase from the carousel, then stumbled toward the exit, wondering if she had missed the 1630 shuttle into town.

The Arrivals Waiting area was chaotic as usual. A small crowd of people waited anxiously for whomever they were meeting; some of them carrying flowers, balloons, a few held signs with bright fluorescent lights that blinked. Spring walked slowly toward the crowd, straining to see a familiar face, Rexlen, Pam, Zavia. Her shoulders slumped a little. There was no one there.

"Spring."

Spring turned her head to her right, her eyes finding Rexlen; standing head and shoulders above the rest of the gathered crowd, making his way toward her. concern on his face. Spring felt her feet move faster than they had in days, flying toward him, enveloped in his warm, solid embrace. His arms folding tightly around her. Spring nestled into his chest, tucking her face under his chin; her fingers clutching his shoulders. She let out a long shuddering sigh. Rexlen rubbed his cheek against her hair, holding her closer.

"Come on," he said into her hair. "Let me take you home."

Spring nodded mutely, allowing Rexlen to take her suitcase in one hand, leading her out with his other arm around her.

* * *

Spring woke up cocooned in Rexlen's embrace, his face softened in sleep, his right arm draped casually around her waist, while his left arm served as her pillow. She turned her head slightly, careful not to rouse him; watching as he slept deeply and evenly beside her, his face innocent, and boyish. She felt her own lips turn upward in an answering smile to his own dreamers smile that played upon his mouth, for the briefest of seconds. She sighed softly, turning her head, her eyes falling on her curtain less window, and the small bluish bulb of the Earth beginning to rise. Spring lay there, hearing the gentle rise and fall of Rexlen's breathing, her eyes on Earth as it slowly began its accent in the ebony black sky of stars. A tear slid sideways down her check. Earth-rise, such a real and surreal moment to her. Carefully, she inched Rexlen's arm off, rolling close to the edge of the bed, before swinging her legs softly onto the floor. The room was freezing. She reached for her robe, thrown on a nearby chair; thankful it was her brand new silky kimono one, and not her lumpy, pilled, Star Trek bathrobe. She tied it loosely, her gaze falling on Gran-Libby's painting, finally hanging over her bed. The bright colors of the painting popped against the muted grey wall. Rexlen had hung it for her while she took a long shower, after her flight.

Spring turned back to look at Rexlen, admiring the long hard lines of his body, a firm, muscular outline; naked except for her ridiculous yellow top sheet, obscuring him from the waist down. He looked like a human man, even though she knew no humans had Pleauxurra pleasure veins or bluish-grey skin. Spring hugged herself, moistening her lips as she thought of the tantalizing pleasure those strange, tree branch veins welded. Running the entire length along his spine, up to his neck …her Alien man. Her Rexlen. She followed the outline of his body, starting at his feet, then up to his broad shoulders; then his firm jaw, his mouth in a soft half smile, his silver eyes watching her sleepily.

"Alma Undaa." He said good morning in such a way, that Spring felt excitement stirring in her. and Her cheeks burning as his eyes took traveled up and down, his pale eyes banked with desire.

"Alma Undaa." Spring whispered, her lips curving into a shy smile. She watched as he sat up peeling back the sheet, rising, proud and gloriously naked. *I wonder if Spock looked this good naked.* Spring's smile erupted into a happy grin as he came closer, pulling her to him. Spring tilted her chin up, closing her eyes expectantly, parting her lips in anticipation. Seconds went by. Nothing. Spring opened one eye a crack, looking up into Rexlen's amused eyes. Spring opened both eyes fully, staring at Rexlen with confusion and an annoying snip of embarrassment. He cocked an eyebrow at her.

"Were you laughing at me?" He asked in a serious tone, despite the faint smile on his lips.

"No!" Spring shook her head, "Why? Oh! Because I was thinking of Mr. Spock!"

"Spock?"

"An Alien on an old TV show, he was a Vulcan." Spring shrugged, watching as the wariness vanished from Rexlen's eyes, replaced once more with amusement. It was on the tip of her tongue to say Spock was half human, but she thought better of it. "Come on, look at the earth-rise! It's the best thing about this place." She stood on tiptoe, delivering a quick kiss, before pulling him along by both hands to the round window. She pressed herself against his solid chest, inhaling the scent of him, mixed with their love making, while his arms came around her, his chin find a place to rest among her curls.

"Isn't it magnif," Spring said. The Earth was already high, the bottom half still cloaked in darkness, as if it was escaping from a large, black velvet pouch. The brightness of Earth seemed to make the thousands of stars around it look dim. It loomed so large, and so close, Spring felt like she could touch it, part the milky white clouds with her hand and expose the east coast. Her old home.

"Would it trouble you to live far away from Earth? Live on another planet perhaps?" Rexlen asked suddenly.

"You mean like Eden?" Spring shook her head, "I can't imagine living there."

"No," Rexlen said patiently. "I meant, Endari. Living there."

Spring's eyes widened. For a long moment she stared at Earth, biting her lip. Rexlen's body stiffened behind her. She looked down at their intertwined hands. Her brown fingers and his greyish-blue.

"I assume your silence means no." Rexlen said in a peculiar voice. Spring twisted around in his arms, her eyes locking onto his unreadable ones.

"It's not that! I mean, I like Endari ...I just," Spring looked away, staring down again, "well, life would be so different there. And it's so far away! I would be the only human. Life on Endari with my handsome Alien boyfriend." She squeezed his fingers.

"We are not that different from your people, Spring." Rexlen freed his fingers, moving away from her, stooping to pick up his uniform which was in a jumbled pile with her sweater and jeans. He folded the pieces over his arm, glancing toward Spring's bathroom, then back at Spring.

"I know you're not that different from us," Spring added. "It's just ...I've never lived with Aliens ...I mean, a whole world. They would see me as your 'Human' girlfriend. I don't want to be in a box." She went past him, sliding open a drawer, handing him a bath towel. He accepted it stiffly.

"Neither do I." Rexlen answered in a clipped voice. His eyes were smoldering with emotion as he stared at her. "I am not your 'Alien' boyfriend. I have a name. Rexlen. And I have never thought of you as Spring, my 'Human' lover. You are just Spring to me." His eyes bore into hers with such intensity that it scared her, "The woman who makes me laugh, makes me smile. The woman I want to spend every moment with. The woman I love. I wish you would see me first, and not my race." He said softly.

He turned away, striding toward her bathroom. Spring hurried after him, tripping over a work heel, that she distractedly kicked aside. She stopped in the bathroom doorway, her hands holding on to the door frame, "But I do!" She protested breathlessly.

Rexlen stood by the shower, testing the water, before slanting a look toward Spring. He shook his head slightly, "No, you do not. I wonder if you ever have." He held her gaze for a moment, both of them staring at each other. The rising steam from the shower seemed to make his eyes glossy, his mouth set in a grim line. He stood by the opaque shower door, facing the mirror, his hands pressed firmly on the counter. Spring took a small step into the bathroom, her heart beating wildly. She reached out, placing her hand over one of his, the muscles in his hand flinched under her touch. She stared at their hands, noticing the contrast in their skin tones, and how long his fingers were. She traced his fingers, spreading her hand out over his large one.

"Now, if you will excuse me," he said in strained, formal voice. Spring's eyes flew up to his, startled by the coldness behind his words. Rexlen quickly looked away.

"Of course." She heard herself say. She backed away, dropping her hands to her sides, plucking at the silk, "I'll…I'll use Pam's shower." Slowly, she slid the door shut, pressing her cheek against the cool wood, her fingers on the frosted glass. She wrapped her other arm around her waist, hoping to stop the throbbing pain that seemed to squeeze her.

A few minutes later, Spring reentered her room, toweling her wet hair. Rexlen sat on the edge of her bed, pulling on the black socks she had knitted for him. They were her first (and probably last) knitting project. The misshapen pair looked out of place with his immaculate uniform. The right foot was slightly thicker, but the correct length, but the left sock only reached his ankle, bunching awkwardly.

Her throat closed with emotion as she silently watched him pull on his tall boots. *No one will know he's wearing socks made by me, his human…* Spring stopped herself, *his girlfriend. By his girlfriend.* She took a few steps closer, hugging herself. He stopped, looking up at her, frowning slightly as he scanned her face.

"What?" He asked, his hand on his left boot. Spring stared into his face, her throat tightening.

"The socks." Her voice sounded small, childlike. "You're wearing the socks I made." She tried to smile, but the corners of her lips trembled. "I ... I should knit you a better pair." She placed her hand lightly on his shoulder, her fingers inching toward his collar, itching to touch the black hair curling at his neck, still damp from his shower. Her fingers slipped slightly as his shoulder shifted as he pulled on his boot.

"I like this pair well enough." He slid a glance her way, a faint smile on his lips. He stood up, facing her, opening his mouth to speak, when they both heard a commotion at the front door. The door slammed, and the sound of luggage rolling to an abrupt stop followed. Spring exchanged a look with Rexlen before heading into the living room. Zavia stood by the coat closet, shrugging out of her uniform coat. Her hair was pinned up, exposing the same tree-like branches Rexlen had on the back of his neck.

"Hello, you two," Zavia said without turning her back. She always buttoned every button on her coats when she hung them. She gave her coat a little pat, then turned facing them, her smile fading as she looked at them.

"Na'allo." Spring and Rexlen managed to say at the same time. They both seemed rooted to the floor by her bedroom.

"Spring," Zavia came forward, hesitating for a moment, before hugging Spring. StarShip smell filling Spring's nose. "I am so sorry about your Grandmother Libby! Did your family get the plant Pam and I sent? Spring vaguely remembered the large green leafy plant with the white, fan-like blooms. Her mom called it a 'Peace Plant'. Hunter had pointed out that it was actually called Spa- something.

Spring nodded, "Thanks. It...it stood out among the flowers, thanks." Zavia released her, standing back, studying their faces once more, before smiling.

"Would you both like some breakfast? I can make some French toast? I have a new recipe. Blueberry pancakes?" Zavia was already heading toward the kitchen, still in full uniform. "How about some delicious omelets and roasted Endarion Meltariss potatoes?"

Rexlen glanced at Spring, raising an eyebrow, before striding toward the door. He cast a curious stare at Zavia puttering around the kitchen, an apron tied around her blazer. He paused by the door, turning back, his eyes on Spring. Spring stumbled forward.

"I have work to do at the base, I will have to experience your cooking another time, Zavia." Rexlen pulled on his gloves, flexing his fingers.

"Are you sure you can't stay?" Spring hated the pathetic pleading tone in her voice, "We can have some tea or coffee? Toast?"

Rexlen simply stared at her, his face unreadable. He looked down at his hands then back at her face, shaking his head. "No. I am afraid I have no appetite at this moment. Good morning, to you."

Spring's eyes began to smart at the curt tone of his voice. His 'good morning' felt like 'goodbye'. "Okay, I'll see you later then." Zavia came out of the kitchen, whisking a bowl of eggs, watching the exchange with interest.

Rexlen smiled faintly, 'Yes, later then. I have much to discuss with the EF. He gave them both a small nod, then opened the door letting the chilly hallway air blow in; before stepping out, closing the door softly behind him. *He didn't even look back.*

"Two omelets then." Zavia said matter of factually. Spring looked at her, then bursts into tears.

24

WISHING ON A STAR

Spring lay on her bed, blanket up to her chin, staring up at the ceiling, while music blared from her tiny sound cube. She was just getting to one of her favorite songs when someone rudely started pounding away on her closed door. She sat up on her elbows, glaring, debating whether to throw a pillow.

"Go away!" She yelled, falling back on her pillows, snuggling deeper, closing her eyes. The door slid open, slamming loudly into its pocket. Spring opened one eye, spying a pair of Decco Mok shoes coming around to the edge of her bed. Eggplant slingbacks with the chunky golden yellow heels. Her shoes! Pam! Spring sat up fully, eyes wide open, staring at Pam crossly.

"What? Can't you see I'm busy?" Spring snapped, leaning back against her headboard, crossing her arms. "Love the shoes by the way. Wherever did you find those?"

Pam gave her an equally snarky look, before going to Spring's wall, tapping at the little buttons controlling the music. She slanted a look back at Spring, "Your closet of course. It's not like you're wearing them, moping around here, listening to what is this crap?" Pam looked back at the wall, squinting, "Ah, 'Music to Cry By'. Great title." She smirked at Spring, "Do you have a 'Woe Is Me' playlist too?

"If I want to listen to that, I can." Spring growled. "It's not bothering anyone."

Pam made a face, "Riiight. The past three weeks you fly, then hibernate in here listening to this stuff. It's driving me and Zavia nuts! Spring," Pam's tone softened, "Why don't you just contact Rexlen? I know he misses you."

Spring perked up, "Really? You've seen him?" Pam was spending a lot of time on the EF base with her new man. "Does Adam work with him?"

"No, but he's seen him a couple of times. He said he looks kinda, stony, brooding kinda."

Spring snorted. "That's what he's normally like. I mean at work. That means nothing." Spring sighed, pulling back the covers, swinging her feet over the bed, staring down at her toes. *I totally need a Pedi.* "I bet he's probably still mad about the 'Alien' thing."

"What Alien thing?" Zavia's voice popped out of nowhere. Pam and Spring jumped, their eyes shooting to the doorway. Zavia leaned against the door frame, yawning, a coffee mug dangling casually from one hand.

"When I, well, kept referring to him like that...as an Alien." Spring looked away from Zavia's penetrating eyes with embarrassment. "I should get a hold of him—"

"When do you fly again?" Zavia interrupted.

"I dropped my Earth two day, for tomorrow..." Spring bit her lip in concentration, "I don't fly again till next month. I'm on vacation next week. Why?"

"How about you coming with me to Endari? It is our warmest season, and there will be so many parties and..." Zavia winked. "So many handsome men to choose from!"

Spring shivered, thinking about that mausoleum of a palace, loaded with gaudy opulence, and icy courtiers. "Um..."

"Oh, we do not stay at that palace in the summer!" Zavia laughed, as if reading her mind. "No, we stay at my favorite palace, Canasarra. Right by the sea. I was born there. It is smaller, and more modern. Not like Snowendorrica. Not a mosaic or hideous antique in sight!"

"Will Rexlen be there?" Spring said in a low voice. Zavia blinked, before smiling slowly, shaking her head.

"Only courtiers. I think your commander may be way too busy to party on Endari. Well, what do you think? Do you want to join me?"

"Sure."

"Vunda'klat!"

* * *

Zavia was right, Canasarra Palace was completely different than Snowendorrica. It didn't even look like it belonged on the same planet. The small imperial StarShip that picked them up on the Moon, flew them directly to Endari, and to the lush looking island of Solak, floating in the middle of inky blue waters. Solak was the biggest 'island' Spring had ever seen, more like a small continent; with softly rolling mountains and miles of beach, a few mansions dotted the coast.

Canasarra palace took up one half of the island, sitting on a hill overlooking its own private beach. It reminded Spring of a Spanish villa with its brick red tiled roofs, airy verandas, arched windows and creamy vanilla walls. All of the island residences sported the same clay red roofs, although some of the homes were painted in warm shades of green and pink. Relatives homes, Zavia explained as their small ship landed slowly on a landing pad on the manicured parkland of the palace.

As the shuttle doors slid open, Spring braced herself for the cold, despite being bundled up in her thickest coat, scarf, wool skirt, tights and boots. Instead of a gust of frigid air, a warm slightly humid breeze wafted into the shuttle, smelling of sunshine and fresh flowers. "I told you it was warm here." Zavia smirked as she hopped down, waving away several bowing courtiers and imperial soldiers. She turned around waiting impatiently for Spring to jump down.

Spring stood at the shuttle door, gazing at the crowd, all of them dressed in light summer clothes. A guard offered his gloved hand, Spring took it, hopping down onto the bright green lawn. *I must look like I'm dressed for Siberia.* She glanced around shyly, quickly taking in the blossoming trees and bushes in every color imaginable. The palace lawn went on for miles, sprinkled with brightly dressed courtiers strolling casually. She spotted a few couples walking hand in hand toward the beach, or lingering lazily on tiny boats floating in the small pond near the palace. Children dressed as regally as the adults sprinted around, shrieking, jumping, playing. A small group spotted Zavia and ran excitedly beside them, gathering around Zavia in a garbled rush of Endarion. A few walked slowly beside Spring, their faces curious, but shy. Spring smiled back. *Probably wondering why I'm dressed for a blizzard.*

Spring allowed herself to trail behind Zavia and her welcome entourage, walking as slowly as she could. Taking in everything. Most of the men wore their stiff looking uniforms, a few wore brightly colored tunics and pants. The women still tittered around balancing headdresses, although a few had their hair wound up high, enclosed in ribbons. The women still wore fan shaped eyes makeup. They all looked as still and formal as Spring remembered, just lighter clothes. Painted eyebrow-less eyes,high necks and wasp waists of course. Spring looked down at her feet, her hands going up to her loose curls, *Do they ever let their hair down here?* Spring blinked up at the cloudless purple sky, the planets rings a faint series of lines. *Well, I'm certainly not in Kansas anymore.*

* * *

"Are you sure I look okay?" Spring turned away from her reflection, casting an uncertain glance toward Zavia, already decked out and princess looking, her 'human' eyebrows obscured with decoration. Spring felt her own hands climb up to her face, her fingers lightly tracing her new eye makeup. She was not sure she liked covering her eyebrows up with a vivid fan sunburst pattern trimmed with tiny stones. But she did feel a bit Endarion now. Like Uhura on an undercover away mission on Star Trek.

"The men will love it! And do not worry, the stones will not come loose and blind you…just do not touch them!" Zavia glided forward, slapping Spring's hand away from her face. Zavia turned her slowly toward the mirror, standing behind her, beaming like a mother hen. A rather tall, Alien mother hen in a shimmering ball gown and headdress. "No one will guess you are not one of us."

"One of us." Spring echoed, starring at the unfamiliar vision before her. Her borrowed gown was light and gauzy with only a small belt at her waist, while her hair was piled on her head, behind a junior sized fan headdress that glittered. Her eyes jumped away from her face, looking wider, like two discs. Sunburst discs. Maybe she should have insisted on dressing like the Earth girl she was. She turned her head, casting a look toward dressing room where her suitcase was stored.

"Oh, no Spring" Zavia followed her stare, "you look fine. Come on, girl!" Zavia grabbed her arm, pulling her into the wide corridor. Spring clutching her headdress with one hand, looking longingly at the dressing room over her shoulder.

"Zavia, maybe I should sit this one out ? You know, since it's my first Endarion shindig and all?" Spring struggled to keep up with Zavia's long excited strides. Spring could hear the distant music and laughter, it seemed to coincide with the nervous drumbeat of her ears.

Once they reached the ballroom, Spring's nerves relaxed a bit. It looked like something from home. Well, almost like home. Along with the standard group of couples dancing under soft lighting, there were dancers covered in glowing lights that slid around their bodies like snakes, floating high above the dance floor. The dancers seemed to leap and twirl within giant, luminous bubbles of shifting color, while their trail of lights roamed around their obviously naked bodies. Dancing chandeliers. Or planets, Spring realized as she watched the balls rotate around a brilliant duo enclosed in a bright prism of light. Every few seconds, tiny stars would rain down on the crowd; like falling fireworks, only the guests would catch the stars and drink. Drink! The stars were small glasses filled with luminous liquid.

"What are they drinking?" Spring asked Zavia as they breezed through the crowd. The BelReginar and her entourage sat on an elevated dais a few feet away. Spring's feet heavy as Zavia led them toward The BelReginar.

"It is called LuneArdari," Zavia called out loudly over the music, "The drink of the stars and the moons. Very potent stuff."

"Oh," Spring said thoughtfully, her gaze falling on two uniformed Endarion men. Cute, but not as handsome as Rexlen. "You mean it's like an aphrodisiac?"

"What?" Zavia yelled. The crowd was breaking as they approached the imperial dais.

"An aphrodisiac!" Spring shouted, suddenly aware that the music had stopped and all eyes were on her. She felt her cheeks burn. The only sound was the swish of fabric and the soft whirl of the dancers in their bubble planets above .

"Right." Zavia linked her arm with hers, leading her up the stairs of the dais. The BelReginar's eyes bore into Spring's with mild disdain. Zavia stepped away from Spring, allowing Spring to dip into the formal curtsey she had practiced all afternoon. She rose, chin held high, staring directly into The BelReginar's eyes. Rexlen's grannie. The BelReginar stared at her for a long moment, her eyes narrowed slightly. Finally, her mouth shifted into a small smile.

"Welcome, Miss Stevens. It is a...pleasure to see you once more. How do you like Canasarra?"

Spring smiled back. *Pleasure? Liar. I ruined your family dinner AND was kicked out of your other palace!* "Thank you, my lady, BelReginar. It's a pleasure to be here, and to meet you again. Canasarra is beautiful...I feel like I'm in Hawaii!" Confusion flicked over The BelReginar's face, and a few courtiers exchanged looks. "Oh, um, that's a popular vacation place on Earth. Of course, Hawaii is not as pretty as Endari. I mean, you know, no rings, or a purple sky and all..." Spring's cheeks were burning. A few courtiers coughed and snickered.

"Oh, I see." The BelReginar nodded. "I am sure your Hawaii is just as beautiful. Please enjoy yourself." The BelReginar smiled again, this time it reached her eyes, lighting up her face.

"Thank you." Spring sank into another curtesy .

"Savatareena. Back from your adventures as a servant?" Spring and Zavia both turned, staring down the dais steps at The BelFilius and his wife. Onaldi, dressed in green as usual. Onaldi's small eyes fell on Spring, giving her the once over. "The commander did not mention that he brought his Human with him."

"The commander?" Spring said faintly, her heart beating wildly in her chest. "Commander Baldric? He's...he's here?" Spring shot a look at Zavia. Zavia shrugged, looking as shocked as she was.

Onaldi bared her teeth in a smile, "you did not know? You are not his guest?" She said innocently.

Spring felt dizzy and hot, "Where is he?" Her eyes frantically scanned the room.

Onaldi inclined her head, nodding toward a tall, handsome couple dancing slowly. Rexlen. Rexlen resplendent in his dress uniform, dancing with an ethereal; willowy beauty with the swan neck Spring always wanted. Spring's heart dropped in her chest as she watched Rexlen laugh at something the woman said.

"Rexlen." Spring whispered, swaying, her eyes filling up. Rexlen suddenly looked toward the dais, his smile vanishing from his face, his eyes locking on Spring. Spring swayed again, and was dimly aware of Javarr and Zavia steadying her. Rexlen broke away from the woman, shouldering his way through the dancing couples, just as large black spots began to fill Spring's vision.

"Rexlen." Spring murmured as she sank into blackness.

∗ ∗ ∗

"Give her room! Give her room! She is all right!" Spring heard Zavia's commanding flight attendant voice even before she opened her eyes. She was leaning against a warm solid, shifting wall, achingly familiar. She kept her eyes shut, relishing Rexlen's firm hold on her, his fingers pressed worriedly into her shoulders. It was a crying shame her prickly headdress was probably poking him in the chin. *If I marry Rexlen, first thing I'll introduce: Tiaras. My contribution from Earth.*

"Spring?" Rexlen's voice sounded so concerned, he gave her shoulders a little shake. Spring moaned loudly, sinking deeper against his chest, a slight smile escaping on her lips.

"She looks okay now," Zavia remarked dryly. Spring could hear a rustle of fabric moving away. She opened one eye a crack, watching Zavia rock back on her heels, regarding her with a smirk. "Feel better now?" Zavia asked.

Spring looked beyond Zavia at the crowd of curious guests, including Rexlen's dance partner. The woman stood a few feet behind Zavia; glowering down at Spring, her arms folded, her mouth set. With a deep sigh, Spring grabbed hold of Rexlen's sleeve sitting up against him. She leaned back against his arm, smiling up into his face. The tight expression on his face melted away, his eyes lighting up as a he smiled back.

"You have recovered?" He asked.

"Think so." Spring said weakly. "I guess I'm not used to wearing such a tight thing on my head."

"Perhaps your friend should sit this out, my lady," Rexlen's dance partner said to Zavia, her eyes glued to Rexlen and Spring. "Our garments are too much of a hardship for her to bear."

Spring stiffened. Zavia stood up, glancing at the woman, as she brushed off her skirts, waving away a servant that rushed forward to help. "Spring Stevens of Earth, meet Lolantaria of Tarrantu–Bentorr."

Lolantaria smiled widely, her eyes glinting, "From Earth? How charming! Your people are much weaker, correct? You must be exhausted, poor child."

"Lola..." Rexlen warned, his body tensing.

Spring shook his arms away, rushing to her feet, whirling around to face him. "Lola? You call her, Lola?" Rexlen clamped his mouth shut, his hands behind his back. Spring kept her back to 'Lola', she could feel the woman's gloating smile trained on her back. "Well?" She demanded.

"She is an old friend." He said in a strained voice. Spring looked over her shoulder at Lola. Lola smiled back in triumph. *What is the Endarion word for bitch?*

"Fine. Whatever." Spring adjusted her crooked headdress. She raised her chin, trying her best to stare down Rexlen. "Thank you for your assistance, Commander Baldric. Excuse me." She said coldly, before walking away as quickly as her wobbling headdress would allow. She made it half way to a tall welcoming column, before a hand touched her sleeve. She turned around impatiently, blinking away tears.

"Rexlen, you..." She trailed off, staring up into the face of a gorgeous Endarion man dressed in a formal dark blue uniform. His eyes matched the gold trim around his high collar. He was handsome in a sharp angled kind of way. Razor sharp cheekbones, pointy cleft chin. Tall, but not as tall as Rexlen. He bowed formally. Spring spotted Rexlen a few inches away, stopping in his tracks, his eyes flicking between Spring and the man smiling down at her.

"Arclex Noplin'Arent. May I have this dance?" He bowed again. Spring peeked at Rexlen's unreadable face, then smiled brightly at Arclex.

"Sure..I mean, yes!" She placed her hand in his, ignoring Rexlen as they sailed past him. She could feel his eyes on them as Arclex led her into the mix of whirling couples. Spring held on tight, as Arclex spun her around effortlessly, her feet barely touching the ground. A good thing since she had no idea what the dance steps were. They faintly resembled a waltz of sorts. Spring grinned at Arclex.

"Enjoying our humble planet?" He asked pleasantly, just as Spring spotted Rexlen and Lola among the dancers. Spring smiled wider, her cheeks hurting.

"It's perfectly lovely!" She heard herself, heard the breathy, almost saccharine sweet southern voice. *Where the hell did that come from? Perfectly lovely? What am I 'm going to spit out next, a request for mint julep after suppa'?* "Have you ever visited Earth" She asked. Rexlen and Lola glided past, a strikingly handsome couple. Spring glanced down at Lola's feet. Rexlen did not have to hold her up.

"Of course, that is my goal..." Arclex was saying as he spun her backwards, "Even if it is a modest one."

"To visit Earth?" She grinned manically at Arclex. He frowned, looking confused for a moment, then grinned back shaking his head .

"No, I meant my goal is to leave Endari one day. I have never traveled off of it yet. Small goal I know. However, Earth would be a intriguing place to visit."

"Oh, it is! It is!" Spring laughed. Rexlen glanced in their direction, tight lipped. Spring watched as Lola reached up with a glittering hand, gently steering his face to hers with a sensuous smile. Spring felt a wave of heat rush up to her cheeks, her eyes glued to Rexlen as he danced with a smiling Lola.

"Miss Stevens? Is something wrong?" Spring tore her eyes away from Rexlen, focusing on her dance partner. They were both standing in the middle of the dance floor, dancers spinning past them and around them. "Miss Stevens?" Arclex asked again, a puzzled expression on his face.

"I…I think I need some fresh air. I'm…I'm sorry. It's been a pleasure, excuse me." Spring bobbed an awkward curtsey, before walking as fast as she could toward the open doorways. Her cheeks on fire, her eyes stinging.

Spring stepped out onto the terrace, gulping in fresh ocean air, crisp and so much like being at home. The terrace was already a little crowded, a few couples stood in the open light of the doorways. Spring moved off to the side, into the shadows, leaning against the cold stone railing, her eyes on the ocean, the waves breaking with white caps. She blinked up at the night sky, trying to clear her vision, her eyes slowly focusing on a cloudy night sky. Thick, puffy rain clouds. She closed her eyes, inhaling deeply, hoping to catch the salty smell of seawater, but apparently that must be an Earth thing.

"Spring."

Spring turned, spotting Rexlen half hidden in the darkness. She looked behind him, expecting to see Lola, but he was all alone. She met his eyes briefly, then looked away, watching the waves. "Hi." She said.

She heard him come forward, felt his presence as he stood beside her. He seemed to fill up the area, with his scent, his warmth, his soft breathing. His hand rested a few inches from hers, the fingers long and relaxed, dwarfing hers. They were both silent for a long time. "I thought you were on the Moon." Spring broke the silence, staring at the white caps.

"I have finished my business on your Moon earlier than expected." He answered. "I wanted to come home…needed to. I heard someone would be here, and I needed to speak with her."

"You mean, Lola?" Spring bit the name out, glancing sideways at Rexlen. He was staring at her, his pale eyes intense, scanning her face. He moved closer, his lips curving into a faint smile.

"I meant you." He placed his hand over hers, just as the first drops of rain began to fall. Spring jerked her hand out from under his, taking a step back.

"Could've fooled me." She said hotly, "you looked very comfy with her."

"She is an old friend. I had a history with her…long ago. It is over now, has been for a long time."

"Didn't seem that way to me." Spring looked away, watching the couples hurrying inside under the light droplets. The smell of rain was not here, just the scent of flowers and nighttime air. Spring shook her head. "Were you engaged?" She asked dully.

"Engaged?" Rexlen repeated cautiously. His eyes lit up in understanding. "Engaged. Yes, but we…it did not work. I am glad it did not."

"Why not? She's pretty enough. Glamorous. Tall…can dance. Lives in your neck of the galaxy. What could be wrong with her?" She peeked up at him.

"She is not you." Rexlen said softly, his eyes locked on hers. "She would have never braved the stars, never leave her home world. She would never soothe the fears of travelers as they move to new worlds. She would never be curious about others and," He added, his eyes twinkling, "curious about certain palaces of pleasure on space stations. Or knit a pair of socks. She would never risk her life on an unknown ship, just to save a friend, and then stand up to the commander when he made a mistake."

"I was kinda hoping you had forgotten about the pleasure palace." Spring felt a smile tug at the corners of her mouth.

"No," Rexlen smiled, pulling her away from the railing as the sprinkles turned into a steady shower. He pulled her into his arms, leaning against the palace walls, under the thick terrace roof as the rain sounded like loud applause as it hit the terrace. They were the only couple outside. She shivered, leaning into him. Rexlen pulled her away for a moment, taking off his formal jacket; draping it over her shoulders, pulling her back into his arms, his mouth finding hers. His kiss tasted of the rain, safety, warmth...love. He crushed her to him as he deepened the kiss, his hands coming up, his fingers at the nape of her neck, in her hair, pressing her closer. Spring shuddered, moaning softly as little shocks of pleasure shot up her spine, then back again. The Endarion thing. Or was it?

Rexlen broke the kiss, staring down at her with hungry eyes that seemed to burn in the semi darkness. Spring stared back, mesmerized, her heart beating wildly, as he reached out to smooth a wet tendril away from her cheek. "We should go in. Come, you do not wish to be outside during one of our storms."

"Why not?" Spring looked up at the purple sky, watching as small flashes of light lit up the storm clouds. "I kinda like storms. Great ghost story weather."

Rexlen led her toward the open doorway, glancing up at the sky, "our storms are very violent, lighting filling the sky." He looked at her, "it looks like daylight."

"Oh?" Spring cast a nervous glance up, before stepping back into the overly bright ballroom, her eyes adjusting to the music, people and smells of food. Rexlen followed behind her, stopping beside her, offering his arm. He smiled down at her. Spring grinned back for a moment, before a thought crossed her mind.

"You said you were finished on the Moon," Spring said, feeling dread spread in her stomach. "Does that mean ...does that mean you're staying here? I mean, are you coming back to the Moon?"

His smile faded. "My mission on your Moon is complete."

"I...I see." Spring stared hard at the scroll-like braid on his sleeve, before daring a peek up. "Will you stay on Endari then?"

Rexlen was silent, then he opened his mouth, preparing to answer, when loud horns sounded. Spring looked around for the source, noticing how the dancers stopped, dipping in low bows and courtesies, and how the guests cleared a wide path. Spring cast a puzzled look at Rexlen, who simply slid a glance her way, before bowing stiffly, his face a mask. "The BelReginar." he said low, under his breath. Spring scrambled to curtesy, just as The BelReginar made her way out of the ballroom. Outside rain pounded the windows, rattling the glass, sending flashes of light. Spring straightened up as The BelReginar and her stuffy looking entourage walked by.

"Perfect timing." Spring muttered, adjusting her headdress. It took her a moment to see Rexlen's outstretched hand. "Is the party over?" She asked.

He led her onto the dance floor, one arm closing around her waist. He grinned, "No, now you will see a real Endarion gathering."

All around them, people were literally letting their hair down. Loosening uniforms, setting headdresses down. Most of the women had removed their over-dresses. Even the music was different, faster. Wilder, with a nightclub feel to it. Spring smiled, "while the cats away, the mice will play."

"Very true." Rexlen laughed, spinning her then holding her close. "Miss Stevens, is your schedule free tomorrow night?"

"Uh, huh."

"Good. Join me for dinner. I will pick you up. It is time you saw more of Endari than palaces."

* * *

"He did not say where he was taking you?" Zavia asked, sitting among a pile of dresses, gowns and jeans. Zavia was dressed for some evening soiree on a boat. "You both can come with me, you know."

Spring thought of Zavia's Endari crowd, all carefully approved junior members of the court. They all knew each other. Practically from birth. A wild bunch, full of pompous titles, and snide back handed comments. She had had enough, and besides, she was curious about where Rexlen was taking her. "No," she said shaking her head, before stepping into her favorite green V-neck, silk jersey dress. She wanted to look 'human' today. No headdresses. She moved toward the dresser, putting on a pair of dangling earrings, "I can't wait to spend time with Rexlen, I mean, I leave in two days. Maybe he'll cook dinner for me?"

Zavia made a face, "maybe he will fly you to Kelti, and you can meet Lady Dreux'Jalio!" Zavia rolled her eyes at Spring's confused expression. "His mother. She is Lady Dreux'Jalio. She lives on that Moon."

"That would be nice." Spring slipped into a pair of strappy sandals, before surveying herself in front of the mirror. *I probably shouldn't meet his mom dressed like this.* She glanced over at the discarded pile, her eyes lingering on an Endarion dress. Zavia followed her gaze, standing up with a chuckle.

"Do not look so worried, Spring! Kelti is too far away, and I am sure he is not taking you there...yet." She giggled mischievously, steering Spring toward the doors. "Have a wonderful time, fill me in later, and I shall do the same!"

* * *

Spring was relieved to see Rexlen waiting for her in a pair of dark blue jeans and a black button down shirt and blazer. She happily hurried down the wide staircase, ignoring a few stares from over dressed courtiers headed god knows where in the palace. Rexlen met her halfway, leading her down the stairs, his eyes roaming over her approvingly. "You look beautiful. I was hoping you were dressed like yourself tonight."

He led her out into the front lawn, toward a strange looking moped /motorcycle parked a few yards from the edge of the cliff. It looked like a motorbike with fighter jet wings, dark blue, streaked with silver trim. Probably not a device for traveling off-world. "Guess this means we're not going to Kelti." Spring mused, slanting a look at Rexlen. Rexlen's eyes widened in surprise.

"If you wish to, we could go to Kelti. Do you want to?" He asked. She shook her head.

"Good. It is the middle of winter there anyway." He helped her onto the flying motorbike, before climbing on in front of her. Spring wrapped her arms around his waist before glancing down to make sure her dress was not bunched around her waist. She placed her feet on the narrow platform behind Rexlen's, the wings directly under their feet. Her stomach flipped nervously. Maybe they could join Zavia and her friends on the boat? "We will save Kelti for another time...unless you change your mind that is." Rexlen said.

"Do we need helmets or something?" Spring asked nervously as Rexlen steadied the vehicle, bringing it to life with a loud Varoom. Silver and blue lights glowed around them. "Rexlen, do we need helmets?" Spring shouted over the noise. She clutched him harder, letting out a high pitched giggle.

"No." He said, guiding the machine forward toward the cliff. The motorbike had a soft hum now. Spring glanced out at the ocean, spotting a few tiny looking yachts. She squeezed her eyes shut, letting out another high pitched giggle. Rexlen stopped the machine/motorbike a few inches from the cliff. One of his gloved hands found hers, giving her a reassuring squeeze. "Relax. Breathe." Spring nodded, taking in great gulps of fresh ocean air. After a few moments, her giggling stopped. "Better?" Rexlen asked. Spring nodded again, but kept her eyes shut, leaning against his back. With a quick jerk, they were airborne, instantly covered by a softly illuminated, protective bubble that still allowed a soft breeze to come through. Spring relaxed her death grip, opening her eyes.

They flew high above the ocean, dipping low enough for Spring to spot the yacht Zavia was on. It was the only one with a woman waving madly at them, Spring waved back assuming that was Zavia. They flew higher, joining a few others as they sailed in the clear sky. Most were couples, Spring waved at them, excited to see others out on 'dates', dressed in various get ups. Everyone waved back. A few were so far away, they looked like shooting stars. The sky was a kaleidoscope of 'Northern Light' style colors, caused by the planets rings. Spring pressed her cheek against Rexlen's back, smiling.

Spring squeezed Rexlen excitedly, "I love it up here!" They flew higher, the palace just a speck of light below. The stars and the Endari's three moons loomed large, She wondered which one was Kelti. The planets rings were clear tonight, shifting in colors that reminded Spring of Aurora Borealis, in a deep purple sky. They flew through a misty cloud, Rexlen chuckled as Spring reached out, trying to touch the cloud.

Finally, they descended, flying past the yachts, the palace, to a smaller island in the shadow of Solak. They landed softly, a few yards from a modest cottage, perched on its own ledge over the sea. The large round windows of the home were ablaze with light pouring out onto a small garden, the savory aroma of food made Spring's stomach rumble.

"Who lives here?" Spring asked as Rexlen helped her off the flying motorbike. She liked the curving shape of it, a bit like an observatory; except it was larger with a glass domed roof and the largest round windows she had ever seen. It looked like the house was the only building on the island. The rest of the land was cloaked in that spooky nighttime darkness, where unseen trees rattled in the wind along with the crashing waves of the ocean. Spring shivered, following Rexlen.

They reached the door, Rexlen swinging it open, grinning down at her, "I do. This is my home." He stepped aside, bowing grandly, "welcome." She moved close to him, standing on tip toe to deliver a soft kiss.

"Thanks," she said softly. The roundness of the main room felt like being inside a large bubble. Tall windows curved upward to the second landing, the ceiling itself was a gigantic glass dome, the shifting colors of the sky clearly visible. Other than that, it did have the basic bachelor air, awkwardly placed bare minimum furniture.

Spring had to give Rexlen a gold star though; the place was clean. He even had beautifully sculpted statues, displayed in little niches in the walls. She walked over to one, gingerly touching the life-like miniature tree, made out of a shimmering light blue stone. She glanced over at Rexlen, he was watching her with a carefully neutral expression .

"I love it! And these little statues are amazing! Where did you get them?" She said and she meant it. It was much better (and cozier) than a palace. She felt her heart jump at the delighted smile Rexlen flashed, relief and pride playing across his face.

"Thank you. I made the statues—my hobby when I have the time." He said casually. "I have pizza …green peppers and tomatoes. Your favorite. Hungry?"

* * *

The pizza was delicious, especially eating it outside on Rexlen's balcony. A fresh vase full of Earth sunflowers sat on the small table. Replicated? It was still delicious, even if the tomato sauce was bright orange.

After dinner, they strolled down to the shore, walking along the edge, the three moons shimmering on the water. They walked barefoot in the powdery sand, still warm from the evening sun. He seemed more relaxed here, on the private island that his father gave him. He even spoke about his family and life on the tropical moon Kelti; where the oceans were emerald green and clear all the way to the bottom. She wanted to hear more on the Radi water people. Actual mermaids that lived in massive cities in Kelti's vast oceans.

"They are not like your fables," Rexlen stressed after Spring told him about The Little Mermaid. "They are scaly beings that reach no higher than your knee, with webbed arms and sharp teeth." Rexlen laughed at her crestfallen face, chuckling, "Do not look so sad! I believe planet Loftarri has the mermaids your fables describe. No sharp teeth."

"We could visit Loftarri?" She asked hopefully. The Little Mermaid had been her favorite fairy tale.

Rexlen paused by the shoreline, gentle waves lapping against their feet as he pulled her up against him, gazing down at her with gleaming eyes. Spring nestled even closer, her fingers lazily playing with the buttons on his shirt."We could. It is a pleasure planet. The wildest place in our system. But, I think we will avoid Loftarri for now." His finger traced the dimple in her cheek, before traveling to her parted lips. He lowered his face toward hers, his mouth curved in a sensual smile, "one planet and moon at a time."

Spring stood on tip toe, reaching up, pulling him closer, till his lips were brushing against hers, "Who needs a pleasure planet for pleasure?" She said huskily. "We can make that anywhere...here." She sealed his mouth with hers, tasting of him greedily, weeks of being apart slipping away, as she was rewarded by the low groan in his throat, as he deepened their kiss. His hands smoothed down her back, sending tiny sparks of pleasure down her spine, as his fingers cradled her bottom, drawing her tighter against his hardness. Spring moved her hips against, slowly, rhythmically, relishing the feel of him, the taste of him.

Rexlen dropped to his knees in the wet sand, pulling her with him, as his tongue moved to explore her neck, going lower, while the tide sent wave after wave over their legs.

25

ACROSS THE UNIVERSE

THREE DAYS LATER.

Spring sat nestled between Rexlen, his legs swaying her gently, their fingers intertwined as they sat on the warm sand, watching as a few yachts sailed by in the distance. Of course her last day on Endari would be the one rare day that Endari's rings, luminesced during the day. The sky was filled with vivid streaks of color, pinks, red, blue, green, competing with a blue sky.

"I wish I could stay here forever." Spring sighed, leaning against Rexlen, feeling the gentle rise and fall of his chest. She had borrowed a few extra off days from Pam, who happily swapped days off in exchange for Spring's collar necklace. "I don't want to go back. Why should I go, if you have to stay here?"

"Stay here then. Stay with me," Rexlen said into her hair. "What would happen if you stayed here on Endari? Would you stay here with me...could you stay here?"

"I want to but...I'm so far from home..." Spring felt foolish tears gather in her eyes, "Endari is just...so different from everything I know. I can't even speak the language, or endure those stupid headdresses..."

Rexlen chuckled softly, holding her close, "You do not have to wear what the others wear, and I can teach you Endarion. Do you know what 'Am arma'stann' means?"

"Arma...?"

Rexlen paused, his lips close to her ear, "Am arma'stann, Spring."

"Arma...what, does that mean?" Spring turned around, gazing up at him. "It sounds beautiful."

He gazed at her, his intense eyes full of emotion, "It means, I love you, Spring. I've loved you since the day I met you in the captain's quarters, on your starship hit by asteroids. When you smiled at me with your—what are they...dimples in your face...you captured my heart then, and have had it ever since, my dear, sweet, Spring."

"Oh, Rexlen," Spring whispered, her eyes filling with tears.

He looked confused, wiping a tear as it strayed down her cheek, his hands cradling her face, "My words upset you?"

Spring shook her head, "No, no its not that! These are happy tears! And I love you, Rexlen...more than anything in the world...more than anything in the universe!"

"Then don't go back, stay on Endari...be my wife."

Spring stared up at him, his eyes shining with love...for her. She could not stop her tears. "I'm so far from home, Rexlen...my family...my parents. Earth is so far away. I'm so far from...home."

"Make Endari home." Rexlen said, leaning down kissing her tears, "Earth is only a week away by ship."

"I...I don't know," she hated seeing the hurt filling his eyes. "I'm not sure...I..." she gently pushed away, standing up, rubbing her eyes, "I think, I better go back to the palace," she said in a ravaged voice, looking at her feet. Minutes passed, before she heard Rexlen rise, taking heavy steps toward her. Spring raised her eyes, staring up into his face. His beautiful eyes glistened with raw pain, his mouth a firm line. "Rexlen," she said brokenly through her tears. She put her arms around him, leaning against him, "Rexlen, please...give me time to..."

He held her close, taking a long shuddering breath, pressing his cheek against her hair. Spring closed her eyes, listening to his heart beat, tasting her salty tears. They stayed like that for a long time. "I'll wait then," His muffled voice said into her curls. "I'll wait, Spring."

* * *

"You told him 'no'?" Zavia stared at her in stupefied shock. Zavia sat on Spring's bed, watching her pack. Rexlen had dropped her off a few minutes ago, his face a blank mask.

"No! I never said that! I just need time..." She felt another tide of tears threaten as her fingers wrapped around the delicate pendant necklace with the multicolored fiery stone Rexlen gave her, a couple of days ago.

"Why? Do you want to live on the Moon forever, going back and forth to Earth? Endari is wonderful!"

"So wonderful you ran away, so you could fly back and forth to Earth, right?" Spring snapped.

"Well, okay, you have a point there, but Spring,...why are you so afraid?"

Spring sat down on the bed, looking down at her clasped hands, "I just wish..."

"He was human? From, uh...Virginia?"

"No. I...just wish he was just a regular guy...for regular, boring me... not the son of a future king!"

"BelReginar."

"Whatever! I can't fit into this world...I...I'm..."

"Do you think you are not good enough?" Zavia asked in a low voice. "That you should not be at his side? Would you prefer he marry Lola?"

"No! I love Rexlen, he's mine...I just need time to think." Spring looked at Zavia through a veil of tears, "If I stay here, marry Rexlen, I'll be so far from home...my parents. At least on the Moon, I could see Earth...but Endari is a whole solar system away. I'm...afraid. I'm not brave like Spock's mom on Star Trek." Spring rolled her eyes at the confusion on Zavia's face. "That was a TV show. Spock's mom was human and she fell in love with Spock's Vulcan dad. She moved to Vulcan with him."

"Can you live without Rexlen?"

"No." She whispered.

"Follow your heart, Spring." Zavia stood up, gazing at her with Rexlen's eyes, "I am sure that is what Spock's mother decided. It may not have been easy for her either. And Rexlen will be with you. You won't be alone. "

* * *

Rexlen surprised Spring by waiting for her by the shuttle. Zavia gave him a quick hello, before hopping into the shuttle, slamming the door in Spring's face. Spring smiled hesitantly at Rexlen, her heart aching as he looked at her. His eyes bore into hers, scanning her face as if memorizing her features.

"Na'allo." Spring said softly. *I will not say goodbye. This is not goodbye.*

"Hello," He said with a slight smile. He led her away from the curious courtiers that hovered near the shuttle, stopping by flowering bushes a few yards away. "I know you need time to think..." he said as he held her hands, stroking her fingers with his thumb. "I just want you to know, that I will wait. As long as it takes." Tears stood in his eyes as he gazed at her, his curved slightly.

"Rexlen, I love...Am arma'stann," Spring walked into his arms, immediately held tight in his embrace, "I'll be back, I will." He pulled back, his hands cupping her face, his fingers rubbing away the tears that dampened her cheeks. She gazed at him, his eyes locked tenderly on hers, filled with the same pain that filled her throat, closing her lungs. "This is not goodbye," Spring shook her head.

* * *

THE MOON. TWO WEEKS LATER.

Spring fastened her new gold wings against her blazer. She couldn't believe it had been a full year since graduation. She double checked her reflection before leaving her room, closing the door. In the living room she nearly collided with a radiant Pam, actually wearing her own clothes for once, dressed in her designer coat and carrying a cute overnight bag.

"Pam, where are you going? Deadheading on my Earth flight?"

Pam beamed, "Adam and I have a date on Pegasus I! We're staying at the Constellation...tastic, huh?"

Spring felt a stab of jealousy, The Constellation was one of the finest hotels off world. Every room a three story suite, with actual holo chambers, with 360 views of stars and planets. The restaurant was to die for.

"Sounds like you two are getting serious!" Spring smiled, "I'm so happy for you!"

"Thanks, but Spring...how about you and Rexlen? I mean, when you came back a couple a weeks ago...are you going back?"

Spring slipped on her heels, her mind filled with Rexlen. They spoke everyday. She turned to Pam, wishing Zavia was there to hear what she had to say.

"I have decided, I mean, made up my mind." She said.

"Does this mean I'll need a bridesmaid dress?" Pam gushed excitedly.

"Well, I don't know about that!" Spring laughed, wheeling her suitcase to the front door, "I'll let you know. And you let me know when I need to pick up a bridesmaid dress!"

"We could have a double wedding! How magnif would that be! Oh, Spring?"

Spring looked up, Pam held up Spring's brand new collar necklace that blazed with a rainbow of color. "Uh, mind if I borrow this?"

"Sure." Spring said absently, opening the door.

"Tastic! And how about your..."

"No. Later, Pam." Spring shut the door.

* * *

Spring's return flight to the Moon actually had trainees onboard, and Spring found herself sitting in the back, mentoring a trainee. Her trainee reminded her of herself, nervous but smiling bravely. Kayla, (the trainee), even had curly hair that hovered an inch above her shoulders, held back by a thin silver headband. Kayla also reminded Spring of Gran-Libby. Almost the same warm cocoa brown skin, brown eyes. It was like seeing a younger version of the flight attendant Gran-Libby had been, so long ago. Spring smiled at the thought.

As their shuttle roared up into space, she glanced at Kayla, buckled tightly into her jumpseat, her eyes still squeezed shut, her ebony brown face tense. Outside Kayla's window, Earth swirled, bright blue and milky white.

"Ladies and Gentlemen, planet Earth on your righthand side..." The rest of the pursers PA was drowned out by cheers and loud applause. Spring leaned over, tapping Kayla's sleeve. She opened her eyes a crack.

"You don't want to miss this, look!" She pointed out the porthole sized window. Kayla's face instantly transformed, her eyes widening with awe.

"It's...beautiful! I..I can't believe I'm seeing this!" She exclaimed, her eyes glued to the window, "Do you ever get tired of seeing this? I mean, you probably do right? The Moon is your home now, huh?" Kayla asked slanting a look Spring's way. Spring felt like an old veteran, smiling back at the trainee. "I guess Earth will always be home. Even if I'm a million miles from it."

* * *

"Welcome home." The customs agent smiled at her, handing her passport card back. Spring turned to wave to her crew and the two trainees, before heading to the arrivals area. As usual the arrivals area was packed, organized chaos of welcome signs and confused tourists. Spring navigated her way through the crowd, taking in the family's greeting each other, a group of students wearing matching T-shirts, reading 'Beam us up!'. Spring's eyes landed on a tall, familiar man, standing at the end of the arrivals area, head and shoulders above everyone else, the light of the hall bouncing off his eyes, making them shimmer. Rexlen's eyes locked on her, his face breaking into a grin as he made his way toward her, sunflowers in his hand.

Spring hurried through the crowd, her heart beating excitedly as she grew closer, finally breaking into a run, abandoning her suitcase. She laughed and cried as she threw herself into his firm arms, folded in his embrace, lifting her face to his, his mouth claiming hers, among deafening applause. Rexlen broke off the kiss, resting his forehead against hers, grinning.

"Ready to go home?" He asked, still holding her close. Spring nodded, her hands clutching his arms.

"Yes! Yes, to everything! I'm ready to go home…with you to Endari. I'm ready to wear those headdresses and learn Endarion!" Rexlen let out a deep laugh, squeezing her.

"Well, perhaps we should swing by Earth first." He said leading her toward the exit doors.

"Earth?"

"Well, I have to meet my future in laws." He winked at her, "and I want to see this place called, Virginia Beach. Do you mind showing me around?"

Spring looked lovingly up into his beautiful eyes, filled with love, "It would be my pleasure! Maybe I'll even cook dinner too!"

Rexlen made a slight face, "any restaurants in your home city?" He laughed as Spring nicked him in the ribs, giving her a final squeeze before setting her down. Arm in arm they walked toward the shuttle, Spring feeling like she could fly.

CPSIA information can be obtained
at www.ICGtesting.com
Printed in the USA
BVHW040956251021
619811BV00016B/508